BLOOD
TIES

BLOOD
TIES

JENNIFER LASH

BLOOMSBURY

First published in Great Britain 1997

This paperback edition published 1998

Copyright © 1997 by the Estate of Jennifer Lash

The moral right of the author has been asserted

Bloomsbury Publishing Plc, 38 Soho Square, London WIV 5DF

A CIP catalogue record for this book
is available from the British Library

ISBN 0 7475 3504 3

10 9 8 7 6 5 4 3

Typeset in Great Britain by
Hewer Text Composition Services, Edinburgh

Printed in Great Britain by
Clays Ltd, St Ives Plc

ONE

In a moment of discontent, a moment of dull charm, a moment of proud rejection, Violet Farr crumpled that piece of paper and its contents until she heard the small, mocking sound of those frail bones shattered. She was standing in the sun. She was standing just at the edge of the porch. It was evening. It was late September, but there was still considerable warmth.

The day itself had been hot, muggy, exasperating; full of a solid thick dead kind of stillness, like rotten marrows on warm ground. During the afternoon she had wandered slowly about the house, staring out from the wide dusty windows of empty rooms. Now and then she had moved random objects; a wrinkled apple, a single sock, an empty medicine bottle. She had not been busy, she had hardly been occupied, nevertheless the day had gripped her, it had almost driven her; she had felt within it echoes of ancient ferocity. These echoes applauded her reticent memories until gradually they rose within her full of summons and authority.

'It's too late,' she said aloud to the long grass and rich sharp evening shadows; to the distant hill, a strange, thrusting, irregular shape, that seemed sprung unevenly from some kind of pain. It was her Mont-Saint-Victoire. She had watched it in every mood and all weathers for over fifty-seven years. The stretch of hills and woods and river between the house and that hill seemed to be the space of her life. That silent, attending, unnamed space was to her a vast, mysterious receptacle, one that she both loved and hated. It was a view that could trap and inspire. She looked away from the hill to the flourishing weeds close by. 'It's too late,' she said again. 'It's all too far gone.'

She turned back into the porch. For an instant she looked down at her clenched fist; the freckles, the pale skin, the arthritic knuckles. She was tempted to put the paper down on the faded wicker table. She was tempted to ease the fraught, crushed centre and spread the paper gently outwards; she was tempted to smooth it back into its first, square, handkerchief shape. She was tempted. But then those fragments so purposely crushed by her might still exude unimaginable memories; in fact, some small portion of beak or skull might still remain undamaged, intact – then this little exercise, this spontaneous second of exorcism that had happened up there by the box-room window, in the dark full dusty heat of the afternoon, that second, would like some eager tributary resume its course, regain its vigour, and an act of purposeful banishment might become a fresh proposal of intriguing pain and restless doubts all demanding reconsideration.

'What is past is over,' she said to the thin grey cat which had just come into the porch from the garden and was leaning against her ankle, purring. 'What is past is really quite beyond one . . . out of the way . . . different. And what is now . . . What is now is almost without any presence whatsoever. But then, nothing is as it seems, so they say . . . and who knows . . . who knows anything.'

She sat down on the battered oak bench, a bleached and weathered thing, full of cracks and creaks; not unlike herself she thought. The bench was at the back of the porch against the outer wall of the house. As she sat, a shard of peeling plaster fell on to her cardigan; and she heard that fine subtle electric splinter of sound as a cobweb broke surrendering its remarkably sensitive strength into the dull grey gathered knot of her combs and her hair.

She was stroking the cat.

The purring was very loud. An extremely palpable display of pleasure. Her voice dropped; it was less sighing and strident, more resolute and reflective now that her hand was in touch with the fur and warmth of this thin creature. Her cat. Well not really hers, not at first anyway. At first it had been 'that pathetic grey person' then it had become 'you dear puss person . . . you fine brave creature . . .' Then gradually, after regular feeding and care and nurture, the cat had regained confidence and a sense of its own personal identity. Its initial timid ways became definite; purposeful displays of choice. It was not to be put upon. It was never to be assumed to be servile or tender. By now and then delivering a hiss or sharp claw, a quick run into the coal shed or barn or wood store, it maintained its freedom, its own dynamic, its individual status. It was not a possession. It simply lived about the demesne. It was named and called and fed and loved, but it was not possessed.

They had called her Shiva. It was the dart . . . the dance . . . the jangling power of her that had made Violet suggest the name. Also . . . in some way, it was a quiet acknowledgment of gods and myth.

Violet, having lived for so many years in Ireland, felt enormous distaste and irritation for the gross, vulgar power of gods and myth and dogma over the lives and minds of simple people. The terrible grip of superstition. All that dreadful mumbling magic. Of course she had many friends who were intelligent and kind and Catholic, but their commitment to all that stuff definitely created a gulf, a division, a sort of no-man's-land between herself and them. That gulf was the very space into which she now stared, as she stroked Shiva and watched the shadows increase and felt the warmth of the sun gradually fade.

3

'Well, we did our best,' she said. 'We did our best and God knows, we were old then. Now, my dear Shiva, we're practically dead. We're overgrown, faded and rank. Peculiar. Definitely peculiar.'

She said the last word with a certain amount of pride. There was some kind of licence, some sort of freedom in it.

The cat walked off into the house. Violet stayed there. She stayed in the porch staring at the hill and the long narrow shadows. Then she looked down again at her hand; at the knuckles, and the wrinkled keen white edges of the piece of paper, just visible between her thumb and forefinger. Her hand was on her lap, on her faded brown skirt, that worn and torn and scarred material that hid the wide shape of her thighs. She was a big woman; age had not altered the impact of her size, taller than many men, towering above most women, but with unexpected small, pale blue, very piercing eyes that were set wide apart and very deep into her head. The fine arched nose was deemed to be her father's, the high cheek-bones, the long neck and sloping shoulders her own. Her mother had been a small fussy little woman with little to say for herself. Her father a vast intelligent human being had died of typhoid when she was only fifteen, so her romantic knowledge of him owed a great deal to his considerable library, now in her possession, his strong precise handwriting, his intense stare from faded sepia photographs and the abundance of anecdotes and references that were to be found in so many monographs and biographies of the once 'indomitable Irishry' of that poet's fancy. Her father, Lumsden Fitzpatrick, had frequently stayed at Coole Park where he had met Yeats. He had not liked him. He distrusted his arrogance and what Lumsden called the wretched whimsy of the man, an arch-dabbler held in chains by the quite extraordinary grip his virginity seemed to have had on him. No real excursion into manhood until practically forty so Lumsden Fitzpatrick had always maintained . . . 'so much Maude poor

4

fellow but never far Gonne' was one of his favourite remarks about the poet.

Where she could not actually see the edge of the paper she could feel it. It was lined paper. A page torn from a child's exercise book. How smooth those pages were before they were crumpled, as smooth, as cool as linen, as smooth as cool as that.

She had not told Cecil about the letter. It had been addressed to her, but of course the contents were definitely his by right, by birth, by blood, all that ridiculous fuss of kith and kin.

What a travesty it had been. What a charade. She kept telling herself that it was all best forgotten. What was the good of raking up the past? What was the good of that? She had not even told Cecil about the boy's death; after all, from her point of view all his life had been to her a kind of death; their so-called grandson's life.

What might have been for them both, what might have been for them and for their son, whose name they rarely even uttered now – friends were kind enough to refer to him as seldom as possible – what might have been somehow or other simply ended when Violet had thrown in the sponge. When she had at last really let fly.

It had been a fearful but fascinating feeling, that second when she discovered her grandson beyond the red barn by the stone trough across from the broken gate, propped by weeds and debris against the fallen stone wall. That yard was a dank, disused place; the broken concrete slabs were wet and slippery, strewn with leaves and the mossy remains of torn sacking, dented and chipped enamel jugs, and a basin, all rotting and resting in soft silt mud.

Of course his shoes were dirty. He never changed into wellington boots although repeatedly begged by all and sundry to do so.

Whenever Violet had had to go and hunt him out for a meal or bed, it was always the small pale face she saw first, like a thin cut, stiff, circle-crust of dry cheese hung unexpectedly in the giant gothic dark of tall trees, rusting gates, chipped urns, stone rubble, piles of leaf mould; he was always in some banished or discarded place.

He never answered her calls. She had grown used to that. She fully realised that her cry of 'Spencer. Spencer' was more to herself. It eased her frustration. It marked her passage through the damp thick heavy air.

Spencer. Such a ridiculous name for a child. It made her think of socks, vests, elastic, old underwear. She certainly never thought of a poet as her son had insisted she might. There was certainly no poetry about this child; the painful result of an untimely irresponsible liaison of their gifted son, their hope and fortune, their miracle after ten barren years and various medical difficulties. How could what had seemed such a gift then become so utterly squandered, so lost, so drowned out, so bleak, so cruel? That time of joy. It was so long ago. It was too far back, too painful, too full of lesion and wound and blood for her ever even to attempt to recognise it or remember.

'What son?' she had heard herself say sharply when at some dismal gathering of newcomers to the area an Englishwoman had referred to . . . 'Oh Lums. Of course, that trendy old rogue is your son!'

At Violet's first rhetorical response the small over-dressed woman had burst into a provincial clatter of forced, nervous laughter, it popped like cheap bright bubbles from her thick, ridiculously red lips.

Above all else Violet Farr regretted that at her son's birth she should have insisted he be named after her father. Lumsden. A name that had had for her a ring of safety, style and solution about it, until she inadvertently lost it to this new, feckless, hedonistic generation. At Lumsden's christening, in the cold simple Church of Ireland chapel, she had felt that she held in her arms some fine rare fragment of her father. She gazed down then, so she felt as she stroked the fair hair, at some poised and perfect vessel within which surely some small flame of mind and spirit would grow with courage and certainty towards a distinguished manhood.

What bitter irony his ensuing life had been to her. Dishonest. Sexually deviant. A parasite. A liar.

When he left the country in a haze of dishonour soon after his seventeenth birthday she admitted it all to herself, and the bitter facts burnt some sour place in her mind where a great angry tethered pain seemed forever after to abide. She could not budge it. She could not disregard it. She could not take it or break it. It was the unseen centre of her life, a great black cauldron bubbling with anger and shrill pity. Pity for herself. Pity for this irredeemable injustice she had suffered. It was as if some unseen force had taken her body and heart and hope and had spread it like a stained hide, to be trampled and marred and generally disfigured forever.

Of course they had sensed trouble early on. There had been signs. But Lumsden had been sent over to England to various boarding-schools, and the brutal, insensitive, snobbish ways of the English were blamed for everything. After he left the country there were rumours and debts. But they were worlds and waters apart. Nothing too particular infringed on them. At least until this wretched child was born.

They knew nothing whatsoever of his birth at first.

It was three years later that quite literally one quiet summer evening the child had been summarily dumped on them.

A beaten-up truck had careered noisily on to the gravel directly in front of the house. They had assumed that it must be some lost tradesperson. But the girl who was driving the van leapt out distraught and aggressive. 'You Mrs Farr . . .?' she said, and Violet naturally enough had not denied it. 'Then you've got to take the kid . . . you've got to take him now.' 'What "kid"?' Violet had said, but sufficient rumour had come to her often enough for her to know to whom this bulky dishevelled girl referred. 'Your bloody fucking grandson . . . that's what.' Violet had tried to draw herself up, to murmur things like 'Please don't use that unpleasant language to me.' But her words were lost like a trail of woodsmoke. The girl was dumping baskets and plastic bags and a filthy blanket of multi-coloured knitted squares on to the gravel. 'He won't do anything. He won't be difficult. He's quiet. He's bloody stunned. She drinks. His mother drinks. These are his papers, birth certificate and things. They've fucked him up enough, there's nothing left for him over there . . . so I said I'd bring him here . . . Right?'

Violet in disbelief, as if witnessing some staged drama, had watched the girl crash open the dented rear doors of the van and then clamber into the dark and drag forward a bundle of blanket. 'It may seem tough to you . . .' she began. 'It seems quite absurd,' Violet had said, trying not even to acknowledge the bundle, the small grey fallen sock, or the matted crown of dark hair. 'But it's a fact,' the girl continued as she struggled towards the porch. 'You're family . . . kith and kin, all that crap about blood being thicker than water . . . that's why I've brought him. It has to be better than how it's been before. It has to be better than that.' 'It's ridiculous. We're quite unprepared,' Violet tried to interrupt her. 'Don't give me that shit. You've got a house and space; rooms, doors, fields, sky, water, cows, milk . . . priests!' The child stirred. Another sock fell. The girl put him down. She was nervous. She was afraid. Violet grudgingly acknowledged that some of her vulgarity stemmed from a kind of distress. The girl bent down, resting on her hunkers; her wide thighs. She was strong. One of the blankets fell from the child's shoulders.

8

The girl took the other, a matted, yellow, crocheted object that could have given neither warmth nor particular comfort. The girl crumpled it into a ball on her knees.

'Spencer . . . we're here . . . Spencer . . . you know, your Nana's . . . We're here like I told you. Come on . . . come on.'

The small thin child was standing impassively there in front of the girl. He was staring at the ground. His head, which was a mass of dark unruly hair, hung down as if it were a great weight that he wished he could release to crash to the ground, to roll away.

In the terrible, choked, mad silence Violet could hear the sound of her own breath as she struggled to find some word, some sense or other. She heard her husband walking on the floorboards in the hall. He had watched the van from the library window. He assumed Violet would redirect it, after all they were expecting no one. Then he witnessed the peculiar commotion of this girl strewing the gravel with bags and various improbable paraphernalia. At first he assumed she must be selling something but the tenor in the voices was heightened, emotional. Cecil became intrigued and decided to come and see for himself. He was not a fit or particularly intelligent man. He had been invalided out of the Army. Violet was the force, the power, the condition under which he lived. She filled the dull space one way or another. She summoned him, sent him on errands, told others what he thought and felt. It was a map to which long ago he had conceded gratefully to belong. He concerned himself with small decisions; which bag was more appropriate for the market or the picnic, which toast rack, which nutcracker; the hall barometer was his only real possession.

Violet was standing far out on the gravel looking back towards the house. The fat girl's tears were quite unseen by her.

'Come on Spencer . . . Come on . . . fellow.'

Her words made no sense. There was no sense to him. The child had given up long ago. The world was simply noise and space, shape and texture. He did not belong to it. She had her hand on his cheek. She was sniffing. Her fingers were warm and rough. Very slowly he turned and walked through the porch to the shabby marked white wall, where he stood with his back to them. It was as if he might melt himself into it. His extraordinary stillness seemed to cast a spell. Even as the Captain, as Cecil was always referred to, got to the door and stepped out into the porch and saw the fat girl crying and this small tinker's child leaning against the wall of the house, and Violet, pale and tense and huge by the beaten-up blue van; even as he stood there he felt the pain, the discord; an uncomfortable disarray that completely banished the warmth and sweetness of the summer evening. The brilliant light on the hill beyond the house, the smell from the tobacco plants, all, everything, seemed stricken, brittle with anger and shame.

Cecil began to walk towards his wife. Her usual command and authority seemed momentarily to have deserted her.

'Can I do anything, my dear?' he said in an ordinary way, as he always did, about everything.

His voice shook Violet. She looked directly at him; his loose coarse reddened skin, his deep-set pathetic pleading eyes, his highly polished shoes, his food-stained shirt, and the worn cardigan with its leather patches and leather cuffs. She realised that she longed to scream . . . to pitch her voice higher than that mountain behind her head and yell. 'Drop dead, Cecil . . . just drop dead.'

The horror of such a thought so definitely in her mind gave her back a sense of control, a sense of herself, her position. But she was not quick enough. The girl unable to bear the sight of the child's back any longer had rushed round the van and to avoid Violet had clambered across the passenger's seat. She reversed; the van spun round spraying Violet with stones and dirt. The child did not move. The bundles remained. Cecil hesitated. He did not quite like to propose himself again to Violet.

He glanced at the child but could not see how something so obviously alien and inappropriate could possibly concern him, so he said to Violet who still stood beyond the bundles on the gravel, 'I'll lay the table . . .'

And he went back into the house. Back to the green baize in the cutlery drawer.

Violet was rescued from her indecision and horror, her anger, rage, bitterness and contempt by the arrival of Maura who had cycled up from the village to see to the supper. She knew enough of Madam, her sorrow, her anger and her life, to know instantly whose the poor child was. The village knew much more of it all than they did up at the house. The mother was a simple girl not twenty when she fell for Spencer. Her friend Teresa had written several times to the priest asking for money and advice.

But Maura's arms and whole heart and whispering, gentle, tender voice were not enough. Disregarding the child's impassive expression she gathered him up. She fed him, but he would scarcely eat. She chatted to him of his father, the house, the toys which she knew were up there in the attic, the old donkey Flora who was gentle as a mouse, and down there by the barn the birds, her own grandson's tame jackdaw, and the sea, not really so very far away. Her voice was even like a flow of bubbling clear water. She knew that it would be some time before the poor little mite would respond at all. But it was not response she was after. She would talk so to ducks, chickens, even sometimes her pots and pans. Her whole life was a busy, practical flow of loving and doing, minding and caring and keeping. But of all the creatures ever to come into her care, none was so pathetic, so numb, so poorly as this little lad. She ran a warm bath for him but he seemed very fearful of it so she made a game of the tooth-mug and flannels and soapy water letting it run away, gurgling and bubbling. She managed to quickly wash his bottom and his back and his knees. She left the face, it was grubby and sore, but she left it. Out of the corner of her eye, as she knelt on the cork mat by the bath, she thought that just for a second he almost looked at her. Well she knew that like with any wounded creature you must bide your time, bide your time. She did at length have him finally into a warm bed, with fresh clothes. What a terrible cruel thing it was above all else to be so small and have no one wanting you, no one really to call your own. But they would try. They would certainly all do their best for him although it was no ordinary home, not a natural spot for a young lad to be reared in, but nevertheless, and she sighed so heartily to herself as she left him that he looked almost directly towards her. Nevertheless, when all was said and done it was probably a better, safer place than he's known yet. She would hope so anyway; and by the grace of God it would be so.

It was much later that night after the priest had been, after talk and telephone calls, that Violet having picked at her cold supper had heard, suddenly, tearing through the house a terrible, raw, stifled, animal sound. There was nothing within the bounds of her experience to prepare her for it. She could not attach it to any concrete reference. She could not disarm it with any kind of quality of reason. It seemed like the very wrath of blood. A curse. A cursed creature. Those were the very words that came into her mind as she left the dining-room, and gathered up her skirt and made to climb the broad central staircase. Maura had put him she supposed in the old night nursery. She made her way up the second flight of stairs. The sound peaked like a sharp narrow point into a most painful place. Then, just as she reached the open door there was silence. A peculiar, hung, poised silence not at all the kind of heavy, old silence to which they were both so used. A pending, strung silence. The light was on in the night nursery. As she moved slowly towards the open doorway she was for a second strangely fearful to look towards the blue painted bedstead that she knew only as Lumsden's, only as her son's. She rarely came these days up to the second landing, there was no reason to. So, in her mind's eye, the room was still full of Lumsden, that part of him that she had always felt nothing could take away from her. His eyes had always been bright, his skin soft and clean, never rancid and rough and sore. The bedstead was directly in front of the door. Her huge figure almost filled the space. The child lay ahead of her. This time he looked piercingly at her. He made no attempt to turn his head. He had kicked off the covers. He had on nothing but a T-shirt and pants. His face was flushed and yet still pale around the temples. His left hand was up at his face, the thumb in his mouth, while with fierce regularity he pulled with his forefinger at the sore, puffy upper lip. His right hand clutched and moved, with what was to Violet horrid and wretched monotony, a small, swollen, uncircumcised penis.

He stared at her but never for a second did the rhythm falter.

For the first time in that terrible evening, which she would never forget because it altered utterly the whole flow and sense of her life and finally at the end, of herself, she was troubled by a gust of emotion. It rose through her like a powerful wave. It was close to another feeling; at her father's funeral in the brilliant sunlight as they lowered the long coffin into the dark ground. Fighting her tears and her anguish, she had suddenly seen him there, as if miraculously the lid of the coffin had been lifted. But he had not been clothed; he had been marble and chiselled like a god. Below his hips there had been a smooth fan of fig leaf and in the instant of her tears and worry she had felt such shame, because she had longed to lift the fig leaf and, in some way she did not understand, to know him truly. That peculiar fraction of shame and sorrow had in a way persisted all through her life, becoming gradually disappointment and almost disgust within her own marriage, until in the early years of her son's life it had almost been rescued to joy and charm as she had seen him bathe and sleep. Now, in this moment of unexpected torment, it seemed to her as if this crumpled, bleak child, apparently proven to be her grandson, had brought back to her out of darkness and buried time a rude reminder of some host of herself unknown and unlived. He was so pathetic and yet he seemed monstrously to mock her.

She came into the room. 'Never make that cry again,' she said. 'Never.' She picked the covers up off the floor and tossed them back over him. He never made that cry again. Never quite the same. Never for so long. Never so determined. But the sound of it to Violet, its reproach and mockery, seemed burnt forever into his wide brow.

She never looked at him again without there being some substance of it there. In this way she was never able to see him simply for himself.

So when that moment came years later, that moment by the red barn, by the stone trough, when she found him, when she really let fly at last . . . after so long . . . It was all these buried but substantial forces that came into form, into strength, into a triumphant withering rage. It was as if her mind and feet and throat, the whole thrust of her, were suddenly seared free with some kind of justice and certainty that would release her and obliterate the rest. In a flash it was so clear to her. The damp and dark. Her voice calling. Then the glimpse of that pale face, and him found there but found this time with all the evidence that she had sensed before, but that had as fact so long eluded her. Here he was with the gleaming soft feathers lying across his bare knees . . . and the dead head down in the green slime of the water and the strong, brilliant yellow claws dangling by his rolled-down socks and muddy shoes . . . and spatters of blood, and a great stain of wet on his shrunken, burr-spotted jersey. She came running. She came very close. He felt her panting and her breath before he said:

'I didn't do it. I didn't do it.'

He so rarely spoke. That was the maddening thing, his deafening, frightful silence. So when his voice was suddenly clear and calm, its very sound, which for years, months, she had tried to summon, tried to cajole, tempt, scream apart, wrench out from him, when finally and in such circumstances she heard the calm, complete, gentle, childish, vulnerable sound, all the pain of her mockery by him, his utter banishment of her, all that buried pain and stagnant self-pity raced into clear, violent, uncontrolled anger. In a split second a terrible certainty lodged in her mind. Brandished its belief to her. He is mad. He is bad. He is a cursed child. He has killed this hen, this innocent bird, he has blood on his hands.

She accepted the terrible certainty of it and all the implications. It must be recognised. And she would do that. Now. She knew. Now she certainly knew. There might be reasons for everything but that was not the point. There might be tenuous links, peculiar patterns. But . . . and this was what she took hold of to brandish forever in that bleak empty part of her that was too cold for sorrow . . . he is bad blood. Bad blood will out. Bad blood is a fact, it cannot be denied.

She remembered how she had sensed it from the very beginning when she heard that scream the first night he arrived. Cursed. He is cursed. Those were the very words that came to her then and now; this evening by the red barn, here, with the dead bird, she felt absolved of all the threat and darkness of the past eight years.

But it was not screams or fury, questions or accusations the boy witnessed. It was a terrible uncharacteristic control. For several seconds, very close to him, she simply breathed, the loose skin round her throat shook and the strong, wide, shapeless chest rose and fell with such force that the boy could not bear to look at it. She was so close to him, he dared not even slide down from the edge of the trough; her skirt pressed against the feathers of the bird. Spencer longed to free the dead creature from that kind of capture. He eased the dripping soft thing closer to himself. He even put one hand up on to the dry soft part of the smaller feathers under the wing. He had never been afraid of dead animals. It was a kind of resting and pause and safety that he understood.

Then she stepped back. 'Bring it with you,' she said. 'And follow me.' Spencer slid down from the trough and scooped the whole wet carcass up into his jersey in the manner that he often carried kittens and rabbits and fledglings. She turned. She walked ahead of him. In her mind there was this one thought: the certainty and necessity of his immediate departure. He followed her, stumbling now and then. Fear was something so permanently with him that it had become solid, lumpen, a constant moan of dread, always there; he almost thought it was his heart. But he knew as he followed her that something had changed, something had altered. He knew that there would be a new direction now. He did not know what it would alter, but he knew as they came round towards the front of the house that the great hill that was always there ahead of him for as long as he could remember, he knew it might flatten into an empty different skyline. He did mind that because the hill was his magic mountain. He imagined within it an echoing beautiful burial chamber where his guardian angel slept with his other ancestors; warriors and poets; a lion and a unicorn; and a beautiful woman who bent over a small cradle rocking a child who never slept, because of this she always sang but did not turn her head. He had never seen her face, only her hands and her hair.

Violet made him wait in the garage. She telephoned the priest. He was not the same one who had originally interfered and encouraged the fat girl to bring Spencer to Ireland. He was younger, fitter, altogether keener. The hard-drinking and simply ignorant Catholic clergy had given way to a new, energetic, guitar-playing, charismatic crowd whose determined freshness and goodwill masked, so Violet thought, a rough, sexual energy that hurling would help disperse a great deal better than hymns. She was determined now to put all this energy and fellowship at her own disposal. It was after all a priest in the first place whose meddling charitable status had brought Spencer to them. In all that time she had had one letter from her son. The priest had brought it. It referred to 'Everything is out of hand. His mother is young, rather unhinged as you would say, unstable anyway. As I have often heard you say . . . blood will out! What a tiresome mystery it all is. My position at present is utter dereliction but . . . maybe at a later date . . .' Violet still had the letter and this was definitely now; this was the 'later date'. Violet knew that Lumsden was liaised with a rich Italian businesswoman, they must handle the situation. They must take responsibility.

It should never have happened at all. It was not appropriate. You can't summarily give birth and then foist the unwanted child on to elderly grandparents. Apparently the girl, Dolly, was originally from a Catholic background which, Violet supposed, made the Catholic clergy so disposed towards her. Not Irish Catholics Lumsden had told them, but from Aldershot. What could be more unfortunate than that? A mix of beer, khaki and the Sacred Heart. Terrible. They should never have had him. But that wretched fat girl with what the priest described then as 'nothing Mrs Farr but a great and real sense of Christian charity'. The fat girl, with a good deal of popish encouragement, had virtually presented them with a *fait accompli*, and the house was large, and in those days help was not a problem. What had really irked Violet throughout Spencer's childhood was the way the village, encouraged by the priest, went on about what a fine Christian woman she was to take on the child. Of course Maura and many others knew that fine Christian qualities were not central to the themes and schemes of Violet Farr's life, but their own natural charity made them avoid too close an assessment of what really motivated Mrs Farr. The Captain was a strange, quiet man, and she by nature was a powerful

17

woman who had suffered the loss and terrible humiliation of her only son's departure. Maybe England was to be blamed for that. All in all it was a sad difficult place, and they were sad difficult people. So when Mrs Farr arrived with Spencer and the dead hen late one evening at the presbytery, young Father Gerard was not so much surprised as dismayed for the boy who had lived amongst them for so long, and yet in all that time had never really grown close to anyone. Only perhaps to Big Donal, a part-time farm-worker who managed the vegetables and grounds up at the demesne; for this reason, as soon as he had the opportunity, the priest wrapped the hen in newspaper and said to Spencer 'Well, it'll make a fine stew for Donal.' He smiled as he said it hoping the boy would get a kind of absolution, a sense of real forgiveness for whatever had happened. Whatever it was, Father Gerard knew well enough that the scales of curses and sorrow were weighted far too heavily against the poor boy already; he needed nothing but reassurance.

So Spencer was returned to England and Violet and Cecil resumed their certain, stale life as if the dramatic intervention of eight years of Spencer's childhood had been almost nothing more than a bad dream, a drop in the barometer.

These were some of the fragments of feeling, thought and experience that were summoned back to life when now, out of the blue, Violet Farr received the letter. After all it was nearly three years ago. If the letter were genuine, why wait so long? Who did this woman Winifred Chappell think she was? Violet had sent Spencer back to England when he was just eleven, after the blood and the hen; that dank, dark, terrible evening. For Violet, in a flash, that evening was the end, absolutely and entirely. It was then that the evil, the curse, the bad blood of that boy, something she had always known, it was then that irrevocably it finally and publicly declared itself. For her that was the end, so she, with complete justification as she saw it,

18

returned Spencer to England; to his alcoholic mother Dolly and his feckless, rogue father Lumsden. She returned him to the hopeless, post-imperial, over-populated mixed racial mess of that suburban country. It was after all his country of birth and as it later transpired the country of his death. This she had ignored, because for her his death had been when he left them and the demesne and Ireland for ever. She had not told Cecil because she had not wanted to engage in any conversation where the names of either their son Lumsden or their grandson Spencer were mentioned. For Violet, her life, her pain, her considerable anger, which was now the sour sting of old age trailing after a bitter barren life, she could only endure it if Spencer and Lumsden had no part in it whatsoever.

But suddenly now, this September, there was the letter.

It made Violet uneasy; the neat, even, sloping copperplate handwriting was so unexpected, the narrow, soft-cream, heavily-lined writing paper was so cheap. Perhaps she should completely disregard it. Not reply. Leave well alone.

All day she had felt restless so she had wandered about the house going into all the empty rooms; staring at spaces and things; faded carpets and curtains, damp patches, corroded pipes, crooked mats; and it was then, while she was in the attic bedroom, that she had found a cardboard box full of Spencer's things; his pencil-case, his Bible, his book of birds, his penknife, his chipped magnifying-glass and, laid very carefully in an empty cigar box, she had found the skull and several bones of a small bird. It was probably a sparrow. The bones and skull were wrapped in a sheet of paper torn from an exercise book, in one corner written in a very weak disjointed hand were the words 'this little bird is dead'.

Violet did not know why she had taken the piece of paper and the bones up into her hand. She did not know why she had brought it downstairs with her and out on to the porch. And she did not know why she suddenly and very purposefully had crumpled it. She did not know why; but in some way it was to do with this wretched letter and this woman Winifred Chappell, whoever she might be.

These days it was Sally who came to the house; no longer Maura, she suffered badly with arthritis and rarely came up to the demesne. Violet missed her, she missed her more than perhaps she had ever missed anyone except her father, but then that was something altogether different. Maura, while maintaining her domestic position, had managed to offer Violet a kind of natural wisdom and reassurance that transcended the inequality of their relationship. It didn't hurt Maura to punctuate what she considered to be her guarding and guiding role over this awkward family with 'Very well, Madam', and 'Certainly, Sir'. They were simply sounds to her, a particular melody. She never felt servile, or inferior, simply well, or ill, busy or rested. It was the chatter and bustle of her that Violet missed and the extraordinary comfort of hearing her voice from the laundry-room window as she pulled the sheets through the heavy wringer, singing *Tantum ergo* and *O salutaris* long after they were more or less dropped with the Latin from the Liturgy. Maura was a Rosary and Benediction person, but her particular devotion was to Saint Joseph. Her uncle had been a carpenter and had made a sound living by coffins long before fitted kitchens were the thing.

Now it was Sally who came daily to the house and left a little something for their supper after she had cleared away the lunch dishes. Sally could not be compared to Maura. Violet often said of her 'not really a front-of-house person more a natural for below-stairs'. She was a thin girl with lank brown hair falling into a greasy brown bob and fringe which hid a run of very active spots. She undoubtedly did her best but she was nervous and afraid to make any decision whatsoever. Only potatoes heavily mashed with milk and butter and soda bread could be certain of success. Cecil had become increasingly deaf, which meant Violet habitually let her voice rise far higher than was necessary. This was a trial for Sally whose voice was never much more than a hoarse nasal whisper. The Captain never heard her at all and Violet's fierce, articulated, resonant commands flustered Sally until she felt herself to be numb with stupidity. She had none of Maura's faith to comfort her. The laundry-room for her was a retreat for reddened eyes and torn rag pieces on which to blow her nose and summon the courage to appear once again in the public parts of the house, with the dented metal dustpan, the broom, various thin yellow dusters and a huge tin of wax polish.

Sally had left late that afternoon. Violet had heard a loud crash and clatter in the pantry but she had not had the energy to go and investigate, instead she had come into the garden and was now sitting here in the porch with the crumpled piece of paper in her lap.

She heard regretfully the unmistakable sound of Cecil's heavy, slow, slightly scraping tread on the gravel. He came across to the porch. Instantly the cat dashed back into the house darting away from Violet's hand in a strange zig-zag bound.

'Wonderful evening,' Cecil said. 'Very still.'

These self-evident statements on the weather drew a sigh from Violet. If only once in a while he would say something unexpected from which some kind of conversation could develop. She sniffed. She would not reply to a remark that was not a question.

Cecil came a little closer. Standing with his back to the light he seemed somehow more stooped, more worn, more pathetic than usual. He was wearing loose, dark, twill trousers, the frayed turn-ups like collapsed sausage-rolls rested on his brown galoshes, a purple hand-knitted cardigan and a rough check shirt whose small stubborn plastic buttons he fumbled with interminably every morning.

'You have no jacket,' she said. It was a statement of minimal reprimand but the reprimand went deeper than even she knew.

It was reprimand for a lack of manhood, lack of body in every sense of the word.

'It isn't cold, my dear,' he said.

He bent forward. He looked at her closely. She seemed tense, preoccupied.

'I've brought in a few plums, mostly windfalls. Got to get 'em before the wops do. Not many wops about yet.'

He had a small basket which he put down on the low wicker table, the plums were soft and purple. As he picked them over with his stiff fingers, the blotched wine-stains of vivid ageing on the paper-thin skin of his hands seemed equal to the plums' own soft shapes.

'Wretched season autumn,' Violet said suddenly. 'Nothing but damp and windfalls.'

'I don't know . . . the glass is going up. The glass is going up, quite definitely. Quite definitely.'

He often repeated himself. It was a habit. It seemed to round things off; make sure things had been said; make sure that some sound had been made; some sound, some contribution.

'Well windfalls will drop whatever the glass does. That orchard is nothing but a bind. The trees are so old and no one wants the apples. Cooking is a thing of the past, they all want packets and convenience these days.'

'Well, my dear, this plum is a beauty. Quite delicious.'

Cecil gently rubbed the skin of the plum on the sleeve of his cardigan. As he ate, the rich yellow juice ran down the soft creases of his skin, pausing to gather in the deep set cleft of his chin, then eventually falling in one singular spat of juice on to his trousers.

'Look out, you're dribbling,' she said.

'Dear oh dear, how piggy of me.'

Nervously he felt for a handkerchief in his trouser pocket; leaning, heaving, pulling, sighing. What a ghastly effort, what a supreme palaver old age is Violet thought with a mixture of sadness and scorn. Cecil wiped his chin, his lips, his fingers, then he blew his nose with a kind of determined frenzy, turning the handkerchief this way and that to avoid the pale watery mucus.

Violet stared and could not believe that once this frenzy and action, lips and chins and things had been a part of her body with his; their frenzy. The memory of it all was keen and shameful to her because it had never really happened, it had never risen and flown as it should. It had simply been there, coarse and anxious, hopeful, empty and strange. She sighed again. 'I suppose we should go in,' she said.

Cecil folded his handkerchief and put it back into his pocket. She would never know the great regard in which he held her. He remembered constantly her hair as a young woman, loose, fine, reaching almost to her waist. He remembered her freedom, her laughter, her energy above all that, but he knew that for her the sum of things had been disappointment and from that a certain bitterness; now there was no longer either energy or laughter. She reminded him of a flint stone on which anything might suddenly strike and set things to flame. He would like to have been able to communicate better with her; he would like to have had the temerity now and then to have placed his hand on hers, but it was unthinkable. He had lived for so long now within bounds, rigid bounds. He noticed the crumpled piece of paper in her lap.

'Something for the rubbish?' he asked.

'It's nothing,' she replied looking beyond him to the mountain, 'just a scrap of paper.'

'I'll pop it in the wagga pagga bagga,' he said. 'I'm going to the study.' He bent to take the crumpled thing.

'It's full of bones,' she said, 'old dry bird bones.' But he didn't hear her and he didn't take it because she put her long pale thin fingers over it.

They were due to go into the dining-room. Ritual movements

usually preceded this event. He would say 'Seven-thirty, my dear.' She would rarely respond the first time but she would alter the manner and speed of whatever activity she was preoccupied with. She might be at her desk, she might be darning or reading, she might be sorting drawers or papers. Whatever it was as soon as she heard Cecil say 'Seven-thirty, my dear' she would noisily accelerate with sighs and huffs and puffs, and brisk terse movements whatever it was she was doing; frequently something would drop; an envelope, sealing-wax, rubber-bands, embroidery scissors. Cecil would hover closer to the place of action never quite bending to rescue the fallen item, but inferring by his demeanour that any minute he might do so. Then, with a tut and sigh and more bluster she would bend and gather up the offending object and he would say again with more certainty and definition, 'Just past seven-thirty, my dear', and she would reply as she busied and tidied, 'So you said Cecil, so you said.' Soon after that he would go across to the hall and into the downstairs lavatory for a 'wash and brush up'. He would never ever refer in any more explicit way to the real bodily function that his visit to this cold space really involved; this quarry-tiled cell smelling of boots, leather, stale coat collars, encrusted urine, brown transparent Pears soap, bleach; a general congeal of stains, smells, rime and hair.

Perhaps his bowel movements and the slow, difficult, hesitant passing of water preoccupied his mind, perhaps it was for this reason that he liked, at least to Violet, to suggest that a visit to the gents was a brusque, efficient, clear-cut positive action; a chap's action in a chap's space.

In reality the gents, like the barometer, was one of Cecil's few remaining, truly personal territories. It was his fishing-rod in the corner, his waders, perished and dusty and unused, his foxed print of his grandmother's home in Oxfordshire, his cracked, stained ivory brushes, his pumice-stone, his harsh, sharp, transparent Jeyes paper.

Violet never went into the gents. There was another small bathroom on the first half-landing which she and all the guests to the house used; except for on one occasion. This occasion was the visit to Violet of the Dean, their local Church of Ireland leading ecclesiastic.

For many years the Dean and Violet had maintained a relationship of subtle discord; they served together on various committees concerning schools, hospitals, proposed commercial developments in the area. On the occasion of the Dean's visit to the demesne, from his point of view it was to have things out with Violet Farr once and for all, and this time in privacy rather than in public. On the announcement of his arrival Violet purposely kept him waiting in the study where Sally plied him with constant pots of tea. Naturally as soon as Violet made her entry he suddenly felt a compelling and urgent need to go to the lavatory. Violet had been delighted to usher him into the cold, bleak space that was Cecil's proud preserve.

The Dean, greatly relieved to be able to rid himself of the excess liquid, had not been aware of the particularity of Violet's decision. In her mind however it had given her a certain edge, a certain control over the subsequent discussions. Violet felt that the Dean peeing into that dismal pan was an act that would in some way have knocked him a little from his high horse, his flamboyant, singularly tasteless perch; he was a show-off, impossibly self-important and self-regarding.

As far as Violet knew no one else but Cecil had ever used that pan. Sally's cleaning there was very cursory, a slow wipe over the taps and basin and a liberal tip of Domestos into the lavatory once a week. Spencer had hated that cold lavatory, he had always preferred if he couldn't get upstairs in time to use the other downstairs one at the back of the house beyond the laundry-room; it was warmer, softer, kinder altogether.

This evening in late September Violet remained out on the

porch longer than usual. She did not follow Cecil into the house although he had suggested that she might do so. It had clouded over and a chill wind was beginning to blow from the east. Violet had not heard or cared about these meteorological observations of Cecil's.

Inside the house Cecil removed his galoshes. He took the plums from the basket and put them carefully into a white oval dish on the sideboard. He poured himself a glass of sherry from the dusty cut-glass decanter. Violet still remained out there in the porch. He drank another glass of sherry, glancing through the pages of a farming magazine as he did so. But for each flip of a page he glanced over the edge of the paper through the study window to the still, solid, dark mound, back view of his wife. Every so often he thought he sensed that she was about to move, but it was only her hands, the long angular fingers pulling the collar of her shirt closer up round her neck and chin. Eventually, his glass now quite empty for the second time, he went into the hall and opened the front door and said with a mixture of temerity, minimal irritation and considerable anxiety, 'Definitely past the half hour, my dear, definitely well past that.' She seemed not to hear. She seemed hardly even to be there; it was as if she had in some way left the vast lump of her body, and had flown, been blown, had withered with bitter weariness into some kind of flight from herself. She was indeed far away. But however far away she thought and mused, like the silver meander of a slug's trail, all thought, all muse, all vague threads of memory led her back once more simply to herself. She was gazing towards her mountain, that hump hill out there beyond the house. That shape, that form was the store-house of her life, from it she hoped perhaps to find some reason or indication to help her to come to a decision concerning this wretched letter from Winifred Chappell. But the more she gazed and thought and searched, the more she saw her life as nothing but a pageant of pain, denial, trouble and peculiar lifelessness.

'Nearly a quarter to, Violet, nearly a quarter to', Cecil's voice seemed so close that even juicy plums and dry sherry could make little impression on his sour bland furred flat breath.

'I'm coming. Of course I'm coming,' she said. And she looked away from the hump of the mountain shape, and the evening shadows and weeds and gravel. She looked down to her lap and her fist, still clenched over the shattered bird bones in the smooth sheet of now crumpled, almost out-of-sight piece of paper, torn long ago from a child's exercise book. She prepared to stand. She took a deep breath to summon sufficient energy and strength to proceed with Cecil into their glum dark narrow dining-room.

As soon as he heard her move Cecil walked back down the wide hallway. He put his empty sherry glass on to the wooden casement of the radiator and walked towards the lavatory door that was down there in the further dank and dark beyond the wide central staircase.

She came inside. She walked slowly down the hallway towards the door into the dining-room. She heard the sound of a single cold tap running. Cecil always economised so he thought by washing his hands under the cold tap. It was another of the small random austerities that peppered his regimes, like the thin cream single blanket on his bed that afforded little warmth and the tough flat boulder of a pillow he insisted on using. Violet went into the study, she paused beside the desk and looked down into the deep wicker wastepaper basket. She stared at paper, plum-stones, peel and an empty match-box, then, as if suddenly inspired, she turned on her heel and went back through the hall and pantry out into the kitchen. She went over to the solid fuel Aga. She heaved open the fire-proof door. The acrid gassy smell of warmth and anthracite smoke made her cough and her eyes sting, but the smell and the warmth, the small rippling flames, the shape of the heated coals all charged her with resolve and certainty. She flung the tight ball of crumpled paper and its burden of dry bird bones on to the hot coals and then she slammed the door against the heat and smoke and against the intrusion of past occasions.

Cecil heard the Aga door slam. Each of them knew intimately every sound the other might make about the large empty house. Every sound was full of implication; timing, mood, need. Cecil paused from rubbing his cold hands on the small frayed towel. He did not understand why Violet was in the kitchen. The supper would be in the heated cabinet in the dining-room to avoid either of them having to bend. And the wind was enough surely to prevent the greatest disaster of all: the Aga could not have gone out. Cecil dreaded Violet's temperament then; the dust, the grit, the kneeling and scraping and ash and smells, the mean firelighters and the hunt for dry kindling. However, he heard Violet call for him in an unexpectedly cheerful voice.

'It's on the table, Cecil,' she said.

The table was long and narrow. Once in Maura's time it had been highly polished, now in Sally's time it was dull and smeary with various marks and scratches. Violet sat at the far end of the table with her back to the window. There was no view, simply a high hedge, but it was nearer to the kitchen. Cecil sat at the opposite end of the table facing his wife. Although they sat far apart, their opposite positions at the dining-room table were the closest, most intimate, regular appointment they had with one another. To an outside observer this seating might seem to be full of inconvenience. They were not in reach of one another when they were both seated, but each of them had individual salt and pepper pots, sugar bowl, small toast rack and butter dish. And more often than not they served themselves from the sideboard. Sometimes Violet served him. Cecil never served her. The only central item on the table shared by them both was the water jug, but it was Cecil's job to fill each glass with water before the meal so it was very rarely that the inconvenience of the jug standing on a mat in the middle of the table, out of arm's length to both of them, was apparent. Once or twice if the curry was too fierce or the fish too salty they might need a second glass of water, then Cecil would leave his place and pour the water out for both of them.

This evening Violet served him fish in a thin white sauce, mashed potatoes, diced beetroot and boiled parsnips. The food was extremely dull, but they both cut it carefully, gathering each mouthful with precision and delicacy and then eating it slowly as if it was altogether far better and tastier than it really was.

Spencer's eating habits they had found excruciating. He had always taken great gulps of water using it like swill to swallow the large ungainly forkfuls of food he scooped together. His utensils seemed to clatter and spin. He had always eaten noisily, frequently with his mouth open. In the end they had contrived to eat with him as little as possible, using bedtime, homework, jobs, telephone conversations, any activity to avoid the sight of that dark tousled head, the rough chapped cheeks, the gulping and swilling; all that urgent anxious frantic swallowing. But that was so long ago. The rough unsteadying interruption of Spencer's presence in their lives for those mighty and dreadful eight years, from that peculiar, silent, unyielding three-year-old to the final moment of horror by the stone trough in the yard beyond the red barn, with the grown eleven-year-old boy, and the blood and the damp and the feathers, that was all a nightmare now more or less forgotten, bitterly buried. For years now the dining-room had regained its slow pace, its dull stagnant claustrophobic presence; too much unpolished mahogany, too many heavy engravings of stags and highland cattle, too much solid emptiness: empty chairs, empty surfaces, empty urns, empty vases, empty decanters; there seemed to be an unseen shroud that clung to everything denying the room any really pertinent or live function; there was of course laying and clearing, cutting and pouring and eating, but in spite of years of meals the room had never known any kind of celebration whatsoever.

The only object with any life or flow or vitality was a large ornate gilt mirror that hung over the black marble fire surround. On each side of the glass, in a gesture almost of welcome, two candelabra hinged forward into the room. There were stubs of unlit candles in the gilded sockets in case of a power cut, not to light the room with any mystery or gentleness.

Once when Spencer had been alone in the dining-room he had climbed up on to a chair and he had lit the candles. For an instant when he had caught sight of his own reflection in the glass, framed on either side by the flickering live light of the candle flames, he had almost smiled at himself. The small bursts of light made him think of heaven; of kings, queens, angels, heralds. He was sure that the burial chamber in the mound hill beyond the house was lit only by giant candles. But he had dared to enjoy just for seconds the beautiful pleasure of the dancing sharp flames; matches were absolutely forbidden to him. He was terrified that the smell of sulphur, or the smell of the warm spluttering wax, would give him away. Anxiously he lent across and with his hand cupped round each flame, he blew out the candles. He climbed gingerly down from the chair. Some wax had dripped on to the stained floorboards. He knelt down and gently with the tip of his finger prised off the beautiful small circle of white from the wood. He let it lie for several seconds in the palm of his hand, then he had eaten it, pretending to himself that it was a magical pagan communion wafer, full of power, mysterious power.

After the fish, there were stewed plums and top of the milk. And after that Cecil cut himself a small piece of Cheddar to take away the sweet taste of the plums on which he had liberally sprinkled crystals of brown sugar.

Violet watched him. She waited, still seated at the table. She rarely ate cheese. The cat came in from the kitchen. She started to purr and arch her back against the legs of Violet's chair.

Violet, immediately registering this sign from Shiva, eased her chair out from the edge of the table. Shiva leapt up on to her lap and was very soon licking the last remains of milk left in the bottom of Violet's bowl. Shiva preferred meat but she, like Violet and Cecil, had a variety of signs, regimes, displays and orders of behaviour which nourished their sense of themselves almost as much as food and warmth nourished their bodies. Violet stroked the soft, smooth fur of the animal standing on her lap. She ignored the momentary sharp snaps of pain when the claws pressed deep into her skirt, her peach petticoat and her brown stockings, and then the hidden, pale, almost transparent chicken-white skim of skin that covered her thighs. This great round turn of body, her thighs, was so soft, so hidden, that the sharp pain from the cat's claws quite surprised her. It was a shock to be reminded that there was still life there, still a capacity for real bodily feelings. Bodies were to Violet, dull, ugly, brooding places that gave one nothing but trouble. It was to her as if this strange sum of blood, muscles, bones, layers, static and flow seemed in some way to wish to score points; generally to scorn and humiliate the wretched, struggling soul within.

Violet watched her husband with his stiff, swollen-jointed fingers as he concentrated in order to cut his piece of cheese into narrow even slithers.

In such a manner has he lived, she thought; or rather, in such a manner has he avoided life. He has shaved purpose to the bone until all that is left is narrow and dull, a wretched brittle perpendicular. A splinter. Certainly he was never much of a man. He was nothing like her father, that first Lumsden. What breadth of purpose he had had; what resource, what education, wit, drive; what real capacity.

In spite of the many thoughts, feelings and memories which Violet kept hidden, even sometimes from herself, ageing gave both their lives a permanently physical focus. It was his physical clumsiness and general ineptitude which maddened her most.

And somehow from it she found even now, in her seventies, she dwelt uncomfortably often on the utter emptiness of their liaison. There seemed to be more wit, more resonance in one cat's whisker than in any gesture or fraction of Cecil's crumbling, stumbling, disorientated body. And she knew that it was not simply age that was to account for this. She had always felt that in some way Cecil's marriage to her had been an escape, a denial of something or other. He had come to her to avoid life, certainly not to enter into it; not to truly discover it; not to enjoy it.

As she watched him she realised that she could not broach the subject of either their son Lumsden or their grandson Spencer. Both were inextricably linked. Any thought of one or the other might engender the kind of reality that neither she nor Cecil wished to confront. So Violet decided as the cat leapt from her knee that she would not mention the letter she had received that morning. The letter written on cheap, narrow, lined writing-paper. The letter in the ill-educated sloping hand of Winifred Chappell. She would not destroy the letter. She would simply lay it with her other papers in the blue leather blotter in the bottom drawer of her desk. She did not know why but some part of her felt very vaguely that there might come a time when to glance once again at that letter might be appropriate, but it was certainly not now, not this evening, not this September.

TWO

S id and Ruth Frampton did not consider it a blessing when their daughter Dolly was born. Thin as a rail, a chain-smoker who suffered from severe bouts of depression, Ruth Frampton felt nothing but dread, confusion and shame when the doctor told her that she was in fact expecting a child. Her two sons were grown up and away in the Merchant Navy. The small sub-post-office, village store and bakery was run down and dismal. The only thing that kept Sid going at all was the idea of retirement. To sell up. To have a bungalow. To be in spitting distance of the south coast. For them both the conception of a child in middle age was nothing short of catastrophe.

Through the pregnancy Ruth said very little to anyone. She was glad when the shop was empty, glad when each day was done. Glad most of all when Sid's alarm went off at five in the morning and she had the creaking, soft bed to herself.

In the bakery amongst the heat and white and wood, the heaving and pounding, whisking and pulling and shoving, Sid felt as if for some reason not known to himself he was being punished, pinioned, pressed down into the dry cast of his wife's unending gloom. Her sharp stare seemed to fill every canary yellow space in the small house. Only in the bakery could Sid be free from it. Poor Ruth, she tried. He knew she tried. Every

33

night after she had put on the thin mauve nylon nightdress and the worn mis-shaped cream cardigan she would go into the bathroom and dampen the ends of her dull black hair. She wound the ends into tight pin curls which she kept in place by a criss-crossed pair of kirby grips. She smeared Ponds cold cream into her sallow cheeks, and every morning after she had tied her overall and eaten her toast she took a lipstick from an ashtray on the kitchen window-sill and staring menacingly at her sad frantic reflection in the small square mirror by the kitchen window, she drew a long sharp cupid's bow of brilliant red over the thin crimped lines of her lips. Sid never liked to say how sad it looked, it seemed to be something she needed to do; it seemed to give her the confidence to go out there into the shop and face the stares and nudges of the customers.

In fact Sid and Ruth said very little to one another, various voices from the radio programmes were almost more familiar to them than their own. The actual conception of Dolly was almost as much a mystery to them as it was to everyone else. Maybe it had been that night after the barn dance. Maybe it had been then. Sid did remember that they had finished off the sherry when they came home and had sat very close on the settee listening to Ruth's album of *Songs to Remember*. Sid could only remember dreams after that: the bakery ovens were suddenly opened and they were full of fairy lights and Christmas trees, he remembered he had taken hold of a tree but the sides of the oven had collapsed gently round his arm, warm and soft and strangely comforting and the lights had run into quicksilver, little threads of mercury. He remembered he had wanted to catch them for Ruth, to cheer her up a bit, to comfort her. Maybe the comfort he had been was not light or warmth of mercury but the beginning of this baby, maybe, anyway it was no good going on wondering after the event.

Sid's real conversations were in the pub and in the Working Men's Club on a Sunday morning when he had the occasional

34

game of dominos. Ruth murmured to the customers and she had frequent chats with the district nurse and maybe a quick word with Father Noonan after the Mass.

The village was a string of shops and garages on a fast road between Oakdown and Aldershot. There were gravelled driveways to superior pebble-dashed half-timbered houses, there were stretches of heathland with pine woods and bracken and heather and silver birches, and there was the railway. There was a boarding-kennel for dogs and cats up on the edge of the common land. There were three pubs, a church, a graveyard. There were crescents of council houses, red-bricked pairs of houses with metal-framed windows and dark, tarry-looking tiled roofs, just like the pubs and the shops and the village hall. There were various Tarmacadam spaces, a village school and a Boy Scout hut which was used by the Guides as well as the Brownies. And there was the recreation ground with two swings and a rusted see-saw, that squeaked and groaned with regular monotony as if the activities of the children gave it constant pain. Beyond the swings there was the cricket pitch.

Although it was a village to itself, to the harassed commuters, the retired service couples and the various trades people, to an outsider it was pubs, shops and a village hall on an ugly intersection of roads leading to everywhere else. It was not particular in its own right, simply another drab suburban patch in the great southern mosaic of pine trees and people that runs south from London, eating into farmland and woodland, spreading a tired concrete carpet further and further towards the coast. It was simply Surrey.

But there was a good bus service, regular rubbish collection and mostly main drainage, and there were prosperous people to garden for and generally clean up after. For anyone willing to work there was certainly some sort of employment. It was a dull, grey, post-war community, determined to attend to the future by constantly referring to the past.

The district nurse had her own philosophy. 'Take it as it comes my dear,' she would say to Ruth. 'Take it bit by bit.' And that was the way Sid and Ruth tried to do it; bit by bit. Not memories or ambitions, not schemes or plans or horizons, simply the daily shapes of bread and customers, pension books and postal-orders, creamed rice and pork sausages, the *Radio Times* and *Woman's Weekly*; downcast grey wintery days and the occasional heat of summer with flower shows and coach outings.

Dolly was born in December, a scraggy, lively little scrap of a thing with a mop of dark hair like her mother's. She was baptised Veronica, this blessed woman with her cloth on the road to Calvary had always meant something to Ruth, something about quiet women and toil and tiredness, but for some reason Sid always called the baby 'Dolly Girl' and the name stuck. She was baptised in the Catholic church some four miles beyond the village. It was a temporary building made of corrugated tin not unlike the scout hut. It was cold and ugly, but the parish was friendly; no one believed that there would ever be sufficient funds for a real building but they had beetle drives and jumble sales in the hope of one day having a new church.

At the baptism Ruth wore her blue coat and a small felt pill-box hat, cherry red, with a shining black hat-pin to match her dark hair. She had tried, but when she stared at the yellow, red hot, screaming infant in her godmother's arms Ruth felt that this act of baptism was in some way for her an act of giving up; an act of submission. This Church whose fierce dark teachings she had tried to embrace would now, in this moment of water and candles and chrism, the holy oil, in some way it would take the pain and fear and trouble from her. The babe was a child of God now and that was a far remove surely from Ruth and Sid and the bleak, narrow howl, as it felt to her, of the stores and the bakery.

36

The priest had finished, he turned towards Ruth and smiled with benevolence and a certain powerful pride. 'A wonderful moment, Mrs Frampton, the child is now in the arms of Our Holy Mother the Church.' Ruth tried to look back at him. She tried to smile. She searched desperately for some sense of grace of blessing but she felt none. She felt warm tears pricking at her eyes, like the lance, like the thorns; was there really all that point, all that salvation in the piercing and bleeding and pain? She longed now for some Veronica for her, someone gently to wipe away her heap of dark fear and emptiness. The mascara began to run, it made slow fudge marks down her cream white, Max Factor cheeks until it met the bright red loops of the cupid's bow just above her quivering lips. She felt the tears warm and heavy. She peeled the net glove off her hand and shoved her fingers roughly across her face. Sid, who was holding her hand, felt a sharp, uneven tremor run through her frail body.

'She's upset,' someone said. 'It's all been too much. Poor love.'

Sid took Ruth into the sacristy; up there towards the altar, and away from them, and the font, and the pews. He sat her down on a stool beside the great wide chest of vestments; chasubles, copes, like hats Ruth thought, every colour for every occasion. She looked up for a second towards Sid. She wanted to speak, to make some sound. But she could not move her lips, her hands, anything. She was as frozen, as stiff, as pale as the plaster statue of the Blessed Virgin, Our Lady of Sorrows in the corridor outside. It was then that Sid saw her face properly, a terrible circus mixture of clown and frozen animal terror. The mad gash of red across the putty white of the cheeks, the blue-grey, soft mess around the eyes, and all of it moving and running together, but the eyes in it, so desperate, so still and dry now.

The priest came through into the sacristy all smiles and flounces of lace and white over the black cassock. The rest of them remained in the church. They knew. They knew all along.

She was unstable. She couldn't cope. 'Poor Sid,' they said, 'poor fellow,' and they passed the little baby girl from one to another, pausing to sigh sharp nicotine breath laced with cheap scent and cough drops over the irksome little unwanted bundle. Then they went back to the bakery; back to the sherry and beer and sweet cakes and sausage-rolls that Ruth had left out ready for them. It was a sad occasion, no cause for any kind of merriment or celebration.

'These bloody priests have a lot to answer for, encouraging a woman of her age to bear a child. It's ridiculous. Let them try it without housekeepers or offertory boxes, just let them try it,' Lily said. Lily was Sid's sister. She could already feel the burden of this baby being run like a noose about her neck. But on the other hand, Len had just walked out on her; skedaddled off to Croydon the bugger, leaving her with nothing but his unpaid bills.

*

Lily moved into the bakery. Ruth went to the large red-bricked mental hospital out on the Bourne Road. She was in Frimley Ward. It always distressed Sid that it should have the name of a brewery. It was a long narrow ward with red linoleum on the floor and shining cream paint on the walls. It was an open ward with rows of easy chairs and high black bedsteads. Ruth sat day after day in the same chair, sometimes she simply stared; stared at the clean walls and the neat gardens and the huge chimney over by the mortuary, sometimes she just scratched at her thin arms and legs until they were scored to bleeding point. She never read or spoke, sometimes she closed her eyes, sometimes she rocked to and fro and hummed a little. Sid visited her regularly. He came on the bus every Sunday. He held her hand and brought her talcum-powder and Lucozade. Once or twice in the beginning he brought Dolly but the child seemed to upset Ruth so he left her with Lily or a neighbour and came on his own. When Sid came Ruth always managed a crude red splash of pointed lips. He knew when she did it that she did it for him although she barely spoke or acknowledged him in any other way. Sid found her so sad but he loved her. He could remember a girl behind the scout hut with long legs and thick dark hair and a small ordinary tender little smile, a smile from soft, pale lips. He had a snap of her taken on holiday on Hayling Island. 'What happens? Whatever happens?' he would say to himself whenever he glanced at the snapshot in his wallet.

People felt sorry for Sid who was a good, kind, hardworking man. The customers all made a considerable fuss of the child. She grew to be a bright, pert, cheeky little thing who never seemed to be without a packet of crisps or a bag of sweets. Lily made sure to give her a good smack every so often to keep her in line, her father was so soft poor fellow he couldn't say boo to a goose.

As soon as Dolly was old enough she went to the primary school of St Olaf's but the sisters couldn't keep her properly in check. They tried to make allowances for her, after all it's a hard thing for a child never to know her real mother. 'On the other hand,' as Lily said, 'you can't let a kid just run wild on account of a little difficulty. After all,' as Lily reminded everyone over and over again, 'she's got a good home, she's fed and clothed and cared for.'

Lily was a big woman with huge breasts and a large, lively behind. Her legs were thin, she always wore her soft, tan nylon stockings with pride. She had this habit of crossing her legs and then running her plump puffy hands slowly down the sheer fine length of each calf.

Dolly was fascinated by Lily's body. She was fascinated by the painted nails, her short cropped dyed blonde hair and those huge lolling loose shapes inside the pink and lemon sweaters she always wore. Dolly watched Lily intently. She learnt from Lily that a man was either 'a good bet' or 'a rotten sod'. Dolly wished she could have followed Lily into the pub but she had always to stay on the bench outside. When the doors swung open there was a glisten of brass and glasses and the smell of cigarettes and a kind of sweet-stale air and the sound of cheerful voices. Dolly was enthralled by the pub, it was so close and yet so forbidden. Lily went there almost every evening as soon as the shop was closed and the tea was eaten. Before she went Dolly watched her sitting on the edge of her bed, plucking the hairs from her legs and painting her toe-nails, and then squeezing herself into girdles and deep cut, wire-framed bras.

It all seemed so important. Dolly knew that it must all be for something, she was not quite sure what. It was when Lily sat in her petticoat in front of the looking-glass that Dolly felt most able to ask her questions. Lily was so intent then with her face, her hair, her neck, her nails that she said 'yes' to almost anything. She let Dolly use the nail varnish and the powder, the scent sprays, the rouge; just little bits here and there; just a squirt or squeeze or dab. It was a procedure of initiation. It was about men in a way, Dolly guessed that, but not men like Sid, not men like that, more like the Tommies in the Arcade or up at the bus station; the ones who winked and whistled and grinned. Whatever it was, it was about getting ready for something wonderful, something beautiful, something that the sisters at St Olaf's hated, something that was big and free and a good deal of fun. Whatever it was, well before Dolly's tenth birthday she knew she was getting ready for it.

Every time a bloke whistled or grinned at her or brushed firmly against her in the bus, she felt she was making headway. She was one of the girls men saw. She was the one they spotted and teased. She was very proud of this, it concerned her above all else. Only once, when she was about fourteen, hanging around the Arcade one Saturday did she feel a whiff of panic. She was with a couple of girls from the village. They were sharing a cigarette, passing it puff after puff with plenty of giggles and splutters in between, when two boys from the grammar school who travelled on the bus with them walked by. Dolly smiled at them. Maybe she smiled quite a bit, maybe it was a squirm and wobble, a little toss of the head. The boys turned to look at her but they did not smile, they just kept walking and Dolly heard one of them say purposely loud and very distinctly, 'That's that cheap little tart from the bakery.' Dolly felt hurt and she felt angry and in some way she felt afraid.

She began to distrust Lily. She began to fight them all, Sid, the sisters, she was even rude and offhand to the customers. One afternoon she skipped school and went out alone to the mental hospital on the Bourne Road. It was so large, almost like a village on its own. She asked to see Mrs Frampton. She found it strange even to say 'Mrs Frampton' out loud, because she had no picture in her mind, no sense of 'Mrs Frampton' at all, even though she knew she was her mother. 'Who are you dear?' they said. And she replied very quietly but very clearly in a voice that was barely her own, 'I'm her daughter.' They ruffled around with papers and things, asked her her address and her father's name and then finally this short dumpy nurse said, 'Very well, dear' and led Dolly down wide empty corridors and up stairways and down more corridors. Every so often she caught glimpses of paper-thin, slow-moving people, shuffling and standing, murmuring and staring.

'She won't know you dear,' the nurse said as she unlocked a green door to another corridor. They weren't shuffling here, or murmuring, they were hardly even staring, they were like lumps so awkward and so still, just lumps on chairs. There was a smell of knickers and cheap soap; the nurse's brown shoes squeaked on the polished floor.

'She's in here, dear,' the nurse said.

There was a chair and a bed in a small side room. There was a high narrow window with bars and a thin green curtain. There was a little wretched knot of very thin woman in the chair. She had dark hair, thin single very straight strands, her mouth was open, her eyes were closed. She had her skirt up round her waist. Her knees were bent up, almost touching her chin, she clasped them tight with her thin fingers and she rocked to and fro making a very small sound, not a cry, not as loud as that, just a little soft squeak, just a faraway moan.

Dolly stared and then she cried without any movement or sound. She cried because she knew nothing. She cried because all the feelings she'd ever had, feelings of fun, anger, annoyance, determination, suddenly they all crumpled into nothing in this terrible, clean, square space, where something had happened to someone who was her mother, who was Sid's wife, and whatever had happened there had left a gaping hole, something far worse than dying, far worse than that. Dolly felt very cold, very empty. She felt sure that somehow nothing would ever really work again for her. Nothing would ever shine and spin and feel free; well not for her anyway.

After that day and the visit to the hospital Dolly changed. She became moody, sullen, withdrawn and difficult. 'Snap out of it girl,' Lily would say. 'You've no reason to be sorry for yourself. You've got a good figure and a nice pair of legs. You've got nothing to worry about.' Dolly wanted to tell Sid that she had been out to the hospital, but she never did. She just thought, 'I must grow up and get away. I must get away. Maybe to London, maybe there. I must get away.' She felt urgently, desperately, that she must become someone who was not herself. Herself was small and wrong and lost now. She must get away.

Systems of body and soul, recognition of the intrusive complexity of nature, how it is bidden, when and where it succumbs, why it fails and when it rallies and flies, this was the dark conglomerate of mood that in accordance with the nature of things persuaded Dolly and wrung from her uneven attitudes to things and people; all life in general.

It was irritating and exhausting for everyone, but even if

Dolly's behaviour seemed extreme she was at that difficult age, she was, as the sisters said, 'extremely adolescent and ungovernable'. If it pained the sisters it pained Dolly more. If it confused Sid it confused Dolly more. Lily's theory was 'Well, the sooner she's grown through all that, the sooner we'll have some peace.' By 'grown through' Lily probably meant regular periods, regular snogging, a bit of slap and tickle, a good time all round. Lily never allowed herself to be too specific, in this way nothing ever took her by complete surprise.

Because Dolly's interior life felt so turbulent, threatening and senseless, she became very intrigued by anyone who seemed at odds with the rest, anyone who did not conform.

There was Mrs Carter and her daughter Mary. They lived in an old caravan up the lane past the boarding-kennels. They had bodies like tubs, huge and brown. They shuffled very slowly. Any exertion was a strain for Mrs Carter, she huffed and puffed but she always smiled, a wide, careless smile which showed her gold teeth. Their hair hung down rough and straight and greasy, like mops that have been left too long out in the yard. Mrs Carter's clothes were always dark; her worn brown coat was always tied at the middle by rope or baling twine. They came to the village almost every day. Sometimes Mary Carter wore a nightdress under her coat and carpet slippers. They smelt of wood smoke and sour milk and various heaving and sighing bodily smells. From a distance it was hard to tell them apart except that Mrs Carter wore the brown coat and Mary wore a dirty, smog-grey overcoat which dipped at the back where the hem had dropped. They smiled at everyone but they rarely spoke. The tidy, smart, retired service wives, who played bridge and organised the village life; choirs, flower festivals, mothers' union and various amateur dramatics, they always acknowledged Mrs Carter and Mary, but the indigenous local people were less friendly because if it was a sunny day the Carters would sit for several hours on the bench by the bus stop, the only bench in the village centre, which had been presented to the village in memory of Admiral Sir John Bone.

The Carters bought doughnuts from the bakery at least three times a week and tomatoes and ham. Dolly often wondered how it was that the Carters bought tomatoes with a smile when the grander women, the neat, tweedy well-groomed wives, with small yappy dogs on bright leather leads, complained that the price was 'ridiculous. Far too high. Sheer robbery. Extortionate.'

Dolly always made a point to bike past the caravan whenever she could, but she never saw the Carters anywhere outside it, there was only trash and mud, chicken-wire and tin; then suddenly there was Johnny, a beautiful round-faced baby in a huge battered pram. Dolly thought Johnny the best baby she had ever seen. He always smiled a wide open smile just like Mary and Mrs Carter; although he was sticky and smelly with grey-blue dribbles of dirt on his hands and chin it didn't seem to matter.

The intriguing thing to Dolly was that there was Mary Carter, with a thick, dark, dirty boat of a body, hairy legs and greasy hair and yet without any of the fuss that Lily insisted on, there she was, the happy mother of a fine son. Of course when later Dolly heard about dicks and things, what they did behind the scout hut and over by the gravel pits, she vaguely understood. But she still couldn't imagine Mary Carter on the ground or up against a wall with no clothes on. She couldn't imagine a bloke going close enough to her to get it done because of the smell on her. So although Dolly sniggered with the rest of them about 'Sleasy, easy Mary C, left her knickers in a tree', Dolly still secretly believed that there might be something much more special about baby Johnny, like a real immaculate conception. Although Dolly knew that it was meant to be a one-off, with Jesus and everything, Lily always said about tricky things, like war and politics, 'Remember this, if they've done it once, they

44

can do it again.' So Dolly really wondered about Johnny Carter; she always gave him sweets from the shop just in case.

Then there was Stroud-Baker. All the village called him that. Never George, or Colonel or Mr, although sometimes the people in the pub and the trades people just called him 'old S.B.'. He lived in a small bungalow, just beyond the church in Hanger Lane. He had a very red face, very smarmed down black hair and a small moustache. He was very polite indeed, but his politeness never seemed to please anyone. 'That's extremely civil of you, Miss Frampton, very kind indeed,' he would say if Dolly opened the shop door for him. He went to the pub like clockwork every dinner time and then again in the evening. Dolly often saw him when she was hanging around the pub waiting for Lily. He always acknowledged her. He had large round eyes with very dark eyebrows that almost met across the bridge of his nose. His eyes seemed to swim round rather nervously in the loose, tipped-open, red-rimmed sockets. Below his eyes there were giant puffs of soft skin that sagged down towards his moustache, like his trousers sagged onto his brogue shoes. Dolly could never make out why all his attempts at conversation with the other men in their duffel coats and check caps, the majors and colonels and brigadiers and things, were cut off, hastily interrupted or just ignored; almost rude Dolly thought. She knew that there were some women who would actually cross the street to avoid him. Mrs MacArthur was one and Mrs Jameson was another. They would even leave their place in the butcher's queue to avoid standing beside Stroud-Baker.

Sid said that Stroud-Baker had a bit of a past. 'He had no war to speak of,' so they said. He'd been to Kenya where he'd lost everything including his wife. But to Dolly he seemed smart with his blue blazer and brown brogue shoes. It was only when one day she had reason to come very close to him indeed that she realised the blazer was stained and threadbare at the collar and at the cuffs of the sleeves, and that the white shirt was

45

spotted with dried blood from shaving mistakes and that his handkerchief was full of holes and covered with rust marks.

Dolly had been cycling home after doing a few deliveries for the housebound pensioners in the new bungalows when she had suddenly seen him there, flat on his face, spreadeagled on the black run of tarmac outside the ironmonger's. The shops were shut so there were few people about. At first Dolly thought that Stroud-Baker must be dead, he was so still, but when she got off her bike and knelt down beside him she heard his heavy, bubbly kind of breathing. Dolly pulled him over on to his side. She loosened his tie. She'd learnt about that in a first-aid manual. His face was very red. He seemed confused, then he recognised her and smiled gratefully. Dolly knew by then, she had guessed from the smell of his breath, from the reeking drops of whisky-saliva on his moustache; he was drunk. He got himself up in the end. And then he carried on down the road, swaying a little, then pausing, then staggering and then going on again.

So gradually, variously, just by this and that; things, people, sayings, moments, Dolly realised that there were frayed edges, holes, mistakes, mess and muddle always. When to stop and where to go weren't nearly as obvious and cut and dried as the sisters made out.

Dolly took shorthand and typing and domestic science and dropped almost everything else. She peroxided her hair. She played the gramophone as loud as she could. She was fascinated now, not by Lily's body, but by her own. She never let herself think of her mother. It was as if she had wrapped the whole thing in a great grey sack and had tied it down with the ropes of her own determination to proceed; to get up and go; to get away; to get on with her own life, which would be different from the slow, dull sludge of the village, the sisters and the bakery.

The occasion of Dolly's departure from her home was not however in any way how she had imagined it might be. In fact it was more of a dismissal than anything else. She never knew or understood why Sid, who had been so silent, so gentle, so easy going for so long, she never knew why he had reacted so violently.

She must have been fifteen when it happened. She'd left school and was working in a shoe shop in Aldershot carrying on with the shorthand and typing three evenings a week. It was a Friday night. It was August. The day was hot and muggy, it had been like that for several days. Being Friday, she'd left a little late. She had no class that night so she made her way directly up towards the bus station. The streets were pretty crowded, the pavements were too narrow. The streets were always full of soldiers; waving and whistling, nudging and winking. There was always the thump of their boots behind you as you went along. They jostled people a bit, always giving themselves the edge over everyone else, usually walking three abreast. The tired young mothers, the elderly shoppers more often than not gave way to them, after all they had just won the war. Uniform, parade grounds, the scream of a squaddy, camouflaged trucks holding up the green buses, it wasn't so much to put up with after all that had gone before.

Dolly never knew exactly how it had begun. It was just a lark. It was just a bit of fun. There was this truck stopped in a siding down by the railway, and three lads in it, in uniform but off duty. There were a couple of girls with them and crates of beer and a bottle of rum and bars of chocolate. They just called out the usual things, 'Give us a kiss. Come on saucy.' Just the usual. Nothing particular. But it was Friday night and summer and their young free faces bending down over the tailboard of the truck, their tanned arms, with bright hairs on them blond as butter. It all seemed to Dolly then the most natural thing in the world to jump up, get in there and join them. They'd just changed a tyre and they were ready now. They were off to the ponds at Pedlars Ford to swim, to picnic, to have a bit of fun.

Dolly remembered loving the bumps and potholes when they got right out on to the heathland and were on the dirt tracks. The truck bounded and reeled and they fell about on one another, laps and legs, breasts and shirt buttons all tousled and heaped and carefree. Then they picnicked and swam. The boys in their khaki shorts and the girls in petticoats. They used an empty tin can to muck about with, to throw at one another, to douse each other with the murky water. Then it got cooler, dusky. There were two small towels which they all shared. The beer was finished and the chocolate and crisps and ham, there was just the rum. They paired off then to Dolly's delight. She wanted it all, the strong arms, the jokes, the teasing. She felt quite free of that sack in her now, free of Lily and Sid, free from the anxious trap of herself; who she was or who she was not, all that kind of miserable muddle. She was free of that. There was a run in her now, a zest, a spring; she would seize it, go with it, canter free. Rum was better than rum blah blah she thought as she squirmed and then lay there unbuttoned, unbent beside him. The moonlight on the crossed bracken stalks reminded her of the lattice criss-cross on a lemon curd tart. She giggled again. To think she was lying like this, her round, firm breasts bare to the high summer sky like fresh doughnuts! She giggled again. His mouth was soft there, caring and discovering; his head jostled and pushed at her tits like young cattle at the bucket; then suddenly it was painful, rough, greedy; strong and fierce and greedy. Suddenly the laughing, loose, light rhythm that carelessly, only seconds before, seemed to be leading her, fled. She felt his fist and fingers in between her legs and up there roughly into the sharp, narrow dark of her last child's space. She felt afraid, lost, suddenly hurled down into panic and dark. He was so heavy and mad on top of her. Beyond the close shadow of him the moon seemed to spit a poisoned evil light everywhere.

48

'Get off. Get off.'

She screamed. He paused. She closed her eyes and tried to say it again, she tried to say it again but her voice was just a pathetic whimper. There was nothing now but this burst of sharp, stinging pain.

'Fuck,' he said. 'Fuck.'

His voice was hot and furred. He seemed to pause again, to hesitate. Then in a rasping gorge of movement he drowned her in a throb of shame which she would never ever really shift from the map of herself. No one had ever told her it was this. No one had ever told her. No one had ever said. She knew that the moon would never be magic to her again, it would always be like some giant prying witness, a peering, judging, scheming eye boring a hole into her, a gimlet slit of shame. Had every woman with every child, had they all done this?

At last the heavy, throbbing horror of it ceased. He moved over. He sat back alone from her somewhere else. Dolly lay there still; so still. She pulled her skirt back down. She was crying hot coal-tears on to her cool cheeks. She wanted above all else to make no sound. It was as if she could crawl back into the raw, dark pain of it and like an animal, like a rat or mole, become very small, very still, very hidden.

The moon was almost full. It was there above the bracken and the soft brown, elephant ripples of sand and still water. Then she heard the crackle of his boots on the dry stalks. She listened. She stared at the moon, hating its cold power; all its vivid emptiness. She heard the others coming back towards the truck. She heard them open the doors and drop down the tail-gate. Small sounds are huge in still moonlight, she thought. Gradually she sat up. Then she saw the glow of his cigarette and the shadow of him coming back slowly towards her. She was sitting with her knees hunched up to her chin, just staring, staring, staring ahead at the bracken and the bank and the water.

'Come on,' he said. 'We'll drop you off. Hitcham Green, that right?'

He was holding his hand out to help her up. He was different again; quiet, ordinary. She got up. They went back over the sandy ground and dry stalks to the great square dumpy shape of the truck. He helped her up into the back. The others were in the front. He even put his shirt down on the cold metal ridge for her to sit on. She never spoke. There was still the pain and all the mess on her legs. They drove off. It didn't take long. They were soon back among the streetlights. She never spoke to him again except when she saw the lights from the garage and the newsagent's window and then the bakery with S.G. Frampton painted in brown and cream paint, then she just said 'Here.' And he knocked on the driver's window and the truck pulled in and stopped.

He helped her down. She let him, but she said nothing.

The village street was quiet, still, completely deserted. The moon shone on the harsh brown tiles of the village hall roof and on the metal bars by the bus-stop and on the high privet hedge of the caretaker's cottage. As Dolly walked slowly round into the bakery yard she thought of them, of Sid and Lily. Sid was bound to be in bed because of early baking tomorrow, and Lily. She had just thought 'Lily' when she saw them both standing there in front of her in the yard, Sid in his striped pyjamas and Lily in her short nylon quilted dressing-gown.

Dolly was about to say something about Friday night and the girls and a party when Lily came forward to Dolly. With ears as sharp as any guard-dog she had recognised the unmistakable engine sound of an army truck. She had pulled back the net curtain. She had not been mistaken. And now, she came forward to Dolly and grabbed at her skirt, pulling it forward like a large white plate under the spill of the moonlight. Then Dolly saw it; the glaring mess, the blood, the stains.

'So that's what it's all been worth is it? Any bloke anywhere? Just the back of a truck anytime? You filthy little whore, you shameful stupid bitch.'

Then Sid spoke. His voice was different. It was huge and cold and distant.

'Go inside Lily,' he said. 'Go on.'

Lily went inside leaving Sid and Dolly alone together on the smooth black moonlit asphalt.

'Go into the bakery,' Sid said to Dolly. He said it very quietly, very definitely, almost to himself. Dolly wanted to scream out, to run across to him. She desperately wanted to find all the gentleness and quiet he had always been. She wanted to tell him. She wanted to tell him about her visit to the hospital, she wanted to tell him of the dark muddle in her after that which had made her want to get away to find someone somehow different from herself. But she found she could say nothing. She couldn't even mutter, she could hardly move. Sid pointed to the bakery door and she found she was walking quite calmly ahead of him, feeling that everything about her was already written, already planned. She felt very destitute, very empty as if she had suddenly vomited all her life, all of herself into this bleak, steel moonlight air. She was relieved in a way when she was inside the bakery where there was just one small light. She was relieved to be away from the biting glare of the moon.

Inside the bakery it was stuffy. It was full of smells: bread, yeast, warm fats; bountiful smells. It was full of particular shapes that she had always known this was the stage, the real structure, the backroom of all her life; the huge dark holes of the empty ovens, the heavy metal doors wide open, the bulging sacks of flour, the stacked racks, the wooden trays and the long metal arms, like devil's rakes, for pushing and pulling the hot trays in and out of the ovens.

Sid was shaking. Dolly noticed that he was sweating and trembling. He took down the broad leather belt from the hook on the door. It was the belt he wore round his white overall when he was in the bakery.

'Soft,' he said. 'Sid's so soft they all say. Putty. A real pushover. Soft my girl. Too soft, that's what they all say. But no longer Dolly. No longer. Not any more.' The belt was lying there as smooth as soap in the palm of his hand. He was looking down at it very intently, then suddenly he grabbed Dolly by the arm. Her small patent-leather shoulder-bag fell open on to the stone flags hurling combs, clips, lipstick and tissues like a wide throw of dice rolling here and there into the dark smudgy corners under the table. Sid pushed Dolly down across the wide wooden surface where usually he pounded the warm dough. Her plump little arse was barely covered by the short white skirt, her full soft buttocks seemed to shiver in the mad still pause of both their hearts beating with confusion, rage and misery. Then at last Sid brought the belt down across the shivering flesh. At first it fell loosely, then he got the rhythm and the tension right, so that the belt fell again and again, and the sharp even thrash of sound was almost in unison with the kennel yell of Dolly's rigid screams.

Eventually, completely exhausted, Sid slumped down on to the low stool by the pile of bread baskets at the door. He dropped his head into his hands. He didn't move. Dolly, stiff, almost senseless, almost without any fraction of mind left, stumbled back through the dark house to her room and her narrow bed, where she just lay down on the top of the covers. In the dark she stared up at the ceiling, up into the rank, stiff, torn hopelessness from which somehow tomorrow she must make out some sense of herself.

Sid stayed all night in the bakery. He wept as he believed no man could weep. Dolly never ever knew that it was earlier in the day, that day, when Sid had heard of Ruth's death. Pneumonia they said. Very gently. Very suddenly. How could they use words like 'gentle' and 'sudden' to a man who for so many years had witnessed a great withering river of such distress bind and drive and drown the frail, gentle woman he had always loved. In Sid's mind all Ruth's life of pain had in some way been the gift to Dolly of her laughter, her cheek; her life. A life which it seemed she had wrenched from one pit only to throw it summarily away into another.

Ruth was cremated. Only Sid and Lily were at the small ceremony. Later Sid planted a memorial rose bush in the garden of remembrance. He chose it from dozens of catalogues. He chose it with great care. A red rose he had said to the man in the ironmonger's. But they had to sift through fifty or more coloured photographs of red roses until at last Sid found a floribunda. It was a large, full-blown flower; a bright fierce orange vermilion. It will bloom Sid thought with all the freedom Ruth's lips so longed to find but never could. It will flower, he thought, very bright and very red, just for her, season after season.

The next morning Dolly remained in her room. Lily brought her tea and toast on a tray and suggested that she 'lay there for a bit'.

Lily had heard Dolly's screams from the bakery. She had heard it all right, but she had decided that it was not her business to interfere.

She was only there after all as a pair of hands about the place. She couldn't take responsibility if the girl went wrong, and it wouldn't surprise anyone. Lily felt sorry for Sid. Sid's life was the real tragedy. That girl will make out. That girl will get on. There was only one possibility more fearful than all the rest and that was the idea of Dolly pregnant. If it did happen Lily thought it bloody well wasn't going to happen here at the bakery.

It was for this reason that Lily rang a cousin in Basingstoke who had just come out of hospital and suggested that Dolly might go over and spend several weeks with them to help out generally.

When Lily came into Dolly's room and told her the plan Dolly accepted it without any comment or reaction. Dolly stayed in her room for the Saturday and the Sunday. On the Monday she caught the bus while Sid was out doing deliveries. Dolly had thought of leaving Sid a note, but in the end she didn't.

Dolly remained in Basingstoke for several months. Eventually she moved on to Croydon where she got a job in a shop and was able to take a secretarial course in the evenings. After some while she moved from Croydon to Streatham. Wherever she was things were pretty much the same; work, buses, a good crowd of girls, and the pub. The pub became mother and father to her. It was always there, a six o'clock smile seven days a week. It was something she could rely on. It was always the same, like an old song heard again and again and again; glistening lights, smoke, the smell of sausages, crisps, heavy scents and sweat, and old, worn down, beer-swill smells; pretty well always there was a free drink and the feeling, the best feeling for Dolly nowadays, the feeling of being more than a body, more than a boring job, the feeling of being well and truly alive. In the pub she had a voice, she had a pert cheerful way with her that people liked, the girls might snigger but the blokes would bother; one way or another they came round, they got chatting. It was only afterwards that the numb, dead clamp of stagnant lost feelings invaded her, practically overwhelmed her. It was when she woke early with a cracking head and saw piles of unwashed clothes on the floor, the stained carpet and the small cracked oval mirror on the dressing-table. It was then that she tried to conceive of a way out; a plan to better herself. Dolly so badly wanted things to be nice, to be really nice, fresh and shining and new. She didn't want to be raw and cheap and common. She didn't want to grow old and blousy like Lily. She was determined not to fall for the kind of lads the other girls went with. They were

54

all right, but they were so rough, so ordinary. They just wanted a woman for sex and their tea on time with maybe kids later on. Dolly wasn't going to fall for that. She wanted something better, a bit more education, a bit of real class and style.

Although these were Dolly's resolves in theory, in practice there was nothing about her life to suggest they would materialise. Then she got herself a job in a pub in Fulham. She moved from Streatham. She moved across the river. The money wasn't much, less than if she was to work in a store in Oxford Street, but the pub was good. Here she might meet a different class of person altogether. Here there would be real variety. And it was a lovely bar, all brass fittings and old shining mahogany and green leather benches and chandeliers. It was called the Spencer Arms.

THREE

When Violet Farr conceived after ten barren years of marriage, she looked forward to the arrival of her child more as an occasion of curiosity than anything else.

Violet had always assumed that marriage would involve offspring, but it was never from her point of view a particularly central issue, perhaps because her 'point of view' was focused from the rather bleak, stale, uninspired business of her physical relationship with her husband Cecil. Perhaps it was the uniform that had been the betrayer. She would never know. Violet had first met Cecil when they were young people caught in the throes of that difficult transition from schoolroom to society. They had spent several summers in Kilbronan, both their families had holiday dwellings not far from the bay and they had often met down there by the pier, or among the dark rocks, or up beyond, on the stony bare mountain, or down in the cluster of pine trees that led to the ruined cottages on the point at Dunmanah.

The Fitzpatricks had a small white-washed stone house set back a little from the village into the mountain, with its own cluster of Scots pines and several small parcels of land, bounded by loose, crumbling stone walls. The house had two chimneys, one at either end, a slate roof and two dormer windows from which there was a grand view of the bay.

The house had originally belonged to Violet's Aunt Theodora, Lumsden Fitzpatrick's younger sister. Theodora was a wild, eccentric woman whose chaotic life only really made sense at her death, when several bundles of letters were found in the bottom drawer of the press amongst layers of carefully folded embroidered silk underwear and lingerie; there were slips, cami-knickers, bed-jackets and nightdresses all neatly placed between layers of white tissue paper that had grown brittle and slightly brown and smelt of mint and dried lavender. The letters were very loosely tied together with pink ribbon. On avid inspection by the family, the letters were found to be from a passionate and totally unavailable tea planter in Assam. His name was Sam Thorpe. There was no photograph, no physical description, so the family assumed the worst possible attributes to the loyal, letter-writing lover whose continual promises of eventual availability had obviously kept Theodora's heart on a spider's thread of longing and hope that was totally unrewarding. Gradually, after various strange 'flings', random travel, odd friendships with unlikely people; travelling people, circus people, she had made her way to the isolated little house above Kilbronan Bay and succumbed to the power of opiates, tranquillisers and liberal draughts of Powers, or Paddy, to lull her through the waiting, which she knew in her heart was hopeless. Sam Thorpe even referred in the letters to 'our true meeting, my dear, at the end of time, untrammelled then, dearest one, by either History or Society'.

Living alone with a small mongrel bitch, Scraggy, who Theodora had found tied to a rock up on the mountain, two budgerigars, a cat and a goldfish, she withdrew from the outside world, rarely speaking except to her own, flotsam tribe of creatures. She battled with the drink and the drugs until finally the central, yearning longing in her life moved from the memory of three passionate weeks with Sam Thorpe in Paris before the outbreak of the Great War, to the simple, silent, all-enveloping and all-available caress of chocolate, cream fudge, fully sweetened condensed milk over a bowl of tinned pears, Turkish delight, or full cream over smooth, glowing, cling peaches.

Theodora grew so vast, so breathless, so shapeless that she was known only for this bizarre quality of her life. Not to a soul was she known for the deep, painful, real wound of her sorrow and her loneliness. Her death was caused not by heart failure as all her neighbours anticipated, but by gangrene in the hand, and finally raging septicaemia.

Sam Thorpe had given to Theodora during their illicit fling in Paris, a gold ring, embedded with small pearls and diamonds. He had put it gently on the finger of a very striking, very thin young woman, whose lithe flowing body he was never ever to forget; he could see her always on the edge of the bed in the charming, pale cream embroidered silk underwear she always wore.

Theodora knew that the centre, the real sound of her life had been those three weeks and she would far rather die than ever take that ring off her finger. Naturally as her general grossness fleshed out far beyond any design of skeletal reference, the poor little ring became embedded in puffy, throbbing, uneasy skin, where finally, although quite hidden, it caused a complete arrest of the blood flow and so was responsible for Theodora's death.

Naturally Theodora knew that the ring was the cause of the pain. She fully realised the danger to her life if she did not seek help, but it consoled her that her death, the death of a vast, loose landscape of unruly flesh, in a small stone house above Kilbronan Bay, on one of the farthest westerly coasts of Europe, her death was caused by an action; a symbol of love slipped on to her finger by Sam Thorpe in the Tuileries Gardens so long ago. A gold ring slipped on to her finger then, as easily and with as much mastery, elegance, and ardour, as he had slipped into herself.

The considerable pain and loneliness of Theodora Fitzpatrick's death horrified neighbours and relatives, but when the family eventually found the small bundles of letters and the beautiful, scant, embroidered silk lingerie it was Violet who suggested with some excitement that the small ring cut from her Aunt Theodora's huge corpse might be the crucial connection. It would explain so much. It would give meaning to her life. But these romantic thoughts of Violet's were fiercely and summarily denied by the other relatives, who thought it essential to scotch immediately this ridiculous kind of talk by a young girl of sixteen, as Violet then was. Such preoccupations, her mother felt, were deeply unhealthy. Mrs Fitzpatrick burnt the letters and gave the underwear to the poor, who she did not seek out herself but left Mary Daly down at the stores to do so.

Violet was furious with her mother, she wanted to keep the letters herself and the underwear.

'The poor will look utterly stupid in those slips and things, Mother,' she said. 'They'll be so cold. They'll hate them.'

'They'll find some use for them I'm sure,' her mother replied tartly. 'Polishing silver perhaps.'

Violet had always scorned her mother in the way she felt her father had done. Violet scorned her for her fussy, bourgeois, muddled, utter stupidity.

'The poor don't have silver, Mother,' she had screamed at the ditheringly busy little woman who had never been spoken to so rudely before. The occasion resulted in a deep rift between the two. Violet simply avoided any kind of conversation or discussion with her mother. On her part, her mother decided that Violet should go abroad, 'because she was getting quite beyond herself, here at home'.

It was in the midst of this tense family business that Violet, out alone on a brisk walk to attempt some control over her emotions, found Cecil Farr fishing off Kilbronan Pier. To his considerable surprise Violet urgently and excitedly begged him to walk with her up on the mountain.

Cecil Farr was a thin unprepossessing young man, he knew Violet and admired her greatly from a distance. He had always assumed himself to be far too dull a fellow to be in a class with her, so he was delighted and amazed to have her disturb his fishing and blurt out so eagerly such a forward suggestion.

Breathlessly, as they walked up the mountain, Violet told Cecil of her Aunt Theodora's death; the ring, the love letters and the divine silk underwear. The wind blew her hair across her face and she had to pause continually to gather the strands off her lips in order to go on with the saga. Cecil noticed how white, how even, her teeth were, he noticed how strong and pronounced her eyebrows were, how firm and definite her breasts under the thin, pin-tucked, slightly starched blouse. He noticed above all the passionate, defiant energy of her. The way she kicked at fir cones and twigs, the way she jumped up every so often on to a flat stone or boulder and then turned back towards the bay so that the sunlight was full on her face, and declared how utterly stupid and pathetic her mother was, with all the intensity of a preacher or politician; the way she swore if her skirt caught on a thorn-bush. She seemed to be such a master of herself, Cecil thought; he felt beside her less than mistress of his own tentative thoughts and slight, rather dubious passions.

Violet was so caught up in the tale of Aunt Theodora's tragedy as she saw it, that Cecil's presence was simply to her a companion footstep giving her reason to tell the tale aloud. In that remote Kilbronan afternoon there had been no one else. She hardly noticed as she slipped on some loose stones on the way down the mountain that Cecil had taken her arm. 'Look,' he had said, 'your knee's bleeding', and he had offered her his handkerchief. 'Oh fiddlesticks,' she had said, 'that'll soon dry', and she had ignored his handkerchief and had torn instead a large dock leaf from its stalk to wipe away the bright, blackberry bead of blood.

Cecil had put the dock leaf into his handkerchief. He had had little success with women, of whom he was rather afraid. He felt that if he kept the leaf, anyway for some while, he could, without too much dishonesty, declare to his friends the conquest he had made this summer in Kilbronan. He could boast of his walk alone with Violet Fitzpatrick.

*

Violet visited London and Paris. She stayed for long periods in Dublin. On account of her father's considerable reputation she easily became a bright light among the various fringes of the 'literati'. She worked for a while in a bookshop at the bottom of Dawson Street which was close enough to Trinity College to ensure some fraternisation with the students. She was an ardent supporter of the theatre and she played the flute in a small orchestral ensemble. She completely forgot that there ever was such a person as Cecil Farr.

It was several years later that out of the blue one Sunday afternoon when Violet was staying with her cousins in South Kensington that unannounced Cecil Farr visited her. The afternoon, in fact her whole visit to London, was dull and uneventful. She was playing bezique with her cousin Margery, but she was not attending to the cards. She was gazing out over the square; at the children and their nursemaids, the pitch dark trunks of the trees, the sparrows, the ratty, scurvy, ferocious scuttle of the squirrels. She had noticed a cab driving slowly round the square. She had noticed that it had paused very close to the house. But she was totally taken aback when the maid announced that there was a visitor for Miss Violet. 'A,' and the maid paused to smile coyly at Violet, which irritated her enormously, 'a Captain Farr,' she said, relishing the word Captain. Violet was flustered, surprised but nevertheless intrigued. At first the name Captain Cecil Farr meant absolutely nothing to her. She said it several times to herself: Farr . . . Cecil Farr. And then she remembered.

She remembered Kilbronan, the bay, the mountain, the small stone house and Aunt Theodora. Suddenly looking at her prim cousin and this over-stuffed, over-furnished room, she yearned for Ireland, for its freedom, its rich scope of space and melancholy. Violet disliked the English, they were kind enough and very civil in their way but they could not hide their distrust and rather snobbish disdain for the Irish even if they were from within the pale. Above all they were supremely ignorant of the part their country had played in Ireland's sad and noble history. Beyond the pale to them was a mist of violent, routing, ill-educated people led by crazed poets and popish nationalists. The English admired Swift, Burke, Spenser and Sheridan, naturally. But the very act of their admiration seemed to diminish and alter any real acknowledgment of their truly Irish status, milking them of any intrinsically Irish quality, modifying their roots, their blood, their ancestry.

Violet knew that many Irishmen had joined the British Forces but she did not know Cecil Farr was one of them.

When he came into the drawing-room, it was the uniform, its sumptuous brave declaration, the sharp spat and sparkle of it that struck Violet and her cousin Margery. The slight stoop had gone, the skin was healthy and smooth, without blemish. The eyes however were still tentative, unassuming, embedded within this disguise of supreme authority and dash, they seemed to Violet rather touching and really very Irish.

Cecil, whose years of training had been strenuous and deeply unhappy, stood nervously before the two surprised young women. He was immensely grateful for the structure and texture of his uniform which he felt gave him a pretty sound social status from which to proceed.

'Gerry Leinster told me you were here in London,' he said, 'so I thought I might just look you up. I do hope it's not inconvenient.'

'Not in the least,' Violet said. She was most amused that Cecil Farr of all people should be standing here in the drawing-room of 38 Onslow Square Gardens actually impressing her cousin Margery.

Later, in grim harsh moods of hindsight, Violet more or less admitted to herself that it almost certainly was the uniform. The uniform referred obliquely to honour; to the concept of service to fellow men, something like that; a vaguely corporate kind of caring, big schemes anyway; a wider world; a powerful vision of life and death, of course death. But death was no point of reference then in the drawing-room of Onslow Square Gardens.

Cecil and Violet saw each other two or three times in the subsequent week before Cecil's departure overseas. For Violet these were light-hearted, frivolous expeditions enabling her to impress her wretched cousin Margery and remember Ireland, Kilbronan and her poor Aunt Theodora. She attached no other importance to them. For Cecil their assignments were important, even crucial. It was not that he loved Violet. He did not. He respected her. He was fascinated by her and he wanted in some way, which he did not understand, to have a part of her energy and confidence. Strange and disturbing emotions which he had sometimes felt at school suddenly returned to him during the rigorous military training: parades, showers, barrack rooms, messing generally; the endless rough proximity of man to man, the physical, raw, flesh contact, breath and smells and bodies always close, always present. Suddenly those strange and disturbing emotions he had sometimes felt at school battened down on him again; unnervingly vivid and profoundly, miserably, compelling. There had been more than one occasion when he had felt the painful, challenging urge to caress; to hold and to be held by another man. Cecil was terrified of these emotions and urges. He made every effort he could to banish them. But then there would be without warning, in the nape of a neck, a glance, a firm held feel of limbs, purposely close, a second's recognition between another man and himself of this same need. No moment yet had gone beyond the bounds of unspoken instinct, understood longing. But the situation left

Cecil exceedingly perplexed and fearful. He wished that some crisis, some event might intrude on this brooding, complex, mysterious pyre of feelings against which, most unwillingly, he felt himself to be strapped. In order to reassure himself that he was made properly and entirely as he was meant to be he spoke often to the other young officers of Violet Fitzpatrick. To have a known girlfriend, was, he felt, a kind of declaration. He did not work things out too specifically, but in some sense he had decided that maybe if he touched her, even kissed her, then the other disturbing, powerful inclinations might subside, evaporate, be finally and mercifully lost to him. But during the shopping expeditions with Violet, the tea-rooms and the bus stops, no real opportunity cropped up. At their final meeting and farewell they did kiss briefly. For Violet it was a tease for Margery who she knew was looking out of the upstair window. For Cecil it was a hesitant moment of regard with no physical sense in it whatsoever. Disappointed he returned to barracks and from there to action overseas. But he built the occasion up in his mind. He persuaded himself that it had had about it some quality, some physicality. He held on to it desperately. He wrote the name Violet Farr on cigarette boxes and scraps of paper. In the end the written words became for him some kind of a receptacle, some kind of repository.

Although Cecil sent several short letters to Violet during the subsequent months there was nothing in them to prepare her for what was to follow.

Violet was back in Dublin working in the bookshop in Dawson Street. She had set her cap at Finbar O'Dwyer, a man considerably older than herself, who was doing research into medieval Celtic literature. He was a fascinating and intelligent man, but his Catholic roots, he was from Corofin in County Clare, and his ardent republican views made him deeply suspect and totally unsuitable for Violet from the point of view of her mother, various other relatives and the family lawyers. Perhaps it was the nearest Violet ever came during the long course of her life to really holding another human being both in high regard and deep affection.

The afternoon in the bookshop when she received a final letter from Finbar severing their relationship completely on the grounds of her youth and his own unreliable way of life, was the same day that later in the evening she heard violent knocking on the front door of the small terraced house she was living in.

On Violet's return home from the bookshop with Finbar's letter, her genuine hurt and distress became very soon, which was the pattern for Violet, a self-righteous, self-pitying anger. Finbar's letter was so paternalistic, so boringly protective, inferring that she was not yet ready for real life and real responsibilities; it angered her. She cried. She stomped up and down her room thinking how foolish and blind men were; if only her father were alive, he would have acknowledged her intellect, her maturity; he would never have patted her down and patronised her. She rubbed her eyes furiously with her handkerchief. She brushed at her long hair as if she were beating dust out of a carpet, then she threw the hairbrush on the floor and flopped face down on her bed, hitting at the bolster with her fists like an angry child.

Mrs Muldoon, her landlady, opened the door. She saw Violet Fitzpatrick with red eyes and unruly hair, she saw her petulant and distraught.

'Mrs Muldoon,' Violet said, 'please always knock and then wait. Never simply knock and enter.' 'But, Miss Fitzpatrick, it's a bit of an emergency,' said Mrs Muldoon, trying to cover up her purposeful indiscretion. 'Emergency at this time of night, Mrs Muldoon!' Violet said scrambling to her feet. 'Indeed, Miss Fitzpatrick I'm as surprised as yourself but there's a very distressed young gentleman at the door, he seems most anxious to see you and he doesn't seem in too grand a way himself, he's very thin.'

The young gentleman was Cecil Farr. He had been invalided

out of the army. He had become very thin and noticeably unwell. There was blood and albumen in the urine. He was diagnosed as having severe nephritis, a kidney disease which might prove fatal, this was subsequently, years later, proved to have been a misdiagnosis.

That night Cecil told Violet of his illness, but at the same time he told her of his inheritance and his prospects; then desperately, pathetically, he pleaded, begged for her to marry him. 'I know it seems absurd,' he said, 'but I need your strength. Please, please allow me to marry you.' Even as he spoke, Violet translated what he said not as a reference to any physical relationship but as a challenge to life; her life at last. At least Cecil recognised her strength. With him, with marriage, she would show the lawyers and relatives, the small minded prattling gossips who were her mother's friends. She would, as Violet Farr, show them some style, some bite. She would cease to be 'that girl, that child'. She would be a wife, the leader of a household; mistress at last of her own demesne.

It was to Cecil's utter amazement that Violet Fitzpatrick, red-eyed, dishevelled, hair flying electrically in every direction, stood on the doorstep of Mrs Muldoon's small terraced house in Dublin and accepted his strange, urgent and totally unexpected proposal of marriage.

Mrs Muldoon perplexed and fascinated gave the young man tea, a small shot of whiskey and some fresh soda bread with good butter and a bit of her own marmalade. Violet and Cecil sat opposite one another at the heavy mahogany table while Mrs Muldoon fussed and chatted and studied this odd pair. When Violet later announced to Mrs Muldoon that she and Captain Cecil Farr were to be married, she had thought to herself that perhaps their unsuitability was the best thing about it. But they were two of a kind in that they were of the same social standing, poor creatures, neither one thing or the other. Not English and not Irish as Mrs Muldoon understood it. They might have lands and power, wealth and all that, but they'd never know the real God given spirit of the land, so help them!

Mrs Muldoon did wonder what kind of a brood could possibly find their way into the world with that pair. He so thin, so unmanly and she so defiant and quick tempered. It was a sensible thought on Mrs Muldoon's part as ten barren years were to follow the hasty marriage and the one child eventually born to them, who was christened Lumsden after Violet's deceased father, was to prove in a sense a changeling child. Certainly he had an aspect to him that was dark and powerful. There was within his nature a part that seemed to be a jesting intruder, made to pluck at good; to bruise, wither and singe simple sensibilities and so leave disorder, drained belief and dire, peculiar distress behind him.

*

They bought Rathmanagh with Cecil's inheritance. It was a substantial stone house with considerable stabling and out-buildings and several run-down acres of farmland. Most of the meadows round the house were sour and rank pasture, unkempt, unmanaged. The house was just over the humped bridge, at the Claggan end of Ballynaule. Going that way out of the village, leaving Rooney's bar on your left and the small school opposite, only recently built, on your right, the road soon came to a cross. About a mile on from there, just past the field where Pat Mulligan kept his black horse, there was a turn right up the hill, and then very soon, a stride or so on, no more, there was the start of the Demesne wall, with the first pair of gates a little further on, opposite the single great oak tree on the other side of the road.

From the gates the house couldn't be seen. The drive wound upwards for some time; just as the roofs became visible on the right of the drive, the ground sloped away steeply on the left, suddenly revealing the very particular presence of the Mount of Murna. It was a startling view, this strange, powerful shape of ground, unlike any other. The mountain rose up bare and ample, yet tense. From the long, colonnaded porch of Rathmanagh, the mountain had a painful, humped ridge, with a sudden incline and then another small thrust forward again, like the head of an animal. Although Mount Murna was several woods and fields away, and the width of the river, and another climb on from the house itself, it seemed close; a kind of guardian shape to the height and mournful mass of grey-green stone that was the house. Huge trees and dark, high hedges flanked the house on either side as if the eye of the house must be trained continually towards Murna; the moods and the force of the mountain.

It was a great landmark for the whole area, but there was not a better view of it than from the windows in front of the house, or in the long, colonnaded porch. There was even a ballad well known throughout Ireland with the Mount of Murna mentioned in the refrain. The ballad was 'The Lament of Brigid' or 'The Slaying of Croncranach' and the refrain was

> *Weeping beneath the Mount of Murna*
> *She found Croncranach slain*
> *The bravest brigand of the Valley*
> *Had brought her naught but shame.*

Violet knew the ballad and felt that it was Mount Murna that had really sold Rathmanagh to them, or more accurately to her. Cecil, unwell, dejected, his career as such in ruins, his manhood unrealised, wanted only to please Violet; to allow Violet; to applaud Violet. It was a dangerous, far too heady mixture of power and praise for a young woman, who had not yet ever felt deeply enough to have seen others with the same intensity with which she saw herself. For Violet, having been briefly 'unhorsed' as it were by Finbar's dismissal of her, it was as if now she had a fresh mount, a real steed; from this place of power and vantage she could scout out her perimeters and utterly command and possess them. Cecil was very soon quite forgotten by her as being the relevant, the initiating, factor for her new found status and power.

Cecil thought he did not mind. He supposed he was safe; hidden from the charms and claims that had begun to best him almost to a point of madness. There was so much to be done, so many people to meet, so many banal things to say. But the fullness, the practical buzz of their life together, still left Cecil with many many private moments of perplexed anxiety; then he was grateful to Violet for her scorn and chiding, she forced him away from the intense discomfort of himself. This was to be the pattern of his life. Outside observers felt sorry for Cecil; they were appalled by Violet's public disdain of him. Cecil knew this but his love and admiration for her only grew because he was hidden. Like lice in a tomb. Like badgers underground. By Violet he was hidden, with no public status, he was banished, engulfed, out of the sight of light.

Violet entered with verve and gusto into the management of both the house and the farmland. She was determined to cut a dash as a young married woman, to be recognised as someone who was from the intelligentsia of Dublin. She wanted to impress the local hard hunting ladies. She wanted to ensure that they understood that her milieu was sophisticated, intelligent and broadly based. She made sure that they realised she had family contacts in France and Germany as well as London. She had an aunt who lived in Innsbruck and a widowed uncle who was in a home for the elderly in Fontainebleau.

Violet, having inherited a very considerable library from her father, wanted to impress her neighbours with her literary background. She did not want to lose a certain vigour and thrust of language which she knew she had but which she feared might certainly die if her only topics of conversation were brewers, bloodstock, beef cattle, and the general blight of the Holy Roman Church over the mind, spirit and judgment of the local community. Violet's vitality, availability and linguistic drive made her very soon the obvious choice as committee member or school governor, and the obvious guest if any foreigner or arts patron visited the county. Her life outside her marriage was never dull.

There certainly was some musing and gossip on the childlessness of the young couple at Rathmanagh. The small community in the village of Ballynaule and the surrounding holdings and farms assumed it to be a sadness. For they who bred so easily and so often in such trying and derelict circumstances, there was some irony that this young couple, with so much property; so many rooms, so many cows, still showed no sign whatsoever of bearing a child.

Violet fully realised, although she never allowed herself to dwell too much on it, in case further darker considerations would be forced to follow, she fully realised that it was not so much infertility that caused her childlessness, but quite simply a lack of the necessary activity to make it even remotely possible for her to conceive a child.

The honeymoon in Connemara in a fishing hotel, which truthfully was little more than a basic guesthouse, had been a disaster. The bed had been too small, the walls of the bedroom too thin, and neither of them had been roused or encouraged by their physical proximity. Each tried to infer that they were giving way to the awkwardness of the other. On their return to Rathmanagh Violet instantly attended to the redecoration of Cecil's dressing-room. The hint was taken. Very soon there was no attempt made even to caress. Communication was always concerned with practical problems: wages, debts, builders, tenants, markets, machinery, or the social calendar; meets, committees, various small gatherings in vast cold ragged rooms that clung to faded grandeur and bizarre incongruous household improvements; here they were introduced, welcomed and minutely observed.

Certainly the marriage had been consummated – but with anxiety and dogged determination rather than pleasure of any kind. However, as the years passed and the structure of their life established itself, there definitely emerged between them, in the no-man's-land of their relationship, that subtle space, where neither assumed complete control or utter deference; there grew here an unspoken sense that they must try a little harder to come a little closer. Cecil's health had improved. He was not so thin. His life was no longer threatened. Violet had decorated the house with real flair and originality. She had a small parlour sitting-room just beyond the more formal library. It was a marvellous clutter of dog-baskets, plants, papers, magazines and a large collection of sea-shells which lay in ebony trays on almost every flat surface. From her collection of shells Violet made picture-frames and decorated mirrors; she was also working on the small coved ceiling that connected the parlour to the library.

It was in the parlour, with dogs and glue, aprons, scissors and newspaper that she was most at ease. Here, when Violet was fascinated and occupied with her work, Cecil felt he could say things that he found harder to say in any other place.

He would sit on the window-seat and after first remarking on the rundown state of the meadow grasses, the height of the nettles, the newly planted orchard, the broken pump in the yard, the cracked guttering and so forth; all into thin air, never questions; after this statutory preamble, Cecil would obliquely refer to what marvellous space they had here at Rathmanagh, how ideal it might be for children, how safe, how engaging; trees to climb, the river to fish in, the lake and the old boathouse. As he spoke he almost certainly saw himself as the child, as much as he saw any other child. But he did see another child when he looked towards the forceful, strong, dark hump into the air that was Mount Murna; he saw a child there, a child free from doubts, free from guilt and anxiety. It was as if the mountain knew his shame, could share the unspoken thread of the peculiar, keen, rancid half dreams that were Cecil's most constant dressing-room companion.

Violet for her part was now an established married woman; mistress of her own demesne, nevertheless she began to feel with increasing edge that fuller, most ancient part of herself that had never been engaged or even approached, let alone recognised, during the whole Rathmanagh adventure. She went on long walks alone almost every day, just the dogs and her. She went down the front meadows, through the woods across the river and then over to the boggy, treacherous ground at the foot of Mount Murna. Here she would pause to look back at the house, to glance a little at Cecil and herself, then she would go on, gradually making a zig-zag assault on the mountain itself. There were frequent boulders and smooth stones. She would sit. Sometimes she would lie, her finger threading through the rough clumps of the heather as if it were the hair of a hound, or the hide of a cow, or the flank of her mare. The mountain earth had a peculiar life and vitality, it seemed to engender every stubby plant that grew on it with vigour and passion. In these remote private moments Violet felt in her some pull, some real quite painful longing, even need. She wished she could slip into the vast, open, whirling space of the sky. She wished she could participate in the range and fire that seemed to run within the earth itself. Soon the dogs would sniff at her face, wagging their muddy tails over her, eager to be on again; the moment of detached musing would be past.

At home in the evenings she read a great deal: Thomas Mann, George Eliot, Jane Austen, Flaubert; then Margery sent her Lawrence's novels. She felt fascinated and a little afraid when she read in *Women in Love* of Birkin after his row with Hermione 'who took off his clothes and sat naked among the primroses ... lying down and letting them touch his belly, his breasts'. It went on to say 'he knew that nothing else would do, nothing would satisfy except this coolness and subtlety of vegetation travelling into one's blood ... There was this perfect cool loveliness, so lovely and fresh and unexplored ... The leaves, and the primroses and the trees, they were really lovely and cool and desirable, they really came into the blood and were added onto him. Here was his world, he wanted nobody and nothing but the lovely subtle responsive vegetation and himself. This was his place – his marriage place – '

Violet understood something of Birkin's thoughts; they might well be within herself. Violet knew that there could be no physical exchange and expression with Cecil of the kind and with the fervour of which she read in books. That sort of thing by her own choice was, she felt, lost to her. The earth; the pulse of nature, always there, rampant and certain and glorious became more and more the seat of her real affections. She bathed once, completely free of any garment whatsoever, in the dark murky waters of the lake one very hot July afternoon. She lay down now and then in the rides that were kept cut back through the woods; they were lush with flowers; celandine, foxgloves, bluebells, briar rose, hedge honeysuckle, ragged robin, and the small brilliant bright eye of speedwell; and all about these stalks and fronds and petals and smells the brilliant green of the grass, with moss edges stippled up into the damp spread roots of the trees, and over into the dark flank sides of the banks. In this way Violet managed to explore areas of herself that might otherwise have condemned her to even greater frustration and unattainable bitterness.

And so it was by means of their private imaginings that Cecil and Violet came together more often. Always in the dark.

Always an unspoken meeting, where each explored the other by the device of being mentally somewhere else. For Violet it was the mountain, the earth; the tang and burst of energy there. For Cecil, Violet's limbs in the dark were the smooth contours of the paper boy. It was his neck, his hips, his freedom that enabled Cecil to manage with Violet sufficient coitus, on as many occasions, to prompt the conception of their child.

When Cecil heard the news of Violet's confirmed pregnancy he immediately saw in his mind the paper boy as an infant, round and smooth and fair. The paper boy, Jack, who cycled daily up the steep drive to Rathmanagh hardly ever spoke to Captain Farr. He waved. He smiled. He gratefully accepted eggs and apples when they were given to him, then he free-wheeled back down the hill and over the humped-back bridge into Ballynaule. He whistled to himself, to the day, to thoughts of his job in the brewery, he was completely unaware of Cecil Farr's pathetic fascination with him. But undoubtedly without Jack the paper boy there would probably never have been a son and heir to the Demesne of Rathmanagh opposite the Mount of Murna in the Parish of Ballynaule.

FOUR

Lumsden Farr was born in the early hours of the morning. It was not a long affair, and not too difficult for a first baby. Doctor Bracken told Cecil afterwards, 'Your wife is a very fit woman and that's what counts.' Violet supposed she was pleased at the birth of a son. She certainly felt a little fretted and anxious. The newly-born infant seemed so frail, so squirmish, so at odds with everything, so hard to satisfy. A week after Lumsden's birth the black labrador bitch Gipsy had puppies. It was decided that they should keep one pup from the litter for themselves. When Violet saw the firm, roly-poly, snub-nosed, vigorous little black bundle Cecil had chosen, she thought how much more eager and equipped for life the puppy seemed as opposed to her son. The pup was called Birkin at Violet's request. Cecil gave way to her choice as he almost always did; as he had done over the name Lumsden for their son after Violet's father, although he might have preferred to have called the baby Jack.

There was an October christening in the small Church of Ireland chapel at Claggan. Violet tall and thin, her sloping shoulders pronounced by the cut and tailoring of her coat, and her long neck reaching upwards from the soft, pale-cream silk flounce of cravat at her throat, had a bird-like aspect; she seemed more than physically above the rest, she appeared to scout the horizons for recognition and acknowledgment of her self-certainty. She seldom smiled. She engaged another's glance by the intense appraisal in her eyes. Only her laughter showed the even extent of her bright white teeth in the large, wide, generous mouth. More often than not her laughter was a challenge, a gauntlet thrown down to the less informed; it usually followed one of her own remarks or observations. On this serious occasion there was no flicker of humour or challenge in her demeanour; she seemed serious, nostalgic, apart. As she gazed across the font, her high forehead, the deep set dark eyes, the fine Fitzpatrick nose reminded many of those gathered there of her father, after whom the little boy was to be christened. When the godmother, Cousin Margery, slipped the white bonnet off the baby's head, the narrow shape of it, the unmistakably large protruding ears, which Nurse Biddy taped back to the child's head each night with Elastoplast, were a very definite characteristic of the child, as were the pronounced full long lips; it was an unusual head, strong and definite but also loose and sensual. It was as if everything within it was too large, too strong for the infant skin and the small keep of baby bones. The general, endlessly buttoned and bowed clutter of patterned wool, lace-tucks, the embroidered cape, the satin ribbon, the vast fuss of it all seemed to constrict the child, who had a flair even at that age to oppose and confront the arms, the teat, the crib; all the pretty, benevolent spaces prepared for him.

As Violet looked beyond the hats and gloves and necks and chins to her son, as she listened to the words of the service, she tried to imagine with pride, the real, fresh, innocent manhood that must dwell there. In her heart this baby was much more a part of her father than anything else. Cecil's contribution was never very prominent or particular in her mind.

Then the baby yelled; red with fury, poker stiff with indignation, the raging bundle was handed from the Rector to Margery and then as soon as possible to Nurse Biddy.

Everyone spoke later of the wonderful way little Lumsden had quite appropriately yelled out the devil. Nurse Biddy said he was suffering from three-month colic; it would account for the sudden rigid spasms, '. . . and', as she said again and again, 'he has a very definite mind of his own.'

Nurse Biddy was an excellent woman. She had the top floor of the house to herself and Lumsden. There was the night nursery, the day nursery, the sewing-room and nurse's own bedroom and the large sunny nursery bathroom. Everything was simply but very well equipped; and there was Cathleen, a good stout girl from the orphanage, she made up the fires, she blacked the grates, she filled the scuttles, she washed and ironed and polished, and when she pegged out the linen she made that little moment in fresh air go on for as long as possible. Below, in the kitchen, there was always Mrs Donovan among the steaming saucepans, scrubbed tables and the dark pantry corridors, with things steeping and setting and hanging and curing.

It was a busy well-run household. It certainly impressed the older generation of neighbours with its style and modernity but the pair at the centre of it all perplexed people. In public Cecil and Violet never seemed at ease with one another. Their manner in private, naturally no one knew, but it was a source of constant gossip and vicarious wonder. Any gain on Violet's part seemed calculated to be a loss on Cecil's. Their interests were never mutual. She hunted. He did not. The puppy Birkin chosen by Cecil from the litter, presumably for a gun dog, never went to a keeper to be trained, it seemed to become instead the constant, most vital and precious companion to Violet.

Of course there were family occasions; picnics, excursions to Claggan in the pony trap, children's parties, visits to Dublin, visits to Kilbronan Bay on the west coast – Violet was now the sole possessor of Aunt Theodora's house – but all these outings were the exception. By and large Violet and Cecil were remote from Lumsden; they were faces, figures seen from upstair windows or

77

from the library doorway, or in the shadowy, night-light gloom of the landing outside the night nursery.

Lumsden's real life was apart from his parents. He realised early on that although there were always deferential references made to his mother by Nurse Biddy and Mrs Donovan, half cajoling, half threatening, the real authority lay absolutely with Nurse Biddy. Nurse Biddy was the final arbiter.

Every evening Lumsden went to the library for half an hour before bed. Sometimes, it was deemed to be a particular treat, Violet might come up to the nursery in the morning and share a breakfast of porridge and soft-boiled eggs with Lumsden and Nurse Biddy. But these occasions were rare; the only regular private moment Lumsden had with his mother was in the evenings, in the library.

In the beginning when Lumsden was crawling these library visits were to Violet a considerable strain. She seemed unable to sustain the calm, loving presence required of her. Lumsden's dribbling irritated her. His ears maddened her; the nightly Elastoplast seemed to have had no effect. They were ugly, unruly ears, ridiculous clown-flaps giving her son the appearance of a bizarre sea creature. 'Well you won't have to worry about Lumsden,' Margery used to say provocatively to Violet. 'He'll bat his way through life with ears like that . . . dear little Dumbo person.' And then there was the puffy lower lip which slopped forward, a great damp droop of red, whenever he concentrated. 'Please Biddy get him to close his mouth,' Violet would say again and again. 'He's not catching flies.'

So it was that long before Lumsden ever spoke fluently, or ran sturdily, the die was cast in some way between himself and his mother. Nurse Biddy recognised it all. They were destined to seek out each other's frailties rather than their strengths. What might have been friendship became a subtle joust for supremacy. And it was very soon the boy who had the upper hand. He was probably the only person in the parish of Ballynaule who could confront this tall, good-looking woman with the piercing deep-set eyes, the fine Fitzpatrick nose and the wide generous mouth, and unnerve her; distorting her own image of herself enough to encourage in her a kind of angered reticence. Only with Birkin was Violet truly at ease. She never minded his mud, his dribble, his strong, foul, passing of wind, or his coarse black hairs everywhere: on carpets, cushions, stockings, skirts; even sometimes, somehow, into the smooth, pink-white curled centres of the shells in the ebony trays in Violet's parlour.

Birkin slept at the end of the four-poster on a handsomely upholstered day-bed with carved and gilded ends. Cecil was never permitted to throw a sock or silk handkerchief anywhere in the bedroom. Birkin became Violet's shadow; his loyalty, humour and affection became the rich environment for her caged dreams and feelings to bury themselves, and so become a broad, deep, well-made composition of love and certainty that she would never find in any greater measure, anywhere else, for the rest of her life.

It was the infant; those vulnerable, milky, early days that appealed most to Nurse Biddy. In the beginning she wondered if a second baby would follow soon after the first. They often came in pairs after a long waiting period and Mrs Farr was a very fit, strong woman with the structure and dimensions Nurse Biddy associated with easy breeding. However, the way the household was run, the purposely separate lives the Captain and Mrs Farr led, the stilted manner that existed between them, did not encourage Nurse Biddy to anticipate a little brother or sister for Lumsden. She was a very professional person, she would never leave anyone in the lurch, but after Lumsden's fifth birthday she began to hint that her nursery days at Rathmanagh must be numbered. Violet grudgingly took the hint and plans were made to send

Lumsden to a private boarding-school in England at seven or eight.

Having found the infancy of her child boring and slightly threatening, Violet focused on the theme of a disciplined classical education. It was not that she thought highly of England, she did not, but the education there was indisputably better than any thing available in Ireland. No one in their right mind would consider a tutor or governess for an only child.

As soon as Lumsden's attention span appeared to have increased and the dribble had subsided, even occasionally the lips closed, Violet attempted to bring his nightly library visits into the realms of civilization; greater awareness. It was still difficult. She played him the flute: nursery rhymes, marching songs and at Christmas, carols, but he did not attend; he fidgeted, he pulled Birkin's ear, he snagged the upholstery with the buckles of his shoes, and he sniffed endlessly, wiping his nose with the back of his hand. Violet tried simple story telling: Greek myths, King Arthur, Noah, Finn MacCoul. He was always restless, peering into her face, endlessly interrupting with questions. She tried *Struwwelpeter*, Belloc and the Brothers Grimm; 'Blue Beard' was a favourite, but he could never be still; he could never really listen. He had to be active. The stage had to be his. Suddenly, for no reason, after he had appeared to be listening he would say, 'I'm in a dungeon. I'm in a dungeon,' or 'I'm a rotten pumpkin. I'm a rotten pumpkin. I stink. I stink. I stink.'

With more imagination Violet might have been engaged by his ideas, his energy. But she felt put down. She felt rubbished by him. It was very rarely that the library visit ended when Nurse Biddy came; usually, in desperation Violet went to the door and called Nurse Biddy.

One evening in the middle of reading to Lumsden of 'How the elephant got his trunk', he suddenly fell about convulsed with giggles. It was just after the introduction of the crocodile into the story. 'What on earth's the matter with you?' Violet said fiercely. 'I've seen, I've seen, I've seen,' Lumsden said, jumping up and down like a Jack-in-the-box. 'You've seen what?' his mother asked coldly.

'I've seen your mouth. I've seen your whole, wide mouth. You've got tigers in your teeth Mummy . . . real, forest tigers in your teeth.'

'Don't be ridiculous Lumsden. I shan't go on reading if you're going to be stupid,' Violet said it two or three times, but there was something about him, about the eyes, about the laughter. For the first time she was unnerved. There was something more in his glee and energy than simple stupidity or unusual naughtiness.

'Tigers don't gobble,' Lumsden went on utterly inspired, certainly quite unabashed by his mother's tight fury. 'I think tigers just swallow people in one gulp. One huge gulp. Like frogs with flies.'

Lumsden was seven when he saw the tigers in Violet's teeth. He was seven when Nurse Biddy left. He was seven when he discovered the underside to everything and everyone; that hidden, pale, belly-slime space of fear and anger and outrage that everyone kept to themselves unless you could tease it out of them.

Perhaps his turn of mind, his deviant character, the lies, the games, the schemes were only the product of an imagination bounded by endless control.

Perhaps the lies were first told to him when Violet, with utter loathing of his ugly red ears, brushed his hair too hard and then said, 'Goodnight, my darling', when she never really meant it. Perhaps her own theatricality in speech and gesture, of which she was quite unaware, had simply inspired him. There was no way of knowing. Lumsden just discovered a way of life that engaged and amused him. He exchanged salt with sugar, soapflakes for flour. He trapped spiders in glass jars and then steamed them slowly to death by holding the jar at an angle towards the long snake-like spout of the kettle that was always on the hob. He made a greasy, milky run of lard and whey to trap the ants on the larder shelves. In his mind the weird messy white liquid was the Red Sea closing over the Egyptians. But Mrs Donovan found it all unnerving and unnatural. He kept a hoard of treasure in an empty pillow-case under his bed; a button from Mrs Donovan's cardigan, his father's ivory shoe-horn dipped in a lather of shaving soap, his mother's long hair-pins speared into cotton-wool swabs taken from the waste-paper basket in her bathroom. It was the smells he loved. It was the smells he collected. Every smell seemed to have in it the breath, the skimmy, sour person sort of smell that made people different; but they were no longer important or powerful when you had collected that bit, that little shadow chip out of their voice, and old body bossiness.

Perhaps the very poet Violet longed to find in the image of her father, perhaps she narrowly missed him, because what she wanted was her own self-applauding plan for a particular kind of child.

Perhaps Lumsden was simply himself; the changeling, chance conception that Mrs Donovan said had happened before in this house, because the first rath of stones that had been in the meadow by the river had been dug out when the lake was made a hundred years or more ago. 'There'll always be a changeling here from time to time,' she said to Biddy. 'It's their revenge', and maybe it was.

*

It was one month before his eighth birthday that Violet and Cecil set out with Lumsden for Thornborough and the beginning of the Easter Term.

It was a freezing cold day in January. Lumsden had never been to England before. It seemed very dirty to him; noisy and unfriendly with no real hills or mountains like Murna, just houses and roads and more houses and more roads.

Violet was nervous. Cecil was uninvolved; he was only concerned with train timetables and hotel reservations. He had become stale, stiff and moribund even to himself. England reminded him of other times and other energies. He looked forward very much to his return to Dublin.

Lumsden was intrigued by the rough, clacking kind of voice of the London taxi-driver and the strange tipping seat, which forced him to sit directly in front of his mother. She had on a wide-brimmed black hat which swooped to one side, like a chute, like a landslide. She had on long brown gloves which were all soft and wrinkled up round her wrists, like mole skin; an animal pelt anyway. She kept clipping and unclipping the gold clasp on her bag to check for things she never seemed to see when she looked inside.

Lumsden's new clothes pricked at his skin; his knees were red and frozen, his long, home-knitted socks kept slipping down on to his black shoes.

'Whatever you do, don't show off. Everyone loathes a show off,' Violet said clipping her bag tight shut again for the third time. When they got out of the taxi they were at another station. They were to catch another train. This journey was to be far shorter. The railway platform swarmed with boys and caps, labels and luggage. Lumsden sat with his parents in another carriage. Out of the dirty window Lumsden saw a huge graveyard full of chalky white headstones that stuck up in neat rows like tooth stumps under the dark fir trees. He saw roofs and smoking chimneys, telegraph poles, foggy smudgy streets, crows and gulls, and backyards with high brick walls, and small pieces of land with bonfires and tin sheds. Violet said that they were allotments, little parcels of land for the poor to grow their own potatoes.

Eventually they came to the small country station. There were several men with the boys, they had pipes and caps and check jackets and long grey overcoats and nosey, pointed voices. Violet said they were masters. The boys and the masters and the trunks and suitcases all packed into a large cream coach. Violet and Cecil and Lumsden took another taxi. It was called a taxi but it was really a rather dirty ordinary car in which Lumsden was forced to sit on the back seat wedged in very tightly between his parents; he was closer to them then than he had ever been in all his life.

Violet did not accept tea from the matron in the high-ceilinged rather empty parlour. 'I think it would be better', she said, 'if we say goodbye now, rather than dragging things out. You know. These kind of occasions are best kept short don't you think? Better all round.'

Lumsden had never seen her so nervous. The matron was fat and bossy. At first Lumsden thought she might have been a nun because of the starched white hat. He had never seen a nurse before. But there were no statues and candles and things, just general emptiness, with smells of polish and bleach. Everything seemed to be very ugly. As he watched Violet talking to the matron he suddenly thought for a fleeting second that his mother might be rather beautiful. He wasn't sure. Cecil put his stiff red hand on Lumsden's shoulder and said, 'You'll be fine, old boy, you'll be fine.'

It was the very encouragement of his parents, their thin pecking kisses, the fragmented gestures, that began to make Lumsden nervous. What was it that would go on here among all this echoing noise and space and polish, these sliding, scuffing boys, these drawling, thin, noisey men? Lumsden felt nervous but he also felt exhilarated. There was going to be a challenge here; not so much to learn, all that stuff about joined-up writing, spelling lists and tables. No. The challenge would be to himself. He would be as big and loud, as scuffing and shoving as any of them. He hardly noticed Violet's wave from the taxi window, or Cecil's drooping, rather watery eyes under his brown hat. He was alone. He was nearly eight. He had some real money in his pocket; biscuits, fudge and peanut-butter in his trunk; he felt proud of himself, proud and excited.

It was not easy. Lumsden was put in the charge of Baker Mi whose brother Baker Ma was captain of games; a very tall boy with flopping fair hair. Baker Ma was popular and powerful. Baker Mi seemed to feel that his brother's position in the school gave him some sort of superiority. He certainly knew the older boys. On the way into the dining-room they would give him a friendly butt in the stomach, a cheerful grin, tweak his ear. To Lumsden's amazement Baker Mi seemed awed and delighted with this kind of attention. His face would colour up to a deep pink under the rash of freckles whenever these older boys came up to him, teasing and joshing, and just gently bothering him.

The last four hours of Lumsden's first day at Thornborough were for him a most stunning, vivid and confusing initiation into the peculiar, vast fabric of inherited games and schemes, mess and morals, signs and signals that was the accepted theatre for young males from the more advantaged families of the British Isles to grow up in. These small sons of Britain were summarily plucked out, forcibly detached from the soft, small, close comfort of women and gentleness, loved objects, the highly regarded variety of pets and people that are more often than not the sum and definition of a home or family, to be thrown scared and spartan into the churlish, bragging, loud sluice of men confronting men. Here with men, for men, was built a powerful male barricade; a subtle structure whose hierarchy and aims were echoed and remade again and again; the war whoop, lusty challenge of honour, domination, and linear bravery. The focus was always forward, towards the enemy; whether it was in field sports, exams, battalions, or the dark, private challenges of personal lust and desire, an enemy was the utterly necessary adjunct that must be there in some form or another to make the success and grandeur of the game possible.

One day, later, much later, these men might, if they managed to avoid death, dissolution or monetary disaster, they might be welcomed back into a nursery womb of their own making: the club. Here in the dark corners of a panelled room with small lights beside deep leather chairs, they might sleep or snooze to wake later and wander down corridors of male calm; very little recognition of one another; a stare, a sniff, or slight snort is adequate politeness; overfriendly contact, loud cheery embraces is a sign of the upstart or the ill bred. Here in the club dining-room, one of the best of these new-found nursery spaces, the once reviled nursery puddings would be available for them; creamed rice, stewed prunes, spotted dick, grenadier pudding, treacle tart; these dishes were 'madeleines' now, of peace, security and unchallenging female-related safety.

Lumsden was grateful of course for the quiet guidance of Baker Mi. This is your locker. This is your number. This is your peg. When the bell goes Ia wait on the stairs. In assembly Ia sit below the stage on the forms. Never sit on a chair. The chairs are for B2 and B3. Dormitory is utterly out of bounds in the day time. You must get to the Wallow on time if your number is on the list. If you miss your bath that will be a point against your house. Your house is Payne, but you may be moved to Franklin at half-term because Drummond's leaving. The library is out of bounds to Squibs, and the main parlour.

Squibs. Lumsden was utterly mystified and perplexed by it all. Baker Mi talked very fast and confidently as they dragged Lumsden's trunk and overnight bag up the wide wooden stairway. Baker Mi must have guessed what Lumsden was thinking because he said, 'Squibs are Ia and Ib.' 'But where's my house?' Lumsden asked. 'Is it far from here? Is it somewhere else?' It was really the first time that Lumsden had spoken. Several boys were passing down the stairs. 'New Squib?' they said to Baker Mi while staring at Lumsden; his thick mousey hair, his large red ears, his wide cheerful mouth, the very home-knitted, rather too large V-necked sweater. But then they heard him speak. They caught the wretched, unmistakable, soft Irish lilt. They hardly believed their luck. 'The Squib's a spud,' they yelled. 'But where's my house? Where's my house?' they mimicked in broad, stage-Irish brogue. They laughed and then they lowered their three huge faces forwards, very close to Lumsden. 'A house you paddy-whack is a sty for piggy paddy-whacking who daren't fight in a war. Poor piggy paddy-whacks sitting in the bog . . . when it's all clear they'll come piggy paddy-whacking out again.' They paused. They stared. Then they laughed again and were gone.

Lumsden was totally perplexed and for the first time a little afraid. He suddenly felt that he had no idea who he was. He longed to hear Violet's furious high-pitched voice calling him in to bed, or lunch, anything. He wanted to see her sharp white teeth; her hair piled high, with those wisps that always broke free in the wind; her pale hands, and her long thin fingers as she smoothed the quilt every night, just before she turned out the light. He longed for Birkin to bound out and just bark and bark. There were so many sounds in this huge, cold, echoing place, but none that Lumsden knew; not crows or cows or water or cartwheels; just the slap and buffet of boys, all dressed alike, all crowding and jostling in groups or pairs.

Lumsden knew nothing of war and even less of neutrality and any of its implications for him. He thought England was just a very crowded place, with a king in it and masses of cars and aeroplanes and money. He thought Ireland was the real land. He thought the moon, the sun, the stars were mighty and Irish. He'd never thought of Ireland, except as a whole grand kingdom, with Mount Murna in the very centre and a busy edge on one side with Dublin and a wild edge on the other side with Kilbronan Bay. All the stories Lumsden had been told; adventures, mysteries, magic, they had all been old tales but Lumsden thought they were still there in a way, anyway, would certainly come again. But all the talk at Thornborough was of battleships and Spitfires, dirty bosche and bombs, flags and battles, brilliant battles and Britain, brilliant Britain, God save the King, salute, attention, Armed Forces, Allies, rations and Victory. V for Victory.

In the dormitory Baker Mi and Lumsden were alone. Lumsden's bed was in the middle, on the window side, which was very cold. There was a washstand beside the bed and a single small wooden chair. 'We unpack our trunks tomorrow in the games period. For now just unpack your overnight bag,' Baker Mi's voice trailed on. Lumsden sat down on the bed, it squeaked and dipped. He pulled out his striped flannel pyjamas and his hairbrush and dressing-gown from the small battered attaché-case. In the bottom of the case was his teddy, a worn, rather friendly, frail bear, with one eye a stitched-on button and the other eye a really good glass one. There were teddys on some of the other beds. Gingerly Lumsden put Brian Boru as he was called on to the harsh rough pillow-case, but even as he did so something told him that his bear must not have that name, it was too long, too different to be any good here. He thought he would call the bear Birkin, just so that he could think of Birkin as often as possible.

'There's tea now, then free time, then chapel. Have you got a torch?' Baker Mi asked. Lumsden had a torch; it was on the list with garters and shoe polish and writing-paper. He pulled it out of the case. It was silver and quite long with a large flat face where the bulb was. Lumsden was proud of it. Cecil had given it to him. On his last night at home he had knelt on the small table by the window, and with the torch he had flashed towards Mount Murna, whose hump-shape had been very clear in the moonlight. Cecil had told him about flashing and semaphore.

To Murna he had flashed out the message 'Mummy and Birkin are the warriors now. Mummy and Birkin rule Rathmanagh'.

Baker Mi picked the torch up off the bed. He switched it on and off. He swung the long beam round the dull cream walls. He flashed the beam still, now and then, on some of the photographs of tidy, smiling, smooth-lipped mothers that stood in various leather frames on the washstands, with a brush and comb and a Bakelite toothmug.

'Good torch,' Baker Mi said. Lumsden felt as if at last he was to be rescued, something was all right, his torch was all right. Then there was a bang and clatter as the dormitory doors swung open. Four boys came in with their overnight bags. One of them had already seen Lumsden on the stairs. They sauntered over to the notice board. 'How many Squibs have we got? Ah, three Squibs', and they read out the names, 'Finlay, Stanley-Page and Farr.' They turned away from the notice board and looked down the dormitory to Baker Mi and Lumsden and the shining torch and the soft, squeaky bed. 'Who are you?' they called out to Lumsden. Lumsden hesitated, he was fearful to speak again. 'He's Farr,' Baker Mi said. 'He's a little spud.' The boy, who had already seen Lumsden before on the stairs, called out, 'He's a little piggy paddy-whack from the bog. Piggy paddy-whack have you ever seen a fairy?' Lumsden was about to reply that of course he had, but luckily he paused. He paused because the tallest of the boys called Jellicoe had picked up his torch from the bed. He switched it on and off. He let the light glow through his clenched fingers. Then he said, 'Good torch. Really good torch.' Lumsden felt grateful again. So grateful to this good torch, his father's torch. Then Jellicoe came quite close to him and said in a very friendly way this time, 'It's a good torch, piggy paddy. Can I borrow it . . . just for tonight? Give it back tomorrow.'

To Lumsden there seemed to be no possible answer but yes. He didn't see how he would need it, just for the one night.

But he didn't know the rules.

He didn't know any of the rules.

Later, after tea of bread and jam, after free time, just watching
and listening with Baker Mi, after the first chapel bell, when
the whole school assembled in the hall in coats and caps. And
then, after the slow procession across the hard frosted ground
to the small chapel beyond the rusted wire fence and the scrappy
rhododendrons. And then, after the dull prayers and hymns and
the Vicar's welcome and the crocodile walk back towards the
lights and at last the warmth of School House and the evening
assembly. After all of that Lumsden was standing with the
other Squibs and Baker Mi in the front of the assembled school.
Lumsden had noticed that nearly all the boys had torches with
them for the walk to chapel. Many of the torches were quite
small, some were just bicycle lamps. Lumsden knew that his
torch was one of the best; he looked forward to the other nights
when he would beam it into the dark, twisting trunks of the
rhododendron bushes, and then up and out towards the stars,
and down over the faces of the crisp, cracked, frozen puddles.

He was thinking of the cold night outside. He was thinking of
Mount Murna and he was thinking of how Birkin would sniff
the frosted ground before he cocked his leg. He only half heard
the master's droning voice and the boys' sharp, little snap replies,
when he suddenly realised that the Senior Master, who had been
leading the assembly, all check lists and rules and reminders,
Lumsden suddenly realised that Mr Bordon was speaking to
him, directly to him.

'What's your name boy?'

'Farr,' Lumsden whispered.

'Speak up boy, speak up.'

'Farr.' Lumsden said again just a little louder.

'Farr. Farr. Farr what?'

'Just Farr.'

Someone giggled. Baker Mi nudged him. 'Sir, say Sir,' Baker Mi whispered.

Completely mystified Lumsden said 'Sir.'

There were more giggles.

'Are you aware Farr that all boys are required to have a torch in their possession?'

'Yes . . . Sir.'

'You are aware of this?'

Mr Bordon was rather fat with tight clothes and tight skin. His eyes were horribly magnified by the heavy horn-rimmed glasses he wore. His breath smelt, it was a kind of wet, sharp, pantry smell, like some sour thing left too long in a warm cooking place. Mr Bordon was bending down over Lumsden.

'You are aware of this rule? Every boy must have a torch with him for the evening chapel assembly.'

Lumsden nodded.

'Then Farr . . . Farr, who is apparently so aware of this rule', Mr Bordon turned sarcastically aside towards the older boys, they giggled, 'then Farr,' Mr Bordon went on getting very close to Lumsden again, 'then Farr why was there no torch in your hand this evening?' He paused staring at Lumsden. 'Why Farr? Why? Do you possess a torch?'

'Yes Sir,' Lumsden whispered.

'Then Farr where is it?' Mr Bordon bellowed out the question again. 'Where is it?'

'Jellicoe's got it,' Lumsden said.

There was a hush, a sudden tension, everyone was looking at Lumsden. There was a hiss. Sneak. Sneak. Sneak it said.

'Never sneak on another boy Farr, never. Only the weak squeal. Be a man Farr, be a man.' Then Mr Bordon paused and glanced again about the assembled attentive faces. 'Of course it may be difficult, very difficult for someone from your particular background . . .' There were more giggles and whispers of Paddy. Paddy. Sneaky little spud.

Whatever else Lumsden had been during the short, almost eight years of his life, he had been brave. He had always been brave. Brave in the dark. Brave when he fell. Brave with injections. Brave with wasp stings and nettle-rashes. But suddenly now it was as if that boy, the daring, inventive, rather wild, unruly child of woods and walks and birds and barns and bicycles, hidden smells and peculiar treasure, it was as if that child had suddenly had his vision and senses sliced in two. It was as if he had been quartered and thrown to the dogs.

Lumsden's only thought was that he must not cry. He must not cry. He had told the truth. All his life that had been the main thing. That's what they had all kept saying: tell the truth, tell the truth, tell the truth. Suddenly here, the truth told was weak and wrong and terrible. He was a sneak. That might be a disease. A plague. He didn't know. He had never heard the word before.

A bell went. The boys moved in to supper. Baker Mi went with them. The only place Lumsden could go was the lavatory. A cold, small, smelly lavatory. In the lavatory, in the dark as he searched for the light switch, he tripped on something. It creaked. It was a huge wicker laundry basket with leather straps. As Lumsden held on to the edge of it it creaked again, and as it creaked suddenly Lumsden could not bear anything anymore because in Violet's parlour at Rathmanagh Birkin slept in an old basket that creaked exactly like this one. It creaked when Birkin moved, when he dreamt, when he got into it after his dinner and after his walk, and it creaked when he got out of it, to explore, to sniff, to bark, to greet people, or simply to lick himself. It was these thoughts of Birkin so far away; beyond the sea, that far away, which finally broke Lumsden completely. He cried. He cried so much. He had never cried like that before. He knew that he must never ever tell the truth again. He must hide himself from them. He must hide from them all his thoughts and feelings; all of himself.

Cold and hungry and red eyed Lumsden made his way up to the

dormitory. To his relief there was another Squib there, another new boy to be the butt and centre of Jellicoe's entertainment. It was Stanley-Page, he had the bed next to Lumsden. He was tall with a very clear skin and a serious expression. He had leather slippers, he had a silk dressing-gown and bright blue poplin pyjamas, and S.P. engraved on his suitcase and embroidered on every one of his white handkerchiefs. His voice was quick and clear, quite quiet. Jellicoe and the others seemed to find it very funny.

Lumsden crept into the cold squeaky bed. He just lay and stared up into the dark. He tried to imagine the Mount of Murna blowing across the water and filling all this space of England, with its big, dark, comfortable shape. He managed not to cry, but he heard Stanley-Page doing so very quietly into his pillow.

Of course as time went on Lumsden more or less learnt the ground rules. Laugh when the others laugh. Never argue or answer back to bigger boys. Give in. Say what they want you to say. Do what they want you to do.

When Lumsden returned to Rathmanagh for the Easter holidays Mrs Donovan was shocked. He seemed shrivelled, smaller, thin so thin. 'Not our Lumsden at all,' she said. 'Quite a different boy now, not the spark there was.' Violet disagreed. 'It's just the change, other people to think about and a little real discipline,' she said, and she managed to believe in that idea, against all the odds, for a very long time.

'He must learn to take the rough with the smooth, learn to paddle his own canoe,' Violet said and Cecil didn't disagree with her.

For the first year at Thornborough Lumsden went on more or less with the general tide of things as best he could. He got used to the cold and the dull over-cooked food. He got used to the cries of Far---r---r---r---T' whenever he walked by a group of boys. He preferred it when they simply called him 'Spud' or 'Paddy-whack'. He made important friendships that were full of secrets and plans; loyalties were intense, but often short lived, they never came to anything, but the sense that never really left him, the sense that stayed with him always, even after he had managed to create and project a very particular manner for himself, the sense that remained, was that of not really knowing who or why he was. There was always this void; this anxious, empty space, uncontrollably open to every diversity of thought and feeling, social whims, sudden personal demands. In the end the manner and make and purpose of his life became a sophisticated circus act of how to fill, with as much noise and vivacity as possible, that void, that crippling, numbing, anxious space.

After about three years at Thornborough various events gradually changed Lumsden's focus; the way he saw himself and the way he wished to be seen. He was determined to have it recognised that he was a power, a singular force in his own right. He disliked games; the mud, the wind, the interminable waiting, whatever the season, for real action. His academic progress was uneven; appalling in mathematics, average in Latin, but in English and History there were, every so often, sudden flashes of originality and unusual understanding. It was these moments of public praise and high marks that led Lumsden to look with real intent into the lives of poets and artists. They seemed colourful people, powerfully present even in states of wretchedness and languor. Perhaps words were the thing to hoist and parry with. His mother would approve. She definitely had this obsession about Irish literacy.

Lumsden still sought for some kind of approbation and enthusiasm from his mother, but each holidays she seemed more distant, more remote, more aloof. When Lumsden visited the homes of other boys for half-term or odd weekends, he began to recognise how different his mother was from the mothers of his friends. Their clipped language, the kempt curls, the rigorous order, the attention to endless detail in small things; clean hands and nails, polished shoes, aired beds, folded table napkins, and the exact way the cutlery was placed on the table, apparently pudding spoons above the plate were less appropriate than pudding spoons at the side of the plate. There seemed to be this sense of dull ceremony; the right and wrong way to do almost anything. Anger, distress, burdens of grief, pain, or remarkable joy, were always dealt with with restraint. Excess of any kind seemed to be bad taste, an affront to the pleasant, safe, even keel of life. The food, the gardens, the cretonned living-rooms, the puffed and pounded cushions, the dull bedrooms, the cold bathrooms; all served the same purpose. They all affected a sense of regime and order; a certain prosaic control, too sensible, too utterly understood ever to give rise to awe, mystery or passion, any real acknowledgment of human disorder or complexity. 'Manners maketh man' so they said and they seemed to tie the whole thing up in that.

Lumsden absorbed it all; but two things which he had always accepted as the best, the most central, became less central and less certain.

These two things were Ireland and Violet.

Lumsden gradually understood that Ireland was thought of as a peasant land, wet and violent; and less much less than England; just a bog, a Catholic bog.

It was the jokes, the snide references, the dismissal of Ireland's history, except for the famine, that irked Lumsden, but as one not particularly initiated voice alone in an alien territory there was nothing he could do but add this sense of uncertain identity and validity to all the rest.

Then there was Violet. Her vivid cluttered bedroom, her wild, long hair pinned up with passion each morning as if she were penning in some unruly creature, and then, after the day and walks with Birkin and farm and stable visits, there would be the loose, long, free wisps of hair that flew everywhere, they lodged on the collars of coats and cardigans, and were even found in the food occasionally if Violet had mixed the salad, or on a Sunday she had heated the soup. Throughout Rathmanagh there was a conglomerate trail of boots and dog baskets, papers, cuttings and books, mountains of books in zig-zag piles on the floor, under the piano in the library, under the tables in the parlour and even on the stairs. There were chipped pails and jugs everywhere to catch the drips and leaks. There were bits and pieces of faded embroidered fabric thrown over worn chairs and over the *chaise-longue* in the parlour. There was the scrap screen in the parlour, made by Violet from her father's photographs and his small line drawings, newspaper cuttings, odd fragments of poetry, epigrams, quotations, all written in Lumsden Fitzpatrick's neat, slanting hand, all written in pale brown ink. Rathmanagh was different quite different from the English homes.

Then there was Violet's anger, when words flew as abundant and devastating as a scatter of starlings, or the cry of hounds, or the moan of calfless cows; regular bellows of pain. And there were her long staring silences, when only Birkin would dare to interrupt her. And the gramophone, with the same record again and again: Schubert's 'Trout Quintet', 'The Emperor Concerto', Caruso's voice 'O Bella Napoli' and 'La Donna e mobile', and then high voices, 'Bist du Bi Mir', 'O for the wings, for the wings of a dove', 'I know that my Redeemer liveth' and extracts from 'The Messiah'.

These sounds were etched into the sum of Lumsden's Rathmanagh experience like the lines on the palms of his hands. They were seams of feeling that were in some way the buttress, the ramparts, that shored up a lurking, uncontrollable chaos; those ungrounded mists of personal anxiety that were never ever really hidden. This chaos of feeling and longing sought a parade, some wide stage, some free unrecriminating space to exercise itself.

Gradually, Lumsden's view of Ireland altered, it became a strange backroom where belongings might be stored but not addressed. His mother became like some character in a dream whose powers by process of denial could be tamed and left. Increasingly Lumsden returned to Rathmanagh with less grace, less overt interest, less involvement of any kind. Only Birkin and Mount Murna remained full of presence to him. Only Birkin and Mount Murna could stir him to feel any kind of commitment or intrinsic belonging.

Birkin did not notice Lumsden's anglicised voice, the curt, careless manner, the languid, purposeful boredom and disdain for any information concerning people or events in Ballynaule or Claggan. Birkin's bounds and licks and little squeaks were always completely generous, unerringly certain. For Birkin, Lumsden was the smell of his own, the smell, even after dirty trains and weeks and months of absence, the smell of a tribe presence; of some part of Birkin himself; his pack, his band, his being. Birkin's loyalty on odd occasions almost tripped up Lumsden's increasingly detached and self-important view of himself. This large, rough, friendly black beast, with considerable appetites that took him every so often far from home, to howl and starve in some yard or by some windy hedge in anguished pursuit of a bitch in season, this loyal, even-tempered creature seemed to embody in his uncompromisingly animal self many cherished and longed for human attributes that for Violet and Cecil and Lumsden were banished, trapped, hidden from themselves and from one another.

And then there was Mount Murna. Lumsden never returned to Rathmanagh without a real pounding in his heart when he caught the first glimpse of that great weight of particular ground. It seemed so comfortable and necessary in that space below the sky. Its timeless grandeur, its uncompromising shape, made all the vivid, trappy little details of life fade. To look on it was to look beyond oneself. But in that 'beyond' there was thrall and devastation, if self-importance gave no ground, no leeway, no acknowledgment to deeper mystery; less certain and less obtained values.

Even so, as the years passed and Lumsden's orientation seemed to be just like all the other boys, he knew that he was different. He knew also that to create any kind of real freedom for himself he must somehow capitalise on this difference.

In the first year he had been alert, but constantly unnerved, constantly confused. In the second year he made little real headway. But in the summer term of his third year at Thornborough, a certain event led Lumsden to make an intriguing and very positive decision about the manner and direction of himself and his life.

There was a boy a year above Lumsden, in the same year as Jellicoe, a boy called Morton. He was rather podgy, but still not exactly fat. He was a real swot. He was always being ragged, but he simply smiled, he never got worked up or angry. He seemed able to pick his way slowly and carefully past people and very soon resume his studies or his reading. He walked in a rolling, odd way. He never slid and ran, scuffed or swooped like the other boys.

One afternoon, Lumsden had learnt the advantages to be gained by sucking up to the older boys, one afternoon Lumsden agreed to go up into the Lower Dormitory immediately after lunch and take some of the blackcurrant pastilles that it was known Matron kept in the sewing-room. The reward for this daring act was for Lumsden to be shown by Carter and Newley the route, out of bounds, to the gulley and then on from there, through the wood, to the alley-way, past the allotments to the small paper shop by the railway where sherbet could be bought and liquorice sticks.

Lumsden was not really so afraid of the matron as some of the other boys. In a way he felt rather seduced and engaged by female fury, perhaps because throughout his childhood it was only when Violet was driven to rage that she really came close, physically close to Lumsden. Her scorn, her sarcasm were the means by which Lumsden had known that he was really some part of her. So it was with eagerness rather than too much anxiety that Lumsden approached Matron's landing.

The sewing-room was a small sitting-room, just off the linen room where the boys' clothes were kept. The sewing-room smelt of Matron's cigarettes and starch and iodine. The pastilles were on a little tray beside the kettle and a glass jam-jar, with scissors and pencils and two thermometers in it. Without difficulty Lumsden went into the empty sewing-room and took the pastilles. The tin was practically full. Then he heard voices and the unmistakable sound of Matron's feet on the polished linoleum. The only hiding place was the sluice beside the linen room. It was a narrow room with a double sink and a long wooden draining-board. Under the sink and draining-board there were various buckets and enamel jugs. At the far end of the room there was a pale green curtain pulled across a few pegs on which Matron hung her caps and odd aprons and things. Lumsden dived behind the curtain, shoving a cardboard box in front of his feet so that his socks and shoes would not be seen, the curtain didn't reach the floor.

To Lumsden's surprise Matron paused by the open sluice door. Then Lumsden heard her say, 'You're late, Morton. You're late again.' Then through the gap in the curtain Lumsden saw a red-faced, downcast Morton come slowly into the sluice.

'They're in the bucket. Two pairs.'

Morton bent down. He slowly took two pairs of grey flannel shorts out of the bucket.

'Water. Run the water,' Matron said.

Morton ran hot water into the basin. It was cold at first but then Lumsden saw the steam.

'Soap,' Matron said.

Morton took a solid lump of green soap and with every inch of his body seeming to be stiff with a most terrible pain, he gingerly unfolded the flannel shorts. A terrible acrid, pungent smell of human excrement nearly suffocated Lumsden. It was far worse than any farm smell, or any fart Birkin had ever blown. Lumsden thought he might be sick. Then he heard Matron say, 'Wet the soap first.'

Morton, his hand visibly shaking, put the cake of soap under the tap. Then he opened the shorts at the offending, miserably stained place between the legs. Gently he pushed the softened soap back and forth over this place. He seemed to have stood there forever. He seemed to be glued, utterly stuck to the cracked brown linoleum on the floor.

'Now scrub,' Matron said as she handed him a scrubbing brush.

Morton took the scrubbing brush and with the same painful even action he scrubbed and the soap became full of brown sticky bubbles.

'Rinse,' Matron said.

Morton put the weight of stiff grey cloth with its stinking wound under the running tap.

'Right,' Matron said. 'Now the other one.'

She walked to the door and then turned, her heel squealing like a pig. 'Properly,' she said, 'do it properly.' And she turned again and went back down the corridor.

Lumsden wanted more than anything else to be swallowed into the ground, buried, away, just away. He did not want to smell this smell. He did not want to see and feel Morton's terrible pain. He did not want to be any part of it. All this filth. All this crumpled sticky stink of Morton's. Morton. Morton, who could write in Latin, his own verses. Morton who could translate

Greek. Morton who could paint coats-of-arms, and made masks, the long detailed frieze of dinosaurs and Tyrannosaurus Rex and King Arthur and Sir Galahad all converging through forests towards the distinct shape of Thornborough by a giant lake, that was his. Morton, who read a book a week as well as everything else. Morton, who knew ballads by heart; the whole of *Sir Patrick Spens*. What was wrong? What was wrong with everything?

By now there were many less than laudable things Lumsden was in the habit of doing.

Stealing certainly: pens, nibs, paper, biscuits, elastic-bands, cigarette-cards, garters. Cheating definitely: copying other people's homework, taking cribs into the Saturday exam periods. Lying naturally: how else could he hope to survive the taunts of others.

Most of his lies were fantasies. They were to build himself up, both in his own esteem and in the esteem of the masters and the other boys.

He had invented an Arab horse that was his, stabled at Rathmanagh. The horse was called Troubadour and was jet black with white socks. He had invented his father's stud and successful racing stables. He had invented marble floors and pillars and huge family portraits in the hall at Rathmanagh. He had even invented a beautiful cousin who had shown him her breasts when they were out blackberrying. He had invented a great deal. But without hesitation, he knew he would never ever betray Morton's painful secret to the others. Lumsden knew in some way that this gentle clever boy was a victim of something bigger than the ordinary smarts and torments and injustices.

But the sight of Morton by that sink; stiff, stunned, quite thick with shame and humiliation, the sight of him stayed in Lumsden's mind. It gathered about it all the darkness and edge of Lumsden's own anxieties, until it was a dreadful clamp of worry, a great midden-mound of deep wretchedness. Lumsden wanted to find a way to hurl it out of his mind. He wanted, in some huge, final gesture, to jettison, to utterly evacuate all the dumb hurts; all those secret, measured stings and shadows. He wanted to threaten and shatter this terrible, stale cage that seemed to have captured them all, without any explanation or invitation.

Lumsden decided to become bad; as bad as possible.

Very soon he knew all the bad words in the dictionary and most of the dirtiest bits in the Bible. He no longer feared being beaten. Now he challenged the headmaster and his whippy little cane by his smiles and unctuous politeness. Lumsden learnt to take a beating as if it were a compliment. He noticed how it maddened the masters and how it enthused the boys.

By his last year at Thornborough Lumsden was a very considerable thorn in the flesh of the staff but he had developed sufficient powers of imagination and deceit within himself to feel powerful and unruled. Although behind his back many of his contemporaries were irritated by his interruptions in class and his endless flamboyant bragging, they were all so thoroughly entertained by him that they kept any reservations they might have had about his disruptive behaviour to themselves.

During his last summer term he and another boy bathed without clothes in the small stream beyond the gulley in the out-of-bounds wood, beside the railway. They kissed and caressed, rousing one another with the warmth and peculiar softness in those usually trousered and hidden parts. Lumsden knew as he watched the spatters of sun through the trees while they both dressed, he knew that very soon he would feel a girl. A girl, even more beautiful than the cousin with firm breasts whom he had invented.

He was like an arrow notched into the bow ready to take its leap, its chance; he was ready to get away.

Lumsden was thirteen when he left Thornborough. He had scraped into an East Anglian public school by the skin of his teeth. Violet was not impressed. She loathed that bitterly cold, relentlessly flat East Anglian landscape. But already, in her heart of hearts, a very hidden place, she no longer imagined any particular future for Lumsden. He was certainly not academic. He was certainly not athletic or particularly beautiful. He had, she did acknowledge, made the most somehow or other of those extraordinary, ungainly ears. He had shot up during his last six months at Thornborough. His neck had lengthened. His shoulders had broadened. He had begun to cultivate a new manner, casual, open, with rather over-generous gestures. A sort of clowning, manipulative charm. He was still clumsy. His limbs like his ears always seemed to be too big for him. But as he grew, as he filled out, there was an inkling of order and relatedness about his body. A body, Violet found it hard to think of, that once long ago had lodged within her, and that after a fumbled, frantic intrusion of Cecil's improbable, sad, rather derelict member. Violet never dwelt on these things, but every so often some random connection would suddenly jolt her memory and force her, for a fleeting moment, to acknowledge those uneasy lumps, those sour seconds of experience that had been, however forgotten they might seem now. Brutal, burnt moments without liaison or harmony of any kind.

When in conversation friends referred to odd couples, extraordinary partnerships, 'never a grey goose without a grey gander', Violet would laugh with them, but she always half knew that she might just be laughing about herself and her husband and her son.

Lumsden's eyes were lively. Lumsden's eyes were the best part, although Violet felt that they were not particularly kind. But then she might have gained that impression simply from the looks Lumsden directed at her. She might have read as unkindness the rather challenging detachment Lumsden felt towards her. He had to keep his mother at bay.

In the dining-room above the sideboard there was a large engraving in a maple frame of a stag at bay. During the many dull meal-times in that room, Lumsden had always sat with his back to the fireplace, opposite the sideboard and the engraving, with Violet on his left and Cecil on his right.

The eyes of the stag, great ovals of alert sadness and power, had always seemed to Lumsden like a third pair of eyes in the room, a third person staring, gauging him, monitoring him.

One morning when Lumsden was just fifteen, during a long, tedious, rather empty summer holiday, he had a dream which spilt over suddenly without warning into a strident, absurd, ferocious encounter with his mother.

For Lumsden, Ireland, and particularly Rathmanagh, had become a dull, boring backwater, devoid of any excitement whatsoever. The summer holidays dragged by, a great weight of lush, worn growth, ham and salad, sun and sudden storms. There was so much emphasis on the farm, the calves, the quality of the hay, the yields of this and that, but worse than the farm was the endless abundance of vegetables in the walled garden.

This large, south sloping vegetable garden, with its high brick walls and its narrow cinder paths, just wide enough for a wheelbarrow to run between the box hedges, was a flourishing well-organised place; there were medlars and pears espaliered against the high walls like some tree of Jesse; there were two long greenhouses, one almost completely given over to tomatoes, the other, with a mixture of early seedlings, bedding plants and house plants; there were redcurrants, blackcurrants, gooseberries and loganberries. The garden was large and it was completely enclosed. At the far end there was a single wrought-iron gate into the orchard. At the lower end there were two separate wooden doors into the stable-yard.

This enclosed garden was the one place where Cecil and Violet seemed to be comfortable with one another. Here Cecil's labours were of great assistance to Violet. She almost overtly welcomed him and his trug and hoe, or spade, or watering-can. Violet and Birkin spent many hours in the vegetable garden. The considerable excess of plants, herbs, tomatoes, lettuces, potatoes, spinach, celery and much more besides were lifted, gathered, weighed, and marked and priced, and then sold in the Claggan Market at the produce stall every Saturday. This real money handed over for real goods sold, although insignificantly small in value, assumed for both Violet and Cecil enormous, crucial significance. It was the very real fruit of their very real labours. It connected them in their own minds with the labouring truth of a simple, God-given working life, with its own rewards and very real values.

Delivering the goods early each Saturday morning, taking their place at the market stall; the flasks of tea, the greetings and the gossip, all gave a wholesome, ancient shape to Cecil and Violet's sense of themselves, which in every other direction was incoherent, difficult and sometimes extreme.

Obviously August was one of the busiest months with sudden floods of lettuces, courgettes and marrows, and then the glorious profusion of herbs; mints, parsley, dill, coriander, oregano and lovage, all needing to be cut and tied and labelled into little bundles, or the roots divided into small pots.

Lumsden's appallingly provocative laziness on those Friday evenings of gathering, tying and marking, and then after that, his hopeless, ridiculous, unhealthy sloth every Saturday morning, gave Violet ample opportunity to find occasion to voice her fury and distaste for the whole manner of Lumsden's life. His self-indulgent, soft, boorish ways.

In the beginning Violet and Cecil had naturally insisted that

Lumsden should breakfast with them from eight o'clock on, certainly never later than nine. Increasingly Lumsden disregarded their wishes, never even referring to his misdemeanours. 'At least apologise to your Father,' Violet would shriek out at the end of some wrangle or other. Lumsden used to succumb. He used to mumble something or other before he slammed a door, but now, this summer holiday, since his fifteenth birthday, he showed complete contempt and utter disregard for anything his parents might say or suggest. Lumsden had even said to Violet, after a row over his clothes and the making of his bed, he had actually said in that loud drawling awful English voice, 'Oh can it Mother, stuff a sock in it, you're just out of date, off the moon. Not remotely in the real world my dear.'

It was the 'my dear' that had thrown Violet beyond control of herself. 'How dare you? How dare you speak to me like that, Lumsden?' And she had thrown the book that was beside her. It was a small red copy of Conrad. It was an involuntary action. The book missed her son and landed instead on a surprised and sleeping Birkin. The large dog had leapt hurriedly to his feet and in all the commotion he had knocked over a small table with a tea tray on it. There was suddenly spilt tea on the carpet and broken tongues of white china and in amongst all that, Lumsden's great, ungainly body; the long tree-trunk legs, the great hooves of shoes, jutting like breakwaters into the small space, and then his wide, soft hands were all over Birkin so that the hairs flew and he jumped and bounced continuously, encouraged by Lumsden's strange, quaking, unsure up-and-down voice.

'A bit of an over-reaction Mother,' he had said.

Together they had cleared up the mess. Violet had longed physically to assault him. What could she do? She could no longer pull his hair, or his ears. She could no longer whack his behind. He was so large, like a young ox. There was so much body about him. Violet realised with horror that even her voice meant nothing to him. Her words would never even be heard by him. With his wide, supercilious smile he would simply stare her out. He was quite beyond her control; out of her orbit and yet like some greedy interloper he mooched about the place, a noisy, brooding, ugly presence everywhere. Idle. Always idle and yet always managing to make himself the centre of debate by his purposeful absence. Late for meals, no appearance at breakfast. Never a helping hand. Never available even when asked a thousand times. It was to Violet a quite intolerable situation. It underlined for her Cecil's complete inadequacy and her own bitter isolation from many threads of life that might still beckon her if she ever allowed them to.

Lumsden's presence in the parlour, in the library, the way he altered the angle of the chairs and tables, the way he took books from the shelves and then left them open, face down so that the spines cracked, the way he left his huge shoes just anywhere, great evil scabs of dented leather. All these irritations were to Violet a gruesome reminder of her failure as a parent, as a mother, as a woman. They charged the fragile personal spaces she had carefully and stylishly made for herself with taunts. The bestial, swaggering, unkind disregard of her by her son; a creature who seemed to have been born simply to dredge the fine memory of her father from her. He had destroyed his potential inheritance and now he dragged down what was left into an ugly, unwanted mess.

There were many incidents, many slammed doors, many silent, terrible meals where only Cecil spoke; little comments on the weather or the world made nervously as if only to himself. 'Wretched business at Mulligan's.' 'Good bet that gelding of Parker's.' 'We'll have an easterly before long – glass is going down', and so on. These phrases might have been the sound of a Hoover or a steaming saucepan or a rattle of coals into the scuttle, so little attention was paid to them by either Violet or Lumsden; they might really never have been words at all.

There were days of heat and abundant vegetables, wonderful borders full of flowers, marvellous drying days for the linen and rugs and blankets; long, still evenings, good for bonfires in the orchard or at the edge of the wood; glorious, quiet, windless days, with the scythe swinging continually over the long rank weeds and wild grasses; the timeless keen purr of the mower over the neat dry lawn beyond the library windows; hot piles of sweating yellowing grass clippings; the continuous drip of the yard pump on to the large flat stone as the watering-cans were refilled again and again to succour the plants, the drying urns, the seedlings, the roses and daisies and dahlias, the delphiniums and lupins and hollyhocks.

During these long summer days the fret and fury and tension within the house scoured the beauty of the natural season leaving a strained, uneasy, almost bleeding, ticking kind of dangerous calm over everything. Like the very cloudbursts and heavy, crashing, natural storms of thunder and lightning outside, there would have to be at some point a burst; a break beyond any pretence of control, or civilised continuity, within the house itself.

It happened on a Saturday morning. Violet had worked particularly hard the evening before preparing for the market. Lumsden of course had been absent. He had taken Birkin for a long walk over the hill and he had returned late, without Birkin.

One of the most painful things for Violet, because of the intense and wonderful pleasure he gave her, was the very idea of loss or worry for Birkin. Without Birkin she knew she would lose all sense of her life. Birkin was the external reason for almost all she did that gave her pleasure. Her long tramps and meditations over the hills, through the woods, by the bank of the river and on the very crest of Mount Murna itself, were made possible and so precious because they were shared with Birkin. There were very few occasions when this great black dog was not lying somewhere close beside her. Whenever she went from one room to another, or up the stairs, or out on to the porch, even though Birkin might appear to be sleeping heavily, as soon as Violet moved, Birkin would stir, he would sit up and prick his ears, and then instantly, with considerable eagerness, he would follow her wherever she was going.

In some way, for as long as he could remember, Lumsden had been jealous of Birkin's ridiculous place in his mother's affections. Latterly Lumsden had discovered that the one way to wean Birkin from Violet was to take him for long wild walks; even longer than Violet's. Most of the time it was difficult because Violet walked him so much. But during August, during the busy, fruitful season of endless vegetables, Violet walked Birkin far less, perhaps sometimes only a short run when it was almost dark. Birkin did grow bored of lying in the heat on the narrow cinder paths in the walled garden. He was easily seduced by Lumsden's invitation to 'walk'. After one or two walks with Lumsden, Birkin, to Violet's immense dismay, began to wait, to listen for Lumsden's voice.

Lumsden had taken Birkin out early that Friday afternoon. Violet had been busy, very busy. She could not find any reasonable way to forbid Birkin's obvious pleasure, but his long absence had got to her. She imagined the poison in the hills that she knew the neighbouring farmers put down for the foxes. She imagined the bogs, sudden runs of treacherous, swampy ground. She imagined single cars suddenly speeding round the corner of a narrow lane where Birkin might be following some scent, zig-zagging the open road from side to side.

Violet had tried to hide her anxiety from Cecil because nothing was more appalling to her than his attempts at kindness and understanding. But when at last in the darkness she heard Lumsden outside, kicking his boots off in the porch, she ran eagerly to the front door waiting for the wet, wagging bound of her dog, her friend, her absolute companion. But there was only Lumsden, Lumsden grinning and smelling of beer and cigarettes, she was sure of that, but she did not refer to it. She simply said with anger and desperation:

'Birkin. Birkin. Where's Birkin?'

'Oh God, he ran off somewhere, ages and ages ago.'

'Where? Where?' Violet screamed.

'Up on the hill. I dunno. Thought he might be back here by now,' Lumsden said, and he walked straight past Violet whistling.

Immediately Violet had gone out into the darkness. It was a very clear, still, moonlit night. Her voice would carry easily. She had called. Called herself hoarse. Called so hard. Another dog several miles away barked intermittently; the rest was silence, a huge summer silence. Occasionally there was the crackle of a twig, the scurry of a rabbit, the hoot of an owl, but most of it was silence; an intense, wide, sharp silence with the smell of dew in it; a deep, fresh, drenching dew.

By the time Violet came inside Lumsden had gone upstairs to bed. Violet said nothing to Cecil. She knew Birkin had run away before, many times, and always he had returned safely; sheepish and cowering but safe. There was no real reason to think anything would be different this time. But Violet was plagued with both anger and anxiety. She hardly slept.

The next morning she was up far earlier than usual. There was no sign of Birkin. Violet took the produce into Claggan for the market. But she returned to Rathmanagh at once. There was still no sign of Birkin.

Lumsden was quite oblivious of Violet. He was heavily asleep in his room on the top landing, which was stuffy in summer and bitterly cold in winter. The night before he had visited the small bar in Ballynaule. Pat Mulligan had stood him a Paddy or two, chased with a pint of Guinness. In his sleep, a difficult, swimming, turbulent kind of sleep, he had dreamt vividly.

Then, in what was in fact mid-morning, his dreams became acute, full of a painful, particular need. In fact it was ten-thirty and he needed to pee very badly. But he was still asleep. In his sleep he was alone up on some forested hill. A sheep was trapped, caught somewhere or other, and there were hunters calling; strange natives with painted bodies and pumpkins on their heads. They were coming for him, felling huge trees with their bare hands. As they came closer he felt that maybe they blamed him for the lost sheep. Then he saw the sheep, it was just a ragged, muddy fleece; no head, no entrails, no hooves. He felt he must seize the fleece and run. He must not be discovered, yet he must move. Then he realised that a gleaming hoof was on the fleece. He bent down to tug the fleece away from under the hoof. He must move it. Slowly he looked up, past a sweating flank, and a huge, soft, pulsating belly. Then he caught sight of the still, giant shadow of antlers and he realised that he was below the belly of the stag. The stag at bay. The stag like the one in the print in the dining-room. A stag with huge, staring, oval eyes. Eyes that were trained on to him, compelling him not to move although move he must. He must.

Violet had been watching him for some time. She was standing on the nursery landing. She was standing in the open doorway of Lumsden's room. For several seconds she remembered the calm, controlled days of Nurse Biddy, when this room was cheerful and clean and bright, and a soft-skinned, sweet-smelling child had slept in the narrow, blue painted bedstead.

Now, hard-skinned yellow feet pushed through the single sheet. The room was stuffy. It smelt of sweat, not the sweat of a workman, a different, cloying sticky sweat. Everywhere there were piles of clothes and belts and papers, magazines and mugs, with congealed dried-up coffee or cocoa in the bottom, precariously placed on top of them. On the bedside table there was a dirty plate, with an utterly unmistakable cigarette butt on it.

Violet spoke:

'We've had enough of you. Enough of your sloth, your greedy, insensitive use of everyone and everything.'

Lumsden stirred. The stag still had the weight of its hoof on the foul-smelling fleece, which Lumsden could see was crawling with shining milk-white maggots.

'We've had enough. Do you hear me? Don't fake this sleep to me. I know your deceits Lumsden Farr. I know Lumsden how utterly dishonourable you are. You lie. You lie. Now get up. Get up out of this foul bed.'

As soon as she said this Violet tugged on the crumpled sheet and Lumsden woke as the fleece fell from the hoof of the stag.

In the instant of waking, Lumsden realised that the great shadow at the end of the bed, blocking out all the light, was his mother. He realised that her eyes, rather than the stag's, were beaming down on to him. He realised also that he must, whatever else happened, he must get to the loo.

'This sheet is filthy, like everything else about you.'

Violet tugged as she spoke, wrenching, as if she might peel and then discard the whole tiresome, unwholesome experience of her son. She must pull him out from this place, out from her mind and out utterly from her heart.

'Not only do you completely disregard the household, just using it like a cheap hotel. You haven't even any common decency left in you. You lie as and when it suits you. Everything has to be for your pathetic convenience, your whim, your pleasure. You're without fibre of any kind. I despise you.'

Violet tugged again at the sheet which Lumsden desperately clung to. He was immensely curtailed from any real action by the pressing condition of his need to urinate. He had on the flimsiest pair of underpants. The sheet was his guard now, his real lifeline. Lumsden tugged against Violet. There was a moment of tension. The sheet was pulled as smooth as glass between them; then it gave way. Dirty and old, it murmured, then with a roar it tore completely in two. Violet fell back banging her head against the door. With a torn half of the sheet clasped to him, Lumsden leapt out of bed, past his moaning mother, into the sanctuary of the large, sunny, nursery bathroom. He shot the bolt and stood at last, with a relief beyond description, in front of the white lavatory pan. As he relieved himself of the bulk and pressure of the urine, as it bubbled into a fine froth in the pan, he gradually became aware again of Violet's moaning and cursing on the other side of the bolted bathroom door.

For an instant, as Lumsden pulled the plug, he felt unease. A niggling press of real worry. He had taken some loose change from her bag. He had taken a packet of Sweet Afton from one of the men's jackets hanging up in the stables. But surely in a real, adult world, anywhere civilised, surely these would not be crimes but simply a case of poorly organised logistics.

Violet banged on the door.

'Jesus wept,' she screamed. 'My head's bleeding and all you can do is lock yourself into the bathroom. You should be thrashed. You should be thrashed.'

Lumsden did feel uneasy. But this woman was no longer his mother in the manner mothers sometimes seemed to be with their sons. She was huge, she was animal, she was at bay, bellowing her own mad pain at him and he simply would not receive it. He would never receive it. He would never allow himself to be a receptacle for the frantic, hopeless, shrieking pain of women. Never. Not in any circumstances.

Although Lumsden in his mind felt he was regaining some kind of strength, some sort of position, he was still uncertain of what to actually do.

Then, as in a dream, a fresh, utterly wonderful dream, he

saw the distant figure of Birkin skulking muddy and exhausted round the top end of the lawn.

'Birkin's back,' he said in a new voice. Lower. Calmer. 'Birkin's back.'

At first Violet did not hear. She was dabbing her forehead with a small scrap of torn sheet. Then, as if rescued from some terrible drowning, she heard what Lumsden had said. She heard that Birkin was back. She ran down the stairs and out into the garden.

To Birkin's considerable surprise, there was no fury from Violet, nothing but a marvellous, utterly forgiving welcome.

Although Birkin's return had to a great extent rescued them both from one another, a rift, a deep despairing rift was now between them. Both began simply to avoid, to ignore one another. Both would build, block by block, a defence between them, that would numb and blind them from any shoots of feeling that might inadvertently quicken and display themselves. Both would seek a kind of death to what had been a kind of longing. The longing for a mother to be recognised and cherished by her son and the longing for a son to be wanted and loved, simply for himself.

But long ago Nurse Biddy had clearly foreseen that Violet only anticipated discovery of what she wanted, what she deemed to be appropriate.

For Lumsden Farr to be himself, which is the natural, God-given charge to everyone, it would be, Nurse Biddy always knew, it would be difficult, very difficult, if not almost impossible.

*

Lumsden Farr was not popular at Hitcham. He was undoubtedly a force in the school. He was certainly one of its more flamboyant and unruly pupils. Hitcham was a large eighteenth-century house built in the Palladian style. There were practical contemporary additions but nothing could take from the elegant substance of the house itself. The house was set in flat but nevertheless imposing grounds. There was a large lake below the house on the south side, beyond a series of terraces. Beyond the lake there were marshes, and beyond that the sea. The central section of the house was a rotunda; this large circular hallway with a cupola ceiling had three elegant stairways leading up from it to the galleries above. Various classrooms and libraries opened out on to the gallery, they were high, well-proportioned rooms, with decorated ceilings and substantial marble fire-surrounds. Beyond the centre of the house there was a splay of practical modern buildings: flat-roofed laboratories, a gym, changing-rooms, the new kitchen, the refectory and the art block, but for all their ugliness and mundane practicality they did not seriously impinge on the impact of proportion and classical elegance of the main house, the orangery, the terraces, the cedars on the front lawn, the beech avenue leading up from the main gates, the various temples and follies hidden and crumbling in the grounds. The traditions of the school, which were broadly aligned more to Arts and Humanities than a rigorous classical or scientific base, stemmed to some extent from the inspiration of these noble eighteenth-century surroundings. Drama, particularly verse dramas, were constantly performed. There was a school orchestra and a very dedicated choir that from time to time toured the country and had been recorded. Lumsden might once have been a natural candidate for some of these activities, but his distaste for authority, his constant bragging, full of obvious apocryphal detail, his absolute need to scorn his more disciplined peers, made him unattractive to any group that needed to work as a team.

Although Lumsden's voice was now without any Irish lilt as such, it was still particular. His delivery of speech was rapid, with keen, forceful, pelted diction and stress; a certain rather flowery panache, involving gestures of the hands, a raised eyebrow, a toss of the head, to throw back a mane of loose, wavy hair. His ability to shock and discomfort engaged him enormously. To be the bearer of lurid detail, to amuse at the expense of truth and other people's reputations, were unquestionable delights to Lumsden. He seemed completely careless to the very real dislike the majority of boys and staff felt towards him.

The old void, the chaos of threat and anxiety he had felt at Thornborough, that unease, the sense that he was not 'right', not appropriate, had billowed into a determined, arrogant flounce of assumed superiority. It was as if he had to place himself above and beyond all the rest. To do this successfully a certain distance from the others was needed. This distance Lumsden achieved all too easily by being quite simply, irregular, sarcastic; unreliable in every way.

That silence of soul, which might gnaw and question, intimidating self-certainty, Lumsden managed to fill with the bright bubble of his own loud and arrogant vision of himself. His greatest ambition was to train his sensibilities, the whole substance of himself, in such a way that there would be no part of him left vulnerable to the insidious infections of guilt, worry, remorse; anxiety of any kind.

He seemed to succeed but the energy all this required of him left little over for the ordinary affairs of study and exams.

The staff disliked him. The Head, a lean rather bowed scholarly man, felt such distaste for Lumsden that he tried quite simply to avoid almost any serious recognition of him. Certainly there were many members of staff who were eager to find any excuse to expel him. 'He is not our type,' they would say. 'He just doesn't belong.' 'He contributes nothing.' 'He is quite simply insufferable.' These were some of the constant phrases concerning Lumsden that were bandied about in the smoke-filled staff room.

Lumsden did however have a friend. His friend and inseparable companion was Valentine Duckworth. In the first year they had actively disliked one another, perhaps because instinctively they were both competing for the same ground. During the second year an unspoken truce developed between them. A certain respect for one another took the place of their instinctive sparring. They were certainly two of a kind. By their third year they were hardly ever seen apart. They smoked together. They drank together. They broke bounds together. They developed a passion for Aubrey Beardsley, Oscar Wilde, Jean Cocteau; the cabalistic, the hermetic, any route that they felt might lead to some source of anarchic energy. In fact it was a retired Oxford don, a friend of Valentine's father, who unwittingly initiated them into a hobby that was subsequently to be their downfall.

Valentine's family owned property both in Scotland and London. Valentine's father was an historian. He had four decorative and highly intelligent daughters, who he had summarily ignored while he waited keenly for the birth of a son. He assumed without question that any son of his would inherit his academic powers, in this connection the reality of Valentine was a bitter disappointment. Valentine had been a pampered, sickly, whining child. He had failed despite gruelling individual tuition to pass into any of the major public schools. His mother, who loathed the academic life because it had so excluded her, had encouraged in Valentine a view of himself as precious, refined, artistic. It was she who had thought of Hitcham. She had felt attracted to it for its respect and encouragement of the arts. 'You'll turn him into a raging queen,' Valentine's father had said angrily to his wife. But there were no grounds for any such fears. By the time Valentine was fifteen he had been well and truly seduced by the maid in his grandmother's house; a cheerful, button-eyed little thing, with cheeks that flared up almost as soon as she spoke and a high pitched giggle that seemed to be part of her pleasure.

Lumsden spent the better part of many of the holidays with Valentine, to the immense relief of Cecil and Violet. Very soon Valentine had introduced Lumsden to the rough and ready pleasures of life belowstairs. These deft, carefree experiences gave Valentine and Lumsden considerable edge over the greater proportion of the other boys in their year at Hitcham, who were still troubled by the burden, pain, longings and shame of various uncertain sexual practices, sallow skin, all manner of tell-tale eruptions, those squalls of physical unbalance that so engage the emerging male.

It was during the Easter holidays, while Lumsden was staying with Valentine's parents in London, that the boys met Percival Wetherby-Downes. Wetherby-Downes was a retired medieval historian who lived in a small, over-furnished terraced house in Chiswick. Wetherby-Downes was known by all his friends as 'Pinker' Downes, the origins of this soubriquet were unclear. Pinker Downes had retired early from Oxford under a vague cloud of several rather sad suspicions; debt, drink and various deviant, antisocial activities. No one had any really accurate knowledge of his past. He was now a lonely little man with a great love of Pugin; heavy Gothic decoration, purples and blues and gold, emerging from a rather stagnant, particular, stale darkness. The small terraced house was a full, suffocating mixture of carved furniture, ornate hangings, alabaster figures of nymphs and dryads, brass bells and ornate candelabra; fretted lacquered cabinets full of books and papers, string, snuff and sealing-wax. But Pinker's pride and joy was a rare collection of nineteenth-century French pornographic postcards. Images of little girls, sometimes alone, usually in pairs, who with provocative nubile innocence were draped with furs and feathers, garters, daisies, mantillas, ostrich plumes. From tiger skins and huge ornate leather chairs, or silk screens, or palms, or aspidistras, they displayed themselves, direct to camera or intimately towards one another.

Valentine's father had no idea of Pinker's obsession with little girls when he sent the two boys round to deliver a package of books and papers. Pinker had been delighted when without warning he found himself entertaining these two amusing young men. He plied them with Madeira and rather stale cake. He showed them prints and water-colours of oriental markets executed by himself. He showed them inscribed and valuable rare editions on obscure subjects. He offered them snuff, and then later on he offered them tea with dry biscuits and ginger and raisins and nuts. He wanted so very much for their visit to continue. He rarely had young visitors and certainly very few who were in the least bit entertained by his anecdotes and memorabilia. It was when Lumsden remarked on a photograph of two little girls standing rather charmingly either side of a sun-dial, just as nature intended them, beneath an arc of madonna lilies, that Pinker began to consider the possibility of showing the boys his collection of French postcards.

The boys were certainly in no hurry to leave. This extra-ordinary little man, who sniffed and snorted and hummed as he went from cabinet to decanter and back again, fascinated them both. Whatever he showed them seemed always to lead on to something else. He would draw back a heavy curtain to reveal more shelves; he would unlock more desks, more drawers, chattering ceaselessly as he did so.

Eventually, rather nervously, he asked if they had any interest in early photography. They eagerly attempted to show interest. They had already sensed poor Pinker's proclivity for little girls and they immediately anticipated something along the lines of the French collection, but nothing had prepared them for the abundance of the collection, the extraordinary imagination of the backgrounds, the objects, and the theatrical lighting; the absurd antics, the incredible youth of these unashamed, full frontal little street children. Apparently, according to Pinker, they were rescued from squalor and poverty to be a part of this 'harmless and rather engaging popular art form, a unique celebration of innocence, don't you think?', as Pinker said, and he went on to explain the great value of the collection, the important part it played in the history of photography.

The boys didn't doubt Pinker's claims in the least. They were amazed, enthralled, utterly captivated. They simply could not believe that a dreary errand to Chiswick could have developed into such a fascinating discovery. Above all else, they had to admit that their first impression of Pinker in the doorway; the purple glass rattling in the leaded window, the rather stuffy, smoky, confined smell from the dimly lit hallway; that first impression had been one of a dull little man in a rather dirty house, whose constant, eager conversation through ill-fitting dentures meant that he sprayed them with saliva and little stops of residual breakfast food. They had agreed to enter the house with grave misgivings. They had left it exhilarated. Positively inspired.

It was a surprise to all concerned when Valentine and Lumsden returned to Hitcham for the summer term with a very committed and enthusiastic interest in photography. They both possessed German cameras; twin lens reflex, two and a quarter square format. Valentine's was a Rolleflex and Lumsden's a Voigtlander. They had already done a little developing and printing during the holidays in the Duckworth bathroom. Now at Hitcham they set to with extraordinary energy to make a darkroom out of one of the small storerooms connected to the art room.

The mystery of darkness and intense activity within it, the all-pervading smell of hypo, the yellow stains, the metronome tick of the timer, their soft bleached hands from swooshing the bromide papers about in the fix, the secrecy, the waiting, the final results, all contributed to an air of magic, almost as if they were alchemists. The staff were surprised, but they were prepared to give them the benefit of the doubt. The Head was completely won over on receiving from the boys a print of his elderly mother in the orangery with her small pug dog Brutus.

Although initially their rolls of film covered mundane subjects, such as the cedar trees, the terraces, a hen, a dog, a grinning face, the distant back view of the cook; gradually, as the basic skills were mastered and the prints became less blurred, less overall grey, the boys' vision developed. They set up Still Lives in the art room with sheets as reflectors. They used some of the theatre spotlights for dramatic effects. They tempted sitters with offers of cigarettes; they even experimented with some solarisation. Their first success from their own point of view was a Still Life; various entrails and intestines from the body of a rabbit were taken from the biology lab and then stuck with small red roses and entitled 'Sweetmeats'. Overall the Art Department was impressed. Several members of staff had to admit that 'maybe, after all, now that they had found their metier, they might make a go of their last year and contribute something to the school.' Several of their prints were to be reproduced in the school magazine. The most outstanding was an evocation of 'The Lady of the Lake'. One of the younger boys, with a flaxen Valkyrie plait of gold-braided hair stitched on to one of the wigs from the green room, walked slowly by the lake in a long white robe that had last been worn by Caesar in the Senate. With the ripples of the water to echo the folds of the garment and the long stalks of the bulrushes and marsh grasses, very stark and straight against a wide cumulus sky, it was an arresting print. Perhaps they blew it up too much. Perhaps the negative was a little scratched and dirty. Perhaps the whole conception was over-theatrical, heavy with pre-Raphaelite sentiment; the boy was clutching three white lilies, but it did succeed in persuading the management at Hitcham that they could now definitely boast a thriving, innovative Photographic Department.

So it was that during this season of nets and runs, bats and punts, canoes and careless lounging, this healthy outdoor term, this the very best of seasons, the summer, was in fact spent to a great extent by Duckworth and Farr in the small, stuffy, dark slot of their darkroom. Endless permissions were given them to go into Norwich to get materials: papers, fix and film. Extra time was allowed for them to carry out long-time exposures at dusk and similar such experiments at dawn; the fishing boats returning up the estuary with the early morning catch, the evening flight inland of wild geese and duck over the marshes. They were creators. They stalked their prey; but it was a very different prey from the ones it was assumed they stalked. And the motivation was extremely mercenary. Together they had developed tastes and recreations that needed a constant supply of ready cash.

At last they had left the dull confines of detailed drapery, oranges and jugs, views, gardening implements, boots and shoes, glass jars and eggs and bread. At last they had escaped the art of the three-hour drawing exam. All the charming rural scenes, all those scudding clouds and raging seas, all those pointed wooden prows and upturned boats with coils of rope and tar and stones, all those smiling faces, the standing pairs of cricketers with bats and caps and finely creased flannels, all the architectural shots of pillars and steps and urns, all those masters' wives, with their grubby, toddler offspring; all of it was a cover for the real art. The real art was Nancy Catchpole. Nancy was the plump, smiling niece of Cornelius Catchpole, who was the owner and publican of the small inn at the mouth of the estuary, just where it widens out into the sea. It was really the fishermen's pub. It was called the Eel's Eye. There was one small bar, with a fire in the open grate that was never out, even in summer. Although the bar was small, two bay windows and an alcove divided it into more or less three sections. The fire was up at the bar end, and so naturally it was here that most of the men congregated on the stools and rickety wooden chairs. The floor was made up of large, uneven slabs of stone, with runs of dust and dog-hairs in the dips and crevasses. Cornelius and May Catchpole were great animal lovers. They had three cats and two narrow, rough-haired, indeterminately bred, terrier-type mongrels. The bitch, Scandal, was an over-affectionate energetic creature who always rested her sharp nose on some knee or lap or arm. No one entered the bar without receiving her attentions. Scruff, her son, was less demonstrative, choosing purposely to live a little apart from the fire and the boots and legs and weathered hands. There were seldom women in the bar. Sometimes Cornelius's old mother would come with her port and sit down close to the hearth. To an outsider it would often seem private, more like a fishermen's club than a public bar. The walls were the colour of vellum, the constant smoke from pipes and fire had glazed the old cream paint almost as if a stiff brown glue had been blown over every wall surface. There were several faded photographs in heavy dark frames of boats and nets, and the proud, brave, philosophical faces of bearded fishermen, their skins rough and worn, the eyes keen slits from years of squinting towards the horizon against the onslaught of stinging spray and biting winds. There were several caps and pipes carefully preserved that had belonged to well-loved old fishermen who had passed over.

For many years strangers were uncommon in the bar of the Eel's Eye; they seemed more like suspect intruders than potential customers. Now they were more frequent. They came in bright oilskins and heavy seaman's sweaters. They came with dogs and wives and children but they rarely stayed. The bar was too small, the long hard stare of the locals too appraising.

For Nancy Catchpole, a robust, healthy, outgoing young woman, the Eel's Eye was a dead-end, old-fashioned place, completely cut off. But she was not really of age, and she had always fancied bar work, so to stay there with her Uncle Cornelius and work in the bar as a holiday job, it wasn't bad. In a way it was an opportunity. Officially she was just a niece, just a guest, but in fact during the busy summer months she ran the bar in the daytime virtually single-handed. Cornelius needed to spend time outside. He needed to attend to his own boat and the buildings. Constant exposure to sea winds meant constant dilapidation to the barge-boards and window-frames and the deep wooden window-sills. Slates were frequently slipping from the roof. Potholes in the unmade, unadopted road needed to be filled. And then there was their large flock of geese on the marsh behind the bar. There were the vegetables. There was winter wood to be carted and split and stacked. In fact there was a great deal for Cornelius to do beyond the bar work.

During the summer, most of the men were out with the boats, coming in for their pints but always taking them outside again. Only if the wind was particularly keen and blustery did they come and sit in the bar, most of the time they sat on the bench outside staring over the estuary to the rough marsh grasses, the sleek mud flats and the great concrete slabs that tried to keep the banks in place as the estuary narrowed and then widened ready for the tidal mouth of the sea.

From the Eel's Eye, the spire of Hitcham Church could be seen, and to the left of it the water tower. Hitcham House itself could not be seen. But Hitcham House was known and its presence felt throughout the local community. It was not particularly liked, although the women who worked up there were pleased to do so. They cycled bravely over the open marshes in all weathers, grateful for any job, any diversion that gave them some sense of independence. May Catchpole had worked up at the school before she married Cornelius. 'I don't know what kind of a world these young men think they're fit for,' she would say, 'they certainly wouldn't be fit for seafaring or the land either for that matter. More than likely they'll never know war or want. Maybe there's a soft place for them somewhere down south. But God help this country if they're all we've got.' May was an outspoken, proud woman. Her sister and several of the women who worked up in the laundry and kitchens at Hitcham House thought the young men were 'charming, beautifully mannered, real gentlemen.' 'Manners without the man in it, is like a slop to me,' May would retort vehemently. 'I like meat and I like it red . . . ready for living!'

Nancy had arrived at the Eel's Eye just before Easter. It was late May when she first noticed these two, loud, lounging, thin young men, with their cameras and pale hairy legs and clean, open-necked Aertex shirts. The other fishermen viewed the boys with suspicion. All those antics with cameras just to record a few battered, unpainted boats, dead fish and tangled nets. They seemed a queer pair and the pub anyway was out of bounds to the school, but then that was Cornelius's business.

It was a very hot afternoon when Nancy, having just cycled back from the village, saw the two boys lying exhausted and prostrate on the bank beside the towpath.

'Catch,' she yelled, and she threw two fresh oranges that had just fallen out of her bicycle basket. Valentine caught his. Lumsden missed.

'Butter fingers,' Nancy called out laughing. And then Lumsden really looked at her. He looked at her plump cheeks and the firm, stormy, full breasts under her thin pink shirt. He looked at her tight thighs in the white drill shorts, the tanned skin, the short, free, rather frisky stack of fair hair.

Lumsden ran quickly down from the bank across the smooth stones to this cheerful, cheeky girl down there, with the battered black bicycle and the sun-drenched, wind-slapped skin and those free, 'asking for it' eyes. Together they grabbed at the other oranges still in the bag. They threw them. They rolled them. They caught them. They caught her. They laughed and ran and chased and hid and then stopped and sat together on one of the upturned boats. They shared out the oranges, hurling the bright peel on to the smooth stones, then, with long, happy, insect tongues they savoured the sharp juice and the supple flesh of the fruit, spitting out the pips like pellets from a pea-shooter.

That was the beginning. Nancy had been bored. Now she sensed a kind of fun summer ahead. Later that evening Lumsden told Valentine of his idea. 'Pictures. Pictures of her, Valentine. Pictures of Nancy. Pictures to sell.' 'She'll never fall for it Lumsden. She'll never take the risk.' 'You're wrong, Val . . . you're so wrong,' Lumsden had insisted. 'Women love risk, but above all, women like money. We'll tempt her with the ready. It'll be a really above-board business proposition.'

Nancy did fall for it. First the flattery, then the fun and after that, quite definitely, the idea of the money.

The first pictures were pretty harmless, just ogles and curves, just more or less happy snaps with a bit of suggestion.

It was Nancy who first said:

'Do you think I could model?'

'Of course you could,' the boys chorused.

'Don't models have to be terribly thin?'

'No. There are thin ones just like there are thin cats, thin dogs . . . thin anything. But think of the other models Nance . . . think of the cute and the cuddly.'

'Cute. Cuddly,' Nancy repeated the two words without enthusiasm.

'Well . . . think of glamour . . .' Lumsden said. 'Glamour isn't necessarily thin.' It was like playing a fish, like teasing a wasp on a window-pane. Up and down. Up and down. And then pounce . . .

'Of course, there is money in glamour. Good money. Real money Nance . . .'

'But you have to have clothes. Posh clothes. Furs, shoes, leather bags and things.'

'That is one way. I agree that is one way,' said Lumsden watching her carefully.

'Well, we haven't got that kind of gear,' said Nancy, beginning to sound irritated, almost bored.

'No. No, you're right, absolutely right, we haven't got that kind of gear. But come on, Nance . . . think what we have got. Or rather think what you've got . . . just think Nance . . .'

'Well, nothing. Nothing much. Health, hopes and a battered old bicycle . . .'

'Just a perfect brace . . . a brace of the best Nance,' Lumsden said daringly and he leant forward and gingerly cupped his two hands under her two breasts. He knew he was on the right track. They almost rang bells when he came that close.

'Cheeky bugger,' she said and she giggled. Then she thought. She remembered. She remembered all those sticky, dark, oily walls at the back of garage workshops. Sticky dark walls with calendars and posters pinned to them. Posters of busty girls with blonde hair . . .

'You are cheeky. You should be shot, the pair of you.'

She giggled. Then she laughed. She was tantalised. Why not? Why not? Plenty of girls did it. Why not Nancy Catchpole? What a lark. What a dare.

Lumsden knew, he knew from her face and from her smile, he knew by the way she was twisting and turning the stones with the toe of her sandal. Lumsden knew she was considering it.

'Think of the money, Nancy. Think of the real lolly, girl.'

'Well, maybe I am thinking Lumsden. Maybe I am thinking,' Nancy said, looking as directly and as provocatively as she could towards Lumsden.

Valentine was impressed. Very impressed. These were definitely entrepreneurial skills. 'Lumsden,' he said, 'you'll not only be Farr . . . you'll go far . . . bloody far!'

The whole thing took some setting up. The lights. The barn. The timing. It all needed careful planning. The best time was the afternoon. The long games period when the pub was closed and the place was generally empty and quiet.

In the beginning it was just cleavage and pouts and length of leg. But very soon, inspired by endless talk of financial rewards, the three of them became united in the keen pursuit of a good, sexy range of black-and-white postcards for sale.

The poses got better and better.

The debt they owed to Pinker Downes was often referred to. A young man in the camera shop in Norwich who possessed a motorbike said he could find outlets in the various dance halls of Yarmouth and Hemsby, and he did. By the end of June they had half-a-dozen real winners and with them a regular, reliable turnover.

Nancy bought bangles and rings and cheap scent. She was very proud of herself. Even if she did end up one day with nothing but chickens and kids and a double chin, she would always know that she had been a model. And she would always have the pictures to remind her. It was a considerable satisfaction.

The school was concerned with itself, its end of term, post-exam razzmatazz of plays, matches, choirs and concerts; it was very easy to be skilfully and consistently absent. Consistently unavailable. By the end of the term, when Valentine and Lumsden had their final photographic session with Nancy, rounded off by a bottle of champagne and the settling of the accounts to date, all three were delighted. They had every reason to expect consistent sales through the summer and so receive some good money at the beginning of the autumn term. Although Nancy might not be back for some while, they still had several excellent images that they had not yet even floated on to the market. The prospects were good. The horizons wide. The potential, untapped market enormous.

When the boys drove away from Hitcham at the end of the summer term they had no idea how soon, and how summarily, their lives, particularly Lumsden's, would alter course dramatically. Lumsden could never have guessed that just months after his seventeenth birthday he would be a man with 'a past'. Banned from Hitcham House but banned also from his country of birth and origins.

Lumsden spent the first two weeks of the summer holidays in Scotland with Valentine. Together they drank and smoked away their ill-gotten gains. When Lumsden returned to Rathmanagh at the beginning of August, he was thin and overhung. Already he had a degenerate air. His clothes, his jackets and jumpers and cap, smelt of cigarettes and bars. Everything about him was decidedly unsavoury. His voice was now immensely affected and over-anglicised. His gestures were extreme. His laugh, a vulgar sprawl of purposely uncontrolled, rough sounds, seemed to challenge refinement, any kind of civilised quiet, with raucous, crude, belittling scorn.

Violet was shocked. Lumsden was more than a boor. He was a positive affront to the very tenets of life at Rathmanagh. He seemed able, simply by his presence, to flush out from the house any peace or calm, any indwelling, benign continuity, that over the long, stagnant, battered-down years they had managed between them somehow to put together. There seemed nowhere and nothing that could withstand the insidious, destructive force of his boorish personality.

Violet became increasingly unnerved. A dynamic of real hatred seemed to flare up in her whenever Lumsden addressed her. She knew in her heart that she wished him dead. Over and done with. Utterly out of the way forever. Once, as she was digging over a bed in the walled garden, she even felt that the sharp smack of the shining spade into the soil was a clean sound of the spade into a grave trench; into a handsome yard or so of deep burial ground.

When such dark thoughts as these assailed her she would call for Birkin. She would scold him and love him. She would talk to him in a gentle, warm, soft, murmuring voice, like the tutting purr of a dove. She would talk of walks; of tastes and being and things; of birds, scents, rabbits, hills; the river, the furze, the heather; bumble bees, ants' nests, midges, butterflies; seeded lettuces, rose petals, mildew; greenfly, slugs and spiders and worms. Violet would listen to her voice of loving chatter to dear Birkin; these simple lists, ordinary, and wonderfully mysterious things, that were for them both tasks and duties, irritations and consolations. After some while in this private communication with Birkin, gradually the dark leaps of real hatred and dread of Lumsden would give way again to a more pleasant, reassuring sense of a simple life, quietly sustained in a beautiful place. But increasingly, as the long summer days stretched ahead of them, Violet felt engulfed, suffocated; chats with Birkin were not enough to console her. Only in the cool of the late evening, high on the crest of Mount Murna, with the dew dragging down the hem of her long skirt, owls hooting, rabbits and voles scurrying past rotten lengths of dry timber into the roots and holes and shadows, only then did Violet experience any real sense of sanctuary. Murna was a high and ancient witness of the earth. In some way Murna was beyond sorrow and anger. It was too bold, too thrust up, too God-given to succumb to the mean, dull traps of human pith and scratch; the squeals, stench and scars of mis-shapen relationships. On Murna Violet seemed almost to receive an energy which made voices and houses, people and plans, simply the careless, humdrum excreta from aeons of denial; the residue of some giant misuse; some miscalculation that had cast off man like dropped stitches from the complete scope; from the resounding whole. But Murna was still within the spring of the first sound. Murna still had the breath of complete life, without tally or origin; scale, sense, or mathematical dimension.

There was something else. There was something else.

When Violet lay down in the banks and folds, the drains and dips of this mountain's surface and gazed up into the live, various emptiness of clouds and stars and sky above her, she sometimes felt that the whole heave of this great mound under her could, by a simple swing, somehow embedded in its very nature, roll over, dipping down below every known surface and be nothing but a giant hammock-space, breathing below the moon and sun and stars; a great birth of fresh scope, breathing beneath an entire, free, eternal sky.

Violet never spoke or reasoned these thoughts, they simply stumbled as it were through the bitter, fraught skein of herself like an errant dancer. But the dance resuscitated. The dance was a secret kind of other life; there, but known to no one; known hardly to herself.

Cecil now stooped, visibly. He looked far older than his actual years. He felt completely alienated from Lumsden. The young man's presence in the house was like a vast drop in the barometer. It was a storm to be weathered, not a battle to be won. Cecil knew perfectly well, he knew that the money he always kept in the top left-hand drawer of the chest-of-drawers in his dressing-room was always tampered with whenever Lumsden was in the house. But Cecil could not bring himself to accept that his son was a flagrant thief. He was afraid in any way to confront the subject of Lumsden and his behaviour. Violet's disposition, whenever Lumsden was at Rathmanagh, became brittle, tense, almost unmanageable. Cecil feared for her then. He knew that nothing inflammatory or challenging should be pursued, mentioned, even guardedly inferred. We must just stare it out, Cecil thought. This was how Cecil had managed to come to some kind of compromise with his own personal problem. He had simply stared it out. He had learnt over the years to stare at perplexing and distressing situations in such a way that they faded, grew too tired even to be themselves.

Cecil had discovered that thoughts, unthought, gradually became parched, and like plants denied light or sustenance, thoughts without thought withered, and eventually died. Maybe a great deal died with them if nothing was positively engendered to take their place. Maybe the delirium of utter emptiness to which Cecil had become conditioned was in the end its own final thought. But in spite of everything, Cecil still registered Violet. He felt grateful to have lived in her shadow. In his way he loved her deeply. She had given him what he had asked for. Some kind of denial of life, and some kind of strength to hide behind. But neither could ever have anticipated the alien horror of Lumsden. And it would never have occurred to either of them to detect in the low, negative process towards this final sum of an unattractive, lying, stealing, self-important, self-obsessed hedonistic youth, any trace of a need, to overcome an absence, by becoming a loud, brutally resilient presence.

Nurse Biddy would not have been so surprised.

'If they are not loved and welcomed simply for being themselves, then, sure as day follows night, in the end they'll become something else.'

Nurse Biddy had frequently said that to Mrs Donovan in the warm, clean, kitchen evenings of cocoa and cake that they had shared together so often during Nurse Biddy's time at Rathmanagh.

Lumsden refused to take a holiday job on any of the neighbouring farms or in the brewery, although Violet had made sure such jobs were offered to him. Aunt Theodora's house was let through the summer, as Lumsden had professed an ardent dislike for that 'toothless little community of cringing peasants out on Kilbronan Bay'. He no longer rode, the fag of it all without staff in the stables put him off. He did walk Birkin. He did go off in the evenings shooting rabbits. Mostly he remained in bed. When he did get up he smoked incessantly and continued to make long telephone calls to England. As soon as the bars were open he was down in Ballynaule. He rarely ate with his parents, acknowledged them, or even spoke to them. When the atmosphere was particularly fraught, heavy with such impending violence that it might have been felled with an axe, Lumsden would start to whistle; taking matches from his trouser pocket and then snapping them in two, he would flick the small splinters of wood across the room with his forefinger, with the wood balanced on the tip of his thumb.

Violet would instantly get up and leave the room. She feared any kind of confrontation. She did not feel she would ever be able to muster the necessary degree of self control to avoid some kind of massacre.

When the day of confrontation and final reckoning came, Violet was luckily not on her own. Father Palin was there to support her. In fact, it was he who swore and ranted at Lumsden enabling Violet to remain silent, while vehemently agreeing to the demands being made by the parish priest.

There were three bars in Ballynaule. Brennan's. Rooney's. And Delaney's. There were other smaller drinking houses, but there were only those three on the main street. Lumsden frequented all three. As a young lad he had been warmly accepted by the local community. Rathmanagh was an important part of the parish. Many had lived and worked on the land there. Many fished in the river and shot rabbits and pigeons in the woods. Many remembered only too well the years of Rathmanagh's dereliction, long before Cecil and Violet Farr bought the property. In those days it had been owned by the Keely sisters, a pair of eccentric spinsters who had lived almost in one room, letting the home of their parents and their childhood literally fall around them.

But in those far off days of drink and dilapidation, Rathmanagh had been very close to the hearts and experience of the souls in Ballynaule. In the long years since then, Violet Farr had certainly brought order to the chaos. The lands were now in good heart. The walled garden flourished, full of every sort of plant and produce. The newly-planted orchard was well and bearing good fruit. The river was wide and clear of weeds, although many feared for the family at Rathmanagh for having inherited the spoil and destruction of the rath, when the lake was first dug; long before the Keelys' time even. In the memory of Ballynaule, Rathmanagh was marked with that dangerous presumption; the meddling rout of sacred fairy stones. However, times moved on; things and people changed. But no one in Ballynaule was prepared for the change in young Lumsden since his long schooling in England.

It had been, as they all said at the time, a very unnatural thing to haul a lad out and away from his home, from his mother and father, his very roots, all he knew and loved. But that was their way. It was what they thought they wanted. It was little surprise to the parish that Lumsden became so brash, so awkward, so unruly a lad. Give him time, they said. Sure he's only young. 'Tisn't easy to find your feet on your own. The people were civil enough to Violet to her face, but they found her a cold, unbidden woman. A powerful worker. A powerful horsewoman, with the guts and drive of a man in her. The poor Captain was something else altogether. Not much of the man about him. But he was gentle enough, hurt no one and nothing, that couldn't be bad.

There was never too much attention paid to times and regulations in the three bars of Ballynaule. The drinkers were almost always the same few, standing or sitting; staring and sniffing. The same few in the same places, night after night; their damp clothes crusted dry by the heat of the fire, and their low hungry spirits roused to a glow of positive accepting philosophy. This was the shape of things in the bars. In such a shape, Lumsden, with his angular intrusive voice and his loud ugly gestures, did not belong. He didn't drink quietly, down into himself. He drank loudly, challenging the other customers and their quiet. At first one or two of the younger men would drink with Lumsden; hear his tales and even laugh at some of his jokes, but by his seventeenth summer he had become bad for business. The bars, already quiet, would grow quieter still when he came in. The regulars would move away from him. Even the barmen and their wives refused to bother with him. It was for these reasons that Lumsden went from bar to bar, never staying too long in one place. Very soon, he began to buy himself the odd half bottle of whiskey and just drank alone. In the summer this was easy, there were many good narrow lanes and low stone walls, many open verges and ruined dwellings. Birkin was frequently his companion.

Beside the church in Ballynaule, attached to the presbytery, was the Madox Hut, a lean-to, wooden building originally constructed as part of the tanner's business further on down the street carried on by the Madox brothers. The business had become run down, the yard and hut had fallen into disrepair, but being so conveniently placed beside the church and presbytery, it had been taken over by the parish as a hall and general community centre. It had been bricked out and a new wooden floor laid. A makeshift stage had been constructed with dark green curtains for the school plays and the Irish dancing competitions, the raffles and draws and jumble sales. There was a piano and wooden benches and folded card-tables. Lumsden knew the Hut, as it was called, well. He had often sheltered there with Birkin on rainy, wintery days. The doors were nearly always open.

It was Thursday. It was the third week of August when this incident took place, which was to act as a crucial focus to

135

Lumsden Farr's sense of himself, and the role he would pursue, construct, and play for the rest of his life.

Father Palin had not been long in the parish. He had been a busy city priest and the move to Ballynaule, although technically a promotion, he was the one and only priest, the move had felt to him like a demotion. There was not much drive and fervour in Ballynaule. The women ran their smooth rosary beads through their hands and whispered novenas and lit endless candles. Every Sunday the men congregated in groups at the back of the church, remaining inside for the minimum of time, just enough to take their caps from their heads and sign themselves, and bow a little, as the bells rang out during the words of consecration; after that they would retire to the porch and discuss the price of beef, or the form of a horse, or the death or disease of a neighbour, whose land might then be very soon for sale.

Father Palin found it hard to get the real measure of the people. He seemed incidental to their lives. Although they all greeted him, they had not really warmed to him. They were content with murmurs and candles, the comfort of repeated patterns, the way things were; the fresh, keen white of First Communion, the love of the Mother of God; great faith and great forgiveness. They did not yearn for change, any abrasive theological dynamic. But Father Palin was a modern man. He longed to stir them; to confront them; to shake them out of their damp, sodden, humble, unassuming, undemanding ways. He needed an occasion. He needed a scapegoat. He needed a pariah. And Lumsden inadvertently provided it.

But in a sense, although Lumsden might have been to some extent used by the needs of Father Palin, although other parents might have defended their son, all these strands, all these tributaries of circumstance, seemed to be a presence, slowly and purposely made to bring about the charge of the occasion, which was as much a vigorous beginning as it was a definite end.

It was about three-thirty when Lumsden and Birkin made their way into the cool of the Madox Hut. Lumsden had his half-bottle of Paddy, three-quarters drunk. He lay down on one of the benches at the side of the hall, in the dark of rolled drugget and stacked tables. Birkin gratefully lay down in the dark beside him. Lumsden closed his eyes.

Father Palin was exhausted after a heavy lunch of pork, roast potatoes and cabbage, followed by apple pie; a most unsuitable diet for the stifling, windless heat of the day, but Mrs Dennehay, Father Palin's housekeeper, had no culinary sense of season. To her a priest must be fed, stoked, and primed with the best, plenty of gravy, plenty of pastry, always a real meal, nothing slight or messed about. Good meat and good vegetables.

Father Palin had been irritated by the unwelcome meal. And he was irritated now by the insistence of the women in the parish that Confession should be heard by him in the church every Thursday afternoon from three to four. Few came. And the dark confessional was airless and stuffy. Bridget Lawlor and Sheila Daly always came, with their neat precise voices, and their dull bourgeois scruples. It was they who insisted that the time of Confession should not be altered. They never came together. Perhaps they wanted to be quite sure that Father Palin stayed there for the full hour.

Mrs Lawlor had been. She had confessed once again the same several small sins of carelessness, untidiness, forgetfulness. Is there anything else? Anything else at all? Father Palin would whisper hoarsely through the dark grid, wishing that some real awareness of the rest of the world, other places and other people might fire this woman from her small, complaisant, tidy little personal landscape. Real sin might be a fine thing for her. But Father Palin could never imagine what real sin it could ever be.

He gave her for her penance three Hail Marys. She thanked him and left. Father Palin sat back. He almost slept. He almost snored. Then he became aware of a strange, unexpected, but very consistent pattern of sound that was coming through the air-bricks in the wall, just above his head, from the Madox Hut, just there beside the church. Usually at this time the Hut was shut. Sometimes the women were there tidying up, sorting things, or setting things, but then they always spoke in low voices, he could never hear what it was that they were saying.

Sometimes Mrs Moore might have a pupil for Irish dancing, then Father Palin would hear the beat of her stick on the floor and the relentless Lahla lah lalah la lah la lah of Mrs Moore's voice.

The sounds now were unexpected. Quite different. First there were several rather jarring bars on the piano, then there was a long tense pause and then, suddenly, peals of laughter and the sound of what seemed like a throw of coins across the floorboards.

In fact what had happened was this. Three little girls, recent first communicants, this last Corpus Christi in fact; three little girls, Patsy, Maraid and Eileen, had been passing the Madox Hut on their way to the chemist's to collect various things for Mrs O'Brien. The medications were not ready, so while waiting, just to be out of the heat, the three girls had gone into the cool of the Madox Hut. Birkin had greeted them and they, after a moment's hesitation, had been delighted by him. They shared boiled sweets and secrets between one another. Intense, innocent details of other people's homes and things and promises. They whispered and giggled and made long luscious sucking noises with the large hard sweets in their small narrow cheeks. Then Patsy showed Maraid her petticoat. Peach pink, crisp and new. Then Eileen twirled, and her skirt spun like a flat disc round her waist. The other two shrieked at the sight of Eileen's thin legs, small bottom and, for all the world to see, the sight of her knickers!

It was the shrieks and giggles that first roused Lumsden. The girls had seen him sleeping there at the side of the hall, but they weren't particularly bothered. Then Lumsden sat up and spoke to them. They giggled. His voice was so peculiar. He came across to them.

'Do it again,' Lumsden said.

'Do what?'

'The spin. The twirl.'

'Oh, that. That's stupid.'

The girls were bunched on the bench together, giggling and squirming, putting their hands over their gappy, toothy little mouths and through their fine, long lanky hair.

'Have a pear drop,' Patsy said.

'No thanks,' Lumsden replied.

'Go on. They're good. Go on. Take one. Take one.'

Eagerly they proffered him the small sticky little paper bag.

'I never suck sweets on Thursdays. Never,' Lumsden said. He wanted to keep them talking. In a very vague way he was thinking of asking Valentine over to Ireland, but he never quite liked to because there would be nothing to do, but as Lumsden looked at these three lively little girls, he thought of Pinker Downes.

'Go on. Spin again,' he said.

'It's stupid.'

'Go on, Eileen, we dare you. We dare you,' the others chorused.

'Look, I'll close my eyes, count up to five, and then open them again, and if you're still spinning, I'll give you this.' Lumsden showed them a small coin.

'Go on, Eileen. Go on.'

'Well . . . You do it Patsy.'

'My skirt's too narrow.'

'Then show your bottom. I dare you. Show your bottom.'

It was a joke. A quite unprompted, innocent thought from nowhere at all. They often played dare games. It was like that.

It was just a dare. Just a bit of a dare. But it fitted too well to be lost. It fitted so exactly a thought of Lumsden's and a picture or two from Pinker Downes's collection. Lumsden took all the loose change from his pocket. And so it went on, the giggles and dares and finally the really good game that woke Father Palin in the hot, sticky, quiet gloom of the confessional while he waited for the certain arrival at the end of the hour of Sheila Daly for the sacrament of penance.

The game went like this. Lumsden sat at the piano with his back to the girls and played various open chords and arpeggios. The girls, their skirts flounced above their heads, their bottoms for an instant bare, had to run to the scatter of loose change that Lumsden had thrown on to the floor. And rather like grandmother's footsteps, they had to seize a coin from the floor without Lumsden turning from the piano and seeing a bare bottom. A bare bottom seen, meant the money must be refunded.

The game took good shape. It gathered momentum. It was a really excellent game. Even Birkin joined in.

Father Palin listened. He listened intently. Everything told him that there was some definite wickedness in these unexpected sounds from the Madox Hut. At last Sheila Daly came to the confessional. Father Palin was maddened by the interruption. He gave her a decade of the Rosary as a penance, the longest penance she had ever had in her life. Mortified, Sheila Daly left the confessional. Instantly Father Palin left the church.

Quickly and quietly Father Palin walked round the side of the church towards the half-open door of the Madox Hut. He could hear the piano. He stared into the dark of the hall; then, like a detective, who for years has stalked an unknown tyrant whose ways and habits he knows but whose face he has never seen, he saw there, now, before his own eyes, in this sleepy, dowdy parish of Ballynaule on a sweltering August afternoon . . . he saw sin. Flagrant sin. He saw the sacred innocence of children plunged into the murky, violent whirls of Satan's worst, most dreadful inspiration. The sins of the flesh. A young man's horrible, pagan, animal desires unleashed, and innocent children abused, here in the parish hall, under the very gaze of the parish priest. The holy innocence of three recent communicants lost, besmirched, tainted, soiled. 'Mother of God,' he cried and the combination of his distended stomach with so much pork, potatoes and gravy, the terrible, long boredom of the confessional, and the general dismay and distaste he felt for this humdrum, easy-going parish, all rose in one suffocating, furious howl of righteous anger.

The little girls, like trampled petals from some worn processional ground, huddled at the back of the hall. Instinctively their pale hands pasted their thin cotton skirts down over their thin legs. Lumsden closed the piano. Then he went to the centre of the hall. He bent to pick up the rest of his loose change still lying there on the floor. He was attempting to ignore this coarse, blustering priest.

But then as he bent he felt hands on his collar. He was summarily dragged up from the ground and shaken. Lumsden had never been physically assaulted by an adult before. Father Palin smelt the whiskey on the young man's breath and with it he smelt generations of degenerate weakness on behalf of his countrymen, and he smelt the terrible, evil yoke of the British. He recognised Lumsden. He knew the boy's parents. And he knew of the boy's grandfather and namesake, Lumsden Fitzpatrick. But what Father Palin knew most of all was that Lumsden symbolised to him all the worst parts of pagan power and degeneration of that utterly Godless nation. To Father Palin, Lumsden's presence in the parish, here at Ballynaule, was the presence of the Devil himself, and that money down there on the floor was Iscariot pence. It was as bad, as black as that.

The girls were crying. Father Palin roared and shouted, still shaking the stunned Lumsden.

'We all become so complacent. We just want things easy. Easy

141

and comfortable . . . all we think of is bodily desires . . . bodily comfort . . . bodily care. We are in danger every day . . . every second of losing our souls. We are in constant danger always, of a total fall from grace . . . Those three children, only weeks ago made their first Holy Communion, and now that great grace has been whipped away, torn out from them, with the ferocious maul of a wild beast on innocent, defenceless prey . . .'

Eileen burst out into loud, fearful sobs.

'Go back to your homes. Go back to your parents, your brothers and sisters, who very soon will be sorrowing with me for these tragic deeds . . . in this very building, which is owned by and attached to the church itself. Mother of God . . . what irony . . . what brutal irony . . . Go on. Go now,' he said to the girls, who although more or less silent had still not felt able to budge from the small tearful bundle of themselves at the back of the hall.

'Go.' At last, momentarily, the priest's voice dropped. 'Go back to your homes. I shall visit everyone of you shortly but first . . . first we must send this Satan . . . this foul, crippled creature out from our midst . . .'

The girls left the hall. Father Palin ignominiously dragged Lumsden towards the small humble shape of his Ford Prefect. People had heard the commotion. They stood in the doorways staring in amazed interest. They had never heard Father Palin in such voice before, although he was definitely not a man to button his lip or mince his words if the occasion required otherwise.

Sitting in the back of the car with Birkin, Lumsden stared at the greasy, scarred, bull neck of this apoplectic priest. Lumsden had to admit to rather admiring his great flow of invective. And also, the theme of himself, having such an undisputedly satanic flavour, was rather engaging. Lumsden felt sure that although it might have marginally uncomfortable moments, a life spent in pursuit of nothing but deviant pleasure would at least avoid the problem of boredom. If he was really equipped to be so downright, so thrillingly bad, then he might as well make it his capital. He might as well build on it for effect. He might as well pursue a totally satanic reputation, no holds barred.

Father Palin seemed to have some kind of respiratory problem. His breathing was noisy and difficult; it inserted a peculiar rasping, wet, very visceral sound into the hard-edged, personal silence between himself and Lumsden.

Birkin's large head rested on Lumsden's cramped knees. Lumsden stroked the black ears and stared into the clean, pink-white, waxed whorls of sculpted skin that lay hidden under the black flap of hairy skin.

It was all so bloody ridiculous. Those little girls were about as far from flesh as chocolate truffles were from a jar of Marmite. Palin must be sexually pretty derelict, poor bugger. His whole body must feel enraged against the dreary, unnaturalness of its life. All those coughs and splutters were probably due to the desperate need for everything in the man, all his internal gunge to find some kind of orifice to spit its way out of that ugly tomb of overweight, sticky, red, flaccid, demented flesh.

Thinking of this riot; of this real dump of body that masqueraded as a purveyor of truth and wisdom, Lumsden managed not to give much immediate thought to himself, and his position as it might seem to his parents. The car bumped over the bridge and turned up towards Rathmanagh. They came to the high stone wall. They came to the gates. The car stalled. Birkin sat up sniffing eagerly, a large slather of foamy dribble on his jaw. Lumsden ran his hand through his hair, which was long enough now to more or less cover his large ears.

All the to-ing and fro-ing up and down this drive, in small, badly-sprung, uncomfortable cars. Leaving home. Returning home. That thought 'home', it had always seemed unreal, like a play or game; like a grim charade of frozen syllables. The very phrase 'going home' had a jarring, twisted ring to it. It was like Hunka Munka, doll's house food. A treat of clay.

The car stalled again. Murna was on their left now. Murna seemed very soft and spread against this burnt-out sky. Brilliant blue, beyond a haze of hovering, thin stretches of pale, yellowing cloud. Murna is different, Lumsden thought. No 'home', no bounds, no game or charade can capture it. And in the second of that thought, for the first time for many, many years, Lumsden felt a pinch of real, stubborn pain, that reminded him of those first terrible weeks at Thornborough. He remembered his torch. He remembered Baker Mi, Morton and Jellicoe. Then Murna was behind them. Father Palin parked the car directly in front of the long library windows. Something Violet always considered ill-bred and insensitive.

Violet was weeding the border on the terrace which ran above the high grassy bank that sloped down to the gravel; that large, open, circular space in front of the house. It had been a particularly peaceful afternoon. The considerable heat had made Violet take things easily. There was plenty of shade at the end of the terrace and a low stone bench on which Violet had sat while she had a mug of coffee after lunch. She had missed Birkin. She presumed he had gone off with Lumsden. Violet had not seen her son to speak to for several days. It was extraordinary. It was too bleak, too depressing for words. But at least the kind of sangfroid, the vast distance between them, the unreality of their relationship, meant that there had been no row lately. No vulgar, uncontrollable display of vindictive words and accusations.

Violet had so enjoyed the afternoon because she had been able to make every step between the paths and plants with grace and elegance. She had tried and trimmed abundant stalks and eager shoots, with the sensibility, so she felt, of an artist. She knew that there was a part of her that, if bidden, if allowed, could disrupt and disengage the rest; the elegance, the poise, the obedient synthesis of this middle-aged, powerful, organised, intelligent woman, that was, to all intents and purposes, the proud sum of herself. Only in the night shadows of her long evening walks over the river to Murna, was the other, hidden, discarded sound of her unbidden Fitzpatrick self, ever heard. But the murmur of it was always there; like some distant bass tremble, it lay in wait, to balance and couple with any violent, untamed treble sound that might escape through the devious slits and portals that were engendered by stress and strain, but most particularly by the barbaric intrusion of her son's tormenting, ugly disposition towards her.

She was cutting the grass verge with a tall pair of edging shears. The clip and pause was a distinct, sharp sound into the soft full silence of the afternoon; a different sound to the quiet pull and yield and dump of weeds into the barrow. Then she heard a car. She heard a door slam. She stared for a second at the clump of brilliant, china-blue delphiniums directly ahead of her. Then slowly she turned round and looked down over the steep bank and the wide pale sweep of gravel beyond it, directly in front of the house.

Birkin was bounding up the steps towards her. She disregarded him. He wagged and squeaked and pranced about her ankles. Violet ignored him completely.

Below on the gravel Father Palin stood awkwardly beside his small brown car. On the other side of the car, close to the library windows, Lumsden stood. But his standing was unnatural, awkward. He did not look up or down. He simply stared towards the bank that was directly in front of him, but he stared as if it were a wide open horizon. In fact he stared numbly into himself, where, for the first time for a long, long while, the resolute, bragging, loud flourish of identity and purpose was silent; empty. He felt numb, inconsequential, like a cardboard space; brown, pointless, scooped out and dull; unutterably dull.

Violet sensed that there was or had been drama between them. Father Palin attempted to speak.

'I'm sorry to trouble you, Mrs Farr.'

Violet made her way down the long flight of stone steps. She pulled off her gardening gloves. She fixed the priest with a button-hook, sharp glance of both appraisal and warning. She seemed to glare out to him that she only wanted to hear truth, facts, not a fudge of intimidating suppositions.

'Shall we go inside?' she said. 'The front door is open. Go into the study. I shall be with you shortly, but I'm covered with mud so I'll come in through the back door.'

Violet paused. She almost looked directly towards Lumsden. But she resisted the temptation, and anyway he was looking intently at the library window-sill. He was staring at the lichen and small stones and cracked paint. Violet walked towards the narrow, stone-flagged gulley that ran along the side of the house, below the high bank. Just before she walked away from the bright sunlight into this damp, shaded path, she paused once more. Lumsden's odd demeanour, his stillness, his silence almost engaged in Violet a kind of sorrow where only anger and torment, self-pitying torment, normally would be found. But without moving or looking, she felt she received from Lumsden a definite hurl of banishment. It was as if he had sensed that she might speak, even move closer towards him. Her close proximity to him seemed to pinion him, fix him there without any kind of movement. Neither of them gave any overt recognition of the other's presence, but subliminally with animal ferocity they stalked one another. The priest hovered awkwardly by the front door. Why did neither of them move or speak? Already, before he had told them, before he had even delivered the ultimatum that was in his mind, they seemed to be acting as if they knew. They seemed to be fixed there on some knife edge; on some unspoken strand of understanding. There seemed to be this hair's breadth of need and hate and recognition spun between them. Frozen. Held in this odd, disconnected thrall, they remained physically close, physically bound by a tie of blood that had festered into a septic ditch, where the unspoken detritus of lost years, lost moments, in fact lost life, bowled between them until at last it had so bruised, so cauterised the human bounds that it snapped.

Finally, here, on the hot, late-August afternoon, in the strange compelling silence between them, they instinctively made or wished to make some last tentative murmur towards one another, but the concept of their relationship, the horror of the body-truth that must be at the base of any mother and son idea, was too much for either of them. They withdrew. The hair's breadth snapped. Violet turned into the dark gulley beside the stone house, knowing that no tie now, nothing could hold her in any way to the young man out there in the afternoon sun. He was in trouble; obviously grave trouble of some kind or other. But it was his. All his. None of it was hers. He had chosen to be what he was, and what he was she did not know or recognise. 'He is a stranger,' she said to Birkin. 'He is a complete stranger to me.'

Father Palin went inside the house. He was not at ease. To be close to the mother and her hard, daunting, extreme manner almost imposed on Father Palin some recognition of the boy's difficulties. Hurriedly, Father Palin reminded himself that at the centre of it all was abuse. Abuse of innocence. He said it several times to himself. Instantly he felt stronger. More resolute. More righteous. He was in the study. It should have been a comfortable room, but for some reason the bright colours, the books and papers, the dog-baskets, the dried flowers, the general clutter of haphazard things; seed packets, silver, worn rugs, skeins of wool, threads, buttons, faded petals, a trug, a saddle on a small cane chair with the frayed cane strips fallen out on to the carpet like bright scabs. All of it was frenzied rather than comforting. It was a stock-pot of fragments, a shore line of vigorous flotsam. Father Palin was a disciplined man. He decided that coherent thought would be impossible in such a jumble. So much diversification showed a random, irresolute disposition. It was a loose environment. Careless. A chaos pinned rigid with the trappings of education and social advantage. What a background for a young man. No rule of thumb. No semblance of real order. It would be easy for the devil to play havoc here.

Father Palin mused on to himself because no one came. He blew his nose loudly and then ran the handkerchief across his forehead and round his thick red neck, where old scars bubbled and ran in the sticky heat. Evil is very insidious, very artful and clever in its manner of infection. These people might have position, money, land and a kind of education, but none of that was strength; spiritual strength. None of that was real order. Wholesome patterns. The structure of catechism and dogma, these . . . Father Palin mused on . . . these are the only bounds that can keep our wayward nature intact. Intact. The ring of that word, so knotted and precise, reminded him again of the frailty, the vulnerability of the little girls. Girls in his parish. Girls under his care. His very own batch of first communicants.

Violet came into the study. She was considerably taller than Father Palin.

'I'm sorry to have kept you. I presume it is me you want to see?'

'It is. It is indeed, Mrs Farr.'

'You look very hot, Father Palin. Would you like a glass of lemon barley water?'

'No. No thanks. I'm fine. I'm fine. It's difficult weather. Too hot really. No wind.'

'Well, we can't have everything, can we?'

'No. No indeed.'

Father Palin began to feel his role as aggressor, leader, the pivotal presence. He began to feel it undermined by Violet's tall, assessing calm. By her detached voice. She used words carefully, as if each one were purposely plucked simply for herself. It was as if she would never have shared a word with anyone else. They were hers. Just as Rathmanagh was hers; every weed and stone and bloom and shadow in it.

'I think that maybe your husband should be here also to hear what it is I have to say, Mrs Farr . . .'

'Really?'

Violet sounded amused and surprised.

'Yes. Yes. The boy's father. What I have to say concerns him. It concerns him as the boy's father . . .'

'I have no idea where he is.'

Violet's manner changed. She sounded defensive.

'Do you want Lumsden here?'

'No. No. Not for the present anyway.'

'I'll call my husband but I can't possibly guarantee he will be here. It is very unusual to be summoned in this way, Father Palin, in the middle of the day, without any kind of prior plan or warning.'

'I understand. I'm sorry, Mrs Farr. But there is some urgency . . . that is if I'm to avoid bringing in the Gardai. You see, I want, for your sake as much as anything else, to avoid a public procedure.'

Father Palin began to regain his sense of personal importance; that certain sense of himself and his mission.

Violet refused to show any sign of surprise or anxiety. She would not in any way acknowledge that this wretched man had any kind of power over things. She detested the way the Catholic Church manipulated the laity, using their position of spiritual authority with such practical guile. She was about to remonstrate. She was about to say firmly that if there was a

149

matter for the law, then there was a matter for the law and that was that. Then something made her hesitate. It was strange. She was standing by the mantelpiece. She had just moved a vase of roses slightly forward, she was unconsciously adjusting the objects round her as another woman might adjust her hair. The movement of the vase, this very slight slide along the white marble, caused several of the pale pink rose petals to fall. They fell on to the floor, on to the marble and on to her hand. Violet registered that these petals had a very definite quality of life still, even though they had obviously been ready to drop, ready to make way, ready to resign their proud position. These small thoughts, although so slight, so passing, so untimely, given the obvious gravity of this priest's visit, nevertheless, they were in her mind, as she crushed the petals in her hand, as she watched the smooth, perfect surface cringe into these sharp wounded little lines of colourless vitality. Violet felt as if this very thing, a petal crushed, was the priest's purpose; and her own power, her own identity, was simply to allow, to acknowledge, to acquiesce. She turned to Father Palin.

'I think my husband is in the library. Are you sure you don't want Lumsden here, Father Palin? I presume he is involved with this affair, otherwise I'm quite sure he wouldn't have returned home with you.'

'Mrs Farr, he is involved. He is the wretched, diabolic cause for my visit as I will hasten to explain as soon as your husband joins us.'

'Don't you require Lumsden to be here?'

'Later. I think later, Mrs Farr, would be more appropriate.'

So Lumsden came later. He came after Cecil's sleep in the library had been interrupted by Violet. He came after the bellowing rigmarole of his sins had been vividly, although inaccurately, described to Cecil and Violet by Father Palin.

'Mrs Farr, these children are young, not yet nine years old! Only recently they made their first Holy Communion. They have no carnal knowledge, no possible understanding of what your son made them do . . . He not only made them display their . . . their small bare . . . quite bare behinds, that milk white, soft, childish flesh exposed, Mrs Farr . . . But not only this . . . Your son . . . your son . . . he paid them money for it! He paid them coins, Mrs Farr. I saw it myself. I saw it all with my own eyes, Mrs Farr. Your son could serve time for such an offence but I feel it would be a better thing for the little girls and yourself, the whole parish in fact . . . I think it would be a better thing if within twenty-four hours he leaves Ireland, not to return for at least five years. Not to darken these shores, Mrs Farr. England has educated him, let England keep him and take the consequences. He is no son of Ireland, Mrs Farr . . .'

The priest paused. Like a fighter he was on his toes, ready for ripostes, defensive argument, anger, disbelief. But there was none. There was complete silence. Another petal fallen would have seemed a jarring, positive sound into this throttled, breathless, staring silence. At last Violet spoke.

'Is that all, Father Palin?'

'Is that not enough, Mrs Farr?' the priest blurted out dumbfounded.

'It is enough. It is quite enough.' Violet said and she walked straight past the priest and out of the room. Whatever else, she was not going to give that man any quarter. She would keep him anxious, baffled, guessing. She needed air. She had never before felt so stifled, so hemmed in, so intruded upon. She went out on to the porch. She sat down on the oak bench. She looked down at the small gravel stones, and then at the grass and trees, and then finally at the uneven, animal shape of Murna itself. Her eyes were moist, as they might be from exposure to a bitter north wind. But there was no wind. She stared, trying not to think. She did not want to think reasonable thoughts, of lawyers and crimes and silly little girls. She did not want to think. She simply wanted to calmly embrace what she had for so long, in a bitter and bewildered way yearned for, the final and total estrangement of herself from her son. And if this was to be the manner of it, then so be it. So be it. She did not want to discover anything further. She did not want to know names or deeds. Truth was, she felt, such a transitory thing. One man's certainty might well be another's incredulity. The only dimension civilisation depended on, was a kind of calm; the strength of order; the presence of coherent patterns; the regulation of chaos. Too many questions, too much acknowledgment of alternatives, other angles, other points of view, might lead to fresh chaos and greater disorder. It was the way to anarchy, to the blind, blood-letting pursuit of that wild freedom advocated by the ill-educated mob who sought only for themselves, totally disregarding the balance, the complete picture.

Violet felt better for these thoughts. She felt calmer. She felt positioned once again. For better or worse, this was how things had worked out. So be it. So be it. She prepared to return to the study. She would not involve herself in any kind of argument, simply practicalities. This was an end of Lumsden as her son. So be it. He must move on. Nature, like the river and the day, must take its course.

That hesitant second, of a kind of sorrow, out there on the gravel, just before she came into the house, when she had been so physically close to Lumsden by the car. That sense would never return. She had jettisoned it utterly. Violet felt she had gained strength from disregarding a moment of morbid feeling. She felt that in the tradition of her own family, her father in particular, she had held to reason and clear thought, rather than allowing loose, tyrannical emotions to waylay her. It was well done. This clarity. This control. It was well done.

She got up from the bench. She walked back into the house. The great loss, the drowning torrents of other alternative truths, the bewildered, banished feelings, they were well beyond regard, but not necessarily out of reach. Out of mind perhaps but that was not end or death or even impermanence. Violet's life was to be a long one, and despite her control, and clarity, as she saw it; the manner of the matter, thoughts or things, was that they recurred, came in again on a returning tide, with different voices and different disguises. Control would never be enough. The civilisation that would make whole, must discover a means of orientation beyond organisation.

Cecil had listened to Father Palin with almost childish detachment. Raspberry pips from lunch were rubbing raw the gums under his lower dentures. He had found it difficult to attend accurately to all that the priest was saying. But the gist seemed simple enough. The gist seemed to be the return of Lumsden to England. That was a good thing surely? Violet would certainly find things easier without him. The house would run more smoothly. The only snag, as far as Cecil could see, was the letter he had received that morning, which he had not yet found time to mention to Violet, the letter had been from Hitcham House, stating that Lumsden must not return in the autumn, as it had been disclosed that he had consistently broken bounds last term and was reported to have been seen in a local public house. Cecil, practical enough in his own small way, worked out that the fees he normally paid to Hitcham House could be made into an allowance for Lumsden. He could stay with this friend of his, Valentine Duckworth. He could get a job. To Cecil, there were no insurmountable difficulties. He even had an up-to-date timetable of the sailings from Rosslare to Fishguard. Cecil rummaged through the drawers and files and papers for the timetable. Father Palin waited amazed. He felt let down, confused. He had not expected such an easy ride. He had anticipated more of a fight; more of a confrontation. Cecil found the timetable. Violet came back into the study with a tray on which there was a jug of lemon barley water, three glasses and several ginger biscuits. She poured out a glass of lemon barley water, and handed it to Father Palin.

'This will refresh you, I hope.'

Father Palin nervously took the glass and then said determinedly, 'What about the boy? Shouldn't we call him?'

'In due course,' Violet said, sipping from her glass, 'in due course.'

'There's a sailing at five-thirty tomorrow,' Cecil said.

'Excellent.'

Violet put her glass on the mantelpiece. She moved the vase a little to find space for her glass but there were no rose petals left to fall, so nothing stirred.

Father Palin, for all his anger and bluster, was quite dejected by the staggeringly cold, complete uninvolvement these people seemed to have for their son. He was confused. He longed to drive away. To be back in the neat, empty comfort of the presbytery. He longed to have this terrible, awkward, uncomfortable day over and done with. He could still see those narrow, thin, bobbing, bare behinds of the little girls as they pranced about the Madox Hut, their flimsy cotton skirts flounced up over their heads. He wished the vision would fade. It was disturbing. Cecil too had a vision, which perplexed him, because it had come so summarily, so clearly. When he was listening to Father Palin's graphic description of the little girls, he had been looking out of the window. He had been only half-attending, half-listening, but then, suddenly, in his mind's eye, he saw the cheerful, serried ranks of little boys' behinds; little boys without clothes, playing leapfrog out there in the meadow. With his tongue furiously shifting his teeth to get at the offending raspberry pip, he thought how odd minds were, that he should see little boys while the priest told of little girls. How unexpected the mind is, he thought, and how little we know of one another's fantasies, half dreams, sudden, fleeting visions. Violet would never imagine that he would see in his mind's eye little boys out there in the meadow. The whole idea amused Cecil and surprised him. He tried to attend to the timetable, to put a break on the rather pleasant but unexpected little sortie of the mind that Father Palin's distressing account of his son's licentious debauchery had inspired in him. The timetable was in very small print. He needed his glasses. And he needed complete concentration.

During this time, Lumsden had done many things.

When at last his mother had left the drive and gone down the dark gulley beside the house with Birkin towards the back door, Lumsden had felt such relief. He had imagined that he might speak to her, complain about this insufferable little priest. He knew that his mother was deeply suspicious of any priest's motives. But something forced him to remain silent. It was as if for an instant he was sucked back into that difficult, uncertain, captured nursery-time, when his mother had seemed to have her fingers permanently on the string of a deep, dark bag, in which he was kept. Every time the tension within the bag eased, it seemed to open a little to light and other spaces, other adventures; then she would simply, as it were, pull the string taut and the bag would close tight over his head, putting an end to all excursions and alternative discoveries.

At Thornborough the nursery bag had grown into the void; that anxious, uncertain, terrible terrain of real muddle and fear. Lumsden had not attended to these memories specifically but they were there in Violet's suffocating proximity. He had not looked at her, or moved. He had simply tried to summon up a gigantic force that would defy her. Then she had moved. He had heard her feet and Birkin's paws padding in unison on to the stone flags of the gulley-path beside the house. She was gone. And Father Palin was gone also.

Initially Lumsden had felt fairly sure of himself. The priest would obviously lambast his mother with a highly coloured, sordid account of those pathetic little girls and their 'naughty' games. And then surely that would be an end of it. He might be forced into giving a grudging apology. Surely nothing more?

But as Lumsden stood there alone on the gravel in the bright, full, relentless sun, a peculiar sense of isolation and termination seemed to milk his mind of its usual cavalier buoyancy. He walked across the gravel and out on to the grass. Slowly he made his way down the slope of the meadow until he knew he must be out of sight from the windows of the house. He half expected to hear his name called out angrily. But there was no sound, except birds and the intermittent buzz of insects, distant dogs and the rumble of farm machinery. Lumsden came to the edge of the lake, hardly a lake really, more an extravagant pond. He stood on the bank and remembered all those tales of the rath's destruction when the lake was made, and how ill that boded for those who lived at Rathmanagh. Superstitious bunkum, he thought, and pulled several leaves from their stalks and threw them out on to the dark water. Beyond the river, Murna rose up, a great heaving shadow into the sky. Murna doesn't belong to her, Lumsden thought. Murna is beyond her grasp, out of her orbit. Murna, this great, double-jointed, pap of high ground. He stared at the mountain. He felt compelled and quiet, somehow drawn into the mountain's irresistible stillness and mystery. 'What a fuck up,' he said aloud, hoping somehow to shock the gentle air and free himself from the demands of those deeper feelings that proximity to the mountain engendered in him. He knew that something was over. The mad, angular, irritating thing, his mother, whom for so long he had scuffed about in his mind as an irrelevance; a dated, peculiar woman, quite unlike other people's mothers. This tall, drab woman, Violet Farr, in her loose garbs of dull browns and blues. Her bust, although large, had no specific definition like the pronounced, high, prancing breasts of the English mothers. Violet's bust was simply a slump of heightened shape under careless clothes. She never wore lipstick. Her hair was never 'done'. She was a kind of rockface, a staring, greedy, monitoring promontory, full of unspoken demands. Lumsden felt sure that she had always disliked him.

He turned from the water and began to make his way through the wood and round below the house. Still out of sight from the house, he walked up towards the stable-yard and the red barn. The half-bottle of whiskey, almost emptied, was still in his jacket pocket. He threw it into a hedge of brambles.

He walked across the stable-yard. His father's shirts hung stiff and dry on the washing-line, and his pyjamas and a faded cotton nightdress of his mother's and several pairs of small shrunk socks. They were like scales of discarded skin, they had an air of the same empty, but nevertheless, fierce lifelessness, that Lumsden felt was in both his parents' faces, and their flesh, and their shadows, and the sharp, precise echoes of their voices in between speech. Lumsden passed the washing-line, ducking out of reach of the offensive garments. He went across to the iron pump. He plunged the cool handle up and down several times, letting the water spill carelessly on to the dry ground. Everything was so dry; desiccated, exhausted, shrunk. Even the big stone cattle trough beside the red barn was almost dry, there was just a dark syrupy mulch of water in the very bottom. Lumsden sat on the edge of the trough. He remembered the time, long ago, when he was small, when to sit on the edge was brave. His feet dangled down then, reaching nowhere near the ground.

It was as if instinctively he was gathering up random strands of experience at Rathmanagh, to somehow mark, like Hansel and Gretel with their bright stones, to mark a way back, out of the black, taut nursery bag, if the need should ever arise. But even as he stared at the pump, the red barn doors, the wooden wheelbarrow, the watering-cans and buckets, the stack of split firewood, the bunker of anthracite, the bunker of coal; even as he stared, he planned and sensed nothing except his immediate and final departure. He went into the walled garden and up to the orchard. He put three hard apples in his coat pocket. He was still surprised that no one had called. Any minute he expected to see or hear Violet. He expected to see her head and shoulders just there above the giant tufts of pink and white valerian that thrust out in great stacks of colour from the brick walls. But there was no one, not even Birkin.

Lumsden made his way back down to the stable-yard. He ducked the washing-line and went into the laundry room and then the kitchen. The kitchen was dead in summer. With the Aga unlit, it was like being beside an unconscious, dead weight of derelict animal. The kitchen, without the Aga lit, was a shameful place, devoid of its true purpose and comforting strengths. Lumsden went over to the windows. He ran the cold tap above the deep, china clay sink, which was pitted and marked like Father Palin's neck. He splashed the cold water on to his face and hair. It was as if he was a traveller, a vagrant, gathering stocks and booty for an indefinite journey. A journey that would purposely avoid any idea of destination. A journey that would simply run hither and thither for the pleasure, for the sheer dance of itself. No rules or bounds. No goals or purchases. Simply the thrust and speed and chase of itself.

Lumsden went back into the house. He stood at the bottom of the stairs. He could hear voices; his mother's, Father Palin's. As usual, there was no sound of his father's voice.

Lumsden saw the library door open. His mother's endless preoccupation with her father, his Lumsden grandfather, whose name he obviously never measured up to, this intense preoccupation of hers always irritated Lumsden. He had grown to hate this dapper, good-looking man whose name was written in a slanting, even hand, in brown ink, in so many of the books in the library.

Lumsden decided that for good measure, as some sort of talisman, he would take a couple of volumes. He had not read to any great extent. He had never studied seriously, but every so often a book would make a real impression on him. He felt that books just might become a crucial part of his journey. He had read *Crime and Punishment*. He had read *Gulliver's Travels*. 'Dorian Gray' had been an inspiration, also various passages from the *Seven Pillars of Wisdom* had made him feel that he knew next to nothing of masculine endeavours, the charge of real adventure. His habit was to dip around. Just get a taste of this and that. *Crime and Punishment* was the first book he had ever read straight through.

The library was cool. The shutters were half closed. There could not be much time now before they called him. He decided he should take small volumes, knapsack size. He took a slim, bottle-green volume of Richard Hakluyt's *Voyager's Tales*. There was a much larger edition with maps. So much voyaging, so much seafaring, had inspired Lumsden in the belief that one should always somehow be on the go, on the get out, from the prescribed place that one finds oneself in. Even if the destination was as close as Chiswick and Pinker Downes. Anything was good that was some kind of a departure. At all costs, the trap of female schemes must be avoided. Females certainly had considerable uses, but their demands and dictates must be ignored; their emotional hunger must never be attended to. Lumsden flicked through the volume. He had always loved the old advertisements at the back and front. Heavy black typeface advertising Bunter's Nervine. Instant cure for toothache. Singer's Cycles and The Mexican Hair Renewer. He took down two small volumes of Lamb, *Essays of Elia*. He had never read the text, but the spines were charmingly decorated and the publishers were the Knickerbocker Press, a name that had had instant appeal for Lumsden. He stuffed the books with the apples into his jacket pocket. He let the jacket hang loosely over his arm so that these odd bulges would be less noticeable.

Then he heard the front door. He heard what he definitely recognised as Violet's steps going out through the hall towards the kitchen. Quickly he dashed up the stairs to his bedroom. He put his jacket down on the narrow, blue-painted bedstead. The room smelt stale. It was untidy. There were piles of dirty pants and socks and shirts all over the floor. The bed was unmade. The window was firmly closed. It was a child's room grown ugly and absurd, without a child in it. There were still toys in the cupboard; a train, several puppets, a game of Halma, a Noah's ark and random farm animals without a complete count of legs or markings. He kicked two or three times at the cupboard door. Something fell inside. He would never discover what it was. He went into the nursery bathroom on that landing. He peed. Then he heard them. He heard his name. It was clear, distinct, so carefully pronounced. Violet's voice was always careful, always clear, she carved the words out and then hung them on the air like the wings of butterflies, very fine but very dead.

'Lumsden. Lumsden. We are in the study.'

Lumsden came slowly down the wide staircase. He came in his own time. He came at his own pace. In a way the priest and his passionate moral drama were incidental to what was going on. Father Palin had merely provided in his blustering innocence the means for two so-called civilised and educated people to banish their son, to wash their hands of a life and all its subsequent difficulties. Even before Lumsden entered the study, he was bored by the very idea of his defence. He never wanted to sit opposite that stag in the dining-room ever again. He never wanted to smell the Aga, or hear the wheelbarrow trundle its way over the gravel.

Lumsden came slowly into the study. His usual relaxed, purposely careless manner was restored to him. He was not in the least awkward. There was not the slightest air of anxiety or apology about him.

'We gather,' Violet began without looking at Lumsden. She was looking towards some safe middle distance where nothing would confront or interrupt her. 'We gather you have had a rather tasteless involvement with three little girls in the Madox Hut.' She paused. Lumsden smiled. He did not interrupt her. The priest was the only uneasy, anxious person present.

'We have discussed the matter with Father Palin and we agree to his excellent decision that the best thing for everyone's interests is for you to return to England forthwith. There is a convenient sailing tomorrow afternoon from Rosslare.'

'Fine by me,' Lumsden said. But this time he did stare at Violet. This time he moved. He looked purposely and deeply into her eyes to place there forever the bitter taste of her peculiar and persistent denial of him.

That evening nothing more was said. Violet and Cecil ate their supper promptly at seven-thirty. As usual Lumsden's place was laid. As usual they called for him, announced that supper was ready. 'It's on the table, Lumsden.' That was always the final call. And as usual Lumsden ignored it. He was lying on his bed smoking a cigarette. He was staring at his shoes, at the great, coiled lumps of sheet and blanket that lay at the end of the bed like withered intestines. He kicked them with his foot. He had rung Valentine. Valentine had been impressed and very amused. Valentine also had been asked not to return to Hitcham House. So everything was working out well. Lumsden had been enthusiastic on the telephone, full of ideas and plans for their future.

He had kept Valentine in stitches by his description of the three little girls in the Madox Hut and the scabby little priest, parboiled by the confusion and delirium his celibacy seemed to reek out of him, poor sod. Lumsden had eagerly given Valentine the sailing time, saying how delighted he was to be well and truly 'bog banished'. But he never mentioned Violet; the cool precision of those vowel sounds, the stringent scour that blistered every word she uttered to him. He never mentioned that. And he never mentioned Murna or Birkin. But as he left the telephone with all the arrangements made, as he walked slowly back up the stairs to his room, he felt that old Thornborough fear again; it was as if some dark beast was tracking him down, by the smell of something rotten and putrid, that was there, somewhere deep inside himself.

He heard Violet's voice again, telling him that his supper was on the sideboard, under the lid of the vegetable dish to keep it warm. Lumsden still stared at his feet, at the sheets, at his dressing-gown on the door. There was a gnawing, grinding kind of hunger in his stomach. Normally by now he would have been in one of the bars in Ballynaule. He imagined the covered plate on the sideboard, in the shadowy, gradual darkness of the dining-room. He imagined the stag above it. On the plate, under its cover, he could see a writhing, glutinous mass of creamy white maggots. Of course, eventually maggots would become flies. He imagined that perhaps the plate would remain forgotten, and then after he had left, after his departure tomorrow, when Violet was alone in the house with Birkin, he imagined that she might go into the dining-room, and absent-mindedly she might lift the cover from the plate and a horde of buzzing blue-bottles might burst up into the air, a ferocious dung-cloud of furious life, all wings and buzz, into her eyes and into her ears, into those rosy slits, those frail scoop holes of her nostrils, and on to the wide soft edge of her lips. Then, with the shock of it all, she would surely cry out and the dung-cloud of beastly creatures would surge headlong into her open mouth. Lumsden smiled to himself. The image of the flies both sickened and amused him. But it also reminded him that there was a way round things. Nothing could get your mind. Your mind was surely your own. From it you could bloody well muster a life, a person; you could get in there and make bloody sure no one was going to mess you about. You just had to keep on top of things, always be there before them. You have to go out and bloody take what you want. Sod their schemes and attitudes. Lumsden began to feel better. His actual hunger seemed to bolster his determination. He crunched noisily on the three hard apples he had taken from the orchard. There was no real darkness that night. Murna was visible from dusk to dawn. There was a full moon; a bellowing throb of light above that mass of guardian earth beyond the river, that managed, unlike any human being, to give consistent inspiration and comfort to all who paused to consider her.

Father Palin returned to the presbytery utterly exhausted. The clarity, his earlier conviction of that young man's evil ways had grown distorted, uncertain. There was no disputing what he had seen with his own eyes, there was no disputing that, but in some way the parents' reaction had surprised him. He had been ready to comfort and console a shocked and dismayed woman. But he had not found Mrs Farr that way at all. She had seemed only too willing to banish her only son from his home. Now it was quite one thing for himself, as parish priest, to wish Ballynaule completely rid of the young man; after all, he had to think of the more vulnerable young souls in the parish. But surely, from the point of view of the boy's mother, it would be a different thing altogether. Even the mother of Judas would have had some good word to say on her son's account.

Father Palin definitely felt uneasy, but when he telephoned the girls' mothers and heard their meek, anxious, appalled voices, he began to feel better. He began to congratulate himself on his prompt and definite actions. The next day Father Palin spent considerable time with the three little girls and their families. He tried to assure them of the great wonder of God's forgiveness, but they wept incessantly. He patted their heads and arranged for them all to meet him in the church that evening so that they could make a good and humble confession, but they only seemed to cry the more. In fact the drama in the Madox Hut on that hot, carefree, August afternoon was to remain vivid and painful to the three little girls for many, many years, particularly for Eileen, who felt she had so incurred Our Lady's displeasure that nothing short of a life dedicated to Our Lord would take away the guilt and the shame of it. She entered a convent in her mid-twenties hoping somehow to disguise her body from herself and seek nothing but the pleasure and forgiveness of Our Lord through his work with the sick and the needy.

By and large the parish took the news of Lumsden's departure as more or less good riddance to bad rubbish. But being people whose work and lives were very close to nature, they knew well enough that 'a bad lot' could be the same with pups, or calves, or lambs; there was always now and then a cussed creature, too difficult, or too flighty to be any good. The men were quite happy to have the bars a little emptier without him. Of course no one ever referred to Lumsden's disgrace openly. But one or two of the women didn't miss an opportunity to ask after 'your boy in England, Mrs Farr.' But they met with such a cold, dismissive look from Violet that they almost wondered if the boy had indeed been truly hers.

Cecil took it upon himself to drive Lumsden to Rosslare. Violet was very against the use of the car for long journeys, anything longer than Claggan really. She felt it was an extravagant waste of petrol. But for Cecil, who got about less than Violet, a real expedition in the car was a considerable adventure. It meant maps, oily rags, distilled water and hard-boiled sweets. It meant preparation; the careful assessment, via the barometer, of possible impending weather conditions; small Bakelite picnic tins filled with cheese and chutney sandwiches, a flask of coffee, a rope, a rug.

They left Rathmanagh at about ten-thirty. That kind of start allowed for breakdowns, burst tyres and duff navigation. Violet felt a wave of anger and remorse when the moment came for her to contrive a form of farewell to Lumsden. The anger seemed rooted in self pity; the fact that nature should have dealt her such a shameful, worthless son. The remorse was painful and harder to attach to anything specific. She did not like to look at him. Those huge ears, the lank, dark hair, the high brow, the full lips and the large, strangely floating blue eyes, with long, rather ridiculous eyelashes. She could not bear the way he moved. The careless, loose way all the limbs seemed to lop the space round him, like a clown or lunatic, as if no one else mattered, as if all the area within his reach was his to mangle and buffet and generally disturb. Violet did not realise that Lumsden had wanted to challenge her, to make her stop and see him, simply for himself. His extravagant physical manner in the beginning had been to rouse her, to beckon her attention, but that was a long time ago, gradually it had turned into the noise and gestures of defence. Lumsden never again wanted to find himself alone with his mother when there was a lapse of speech and motion, where subtly she might assert herself over him. With her uncanny powers, she might somehow disengage him from himself and so expose those slum bits, those ragged, rancid, loose ends of personality that really threaten the rest. He sensed that she might, if given the chance, reduce him to a condition he could not control. So, although he definitely felt somewhere a kind of bitterness towards this home, this whole mound of stone and books; hills and trees and paths; sounds and stares and memories; he also felt anxious. To have it all taken from him, with such careless finality, might deprive him of sufficient belief in himself to bluster his way out into that real world of pubs and girls and money, suckers, and the smoky, fascinating trail of social success. Here, a million miles from London and Valentine, gin and tonic, loud music, and Pinker Downes's continuous inspiration, it was hard to believe in anything.

Lumsden loitered about the boot of the car. He was uncertain of how exactly to leave his mother. All he knew was that he must not go close enough to feel the tremble and flock of her actual skin and hair and breath. Arm's length was too close. Birkin wagged his way round the car. Violet stood in the porch. It was cooler than the previous day. Violet wore a long, pale brown cardigan over her shirt. Her generously gathered skirt had two large pockets. Her hands were deep into the pockets. Lumsden was glad he could not see those pale hands and the long thin fingers. Cecil crashed the bonnet down. Everything was checked and in fine fettle. 'Got everything?' Cecil asked Lumsden. 'We should be making a move now if we're going to keep on schedule.' Lumsden did not answer. He simply slammed the boot shut. Birkin barked. Violet took her hands from her pockets. Her handkerchief dropped on the dusty stone flags. She bent to pick it up and two of those long, fierce hair-pins fell out on to the gravel. Lumsden did not move. He remembered how he used to collect those pins, when he collected smells. He remembered how he speared the cotton-wool balls from the waste-paper basket in her bathroom with those hair-pins. He remembered the smell of those cotton-wool balls.

Cecil had the engine running. He got into the car beside his father. He tried to glance towards his mother in an awkward, perfunctory way. He was aware now that she also wanted to avoid any physical proximity, or farewell, and he was surprised how wretched, how bitter, how truly banished it made him feel. The car circled the drive. Lumsden had seen Violet stand there in the porch so often, mostly in the evenings, rarely in the mornings. For the rest of his life, whenever people referred to his mother or to Rathmanagh, he saw her there in the porch. Tall and still and waiting; in some way waiting.

Lumsden looked hard now towards Murna, and in a second of childish fantasy he decided that he could place within the mountain that part of himself that must remain at Rathmanagh. Like a buried child, some part of him would stay; maybe one day it would grow up out of the ground, maybe it would flower with the furze, maybe Birkin would smell his smell there and cock his leg over the spot. Lumsden liked that idea.

Cecil drove slowly but with great pride. It was a wonderful day. Not so hot as the day before, there was a little breeze.

'You should have a very good crossing,' Cecil said.

Lumsden looked towards his father. That bumpy, very set and weathered profile. The thin lips, that moved continuously in a small, anxious, snuffly way, like a hesitant rodent. His father's face never seemed still. There were so many little ticks and sniffs, hums and sighs. His life is so dull, Lumsden thought, all he has left is the organisation of his facial muscles and the control of indiscreet bodily excretions. His nose was large, in proportion to the head it was large, the nostrils were wide and bulbous with very pronounced cavities where odd single hairs often protruded right down on to the small, little loo-mat of a moustache.

He's really enjoying this Lumsden thought. This is his little outing, his jolly, summer's day excursion. My bloody life; no school, no home, just an almighty 'Go and get lost dear boy' sort of journey, simply hasn't entered into his head.

Cecil continued to speak. It made things so much easier to be looking straight ahead at the clear roads, the high trees, the green fields, the rivers, the small compact dwellings, the occasional cart, the occasional black bicycle; it made it so much easier to speak if the environment was peaceful and impersonal, and no very direct glance or stare was possible. Cecil was not the kind of driver who would take his eyes off the road for an instant.

'I'm sorry about Hitcham House, old boy, but you probably saw it coming. You should get in on the ground floor of something. Get in at the bottom and work your way up. Your age will be an advantage. I believe various companies have these sandwich schemes, you know, you are employed by the firm but they release you so many days a week to study at a local technical college, that kind of thing. I'm sure you'll work it all out.'

Lumsden stared at the road, the way it seemed to chase itself up into the sky on the hills. What a drab and dreadful vision his father had. The very words 'work' and 'company' filled Lumsden with serious horror. It was such a joke really, because Cecil had never done a hand's turn in his life. Their frugal poverty, the great strain to maintain the property, however difficult it was, however many leaks there were, or fallen fences, or rotten gates; it would never have occurred to Cecil to have worked. And the idea of work didn't seem in the least bit natural to Lumsden. The difference was Lumsden wasn't going to turn into a timid, stiff little man who tapped his hall barometer and then stared at it day after day, rigid with excitement at the needle swing. Lumsden could think of nothing but the pleasure living might be; there was so much out there, the real noise and gamble, the whole pitch and thrust of people; females. The kind who couldn't wait to give you what you wanted. The kind he'd met already with Valentine's sisters. The kind whose eager, wide eyes gave the clue to how they'd like their legs to be, wide apart, plump and easy for it, no long preamble, just the plunge and capture.

Every mile further on from Rathmanagh and Violet's presence seemed to clock up in Lumsden's bloodstream; a new vigour, real deposits of fresh determination, a feel of giant leaps forward from first base towards a new, completely free future.

Before they turned off from Waterford towards Rosslare, even before that, the gnawing gap, the pit of fear from Thornborough days, the depth of darkness, that awful nursery bag, with Violet's firm hands on the drawstring, it was all lost now in new, ordinary feelings of body and place; any young man's mood in high summer; banishment was going to be good. They could keep their priests and endless green emptiness, all those staring eyes in small crowded bars, all the mist and rain; fine, soft rain. They could keep it. The thing was, so it seemed to Lumsden, the thing was to be so absolutely there, right in the centre, in the real swing of things, letting it all happen, thick and fast, as it was meant to be, no dark corners, no mean thoughts, no guilty, nervous little edges, just head on out there. Live first, ask questions later, if at all. Lumsden loathed his mother's analytical, prising open of people as if they were sardine tins. Her intense scrutiny. All that monitoring of detail. If that was education and literacy, you could keep it as far as Lumsden was concerned. Life had to be what you had in your hand, not what you'd lost, or buried, or simply couldn't find. That way, Lumsden felt sure, was without reward or pleasure.

They came at last to the sea. To the edge of the land; that jagged, bird-spotted, rough and smooth, meeting thread of the earth, to the endless push and slurp of the water. This edge of land, Lumsden thought, is so full of its past, its identity. The turmoil of its history. All that starving and death. All that banishment. People continuously forced to leave real homes to find something more certain across the water.

Cecil parked the car. He had spotted redshank and a dunlin. Lumsden put on his jacket. He opened the boot of the car and lifted out the heavy suitcase that had been Cecil's. It had torn labels on it and Cecil's initials stamped in black. It had a broken strap, which lapped like a sow's ear round Lumsden's leg as he walked across the car-park. But the sea, Lumsden thought, as they got closer to it, as they felt slapped and roused by its smell, the sea is not particular, like a land mass. The sea remains, just a wide windswept pavement of water; some wild Doré precinct, under the spell of gulls or albatross. Whatever land mass it interrupts, the features are the same. The lap and swing and weight of water.

Lumsden stared. He stared at the waves and birds, at the utter endlessness of grey-green, under the wide, empty, keen blue of the sky. Then he turned towards his father. He wanted to move on. He wanted to be alone. He didn't want to hang about with Cecil and the remains of the sandwiches. His father was still by the car, fiddling with maps and things. Lumsden walked towards him. How odd, how random, how intrusive this whole wretched business of parenting was. That small, stiff, anxious, stumbling little man; he didn't look like anyone's father, except maybe a polecat or ferret, something with an important nose anyway.

Cecil walked towards Lumsden. He had in his hand the picnic basket and the battered thermos flask.

'I was wondering if you'd like to finish up the sandwiches, Lumsden, and have some coffee. There's a little left. Enough for one cup, I'd imagine.'

'No thanks. You should get back on the road.'

'Oh no, old boy, I'll wait to wave you off. The boat's in, I know, but it will be a while before you sail.'

'I'd rather wait alone.'

Cecil looked away. He didn't want the difficult, unnerving bother of trying to understand something awkward. He would leave, although he would have enjoyed to have stayed.

'Very well, old boy. As you wish. As you wish. You've got all those papers about the bank and your allowance, haven't you?'

'Yes, I have. Thanks.'

'Well. I hope things run smoothly.'

Cecil felt it incumbent on him to attempt a paternal farewell; some sort of Polonius-type list of 'do's' and 'don'ts'. Priorities in a man's world. But he could only think how annoyed he was with himself for leaving the binoculars behind on the hall table. Seabirds were such joy to watch.

'You'll be fine, old boy.'

Lumsden said nothing. All he heard was the sound of the gulls and other people's voices, other people's cars, Cecil was still there, hovering directly in front of him. Then he came forward, he raised his right hand a little, as if he might put it somewhere on Lumsden, his arm probably, or shoulder, something like that. To avoid the physical contact, Lumsden bent down to fix the strap on the suitcase. For a second, Cecil's hand hung in the air, for an instant it was a strange, meek, dispossessed thing. Then it fell back down on to Cecil's thigh, on the thin, dead, almost transparent feel of his leg inside the grey flannel, that was plucked and rough with wear and insensitive laundering.

'Well, keep in touch, old boy. Keep in touch.'

'I will. Of course I will.'

'Right, then I'll get the old car on the road. She likes a decent run. It's good for the engine. It's good for me too, a little throttle, a little adventure now and again.' He laughed and turned from Lumsden to walk back, back to the car and the land. Back to Violet and Rathmanagh, Birkin and his barometer. He had turned away from the sea, and the improbable, worrying individual that was his son. As he walked away, he waved once more for good measure. It was quite a cheerful, quite a positive, high handed, carefree gesture. But Lumsden never saw it. He had turned already towards the boat and the sea and the milling, easy crowd of people that were waiting there. Keep in touch. The phrase stuck in his head. Touch was the negative trigger. Touch was the vile intruder. Touch was the most important thing of all to avoid.

When the boat eventually set sail Lumsden was on deck, but looking out to sea. He made sure as the boat turned that all he saw was the wide, beckoning line of an empty horizon. He spent almost all the voyage on deck, there was more space, fewer fat women and scruffy, sweet-sucking children. He watched the wonderful lively trail of rough, romping dragon spray that the boat left behind her. Into it, absent-mindedly, he mentally hurled his father, who waved and smiled and floated out to the left, the water billowing into a puff shape, through his trousers and check shirt and cardigan. Then Lumsden tried to hurl Violet. It was harder, much harder, but as he stared into the water, mesmerised by the rhythm and the sound of the propellers, he suddenly saw her, a long, shroud shape; very thin, with her arms reaching up pale and long, like eel ribbons into the wide, spread mess of her hair that straggled up and down, in and out of the waves, like a fine net, ready to catch the small pearl bubbles that frothed out, very small, very quietly from her ears and her long lips, and the small rosy slits of her nostrils.

What a fine drowning Lumsden thought; smooth and quiet and rather beautiful in its way.

It was in the train when this whole rowdy family, with their bags and food and drawing-books, their folded coats and baby this and that, the awful slapstick mess of their games and sleep and general pushing, shoving, place-changing, window-breathing congestion; it was when they suddenly left the train at a suburban station not too far from London that Lumsden had the carriage to himself. He moved along to the window. He put his feet up on the seat opposite. Like an animal, like Birkin, he stretched out, felt down into every smallest particle of his body and it felt good. Apart from being so noisy and so exhausting, that family had been so ugly. He knew that his eyes were quite powerful, they were large and different. People said they were Irish, people said they were wild. It didn't matter, they worked. They went with the thick dark hair and the hidden ears and the long neck and the smooth, clear, slightly sallow skin. They went with the voice that was deep enough now but would grow deeper still, and they went with the free easy way the whole body worked. They went with the vivid, colourful fast speech, the rather tousled, indulgent, mannered way the words hung together, like a string of fruit from a Roman decoration, like a swag of leaves and blooms and berries.

For the last part of the journey, Lumsden slept. He dreamt that he rode up to this high white house, built on some promontory. There were white columns and marble floors, and in the centre, a fine, spiral stone staircase that went past two or three galleried landings to a high room, that was very light and very blue, a warm blue. On the floor there was this wide mattress. He was tired. He lay down on the mattress and slept, but every time he was about to fall off into a really deep sleep, some sound, like bare feet on floor-boards, stifled whispers, or laughter, some sound like that woke him. But when he woke there was always nothing, only the light and the blue room. He thought he should investigate. He left the wide mattress and walked out on to the landing but the spiral staircase was no longer there, instead he was looking down a well, into a gloomy, syrupy circle of dark water. In it he saw his reflection. It was distorted by the water, and it was small because the well was so deep. But also, it was not the reflection of a man, a debonair, hard-riding, good-looking, young man as the dreamer felt himself to be. It was the reflection of a child. A child whose face was upwards, like a pale coin in the tarry murk of the water, but there were no eyes, and there was no mouth. The child was both blind and dumb, but very still, almost resigned to his terrible afflictions.

That strange image stayed with Lumsden for a very long time. Every so often for many years he would suddenly see the pale coin face of the child in the murky, tarry water.

Only when he received a letter from Winifred Chappell some twenty-eight years later did the image alter, but he was conditioned by then to avoid anything thought provoking or reflective. He simply didn't have the strength or inclination to be fascinated. But he kept the letter from Winifred Chappell, although it was vehemently suggested to him that he should burn it. He did not. He slipped it into one of the small volumes of Lamb's *Essays of Elia* that he had taken from his grandfather's library when he left Rathmanagh in August, just after his seventeenth birthday that July.

FIVE

Neville Ponsonby was fat and sweaty, he was also extremely frail. His wealth, which was considerable, enabled him to live among elegant and valuable possessions; it enabled him to maintain a charming first-floor flat in South Audley Street; and it enabled him to purchase and develop a very pretty south-facing Georgian house in a Wiltshire valley. It enabled him to design a most engaging and rather frivolous water-garden, where cavorting stone nymphs hid among fountains and the rich darkness of the still pools of water below them. But the charm and idiosyncratic grandeur of these two establishments, the great variety of life they offered: theatres, galleries, restaurants, opera on the one hand; peacocks, delicious homegrown vegetables, an abundant supply of glorious blooms on the other; the sum of all these advantages could not overcome Neville Ponsonby's sense of isolation and loneliness.

His origins were not so elegant. His family came from the Midlands. The money he now possessed had originally been made by the invention of a variety of sewage filter systems by his grandfather. Subsequently the family firm had gone into refuse and haulage. The business was now run by a nephew, who found Neville and his camp, unreal ways a considerable embarrassment. Even the name Ponsonby was not strictly accurate. It was originally Pounsonby. Neville had it changed to Ponsonby by deed poll, after an unfortunate incident in a public lavatory in Haringey, which had attracted some virulent publicity in the newspapers.

All that was long ago. Now, in his late-fifties, Neville Ponsonby was a very respectable person. His voice was rather high-pitched, with little runs of velvet laughter punctuating nervous, flowery gestures of the hand, nods and winks and rather diffident smiles. But he was exceedingly generous, no boy scout or flag-selling lady ever left his house empty handed. He supported instantly anything connected to the creative arts, the upkeep of historic buildings, the commission of stained-glass windows, or embroidered altar frontals; in fact any kind of local monument. He did not know that behind his back he was known in Wiltshire as 'The Dowager'. Although his manner might cause snigger and comment, his generosity to the community made him a definite and well loved part of it. There was the odd retired military officer, who would not attend a social gathering if The Dowager might be present, but the women loved him. He was different. He was appreciative of their attempts at elegance. He was really sweet to their tiresome offspring. Above all, he was a good listener. There were many married women in Wiltshire whose lives were dull if they did not hunt, or generally pursue an active physical life; dogs, dressage, agricultural shows. Confined to large houses, and all the obvious duties that go with them, Neville Ponsonby was a most welcome friend; a confidant without risk, a great admirer of real cuisine, antique furniture and unusual plant propagation.

For Lumsden a chance introduction to Neville Ponsonby, after a concert one Sunday morning at the Victoria and Albert Museum, was a lifesaver.

For several years Lumsden had managed a precarious and fairly heady life in London. He had worked spasmodically in advertising, in Bonhams, in various bookshops and one or two art galleries. In the first instance, his outgoing personality, his easy manner and the veneer of cultural small-talk he had managed to assimilate, got him the job. But the more civilised jobs were extremely low paid. They could not begin to finance the way of life to which he had grown accustomed. There had been a moment of crisis before, when various creditors were really running him to ground. He had fled the country. One of Valentine's sisters was married to an Italian. She was living in Florence, with a small son. She offered Lumsden a job as au pair-cum-tutor, although the tutoring was more *Brer Rabbit* and *Struwwelpeter* than grammar, or any particular educational skills. The job rescued Lumsden. From Florence, with the English language his only skill, he managed to get a job in Milan and later, for a short while, in Venice. He certainly never made any money but he did pick up some Italian, which he used with good effect. But by the time he was twenty-three, he was back in London once more, with greater debts than before.

Lumsden had particularly noticed Neville Ponsonby because his skin was so taut, so white, so unbelievably creamy smooth. You couldn't help noticing his small hands. The shape of the nails was so uniform, beautifully manicured and even, but the fingers themselves were puffy, they seemed to struggle against the grip of various gold signet rings. His voice was almost falsetto, it piped out from his small flustered lips as if he was about to sing but had not been given any note. He was fat and he wore tight, very tailored clothes; always a waistcoat, always a gold watch-chain. Everything, even his socks, seemed stretched beyond endurance over the tight, smooth body. Lumsden was introduced to Neville Ponsonby by a mutual friend who had whispered to Lumsden as he had stretched out his hand, 'loaded and lonely . . . take my word for it.'

Neville had found the room very stuffy. He had suggested to Lumsden that they might go and sit by one of the open windows. This they did, and before long Neville had unburdened to Lumsden the considerable problems he had with his body; even as he spoke he took various pills, from a small silver box he kept in his pocket. Apparently he had this large house in Wiltshire called Medlars. He spoke of it with great enthusiasm. He had just engaged a young couple for the summer to help him and they had simply not materialised. No letter. No telephone call. It was a scandal to be so inconsiderate. He did have an excellent and most reliable fellow in the garden and two 'hearts of oak' who came regularly from the village to do the house and laundry, but he had need now, as he was not well, for someone who could drive, to be there with him constantly.

As Neville spoke, Lumsden visualised it all. The whisper of the friend 'loaded and lonely' reverberated through his head. At present Lumsden shared a flat in Fulham with Valentine, but he could not afford it; he owed Valentine money as well as everyone else. Perhaps an idyllic Wiltshire summer would be ideal to set things straight again, and maybe develop new contacts and new schemes. Although nothing but debt had dogged Lumsden over the past years, he had enjoyed himself. He was popular because whatever his problems he was never dreary. Apart from being entertaining and good value, he wasn't sure what he was, but he felt that in some way the arts, broadly speaking, should be his natural habitat. It was simply a question of being in the right place at the right time.

Neville Ponsonby blew his nose on a small, soft, exquisitely laundered handkerchief. Lumsden offered himself to lend a hand about the place, just for a while. Neville's bright little brown eyes stared at this healthy, decorative, young man, with his thick dark curls and generous mouth, and his glorious, swimming, brimful blue eyes under dark, almost Spanish, eyelashes.

'Dear boy,' he said, 'it would be the greatest kindness,' and he went on eagerly to Lumsden's great joy, 'I shall see that you are well and generously recompensed for such a spontaneous gesture of goodwill to a mere stranger.'

So it was that Lumsden moved down to Wiltshire and became for a while the personal aide of Neville Ponsonby.

The house was most attractive, although there was rather too much ruching of silk and white marble columns and gilded chairs. It was never a desk, it was always an *escritoire*. It was always the *salle à manger*, never the dining-room. Neville was very generous indeed to Lumsden, who had few specific duties; he was required simply to drive the car and be generally available. The young couple employed for the summer had simply misunderstood the dates. They came a week later than expected and were as hardworking and reliable as anyone could have wished.

Neville settled all Lumsden's debts.

'One must never let financial pressure bleed the soul to stone, dear boy. Usury is a crime. It is a form of rape. It is a delight for me to liberate you from the slaughterer's stare, that grinding knife that bank managers so love to twist in the name of friendship and guidance. Anytime, dear boy. Anytime,' Neville would say. 'Money is not everything. If you have it you may as well use it. Let it fly like a bird. Let it bloom. Let it run with the wind. That, dear boy, is my philosophy.'

Lumsden simply could not believe his luck, and although he knew that various old bags in the village whispered among themselves as to his exact role at Medlars, Lumsden felt that the fondant squares, the chocolate mints, the truffles and the Turkish delight, which were available in every room to satisfy Neville's sweet tooth, Lumsden felt that they were his protection. Neville would never express himself or make any physical demands beyond the accepted bounds of affection and caring. Lumsden wondered if his tight clothes might not be in a way a form of chastity belt. Obviously the climate of the time, the harsh attitude of the general public towards this gifted minority, of whom Neville happily acknowledged himself a member, made the easy and open demonstration of considerable affection a dangerous and difficult business. Neville had settled for the peripheral comforts of sweets, domestic elegance, charming spaces; charming paths and ponds and pergolas. Simply to have a companion whom he could feel he loved, even if the physical side was rather stage-managed and less than complete, simply to witness the vigour and vitality of a young man about the place was, now that he was older and frail, enough to succour him, and take the edge off that lonely, suffocating despair that he had known so many times before.

After the debts were paid, Lumsden looked for some activity, some scheme that might actually give him a positive, even an acclaimed role. Valentine, who came to stay for various weekends, suggested an Arts Week, to be run from and at Medlars. There were many people of real talent in the county. Neville was a natural patron. And people generally had good money to burn if they could be inspired to feel that their investment denoted that they had some kind of quality which put them above, even beyond, somebody else. Snobbery, belonging to some kind of superior, better informed tribe, that's the way to get them. 'The thing is,' Valentine said, 'they long to feel they are moving out beyond their natural provincial limits. They don't realise that their natural provincial limits are their one and only inspiration, their real guiding light. They love to dress up; black tie, a little Chopin, some *Lieder*, readings from Hardy, or Jefferies or Hudson; all those rural voices would go down really well. Maybe Shakespeare's sonnets and a little Donne, introduced by some local character who considers himself erudite, above the rest, there's bound to be one, there always is. You could have Monteverdi in the local church that would give an opening to the local flower-arranging circle.' There was no limit to their ideas and inspiration. Neville visibly flourished with the excitement of it all. No one discussed what it would be in aid of, because, of course, Lumsden and Valentine hoped it would be in aid of them. But they realised that to give credibility to the local community, it must seem altruistic and above-board.

Lumsden paid frequent visits to Fulham to keep himself sane; the one-to-one daily routine with Neville was pretty claustrophobic. Valentine was working with an advertising firm. He had a great many contacts there, people only too eager to have a stake in something creditably cultural. This was to prove Lumsden's downfall. If they had kept it to a weekend and allowed Neville to be sole patron, things might have worked out. But they cast their net wider and wider. They talked themselves into the realms of recording and first public performance. They accepted a large, four-figure sum from a captain of industry whose son had written the music for a performance of a short opera *Jonah and the Whale*. The original libretto was unfinished because the librettist, a friend of the composer, had had a nervous breakdown. As the composer's father feared his son might very soon follow suit, to guarantee any sum to these two personable young men, was, in his view, worth it if it kept the boy going, and stopped those wagging tongues who accused him, as father, of being a bullying philistine. To absolutely guarantee things Lumsden agreed to finish the libretto himself, assuring the young composer that he had done this kind of thing before in Florence. Lumsden found fleshing-out stories with rich apocryphal detail thoroughly entertaining. It was really his own art form, but this time with signatures and deadlines it went too far.

The nearest public-house to Valentine's flat in Fulham was the Spencer Arms. It was a fairly good pub, frequented by Lumsden and Valentine and a great proportion of their friends in navy-blue blazers, or well-cut charcoal-grey, with crisp shirt collars, guarding their fresh skin and their red necks. Loud laughs, and cries of 'Damn good, damn good, fairly drastic.' 'Super girl.' 'Incredible performance.' 'Close shave.' 'Mine.' 'Yours.' 'The old man's coughed up, thank God.' These were the kind of calls usually repeated a couple of times, little barks of applause and encouragement to one another over the curls of cigarette smoke.

Dolly Frampton, who worked behind the bar, listened enraptured to what she felt was the real sound of civilisation and refinement. These were gentlemen; they seemed to her so clean, so well, so lively. She cut the lemons and pulled the pints and smiled as engagingly and with as much friendship as she could. Quite a few of them spoke to her by name. They bought her a drink. They remarked on her looks, her hair, her tan. They smiled and chatted while they waited for their change, which they swept up in a great scoop into their open hands, never checking it, or counting it, simply rounding it up like small stones to be dropped carelessly into the depth of their trouser pockets. If they did get drunk, all they did was laugh a little louder, maybe nudge one another, pull a little on the lapels of a coat, or the colourful tongue of a silk tie. There were no fights. Just a general jostle of loud goodwill. Of course there were girls with them sometimes, but not that many. The girls never paid any attention to Dolly.

Dolly now lived this side of the river. She shared a dark bed-sit on the third floor of a tall, red-brick house not far from the pub. There was a gas-ring and a gas-fire. They shared the bathroom with the other tenants. It was a cold bleak space, but as she often said, 'We're central, we're so central.'

Dolly's friend was called Teresa Ursula Gant. Dolly called her Tug, which suited her. She was a large girl, almost square. Tug always wore trousers and large men's sweaters, she kept her hair short, and her shoes were usually stubby and dull. She came from Croydon. She worked in the Government Records Office in Holborn. She was always nagging Dolly to do something better for herself than just working behind a bar. 'You've got qualifications, you can type, you've got good speeds. You can get a decent job.' But Dolly enjoyed the bar work. Somehow it comforted her. And she did have ambitions. Very definite ambitions. But Tug could never understand. Tug seemed complete on her own, with her library books and her laborious nightly diary. Dolly often wondered what on earth she wrote in that huge day-by-day Boots diary. While Tug wrote, Dolly dreamed. She dreamed of somehow really getting to know the blokes in the bar. The one she knew they called Lumsden she found particularly attractive. Maybe it was his oyster eyes, or the thick dark hair, the way he spoke, so flowing and lively. It must be lovely, Dolly thought, to marry someone who would talk to you. Sid never spoke. She had tried in the beginning to telephone him, but there seemed to be nothing to say. It was just 'Keeping alright?' And Dolly would say 'Fine, thanks.' And Sid would say 'That's good then,' and after a pause she'd be forced to say 'And you?' And he'd say quick as a flash 'Not so bad, not so bad.' And that would be all. Nothing after that. Dolly had almost given up calling. It was too depressing. Lily wasn't there any longer, she'd gone off to Birmingham with some bloke. Apparently several shops in the village had closed. There was a new garage though, and a new stationer's; the bakery just kept going with the post-office. Sometimes, Dolly would suddenly get a whiff of that early morning, bakery smell. It came from nowhere, but it was as keen, as definite, as if she had been there in the bakery in her school uniform. Then the horror, even now, of that moonlit summer's night would come back to her. She sometimes wondered if, before she died, she would ever tell a soul of that night; of that gimlet-eyed moon, and Sid's belt, and the thrashing. She couldn't tell Tug. She'd been out with a few blokes now and again, but she hadn't slept with any of them. She didn't want any stand-up, alley-way hump, or the back of a van, or the pricking rough ground with the moon or sun staring down. Next time, she was going to make sure it was romantic; soft and gentle, and really private. She had her eye on Lumsden long before he registered anything about her, other than the general heave and round display of her bust.

It was mid-May and the dates for the Arts Week had been fixed. Advertising had begun; chairs, caterers and venues had been booked. An account had been opened by Lumsden in the local bank. The account had been very decently filled up and now it was virtually empty. Lumsden was really running pretty scared. There were a great many very verbal and overpowering women that Neville had got in on organisation. Lumsden knew they didn't trust him, and there was the bloody libretto and the composer's father asking for a breakdown of the manner in which, up to date, the expenses relating to *Jonah* had been spent.

It was early one evening before the usual fill of customers, that Dolly overheard a fairly heated discussion going on between Lumsden and Valentine.

'I'm sorry,' Valentine was saying, 'you can't turn back now. You've just got to find someone to do all that typing and secretarial stuff.'

'But I can't pay them,' Lumsden said desperately. 'I can't employ anyone as things stand.'

'Well, somehow you'll have to find a way. You'll maybe recoup some of the losses at the end. But one thing's for sure, you can't go back now. You've got to go on.'

'Chance would be a fine thing,' Lumsden said.

Dolly had heard it all. She had known for several days that they were worried about something. But if it was only typing . . . if it was only that . . . Dolly came round from the bar with their drinks.

'I couldn't help hearing what you said.'

'I beg your pardon . . .'

'I heard what you said.' Dolly paused. The boys looked rather put out. They were very surprised at this gassy little girl having the cheek to break in on their conversation. But Lumsden was desperate. He was quite prepared to hear her out if there might be any mileage in it.

'Well then, if you heard so much, what were we saying?'

'About . . . about typing . . .'

'Typing. We were saying about . . . typing, were we?' Lumsden was playing for time.

'You were. I'm sure you were.'

'Typing.' Lumsden stared at Dolly properly for the first time. She had a bright little face, good lips, good colouring and a rather wistful, almost sad look in the eyes. Too much make up, too much peroxide, but she didn't look stupid. 'Typing. Yes. I did say typing, didn't I, Valentine?'

Valentine grinned. He knew Lumsden was at work. Amazing how he always managed one way or another to ride out pretty well every storm. The advantage was that he didn't seem to have any hang-ups about using people. As he always said, 'What the hell . . . if I don't use them, someone else will, so why not me?'

'You did say typing. Quite definitely you said typing.'

'Well, I can type,' Dolly said eagerly. 'And I've got very decent speeds.'

'We don't doubt it,' Lumsden said. And both the boys laughed heartily. Dolly paused. They had signed for her to sit down at the table with them. That was a real advance. So she didn't mind if she couldn't quite understand why they had laughed. She just went on about her speeds and her certificates.

'It is typing,' Lumsden said. 'All of that, but it isn't exactly a job. Well, it is and it isn't.' And he went on to describe, in glowing terms, the Wiltshire countryside, the artists and the Arts Week. As Dolly listened, she thought . . . well, this is it. Tug can keep Holborn and her wretched Records Office.

'If you were able to help us, which would be amazing, it would mean having to come down to Wiltshire,' Lumsden went on.

'But that's fine,' Dolly said. 'They won't mind here. I've plenty of holiday due to me. And it's a good time, May. It's a better time than August. They'd prefer it really.'

And so it was that Dolly Frampton took out all her savings from the bank, and with a small white suitcase packed neatly with clean summer clothes she found herself driving down from London to Wiltshire in the back of Lumsden's car.

Lumsden drove fast, talking all the time to Valentine. He had the window wound right down, with his bare elbow pointing out into the sun and wind. He kept hardly more than a fingertip or two on the steering-wheel. Dolly tried not to be nervous. It was better if she didn't look. It was better if she just let the draught from Lumsden's open window blow her hair about. It would get messed up, but maybe that would be more countrified. Maybe the kind of curls that came from electric rollers were too tight and fixed to be really free. She wanted so much to be free. Free and loving. Not fixed and tight and anxious. She wondered what on earth it would be like. What would they eat? Would her clothes be the right kind? And what about this man Neville the boys kept going on about? In the end, Dolly simply closed her eyes. She must have slept. She missed the spire of Salisbury Cathedral. She missed Stonehenge. She missed those wide rolling downs, and the neat puffs of white sheep grazing on the short grass. She woke up as they came into the village. It was a very pretty village with low, stone houses, some thatched roofs and very bright, well-kept gardens. There were so many flowers. Honeysuckle everywhere and clematis and jasmine, and loads of other bright flowers she couldn't name. They came to a small stone chapel at the end of the village where the road forked. They took the left fork. Lumsden drove slowly now; over a bridge, past a river and lush water meadows with fat cows. Then the lane was very narrow with high banks. Then it curled up and out on to a wide road, and there, just past a wood and a group of tall beech trees, they turned up into a drive. There was a dear little stone cottage with mullioned windows and a small porch covered with honeysuckle. There were wallflowers and lupins and masses of primroses in the small pocket-handkerchief of a garden. Just behind the cottage there was a weeping beech; a wooden swing hung from it. A white picket fence ran round the garden, with a gate at the back just beside a clothes-line. The gate opened into a long meadow, which ran alongside a dense, high wood. The meadow was full of flowers; bluebells and primroses, campion and cowslips. Lumsden had stopped the car.

'This is your den, Dolly. We've got to go up to the house to get the keys.'

'How do you mean . . . my den, Lumsden? It's a dear little house . . . but . . .'

'It's a lodge,' Lumsden said.

'But . . . will I be on my own?'

'More or less. Maybe a mouse or two. There are deer in the woods. You may see them.'

'But, I'll be alone?'

'Well, old girl, that's the only decent thing, isn't it?'

Both the boys were grinning. Suddenly, just for a moment, Dolly experienced a fraction of real fear. She felt, as she looked at Lumsden's flushed and relaxed face, the tousled, lump froth of hair, the rolled-up sleeves, the long brown arms, she felt that there was in his large blue eyes a cruel, bullying challenge. She felt she must look away. She stared past the cottage towards the huge dark wood. It was pathetic to be afraid. She looked back at the cottage and the honeysuckle and lupins; there was a bright yellow butterfly hovering about the flowers, and a small flurry of sparrows on the little path. It was just going to be different. She wouldn't mind. She mustn't mind because after all, she wanted more than anything else to be different.

'You scared, Dolly?'

'No. I don't think so.'

'Don't worry. We'll work you so hard you won't have time to be.'

They drove up to the house. Neville was sitting out in the sun. He was wearing a white suit and a panama hat and very smart brown-and-white laced shoes with small polka-dot holes in the toes. He greeted the boys very lovingly. Like they were his sons, Dolly thought. Neville nodded towards Dolly rather uneasily. Neville would never be intentionally unkind to anyone, but there was something rather strident and vulgar about this girl, her tightly curled, unreal, flaxen hair, her bright lips and blue-black eyes, frozen like tiny phosphorescent toads in the very contrived, pink and white little face. And the extremely transparent white nylon blouse, with a flounce of a collar, more suitable to embrace a Christmas cracker than a short, thickset little neck. However, Neville tried to overcome his natural resistance to Dolly, which was based more on aesthetics than anything else. He shook Dolly limply by the hand. Her strong little square hand, with its rush of cherry bright nails, grasped Neville's small damp smooth palm too eagerly. Neville flinched visibly, and then retired with the two boys into the house. Dolly was left alone in the sun, surrounded by tubs of flowers and herbs, she tried to be pleased. She knew that it was a very beautiful place. The house was white, with creepers over most of it. Everything was bright. Everything except her spirit. She suddenly felt so friendless. But she made herself think of the bakery and those small, ugly little back rooms; the brown settee, the dull, thick smell of cigarettes and stale life. She was here, she told herself, because she was going to make a better thing of her life. In her life, things would be gentle and pretty. Eventually the boys came out of the house with the keys of the lodge. Dolly felt relieved to leave the grandeur of the house and its pristine, well-manicured garden.

The woods didn't seem quite so dark when they returned to the lodge. And once inside, it felt so bright and clean that Dolly began to feel her spirits restored.

Everything in the kitchen was blue and white. There was a little range, and a small wooden rocking chair. There were two bedrooms, with pretty, flowered curtains and bedspreads to match.

'This is really a guest house, for when Neville has friends for a long stay. But it's all yours. You're a lucky girl, Dolly.'

And Lumsden for the first time actually touched her. He put his hand on her shoulder, and, letting it rest there for some time, he guided her into the small sitting-room. There was a wooden table in front of the window, with a china inkstand and a tall green lamp on it.

'How about there for the typewriter?'

'Fine,' Dolly said.

She hardly moved because she didn't want Lumsden's hand to slip from her shoulder. But it did. And it was quite some time before he came that close to her again.

Lumsden fixed up the typewriter and the papers, the carbon and the folders. He dropped by now and then with pork pies and tomatoes, crisps and Coca-Cola. Dolly told herself that he was very busy when the car spun past the lodge time and again, without even a pause to wave to her. They probably were busy. There was certainly plenty for Dolly to do. After the first few days and nights she got used to the sounds; the clap of pigeons' wings, the scuffle of mice and squirrels, the rustle and sigh and whine of the wind in the trees. She worked long hours, and when she had finished she lay down outside in the sun. Perhaps at the end of it all, when things were arranged and the libretto was finished, perhaps then Lumsden would find more time for her.

Valentine had returned to London. Surely, sometime, Lumsden would come by alone. He did drive her into the village every so often, to buy food and things, but Neville was usually with them, so Dolly sat alone in the back of the car among the posters and boxes of envelopes. Once she telephoned Tug from a call-box. Dolly rattled on about the peace of the country; how quiet, how stunning, how beautiful it all was. 'And the money?' Tug had said, 'What about the money?' 'We're going to fix it all up at the end,' Dolly had replied bravely. 'What end?' And without knowing how prophetic she was, Tug said, 'End of your bloody tether I should imagine.'

The next time Lumsden touched Dolly, came really close to her, actually looked long and hard into her eyes, was when he decided to ask her for some money.

'It's just that it's costing all so much more than we bargained for. I mean, it's only a loan. You'll be a shareholder, a patron. Your name, Dolly, will be there on the programme. Under the list of sponsors it will read, Dolly Frampton. Lord and Lady this and that, the Honourable whatever and then large as life, your name. Dolly Frampton.'

It was a beautiful evening. They were sitting together on the small wooden bench outside the lodge. Lumsden had brought down a bottle of gin. Dolly didn't want to know about the shareholder business. She didn't really care. What was money after all, if you loved someone. And she did love him. She knew she really did. And if you love people, you give things up, you just trust your love. Love is about trust. That's what it really is. Dolly went inside. She went up to her bedroom. She took the small, clean, pink-and-white sponge-bag out of the cupboard where she kept her savings from the bank. She could see the top of Lumsden's head just below the bedroom window. He was whistling. He was feeding the sparrows with crisps from the bottom of the packet. Dolly nearly took out all the notes.

But then she decided to divide them. It wasn't that she wanted to keep anything back. She didn't. But maybe, if there was some still left, well then, maybe he might ask again, and next time he might come even closer. He might even come upstairs. Dolly went down. The sparrows scattered. Lumsden looked up at her and really smiled.

'Here's something towards it all,' Dolly said and she put the rolled notes into his hand.

'You are a saint. Super girl. Wonderful, super girl.'

Dolly smiled. If he did think that, then it was worth it all. Worth all the waiting, all the lonely times, all the typing, all the typing and copying; it was worth it all. Lumsden put the notes in his pocket. What fools women were. And if they weren't fools, they became watching, hovering, serpent creatures like his own mother. There was no middle ground. No man should ever let a fool wrap her way round him; or a serpent either, for that matter. Fool or serpent, either way women were nothing but schemers, trip wires, hidden ditches, ready below the surface to scar and trap and suffocate a man, weedling him into some servile, less than human pastiche of himself, like his own poor bloody father. The trick was to give without giving; to succour, simply by suggestion; to imply, but never make anything definite or clear, that way they would still hang around proffering their, in this case, extremely questionable graces.

He did kiss her. As he left, he put the gin bottle in his jacket pocket.

'Super girl,' he said. And he cupped his hands round her eager little breasts. He squeezed them slightly. 'Super girl, Dolly. This whole thing's going to be a real humdinger.' And he kissed her on both cheeks. He just managed to escape, this time round, the small, fresh little mouth; so eagerly there, like a fish tweaking for air just above the water.

As soon as he had the money, as soon as he possibly could after that little, dry, frisk of a kiss, Lumsden was gone. He had walked down to the lodge. He went back up the long drive at a jog. He was so relieved. It wasn't only the money. Of course that was a help. It was the fact that he'd managed, so he felt, to change gear with Dolly and so be assured of her continuing help, without committing himself in any way. What a gullible, trusting little fool. Still, there must be something in it for her, or she would never have come in the first place. She obviously wasn't a little gold digger. She didn't have the guile. Lumsden assumed it was the considerably improved social status which attracted her. And why not? Pulling pints and being continually vertical had to have its cut-off point. Lumsden told himself that she was bloody lucky to have the chance to spend the summer in the country, to mix with people who did have the semblance of a vocabulary and the wit to do something with it.

By the time he had got to the house and had run a bath, by the time he had done that, Dolly simply didn't figure in his mind at all. She was a practical problem that had been adequately dealt with, that's as far as it went. Just now he had this wretched little composer to accommodate and several of Neville's friends for dinner. He had found, to his relief, that the composer liked the idea of repeated phrases such as: 'and the . . . and the . . . waters . . . the resounding waters . . . resounding waters, whale, whale, water . . . resounding whale waters . . . Jonah . . . Jo . . . nah. Jonah.' That sort of thing. It wasn't bad at all. Whenever he was in any doubt, you just had to have this bass thundering on 'Jo . . . nah . . . Jo . . . Jo . . . Jo . . . nah . . . nah . . . ah . . . ah'. It could go on forever if Lumsden managed to give the composer sufficient encouragement. And luckily, because Lumsden had managed to keep the composer happy, flushed with excitement and intensity about the impending first performance, his father had ceased to be so demanding about the finances. Lumsden began to realise that if he could keep up enough excited cultural energy, then everyone felt inspired, simply by the thrill and achievement of it being on their little patch. No one was vulgar enough to enquire too deeply into the finances. The day of reckoning would come, but at present the caterers, the local wine-merchants, garages, electricians and builders seemed content to subsidise things simply for the privilege of seeing their names in print. More and more Lumsden realised the force of flattery; the appalling hunger people had for praise, for sounds of self-certainty. Compliments were twice as effecting if praise for one managed to be expressed in such a way that subtly it denigrated another. What a game. What a great sham it was, bettering and being bettered.

Dolly very much regretted the amount of gin she had drunk with Lumsden. It made the ache, the real pain of her long solitary evening so much harder to bear. She wondered why they never wanted her up at the house. In a way she knew. Of course she did. She knew that they thought her common, rough; cheap most probably. But surely, if Lumsden felt those kind of things, he would never have kissed her, or brought her down here in the first place. There must be something about her he liked. He made fun of Neville's friends. He made fun of them all, so perhaps it was simply that he wanted to keep their own relationship special and apart. Perhaps it was that. But the thought of it didn't reassure her. It made her weep. It made her sniff and rub her eyes with the tea-towel. It made her sit out there in the garden watching the light fade between the trees while she sucked and chewed the end of her hanky until it was as torn, as wet and worn out as herself.

It had been a subject of some discussion between Neville and Lumsden as to what they should actually do with Dolly during the Arts Week itself. She couldn't very well be simply relegated to assist the caterers, although that was one idea. She could usher, sell programmes, all that sort of thing. What they both felt embarrassed about was the full impact of Dolly on this social milieu of genteel helpers. How could they merge her in without drawing too much attention to her. Neville simply found her vulgarity an affront. It was the only real flaw. He certainly did not dislike her. But Lumsden didn't want Dolly, who was naturally a friendly person, he did not want her becoming too involved with the local village people, whom Lumsden fully realised would be appalled to find out, if Dolly told them, that she was working for nothing and was lending out her own money as well. Money was such a drag. It really cocked things up. Ownership. Possession. The endless pursuit of profit and dreary middle-class security. One day it had to be overthrown. There had to be something better. Freedom. Fun. Licence. Real liberty. The definite decision to live, push out the boundaries, really move on beyond the status quo.

Lumsden borrowed money from Dolly again. He didn't kiss her this time. He was in such a state, such a hurry. It was about having to pay for some goods on delivery. Dolly presumed that he borrowed from her because of their friendship. She knew Neville was loaded, so she felt it rather a compliment that Lumsden chose her in preference to Neville. But of course that wasn't the situation. Neville had paid off all Lumsden's debts, he gave him a good wage, and he had also put a considerable sum in the Arts Week account. Lumsden knew that to mention money to Neville again would be to blow his cover, it would alert people to the state of the account, it would alert people to Lumsden himself.

Lumsden developed a completely fresh tack. He started flogging various bits and pieces from Neville's house to a dealer in Hungerford. Quite by chance, Dolly discovered a box of china and clocks and oddments of silver in the boot of Lumsden's car. She had hardly time to say, 'Wow ... how beautiful, Lumsden ... what's this?' when he roughly slammed down the boot, almost shoving her to the ground in the process.

'What the fuck are you doing?'

'What do you mean?'

'I mean get lost. Jump. There's no business of yours in my car . . . is there? Is there?'

'No. But . . . the groceries . . .'

'I've just put your groceries on the kitchen table.'

'I didn't know. I'm sorry.'

'Sorry is the sort of squirmy little answer I'd expect from you.'

'Lumsden, what do you mean?'

'I mean you're fired. You're bloody fired.'

It was his arms, the mad windmill way they fell about the air. Dolly thought he might grab her, or hit her. He was mad. He was shouting at her like a lunatic. He was making no sense. But the wind in the trees muffled and drowned his voice, just as it muffled and drowned Dolly's screams. Lumsden had been on edge. Neville had noticed one or two things missing. He hadn't seemed too perturbed, but he had noticed. Lumsden was beginning to realise that his days were numbered. The money was spent. The libretto wasn't finished. The whole ghastly business was about to be, very soon, a monumental fiasco, with him fairly and squarely in the provincial dock; a situation he must speedily avoid.

Of course Dolly didn't understand. After days and nights of so much hoping and loneliness, the sudden change in Lumsden, the loss of his charm and jokes, the wild, rough way he had shaken her, it had snatched from Dolly all her brave resolutions, all that careful hard work, all her tentative little dreams of loving tenderness, it even seemed to snatch from her the raw, frail strength that was, so she thought, her heart. She felt, without warning, a surge of terrible shame and suffocating fear. He must hate her. He must really hate her. She was hysterical. She was quite beside herself. She ran away screaming, as if possessed. She ran into the little back garden behind the lodge and then through the gate into the meadow. She ran on, choking and sobbing, stumbling on the lumpy, uneven ground. Every night she had feared the high wood, hating those sudden sounds; creaks, slams, little bursts of sound she could not identify. She felt the high wood scorned her, for her fear of being alone. Night after night she just lay there, terrified by the rhythm of her own breathing. Now, as she ran, she longed simply to throw herself into the darkness of the high wood. She longed to be taken up into it, so that she herself would be nothing more than one of its sounds. There was a ditch between the meadow and the bank into the wood. There were hidden strands of barbed-wire. She fell. She rolled down into the ditch, which was dry, but when she tried to pull herself up and out on to the bank, when she tried to grab at some roots and grasses, she grabbed instead at the wire, and a sharp, little star of dagger stems cut deep into her arm.

Lumsden watched the plump little screaming figure picking her way over the meadow, slipping and stumbling because of those ridiculous high-heeled shoes. He was horrified at his utter stupidity. If he hadn't railed and shouted she would never have guessed. Now she might well be suspicious, suspicious of everything. He was amazed that he'd become so jumpy. Now he had stopped shouting it made her cries much worse, louder, more animal than ever. Sod it, he thought. At that moment a car drove past. Some one waved to Lumsden. He knew he had to get Dolly back. There she was trying to scramble up out of the ditch in those pathetically Persil-white clothes. From his distance she looked like paper litter, some sack blown or thrown from a passing lorry. Anyway, a definite mistake, a definite flaw on the horizon. There was considerable wind now. It looked as if at any moment it might rain. At least that might drown out the sound of her. It would certainly tone down the gleaming white of those clothes. Lumsden knew he had to do something practical about her. He had to have her calm and on his side for a few days longer. It would be fatal if she left now and got that frightful girl Tug to console her. She would definitely try to dun him for money.

Lumsden made his way across the back garden and then through the open gate into the long meadow. She seemed to be having considerable trouble getting out of the ditch. He'd have to calm her. He'd have to bloody calm her, and he only knew of one, more-or-less reliable way to do it. Every so often you had to give them some of what they wanted. At least then you had a kind of control. And it needn't be for long. He'd just sell the last lot of stuff and then on some pretext or other he'd make it back to Italy.

As he came closer to the ditch, he picked his way over roots and stones and rough lumps of ground and dry ankle-deep ruts where machinery had taken thick scoops out of the heavy clay. As he came closer he saw that Dolly had managed to scramble out of the ditch and was running now, through the brambles, thorn, tree suckers and high grass, right into the thick of the wood itself.

Although Lumsden was at this point, above all else, preoccupied with his own extremely serious problems, there was something about Dolly's screaming; the torn, shredded, frantic look in her eyes; and the face, usually so prinked and powdered, positively glued with make-up, suddenly it had altered, shrivelled, dropped. In that quickening of so much pain and fear and fright she had lost the light-weight, cheap, baby-doll look. This was, Lumsden felt, a definite gain.

Maybe because Lumsden's grounding had been in female fury, violent pent-up passion; maybe passion unleashed, violent uncontrollable emotional disorder run riot, maybe it had for him a certain attraction. He was not sure why, but in that second as Dolly ran past him, all sobs and screams, he had sensed an energy there that had a certain, fleeting, bizarre attraction. After the suffocating camp elegance and contrived pseudo-splendour of Neville's house, its generally claustrophobic atmosphere, after all that, and then its opposite; the neat, guarded, unutterably boring life of local retired households and the more prosperous farming families, and fringe craft people, all carefully constructing a life of scrupulous order and middle-class regard, after all that Dolly's red lips, red nails, stiletto heels, the lot; it was at least a stab at life. Dolly was different. And shaken like that, shattered and careless, in a second without any kind of control, Dolly was live; vigorously, petulantly, ferociously alive.

And it was life so Lumsden thought, that he was after. A life big enough, with enough variety, to fill forever any tiresome, self-reflective void, any grim, uneasy reminder of the dark emptiness of the nursery bag. Nothing so specific as dark emptiness ever came close, because instantly there was the merest smell of it, Lumsden would leap in there, with drink, tailors, race meetings, nightclubs, he would make so much sound himself, he would construct such an active hurly-burly, that emptiness and fear were soon stifled out. But maybe in spite of it all, some darkness still lingered in the wings, in the banished, throttled depth of the nursery bag.

By the time Lumsden had jumped the ditch, and negotiated the rusty barbed-wire, Dolly was nowhere to be seen. Lumsden could only follow the track of broken twigs and thrashed-down grasses that he presumed Dolly's panicky, frenzied little body had made. At the other side of the wood a large field rolled down in a wide horse-shoe shape towards the road. There had been quite a thrust of real wind, then suddenly it seemed to pause. Even though it was fairly early, round about nine o'clock, an uncanny, angry weight of purple dark cloud filled the sky. And then, just as Lumsden was at the edge of the wood, the whole sky rattled with thunder and threw down great slaps of rain; a skelter pelt of blinding water. It fell fast, full of rage and surly optimism, disfiguring the summer day, banishing the evening into early darkness. The leaves of the trees trembled with the weight of it all. Lumsden, instantly soaked, ran along the headland towards a wooden barn at the top of the field. The high barn doors swung and creaked in the wind; the sound of the rain rang out so loud, as its direct down course was intercepted by the corrugated tin of the barn roof. Lumsden went inside. The noise was still loud, but much less in the barn itself. Lumsden shook his hair, letting the water run down on to the dry straw bales. Then he heard Dolly. He heard this small, sniffing whimper coming from the back of the barn.

The loud dramatic sound of the rain, the huge quiet of the barn itself; the rafters covered with cobwebs, fine rolled lengths of dust, sacks, implements, a large glistening damp oil stain on the concrete floor, the stacks of bales, both hay and straw; it was such an unexpected environment for either Lumsden or Dolly. It was as if they had both been catapulted by the racing, uneven drama of their personal lives into this timeless place. Here all the sounds, all the smells, all that they looked on, all that they felt against their wet clothes, and suddenly very cool summer limbs, all of it was forever. It was as if the barn was some strange asylum stage; beyond, quite outside, both their lives. Perhaps it was the place, and the pause the storm forced upon them, perhaps it was some of these things, that made them eye each other with greater calm and care than they had ever done before.

Lumsden, as he ran through the wood, had no other thought but simply to get to Dolly first, before she got anywhere else. He wanted to assure her, to assure himself. He realised vaguely that the manner of it might very well be a demonstration of some kind of care. He would certainly have to approach her in a way she wanted, would understand, and would respond to.

Dolly, for her part, felt the miserable, total exhaustion of a child. In her nights and days of careful work and fearful, jumpy sleep, she had, she knew now, she had imagined too much. She had thought so many times of Lumsden, his laughter, his easy manner; she had seen him there, night after night in her mind; careful and tender towards her. It was the shame of so much foolishness that made her bite her nails and sniff again and again, wiping her nose on the back of her hand. Where could she go now, without any money; and so wet, and her arm still bleeding from the wire? He'd said . . . go. You're fired. He'd said that.

Lumsden came slowly towards the back of the barn. He sat down on a bale of straw, more or less opposite where Dolly was sitting.

'Brilliant storm,' he said.

Dolly paused in her sniffing.

'Come on, Mrs Noah, it's not that bad. We could get afloat on some of those old doors. We could certainly feed the animals. It's good hay. Fresh. This season's.'

Dolly attempted a sort of sniffing smile. She wanted so much to say to him that she loved him. That she hadn't minded the work, or the muddle about the money. She wanted to say she was sorry for looking in the car. Sorry for whatever it was that she had done.

Lumsden was not quite sure what he should do next. There was certainly no chance of moving out for a while. The rain was still a blinding drench of throbbing, racing water, filling every hole and gulley, every slit or space in the dry ground, until it stood in great grey puddles.

'What did you do to your arm?'

'Dunno.'

'You couldn't have done that on a bramble.'

'I think it was wire.'

Lumsden moved a little closer.

'Let's have a look.'

'It's alright.'

'Come on now . . . come on . . . Noah knows best.'

This time Dolly grinned, and put out her cold arm, where the warm blood had dried into a scab and smear, with small, bright, pin-prick beads of fresh blood oozing upwards now and again.

'Poor you. It looks horrid.'

It was the fact that he suddenly sounded kind, after all the mad fury and shouting. It was that edge, or real quiet in his voice that set Dolly off again. She turned away from him. She fell sobbing on to the straw.

'I should never have come. Tug said I was a fool. She was right. I am. I'm an idiot.'

And she was away again, good loud sobs more or less in competition with the downpour outside. Lumsden knew he had to rein it all in; all those sobs and tears were definitely a backward step, and a dangerous one, towards possible disaster.

'Come on. Come on. Things aren't that bad. I mean . . . we haven't drowned yet.'

She still had her back to him. She was still shaking with moans and tears. So quite gently, but nevertheless firmly, Lumsden turned her round towards himself.

'Come on, Dolly. Come on. You're a great girl. You've been amazing. No one could have done better. Things have got in a muddle. It's not your fault. I'm sorry I shouted. I shouldn't have done that.'

Dolly was quiet now. Lumsden's hands were firmly there on her shoulders. His hair was wet, it seemed to hang down longer than usual. She hardly dared to look directly into his eyes, they were closer to her now than they had ever been.

'Look, Dolly, there is this bit of a muddle, but just give me a few days. Trust me. Trust me. I'll see us through. We'll get by.'

The way he said 'us' and 'we'. It was enough. It was enough for her to trust him forever. And in that second Dolly felt safe again. You had to try to find real life. You couldn't do it unless you took risks. Dolly wasn't exactly sure what it was she sought so hard and longed for so much. But whatever it was, she knew it was there somewhere; and the rain, the smell of the straw, the dark, heavy sky outside, the damp, warm, softened smell of her clothes, all these fractions of being seemed witness in some way to what she meant. There was a binding between her most hidden self and the small, endless, rough struggle of everything else; nothing, not even dust or rain, could escape the round and round pattern of things. Nothing could stay as it seemed; and what seemed to stay never remained as it was. If all was impermanence, then trust need not be more than now; more than this.

'I love you, Lumsden,' she said.

'Idiot. Poor old idiot person.'

Dolly had never heard him so gentle before. Very quietly he slipped his hands down there into her shirt. He eased her breasts upwards; cold from the rain, the nipples were sprung, very forward and firm towards his hands.

'May I kiss you?' he said.

And it was the most wonderful thing that had ever happened to her, when his mouth rested, gently at first and then more firmly on her right breast. She lay back down against the straw. She dared to let her square hand, with the chipped nails, she dared let it run through his long, dark hair.

She was gazing up at this high barn roof, the woven sacks and poles that rested across the rafters. It was as if the great storm outside was there now simply to protect them, simply to give them this time forever, with one another. It was as if all these waters flooding everywhere were a fountain race to free her of shame and fear; any sense that did not allow utterly this easy, deep, perfect thing. Lumsden seemed taller without his clothes. He took hers from her, one by one; the shoes, with their broken heels, just fell on to the concrete floor. She thought she would be shy of herself, so quietly stripped, so completely bare. But

Lumsden peeled her clothes from her so carefully, as if they were really never meant to be there at all. Like sun moving its way round a garden, he found and loved her. And when he was closest of all, she raced there with him, eager to forget forever that gimlet moon, and that rough, sad, fierce beginning. Later, when the storm had ceased, when a keen yellow light glazed the puddles and the bright green blades of corn, when there was no longer rain or wind, simply the sound of water running from gutters into oil drums and drains, then he handed her back her crumpled clothes, and when they were both dressed he held her very firmly against his own warm body and simply said, very quietly this time, 'Trust me. Trust me, Mrs Noah.'

After that, Dolly remembered the smell of straw and sacks, fine harvest dust and hay: she remembered it differently from almost everything else in her life, which became a dark, beaten down, tired ground of scattered, spilled, bitter things; never resolved, never safe, never complete. But still, she didn't regret that storm, and in it her seconds of trust. She never regretted it, although she knew it was not a beginning; not a start at all; just a dark, very early end. The end of trying to find a beautiful dream truth; the end of longing and mystery; the end of believing anything was meant to be good.

Later Lumsden had to admit to Valentine that Dolly had proved, against the odds, to be a particularly good lay. In fact, Lumsden had found it quite irksome that the way things worked out, it had to remain as a one-off.

It was only three days later that he managed to effect, in theory, a pressing family funeral in Tipperary. People in Wiltshire knew nothing of Lumsden's circumstances, except that he came from Ireland. There was something quite romantic about Rathmanagh, the way Lumsden described it. He told Neville the funeral was his grandmother's. He half wished the truth could have been that it was his mother's; she was old enough to be a grandmother.

Of course, Neville accepted the sadness of Lumsden's news, and the obvious duty he owed towards his bereaved mother. The Arts Week went ahead. Lumsden never dared to enquire how things went; but years later, he did hear the opera *Jonah and the Whale* performed in King's Lynn, and the programme notes referred to it not being the original libretto used for the first performance. It was a back-handed kind of recognition, Lumsden thought.

Dolly did trust Lumsden for those few days. They were very happy days for her. Lumsden popped into the lodge quite often. He was never able to stay long, but he always kissed her when he arrived, and then again as he left; always coming very close, and holding her carefully to himself. Because he didn't give her much work, Dolly spent most of her time in the garden. She fed the sparrows and soaked up the sun. She picked fresh flowers and made cakes. In the evenings she walked out into the meadow; sometimes she sat for a while on the wooden swing that hung from the beech tree. She would rock gently to and fro, remembering the barn and the rain, and the safe, wonderful comfort of Lumsden's body. No one could be so gentle, so careful and kind if they didn't love you. Dolly would watch the sun drop down behind the high wood, until the trees were simply a dark mass reaching up into the sky. She thought how much she loved the wood. She felt she knew all those sounds now. They were no longer threatening or alien. They were just sounds of life, sounds of nature, just as she herself was, in a way, just a sound, just a bit of nature. The hiss of the kettle, the spit of dry logs on the fire, the gentle, slow pop of soap bubbles when she washed her clothes, they were all really just little nature sounds. She began to feel close to the earth. She could understand why it was called Mother Earth. She picked some of the flowers out of the garden and pressed them carefully in the telephone directory. The pansies were best, and the daisies, and some very small blue flowers that grew right down in between the blades of grass, she didn't know their name. When the flowers were properly pressed, Dolly put them into a large brown envelope, between single sheets of loo paper as protection.

It was a Tuesday morning, quite early, when Lumsden came by for what was to be the last time. He seemed very preoccupied, and in a great hurry.

'Remember, Dolly,' he said, 'all life's a gamble. You win some, you lose some. Remember that. But nothing good ever really gets lost. It's all there somewhere, Mrs Noah.'

Dolly felt anxious. She didn't understand what he was saying, but something in his manner, something in the tone of his voice, made her afraid again. All that safe happiness, of trees and sun and flowers, crumpled into a sinister, taunting fear. Was he leaving her? She dared not even think it.

It was one of the women who worked up at the house who, seeing Dolly in the garden that same evening, got off her bicycle. She came over to the fence. She lent across it. She called out to Dolly and said, 'Well, it's a sad business, isn't it? Poor Mr Lumsden. He was in such a state. Dashing about like a mad thing getting everything packed, poor young man. By the time you're my age, you're used to that kind of news, it's more of a shock when you're young.' She paused. 'And what'll you be doing now, Dolly?'

'Me?'

'Yes, my dear, you. He'll not be back, so they say. Not for the Arts Week anyway.'

Dolly hated the humiliation, on top of everything else, of not knowing what this woman was talking about. She had to ask, because she simply had to know.

'Where's he gone?'

'Don't you know? Didn't he say?'

Dolly shook her head. She couldn't bear to speak. She knew her voice would fail her. She knew now that her trust had been for nothing. She had been dumped; just used. She knew now that it had all been lies; careful, terrible lies. She never wanted to feel anywhere near her heart again. Her heart must die. This news; it was like a poison. She felt as if she was drowning in some kind of sickness.

The woman knew how Dolly felt. They had all guessed that Lumsden was a bad lot. And this girl he'd kept down at the lodge, they'd all wondered how and where exactly she fitted in, not his type at all. Now most probably he'd just left her high and dry. Well, more than likely she'd asked for all she got. Pert little thing. Still it was a shame. A shame for any girl to be let down, whatever her circumstances.

'He's gone to Ireland. Southern Ireland. So he said. His grandmother's just died. He must be there for the funeral. It means a lot to them over there, I believe, funerals and things. He must support his mother. That's what he said. Family's a big thing over there I believe. Well, dear, that's it, I'm afraid. He's gone. He'll not be back.'

Dolly didn't stay. She didn't want to let this woman gloat over her. The hopeless, horrid, awful muddle of it. She ran inside into the kitchen. There were freshly-made jam tarts on the table, just out of the oven. There were fresh flowers beside them, and the sun, which was low in the sky, was pointing rich arrows of light across the checked cloth and down on to the floorboards. Dolly grabbed the flowers out of the vase, she crushed the fresh blooms in her hands and pounded the crisp stalks together. She threw them in the bin and then she kicked it. She kicked over the small wooden chair that was up at the table. She pulled at the cloth, a fresh clean cloth, the jam tarts fell off the wire rack, they fell on to the floor, they broke and crumbled. She'd have to ring Tug. She'd have to go back to

London. And that was what she wanted to do, because loving and all that was just shit; just a filth of lies, all lies. Flowers, trees, meadows, peace, it was all lies; it was all stupid shit. Tug was right. She was a fool; a pathetic, idiot fool.

*

Naturally, Tug was not in the least bit surprised about anything. She lent Dolly some money to tide her over. And the Spencer Arms let her have her job back. London was itself, full of summer; lazing people on the hot pavements, tourists, sightseers, pubs and numerous coffee bars, with the whoosh of cappuccino being served and the smell of spaghetti Bolognese. It seemed to Dolly like a great basin of work, people, buses, taxis and trains. It seemed without an edge. Once in the centre, surrounded by the height of buildings and all the traffic sounds, the zest and pulse of it seemed so strong, so permanent; it made the rest, that other world of meadows, corn, high woods, still long days and still longer nights, nights that spread their deep, attentive silence over everything, until dawn roused the birds to start their chip-sharp, trill and whirl of excited, celebratory sounds; it made it fade into less than a dream; just a string of ideas without any truth to them whatsoever. Behind the bar, with heavy glasses soaking in the small sink, and a Hoover over the dark mats, and a soft cloth on the brass and leather, memories of buds and birds, thorns and roses, and all those honeysuckle smells; all that soon faded. But something did remain; something persisted in Dolly's mind, always. It was his face, those dark curls, those wide open, different eyes, and the gentle voice; just that one time; and the feel of him, the feel of him on to herself; and the feel of herself; so bare and free, and so happily complete, back down into the straw. Dolly didn't tell Tug about the storm and the barn. Of course not. It was the money side of things that maddened Tug. She did once say, while she was opening a can of sardines, 'You weren't fool enough to sleep with him were you?' And Dolly had said, very quietly, 'He didn't want that kind of thing', which she knew was true. 'Well, count your blessings,' Tug had replied. Then the tin had slipped out of her hand and the oil had spilt, and in the fluster for rags and newspaper to wipe up the mess Tug had let the subject drop. Dolly was grateful. She was going to keep those seconds of trust to herself. She needn't share that evening storm, and the wet, high wood, and their barn-sheltering with anyone. She would keep it to herself. Maybe it was an idiot hopeless thing to have done, but she was glad it had happened. Glad that she knew something about herself which she had not known before. She put the pressed flowers in the cookery book which had been her mother's before she went into that terrible hospital. The recipes were wartime ones, full of powdered egg and peanut-butter, but her mother's handwriting, very neat and round and careful, was on some of the back pages where there were empty spaces for personal recipes. Dolly's mother had written out one for Irish Stew and one for Welsh Rarebit. Dolly put the pansies in that page. It reassured her, for no reason that she understood. She would never use the book, the recipes were too dull; so the flowers were safe. They would keep, and with them some memory; the sound of rain on tin, and the sense of Lumsden within herself. However wrong and cruel and stupid it might later seem to have been, Dolly wanted, always, to be able to reach it; as it had been to her then, in those seconds of trust.

The obvious thing to worry about never occurred to Dolly. Then, when it did, suddenly one morning, she was glad. She felt that maybe now things might have another chance. Tug didn't notice at first. She left for Holborn far earlier than Dolly left for the pub, so she didn't see her avoid the coffee and have weak tea with dry biscuits instead of anything cooked. It was quite a while later, when Dolly started to lie down for a bit before supper. And then she didn't want the usual things; chips or baked beans or ketchup or anything, she just wanted mushrooms on dry toast. Dolly got this real thing about mushrooms. Then Tug guessed.

'You're pregnant. You bloody fool. You lied. You did screw him. Why did you lie?'

'I didn't.'

'Not his? Someone else's? Not that berk Valentine Duckworth, not him, surely?'

'No. Of course not.'

'But you did screw, didn't you?'

'No. Not really.'

'What do you mean "not really"? Who was it then . . . the archangel Gabriel?'

Dolly didn't answer.

'Well, however it happened . . . immaculate conception or otherwise . . . you are pregnant, aren't you? You think you are, don't you?'

'I don't know.'

'Then, you'd better bloody find out.'

'I don't mind.'

'What the hell do you mean . . . you don't mind. We're not talking about dogs or cats or budgerigars . . . we're talking about a bloody baby. The whole nightmare circus of a human being. Dolly . . . grow up . . . be your age.'

Dolly stared at the floor, the stains on the carpet, her dirty pink slippers, Tug's books and records.

'Dolly . . . Dolly. Answer for Christ's sake. This isn't something you can keep to yourself.'

Dolly stared at everything and nothing. She heard the tap dripping into the sink. She heard someone go into the lavatory on the next landing. She had been sick twice already. It was horrible to have to kneel beside the pan, retching and waiting. Weird, that natural things had such peculiar, uncomfortable ways of getting there. The sickness felt like a punishment;

208

everything seemed to have that smell; even sounds had smells. Everything seemed off colour, wrong, it was like there was this bruised, dead cast over the whole world, it was as if it had been dripped into this stagnant, nauseous, liquid bile. Although so much outside her body seemed different, Dolly knew it was her body that made it happen. She couldn't stand the smell of shoe polish or fried eggs or talcum powder.

'Dolly.' Tug was shaking her. 'Look . . . you're nineteen. You can't just have a child. It's mad . . . it's crazy. That smooth sod. That two-timing bastard. Come on Dolly, you've got to talk about it, face up to it, then we can do something.'

'I'm going to be sick.'

Dolly ran to the sink, because the bathroom on the next landing was occupied. She gripped the side of the basin. It was like waiting for all your guts, all your stomach to be just thrown up out of you. It was better afterwards. The empty drained feeling felt quiet, a kind of momentary forgiveness. Dolly vaguely wondered if she was bad, and this was sin, as the sisters would have said. She could see that it was impractical, difficult, but she didn't think it could be sin. Even if they said so; sin had to be altogether harder, more definite, more planned. It couldn't be sin, she was sure of that. She remembered Mary Carter in the village, and that huge pram and baby Johnny with his broad smile and pale, sticky face. She remembered Mary Carter's dirty petticoat that always hung down below her coat. Lily would be furious. She'd say she'd always seen it coming. Maybe she was right. But anyway, Dolly wasn't going to tell them . . . because . . . because it might be different. Lumsden might care if he knew. She had to give him that chance.

Tug just watched her. The vomit. The smell. Her greasy hair, the utter hopelessness of it.

'Why Dolly? Why?'

'Dunno.'

'You must have let it happen . . . did you? Or did the bastard force his smooth bloody prick on you? Dolly come on. How did it happen? Did he force you?'

'It doesn't matter.'

'Of course it does. First of all, we have to be sure it's his. Was there anyone else?'

'No.'

'Then it is his.'

'I suppose so.'

'And the bastard's not even in England is he?'

'Do stop saying bastard.'

'Come on, Dolly. You can't have this baby, you know that. So don't start getting so sensitive for bastards.'

'I won't get rid of it, Tug. I won't . . . so don't think you can make me.'

'Oh . . . very well then . . . and who pays the rent? Who copes? Who slops out for you? Answer me that. Or will you give it over to some Catholic nuns for adoption?'

'I don't know what I'll do. I don't know anything.'

'I bet you gave him the come on. Were you drunk? Were you?'

'It's none of your business.'

'It is while you're here.'

'Then I'll go. I'll get out of your precious room and its dripping tap and its cracked window and filthy carpets. I'll go.'

And Dolly ran to the wardrobe and started pulling out her clothes and shoes, so that very soon the floor was littered with garments as well as everything else.

Tug ran to her. Awkwardly, clumsily, she tried to hug her. She tried to calm her.

'Dolly. Dolly. Look, I'm sorry. I was just upset for you. Upset for us both. Of course I'll stick by you. Of course we'll work it out. It's just . . . well, it's just shock I suppose.'

Tug was picking things up from the floor. Dolly walked over to the window and stared down into the street; the roofs of cars and taxis, the sound of it all, cats and feet and tyres, a coke can rattling its way into the gutter. There was one thing about this sick feeling, it sort of pushed you back out of things; it put you away, out on to this grey ledge, apart from everything. Apart, so that you didn't think and hear and feel the same way as before. But Dolly was glad that at least something was happening to her. Something was going on. Something to do with real life; and something to do with Lumsden. She could never explain to Tug how she felt. She didn't understand it herself. She knew she just wanted to go on, and if it was a baby . . . But that was where Dolly's thinking stopped. She didn't want to let herself fancy things getting better. Like Lumsden finding out, and caring. Like Lumsden being glad.

Of course they guessed in the bar. You can't hide a thing like that for long. Well, not if you're throwing up all the time. Tug still hoped she'd come to her senses. But Dolly wouldn't discuss it. And very soon weeks became months, and then it was winter, and it showed. There was no going back now. Dolly would certainly go full term. She would have this child sometime in February. Tug just hoped that when it got nearer the time she would consider adoption. It was the only solution that made any sense.

*

If Violet and Cecil Farr ever thought of their son in England, it was never made apparent to anyone, least of all to each other. Life went on the same: produce for the Claggan market, farm decisions, upkeep, maintenance, local committees, local decisions, Cecil had developed problems of wind and acid stomach, and as his gums shrunk his ill-fitting dentures became an increasing liability. Birkin was dead. Violet had found him on the south side of Mount Murna, stiff, yet with his black coat still soft from dew, little beads of bright water glistened on the stark lengths of hair; the stomach was distended, the eyes were open, but glazed, opaque, utterly empty of Birkin, and yet there was in their very emptiness some kind of postscript, some kind of reference to the great, lost spirit of this loyal being. The huge head was dropped down into a little dish of ground, just as it might have lain in Violet's lap. She did not weep. Sorrow such as this had no external means of expression in the battened down, fierce fortress of meshed, banished feeling that was the resolute, guarded structure of herself. She simply stayed there with him until well after dark. She stayed until the cold wind and heavy dew gave her some intensity of bodily feeling; sufficient discomfort, stiffness and bitter cold for her to know this death, this cruel desertion, deep inside herself. She stayed and stared until the dark made the mound-shape of the dog simply a shadow at her feet similar to the outcrop rock and other smooth sides of stone on the mountain. Without Birkin, Violet was deserted; she was truly alone. But for the rest of her life, she would see him, hear him, smell him. There was no path, no root, no open space of ground where she did not remember his boundless loyalty and eager pleasure. She saw his dark shape under the piano in the library, at the end of her bed, and by the fire in the parlour. Donal dug a grave for Birkin at the edge of the wood, high above the house, and together Donal and Violet wrapped him in fresh sacks from the red barn and then they laid him carefully into the moist earth. Later Violet had a headstone carved from a rough slab of stone that was found in the rubble, from one of the fallen cottages on the estate. It simply said BIRKIN and then the dates. Violet did not want any known quotation, that might suggest to other people, at another time, that they might know and understand her sorrow and her relationship to this particular animal. It was not simply a great dog beloved by his mistress. It was more than that, it was passion and trust; it was an alchemy of need, animal thrust and human frailty made whole in a single, celebratory strength.

Violet had finished the shell ceiling that linked her parlour to the library. It was very decorative and most original, and a point of considerable discussion in the neighbourhood. The paper boy Jack was married with children of his own. Donal Barry, known in Ballynaule as 'Big Donal', came to Rathmanagh now on a regular basis. He helped Violet run and manage the gardens, the orchard and all the surrounding grounds. He was a very big man, with broad shoulders and large, wide hands. His movements were always definite and careful. He wasted nothing; no energy, no glances, no words. His silent, gentle, hardworking ways were an anchor to Violet, who had frequent bouts of anxiety and even anger if things did not run smoothly; if animals were sick, or if local people, in her opinion, let her down; Donal, without presumption or impertinence, guided and reassured her. In his heart, Donal worked more for Rathmanagh than for the Farrs. As a boy he had shot rabbits in the woods, snared foxes and fished for pike and bream in the lake. He knew every inch of the property, and although he was happy enough to manage the gardens, lawns and shrubs and flowers, they could never become for him the heart of Rathmanagh, which was in the woods and lake and in the wild banks beside the river. As Donal cycled home each evening, it was the light on Mount Murna, the way the sky ran above her, with or without cloud, that told him what kind of a day to expect tomorrow. Mount Murna was for Donal, as well as it was for so many others, Mount Murna was the real charge and power of the place.

Father Palin had left the parish of Ballynaule long since. Father Bohane, a quiet, gentle, good man, had taken his place. He saw next to nothing of the Farrs, but Donal was a great man in the parish. It was Donal who told Father Bohane that the Farrs were not in fact childless, as he had presumed. They did apparently have a son, somewhere in England. He rarely, if at all, visited Rathmanagh. There were women in the parish who were sure he must have gone to America, or been taken sick; they even wondered if he might not have died.

Lumsden did in fact send his parents an occasional postcard. But there was no reason for Donal to know this, as it was not a subject to which Violet ever referred.

*

When the time came for Dolly to bear her child, Lumsden was living in a flat in Chelsea with an American woman who was slightly older than himself. They were lovers. They were free spirits. Their life together appeared to be a most pleasurable thing, devoid of anything so bourgeois as jobs, or commitment of any kind. They came and went as the spirit moved them; entertaining and being entertained; they were spontaneous travellers, filling days and nights with the discovery of themselves, and many others who were attracted to their seeming freedom and continual generosity. There were those who saw them as degenerate, a dangerous development in an increasingly hedonistic society that was beginning to forget the order and discipline that had won, so they said, two world wars. But, as even Dolly knew, nothing remains the same, and how things seem might very well not be as they are.

For Dolly, things seemed slow, sluggish, cold and uneasy. In the pub they had been very kind. They joked and teased, but they cared for her. Valentine and Lumsden no longer visited the Spencer Arms. But then, Dolly told herself, just as she told everybody else, 'Lumsden's abroad. He'll make contact when he comes back. He'll know where to find me.' 'And what about this great surprise, my dear?' they'd say, patting the tight, drum stomach under Dolly's apron. 'He'll deny it's his,' Tug kept saying. But Dolly managed to keep out of her mind all their talk and worries. Each morning, after she had swung her legs across from the low divan bed on to the floor, she sat for several seconds stroking this strange, hard mass that was still herself, but yet, even now, was well beyond her in more ways than one. The sickness was considerably less, it was more discomfort; aching legs, frequent visits to the lavatory, which, both in the pub and at their lodging, was a cold grim place. The best part was when it moved; when this strong, lumpy, rope thing rose, like some sea creature, twisted, turned, and then settled back down again. Her breasts were huge; they felt strange to her. Standing in front of the mirror, she hardly knew herself. This great bowl shape that she carried everywhere; sometimes it seemed like an intruder that simply hid her. She no longer felt in any way connected to that small, frightened, anxious girl that had sheltered in the barn. It was hard to believe that just those few, quick, full seconds between them, could become so much. The dangerous thing was that although she thought continually of her shape and her condition, somehow, in her mind, it was always connected to Lumsden. It was for Lumsden. It was about Lumsden. The reality of the impending birth, of some quite other person, didn't really impinge on Dolly's continual longing for Lumsden. Dolly could not share these thoughts with Tug. Tug wanted her to contact Sid; she also wanted her to track down Lumsden. Tug felt that when these problems had been faced, Dolly might agree to adoption.

Dolly simply wanted the cold, uncomfortable days to pass. In a way, her condition did hide her from herself. She was this real pregnant woman, her reflection in shop windows demonstrated this, but somehow it seemed to be about the world rather than herself. This shape, that people stared at, made way for, this shape which inspired small children to point and giggle, it was something to do with the tumbling tide of social history; it was too big an event and too ordinary to be simply the stupid miscalculation of an anxious, lovesick, barmaid. It must be something else. It was into this compelling centre of nebulous certainty that Dolly stared. If she thought reasonably or practically that certainty would evaporate, it would fade, and she would be left without resource to any kind of strength at all. Tug tried to be patient. But in the end as the date came closer and closer she could not bear the responsibility on her own. They had spent a dismal Christmas together. Lily and Sid had sent a generous parcel of food, and soap, smelling of lilies-of-the valley, with a gaudy over-cheerful card. Visit us before the weather gets really bad, they said. Lily, deserted once more by her bloke, was back with Sid in the bakery. Eventually, after much persuasion, Dolly agreed to go down there one Sunday with Tug. Tug promised that if things were difficult, they would leave immediately, take a taxi if necessary. 'It'll be worse if you leave it 'til afterwards; they'll be so hurt,' Tug said. Dolly wondered why that mattered; the great weight it was now, night and day, her breathlessness, and a stupid, angry rash, which she had all over her stomach, made her careless to abstract talk of other people and their feelings, she was completely in thrall to the physicality of her condition. It was a kind of shroud, a sack over her; a defence against the quick, sharp, rushing, dashing, other world, to which temporarily at least Dolly felt she did not belong.

Lily was forceful and busy. The shop was much brighter under her authority. It was well stocked with essentials and various new extras; Earl Grey tea, Frank Cooper's marmalade, salami as well as spam. The bakery had become almost incidental. The Post Office was what kept the backbone of regular customers. Sid was tired. He was thin and very stooped. In the mornings he still got up early to do the baking, which was far less than it used to be. There was less call for home-baked white bread, they all wanted sliced white, not a crisp loaf, but there was still some call for doughnuts and pastries. After baking Sid did the rounds, it was mostly pensioners on their own and some of the poorer families without transport. So many had cars these days, and as soon as they did they went in for bulk buying and the supermarkets. After tea at six or so, Sid just managed to stay awake for the news and weather, then he slept in front of the large black-and-white television set that was one of Lily's spoils from her last liaison. Lily was used to Sid's sleep and silence. She came and went as it suited her. She had changed the house; she altered the curtains and covers, they were more flounced, more frilled, china ornaments and decorated tea-towels abounded. Sid, like an old dog, picked his way past the china cabinets, new suites, and small round glass-topped tables. He was glad not to be alone; he was glad to be chivvied and coaxed and fed. Lily was a tower of strength; if life at the bakery suited her, it certainly suited him. There was a large framed school photograph of Dolly in the lounge. She looked bright and cheerful, full of sparkle, full of zip. That was how they liked to remember her. Sid had more or less forgotten the pain and horror of that summer night, with its glaring moon on the asphalt yard, and his own uncontrollable fury towards Dolly, because, as he thought afterwards, the pain in his heart for Ruth's life and death, that very day, had had no means to show itself. When Tug rang they were both pleased. Lily did remark that it was strange Dolly had not spoken to them herself. 'Maybe it was nothing,' Lily said, mentally preparing herself for anything.

Tug and Dolly took the train from Waterloo and then the bus. All the way down there, Tug went on about the shock it would be for them, that they should have warned them. But Dolly just stared out of the dirty windows, remembering various landmarks; the stations and the huge, Brookwood Cemetery. She felt protected by her condition. It put her closer to Lumsden, and apart from them. When they arrived in the village, Tug went ahead. She blurted it all out to Lily on the doorstep. Sid had been asleep. What he heard seemed like part of his dream . . . 'She's going to have a baby', Sid heard. 'The dad's done a runner, but Dolly's fine. She'll probably have it adopted.' Sid woke, thinking of Ruth and her sadness; her red lips and Dolly as an infant in her arms. As he came to the door, Lily turned to him and said, 'Brace yourself, Grandad!' Then Sid saw Dolly in the doorway. Her face looked thin and pale, and her coat, unbuttoned over the unmistakable full stomach, seemed old and worn. 'I'll put the kettle on, Lily,' he said. But he did greet Dolly first. He just said, 'You look tired, my girl, and no wonder . . . no wonder.' And he left it at that. He left Lily to do the rest; the questioning, the furious, stupid bluster about what buggers men were, 'if she could just get her hands on him, he'd soon know what was what . . .' In a way it was a relief to Dolly that all the anger was directed to the father. She couldn't imagine Lumsden anywhere near Lily, so the conversation didn't really seem to be about him. Dolly just drank the tea and ate the doughnuts, and thought how old Sid looked, and how unreal it was to visit a childhood home after a long absence. When they left, Lily gave Dolly twenty pounds, and a new nightdress she had, that was still in the bag from the shop. Obviously, while Dolly had been in the lavatory, Tug had led them to believe that there would be an adoption. Dolly couldn't think or feel that far ahead. But at least they had been quiet and kind; it helped to banish the ghost of that gimlet moon over the stark yard, it helped to soften that memory. It helped Dolly to realise that Sid was simply a rather stooped, sad man, not a devil or tyrant at all. On the journey back in the dark, Dolly thought how impossible it was to ever know a parent properly. That she herself was about to become a parent, seemed a mad, freak idea. She didn't really believe it. When there were kicks and heaves, when the rash over the tight skin of her stomach burnt into her with biting frenzy, so that she scratched herself until it bled, when any of these things happened, it just made her think of Lumsden; longing and hatred became confused into an unbearable pain, that seemed to collect, like storm water, in the live and powerful bundle of this life that led her now, minute by minute, towards the moment she dreaded; the moment of its expulsion from herself.

It was bitterly cold the night Tug made Dolly go into hospital. The waters broke. It was strange, although she had been expecting it, because they told her at the clinic, when it happened, it was like a fearful sign, a sign of doom, a sign of death. It was odd, but that was how she felt as she stomped down the wide hospital corridor. After the sharp, winter cold of the streets, and their own, clutching, damp kind of cold in their room, the hospital was unbearably hot. A suffocating, drying, empty heat, that was instantly exhausting. They put Dolly in a small side-room on her own. They told Tug that there wasn't much point in her waiting. 'Nothing much is happening yet, is it dear?' they said in their crisp, bustling, cheerful way. They helped Dolly to undress. Then they took her things. If you were going to the scaffold, they probably went on like this, Dolly thought. 'Hop into bed dear, then Doctor will come and examine you.' Hop was the very last thing Dolly could do. She wondered, as she heaved herself up on to the hard bed, she wondered if they said things like that on purpose. As for telling her . . . 'nothing much is happening' . . . that was as an understatement. It felt to Dolly like she was waiting to fall off the edge of the world, into a great ditch. She felt as if she was about to be rolled, utterly out of sight, by this pressing, trundle of power in her, that suddenly they were all calling 'Baby'.

'Do you want a baby boy or girl?' the nurse said, as she put this freezing cold, tin funnel object on Dolly's bare stomach. 'Dunno,' Dolly said. 'Baby's heart's fine,' the nurse said. 'Good and strong.' If Dolly thought heartbeat, she thought of Lumsden, not baby. But now, when she tried to think of Lumsden, she only heard his scornful, mocking laughter. 'Dreadful night, isn't it dear?' The nurse cast a last professional glance round the patient and the room. 'Well, there's not a lot going on, so we'll leave you for the moment. You've got your bell?' The bell was rubber. Everything seemed to be rubber. The hot red mat under the sheet, the floors, the nurses' shoes, gloves, their lips, their pushing, practical hands; all rubber. They left Dolly lying there on her back, staring up at this bare light bulb. She seemed to lie there forever. It was as if she had been taken and just dumped in this bright punishment place, where they kept saying 'nothing was happening'. And it was all her fault, it was her fault if nothing happened. Her fault if she rang the rubber bell and the doctor came, because she said there were strong pains, and then he found 'nothing really happening down below'. 'Down below' was hidden from Dolly. 'Down below' seemed to be no longer hers, just some painful squint hole for them to push and pry into, and then tick her off, for calling them unnecessarily. It was all pain to Dolly; the brightness, the stuffy heat, the arid, pit loneliness of it, with just this light bulb for company and peculiar sounds from the hot pipes that ran round the room.

It was hours later when they said, 'Good girl. Good girl. We're getting some good pains now.' Dolly was still lying on her back, staring at the bulb and various stains on the ceiling. During all the waiting time, huge, quiet tears had just rolled out of her eyes on to the pillow, it was now very damp. Doctor came. He peered and pushed with his rubber fingers, and then he said very cheerfully, 'Well, things are looking good down there . . . we'll soon be ready for business.' They didn't leave her alone for so long now. They kept popping back, very pleased that the pains were strong. They kept going on about 'baby'. Dolly felt that she'd never really been alone before. This was more 'alone' than anything. She held on to the cool metal bars of the bedhead when the pain was bad. She cried out. She moaned loudly, hugging the noise, because it seemed to be all she had. 'Well done,' they said. 'It won't be long now. Baby won't be long now.' Every time they said 'baby' Dolly felt resentful; she was afraid of that feeling, it was almost anger. Maybe it was only fear and pain and muddle. Tug had collected all these baby clothes in a plastic bag, and a few small blankets. Terrible bootees that were so bulky they looked more like boxing gloves. She was screaming quite a lot now. There was this feeling that she would be ripped, utterly blown apart; each pause to gather breath again was like a moment of panic in a chase when you know there is nowhere to hide. You have to go on. Then they trundled in this machine, these two cylinders, and they put this rubber mask over her nose. They let her hold it herself. It was the first friend, the first ally for so long. When she breathed in the gas, the pain, her voice, and their voices, it was all distanced, rather beautiful, as if everything was at last further away down some winding echoing corridor. Then it happened. At last it happened . . . 'Well done, good girl, good girl, push now . . . well done.' And there was this splitting whoosh, which was, so they said, 'baby's head', with, so they said, a mass of hair. Hair. That word was mixed up in Dolly's last giant push, and its pain. It was mixed up with her certain, dream feeling that this baby would, in some way, be Lumsden. Dolly was too tired by then to care much about anything. She felt emptied at last; emptied of all life; of all trying and hoping. Then it screamed. A shrill, jerking scream. Dolly was crying. The rubber faces and voices peered down on her smiling. 'It's a boy . . . my dear . . . a fine boy, with a wonderful head of hair.'

They propped Dolly up on pillows, and then they laid this strange, creamy, slippery thing, wrapped in a small cloth, they laid it in her arms. It still cried. It was a wild, frantic, gasping, animal cry. Dolly felt the anger in it. The warmth of her body and the definite feel of her breast and the shy nipple which the nurse pushed towards the soft red little mouth, all that seemed to console him. He grew quiet. Dolly felt his wet straggling hair against her arm. She was crying even as she held him. But they understood. They were sure they understood. 'Poor girl, going through all that on her own, it's only natural.'

They brought her tea and were generally comforting while they waited for the release of the afterbirth. 'Drink your tea in peace dear, we'll take him now.' And they lifted him up, like a rag doll on a totem pole. There was just the hair, and the bright red, wrinkled face, and the little square of coarse white cloth, and below it, pointing down, two little purple feet. He screamed again. 'Come on, little man, Mum needs a rest,' they said. But Dolly felt they were wrong. It screamed, not for her ... not for her at all. It screamed with anger at the horror of its birth. It screamed with an ancient pain that no one could console. It was a scream whose echo rang out in storms and deserts, in public crowded places, and in single staring faces. It was the scream of unbelonging. A scream thread, that scarred every life, in its certain preparation for death.

Dolly slept. Tug came. The baby slept. Everyone said, 'What's his name?' 'He's Spencer,' Dolly said, simply to stop them all asking. It was after the pub. Those thick gold letters which she read every day. Maybe it was after all pubs. And also, Dolly knew that Lumsden had said there was this poet called Spencer. He had told her that in the bar one day. The nurses thought of Spencer Tracy. Tug said it was a bit strange, it should be a saint's name. Tug was still hoping Dolly would come round to the idea of Catholic adoption. 'Bottle or breast?' they said. Dolly said bottle. She feared that damp, crumpled little mouth so close to her.

Tug was worried that Dolly seemed uninterested in the baby; she was so quiet, so different. But the nurses said, 'Give her time, it's only natural in the circumstances ... it's only natural.'

It didn't make much sense; that way you could say murder was only natural, or suicide, or gluttony, even necromancy. Maybe the unnatural things were more in order, more reasoned and understandable than the so called 'natural' things. Maybe they were all really one and the same. Maybe love was the odd one

out; the real triumph, if it could ever be found among the twists
and turns of all the rest.

*

Lumsden, oblivious to any role in life other than the pursuit of
his own pleasure, was becoming increasingly dependent on the
external stimulus provided by alcohol and other 'poppers' and
'puffers'. He was variously roused and soothed, euphoric and
despondent. The periods of despondency were uncomfortable,
a little too close to dark, to the depth and devouring mouth of
the nursery bag. The impulse, above all else, was to circumvent
despondency. The apparent heights and wonders various halluci-
nogenic drugs could release, became for Lumsden the central art,
the pivotal reality, from which the real freedoms of truth could
be discovered. Sensible crime, however lucrative, was a mean
bourgeois little business, involving plans, schemes, endless reasoned approaches. To discover the freedoms of created truth, the
real wonders of experience, one must let go of the contemptible
barriers of rote; times, days, all those useless barren structures of
the establishment; the whole frenzied post-war conglomeration
of commerce, nationalistic organisations that impose themselves
on the bewildered ever-present man or woman in the street.

It was usually a woman of considerable means, and with
property in extremely salubrious streets or unspoilt countryside,
that enabled Lumsden to pursue his life of simple, untrammelled,
devouring pleasure. He and Valentine did keep in touch, but
Valentine, although delighted to 'debauch' now and again, had
various successful commercial interests which he could not be
persuaded to neglect entirely.

Against this background, Tug's final discovery of Lumsden
was bizarre. Tug was in despair. No one seemed able to get any
sense out of Dolly. She showed little interest in the child. She
slept incessantly, even during Tug's visits to her. Very soon the

223

ten days at the hospital would be up. The almoner, the doctors and nurses all did their best, but they were busy people. The child was healthy; the mother was, in their view, naturally depressed. It was common enough in the circumstances, but without her consent no plans towards adoption could possibly be made, and the doctors had noticed that the only thing that roused Dolly to any kind of discussion at all was the idea of the baby being taken from her. From this they deduced that in spite of all the external lack of interest she showed, she must really care deeply for the child. 'Give her time,' they said. 'When she's home things will be different and the health visitor will keep a regular eye on things. Don't worry, my dear,' they said to Tug. 'He's a healthy, strapping little chap. He'll cope. He'll let people know what he wants.'

He certainly had a particularly shrill cry. Tug heard it ringing in her head each time she left the hospital. She could see him lying there; the puckered, crumpled red skin, and the mat of dark, strangely smelling hair running right down in thin strands on to his shoulders, the stiff ramrod way he seized up when he screamed, until he almost choked for lack of breath.

The Records Office, once a dull place of hassle and lost papers, became to Tug a wonderful, complacent environment. The silent filing-cabinets, the large leather-topped desks, the piles of very dusty cardboard files; all seemed to mirror the measured, careful, slow world that was so lacking in the hospital. If only an infant could be put in the 'pending' tray. If only human organisation could be as simple as that. During the long working day in Holborn Tug's desperation about Dolly and the child, and the great vacuum that seemed to surround them, drove her to focus all her fury and frustration on Lumsden. Only he could intervene. Only he could make Dolly wake up and register the situation. Surely he could be made to feel some measure of responsibility if Tug tracked him down. She tried directory enquiries.

On a windy night, her mac buttoned up to her neck, a bright-red knitted bobble-hat pulled down over her greasy hair, and broad working men's boots on her feet, she arrived at the address in Chelsea. She knocked and banged on a smart black door in Glebe Place, where the freshly painted wrought-iron railings glistened in the light which shone out from the windows in the room above. Heavily lined curtains muffled the sound of voices and laughter. Bloody people. She didn't give a fuck what they thought of her. As she stood there in the rain, swearing aloud and banging hard on the brass knocker, Tug became resolute and fearless. The curtains were pulled apart, various faces peered out; pearls and general *décolletage*, red lips and languid, forced shrieks of laughter. 'Wow, look it's a trendy troglodyte,' someone called out. 'Let's get the latest troglodyte news.'

Tug was ushered into the plush, showy room; huge floor cushions, a mass of candelabra, smoke and cigarette lighters, dotty feathers in people's hair, ridiculous bracelets and mad colourful paraphernalia. Faces and hands, twisting waists and long droopy arms converged towards Tug. They held their glasses ostentatiously as if they were pertinent talismans. Tug stood her ground, dripping dark wet spots on to the white carpet. Everyone was giggling. 'Love the hat,' someone said. There were more giggles. 'Where's Lumsden fucking Farr?' Tug yelled out. There was a pause, a rather subdued pause, as if the assembled group were trying to work out a more serious way to handle this extraordinary visitor. Then someone said, 'Lumsden fucking Farr, my dear, as you so accurately call him, is probably, even now, on the job.' Much laughter. 'Then just go and tell him he's a fucking father.' 'My dear,' the voice went on, 'what delightful news. A cause for celebration. You are not . . . surely, the proud mother?' More hysterical giggles. Then Lumsden came into the room. His hair was longer than Tug remembered it. He was wearing a strange, purple, rather eastern outfit that reminded Tug of a bad production of *The Desert Song* which she had once seen in Eastbourne. 'Miss Gant,' Lumsden said, amazed that he had remembered her name. It occurred to him that if there was ever any call for urban scarecrows then Tug would certainly qualify to be one. Through a haze of alcohol and much else Lumsden took some time to link Tug with Dolly. Then he did. And the immediate association after that was Neville Ponsonby. It was that association which made Lumsden nervous. It had rather grisly implications for him. For this reason, with surprising civility, he took Tug into another room where they could be alone. He offered her, of course, 'A drink?' She declined. She would not even unbutton her coat. 'Poor Mrs Noah,' Lumsden said. 'A disingenuous fool by birth and origin I'm afraid, but not without some robust qualities.' Tug intervened. She shook him. Her claggy, thick, furious face so close sobered Lumsden instantly. Tug threatened him with Neville Ponsonby and proceedings to be taken against him if he didn't co-operate. The name alone, on Tug's rough, uncivilised lips, was enough for Lumsden. What did she want him to do? Have tests? Acknowledge paternity, at least. That way, Tug felt, she could put real pressure on Dolly for adoption, because she might realise that there was definitely no mileage for her or the child from Lumsden; but at least the child would have an acknowledged father, for what it was worth. 'You don't have to see her, it would only make things worse,' Tug said. 'I hadn't the slightest intention,' Lumsden replied.

Virtually blackmailed by Tug, Lumsden agreed to the sordid little tests; men in white coats with test-tubes and things. Anything was worth avoiding a court case with Neville over the loss of sundry objects and funds. And there was something quite beguiling about the positive, indisputable germination of one's wild oats.

Lumsden did write a letter to Dolly after the outcome of the tests was positive:

'. . . What a blessing, Mrs Noah, that it wasn't a brace! Let the fellow be some pious family's novena miracle, I'm sure that would be best all round. But remember, Dolly . . . any port in a storm is a dangerous maxim! Sorry, I can't do better. No funds. No ties possible. No inclination for bricks and mortar, all that sort of thing. Good luck.' He signed it Lumsden Farr and in brackets (Noah now and again).

Lumsden felt his letter was rather good. It was in keeping with the *laissez-faire* cool he was cultivating. An uncommitting but human approach to everything. As Tug didn't get in touch with Lumsden, he assumed a good Catholic adoption had been organised. It rather amused him to imagine Violet's indignation if she ever realised she had a popish grandson! For the present, Lumsden assumed a rather remote difficulty had been adequately and quite appropriately dealt with. He had no reason to dwell on that summer saga, with its rather raw, unexpected wintery end. Many other events and dilemmas quickly superseded it. Fathers and sons was really outmoded, imperialist fantasy; the new truths of real brotherhood did not need the dreary edge of possession and hierarchy to determine responsibility. All is one and one is all. With these verbal gymnastics, Lumsden found himself free and flawless; so long as despondency was controlled.

As Dolly's body regained some semblance of its original bounds, her sense of herself seemed to diminish. She did not smell the same. She smelt those sour, milky, infant skin smells, in her hair and on her clothes. The night, which had been an asylum to her, however worrying and uncomfortable her mind and its moods might have made it, the night was now a frayed, disordered tunnel of jarring fragments. Fragments of deep sleep, fragments of screams, fragments of hopeless rocking tussles, with this small starfish creature and its continual discharge from either end of foul-smelling fluids and general mess. Sometimes when he slept she did stare at him. She even stroked the strands of dark hair with the tip of her finger. His face and upper chest were covered with angry little spots; tiny sprouting heads, as if the body as well as the spirit didn't know its proper use, was, all the way round, a wrong mixture. 'Milk spots,' they said. 'Don't overheat him,' they said. But the only thing Dolly could bear to do when he howled and struggled was to roll him tight in the woven white cotton blanket the hospital provided. She didn't want to see those broad, soft, little monkey fingers shiver up into the air like frightened hydra, desperate for attachment. Dolly did not want attachment, and yet when they spoke to her of his adoption; the great joy he might be for a childless couple, the quality of life he would have himself which she, simply on account of her age and circumstances, could not possibly give him, when they went on to her about 'baby's future', she could only sense the gnawing gap out of her reality that his departure would make. In some way, he pinioned her into a physical place. Without this, she doubted if she had any physical presence at all. It was as if her eyes, her arms, her feet, would have no gauge, no centre, and therefore no coherence. She could not express these feelings in words. She simply said like a small child . . . No . . . No . . . No . . . and buried her head in the pillow if anyone mentioned the subject of adoption.

Tug had to admit that the hospital had been very long suffering. They had let Dolly stay longer than usual. They hadn't been too brusque or bossy about dressing and walking about after her hot salt bath each morning. But the day Tug dreaded came, and despite all her attempts to achieve an alternative, Dolly and Spencer returned home in a taxi with Tug, and the three of them made their way up the dark communal staircase, to the top room and its gas-fire and cracked window and stained carpet. They had been lent and given various things; among them was a Moses basket, which they put inside the rickety, dropside cot. Tug had made a makeshift screen with an old towel-rail, to shade the baby from the light. She had done her best. She had even bought some daffodils; and her own present to Spencer, three flannel nightdresses from the market, on which in blue feather-stitch on the yoke she had embroidered the word *SPENCER*. It was something personal. Tug felt he needed that. Dolly seemed to hold him and change him as if he were not a real person at all; just sounds and limbs, a hopeless, restless contortion mistakenly demanding space and food, and endless attention.

The Spencer Arms gave Dolly four weeks off for a start, with reduced pay, but it was enough to keep things going. The health visitor on her first visit remarked 'how cosy' they were, 'how nice and high up, not too noisy'. On her subsequent visits, the smells, the general disorder of damp nappies, dirty bottles, condensation and piles of unwashed dishes in the sink and on the floor, the obvious chaos and overcrowding, made her suggest that Dolly and Tug should apply for a council flat. It would take some time, but with Spencer they would be a priority. They agreed and Tug gave up any more talk of adoption.

For Dolly the days were long, lonely affairs. She rarely got her clothes on before midday, and sometimes not even then. In a dream, she dunked the sticky, empty bottles in soapy water, then she boiled them, and then she made up the mixture of milk. Then she fed him. She would sit on her bed, her legs crossed, with him like a strand of cat's cradle between her knees. He had favourite teats that were too fast and others that were thick and dumpy and too slow. After the feed she would wind him, resting him up against her shoulder as they had shown her in the hospital. Sometimes as she did these various things, as she laid him on the towel, with the nappy pin in her mouth, as she stared down at the restless body, the lop-sided, dangling willy, that seemed out of all proportion to the rest, sometimes she cried, but mostly she was silent. It was as if his birth, that moment of expulsion and scream and life, it was as if it had dropped her into this automatic cage where there were no longer real feelings or sounds, just a pattern; a series of reactions for her hands to make. She was just this thing that moved into the spaces he made on her day. It was a relief to be able to be so close, and yet to hardly hear the cries. It was a relief to be able to block out the constant smell of this liquid shit, and the fine endless sprays of urine shooting out at odd angles over everything; it was a relief to move about among various objects and to hardly know the difference between the pillow and your own cheek, a bent knee and a rolled towel. It was a relief to do things without thought. To hear those gasping, choking, greedy noises, yards from your head, and yet not to hear them; by just lying still, almost frozen still, the sounds became a fossil pattern printed in the space just a fraction beyond the skin of the forehead.

The only thing was, as the days passed, as Dolly's movements became increasingly sluggish, the baby seemed to hunt out every particle of silence, every atom of air near its small, tormented circumference; he seemed frenzied to make the airless, silent, uncomfortable space around him respond to his presence. By the time Tug returned home, Spencer was exhausted. Tug fed him, nudging him against her bulky, comfortable body. Then she would put him down, with continuous chat, little pats and tucks and whispers of affection. Then he would sleep, as still as a lizard on a warm rock. 'Good as gold,' Tug would say. And Dolly would reply, 'You should have been here today.' Tug would laugh. She had no idea what a strange theatre of disjointed, brutal alienation she had missed. In the evenings, things seemed untidy, but normal enough. Tug had no idea what was really going on. In a sense Dolly knew. Dolly knew that each day made a cruel, wooden, angry shape around her; she knew about the pattern of these days and nights strung together; she knew it was a pattern of some force. Maybe, as the threatening movements of his choking screams and her unperturbed stares became more frequent, more pronounced, they almost combined, coagulated into this unseen, fixed battering ram. Dolly could almost feel it growing there. Taking up every space, every shadow, every fraction of objectless atoms, seen or unseen. Everything that was not a named, particular substance became this heavy, full, diabolically drenched thing. Dolly knew it was there. She knew in some way that she was making it, but she was not sure to whom it belonged. She knew that in the end it would become bigger than her or him. It would fill his screams. It would still his body. It would drown her. In some way it would shatter them both. Things would begin again. It was like sweeping the counters from the board or pulling the cloth from the table, it was like that; it was just cleaning a space, just forcing a gap. It was trying desperately to end something, in order to begin. But of course there were no real beginnings, simply interruptions, changed positions, changed focus; the extent would never be entire if mind kept pursuing a kind of control. The seemingly discarded thing was only altered, over and done with, an effect, the reaction to a cause. But the causes were so hidden. What was found could never be the full story. Dolly understood the giant emptiness of everything. She understood that living was lies, as it was told; but to dare to doubt its lies, surely that was to be mad. Madness was an understanding that didn't fit because its shape was so natural, so complete, so all embracing. All embracing, complete, was not how things appeared to want to be.

She said the word 'Mad', to her reflection in the small, cracked looking-glass above the sink. First she whispered it. 'Mad.' She watched her mouth; it knew exactly how to move. 'Mad.' She said it again and this time her eyes seemed to catch it. 'Madness.' 'My madness.' And this time, when she said 'my madness', she knew that the thing that had been building up everyday, coagulating and combining, she knew it was hers. It was a kind of tool, a kind of weapon. When it became too large, too huge and total, then something would happen.

It had been a bright day. The sky was an intense spring blue over the rooftops, the shadows were rich, the sparrows in the

gutters were particularly noisy. Dolly had just fed him. He
was laid back down in his cot; he had outgrown the Moses
basket already. His eyes were open, they trailed round the
room, the gaze never resting for long in one particular place.
His little fists punched the air and himself, until at last the
regular sucking sound on to his knuckles made Dolly realise
he might be settling down. She was sitting on the edge of the
bed. The cot was immediately opposite her. The carpet was a
scatter of nappies, clothes, plastic-bags and scuffed strands of
cotton-wool. Something about the blue sky and the sound of
the sparrows made Dolly think of the spring, and then summer;
it was as if an old freedom calling her name was creeping in from
the light outside, like a gentle spin of smoke from a bonfire. She
had been in this cage of non-being for so long. She had grown
used to the bland, thick, dull feeling of namelessness. She stared
down at her feet; they were small feet, with tight, crunched-up
toes, the end ones red and raw from being constantly forced
into tight, pointed shoes. She moved the toes up and down. She
moved them again. It was almost as if they might make some
little sound of herself, towards herself. They might greet her.
They might acknowledge who she was. By looking down like
this, from her eyes to her toes, there was a line made, a link.
She sensed that private thread which bound the lost scope of
herself. She was there, there within it; but somehow she must
break the bounds.

Then she looked up from her feet, she looked slowly towards
the cot, the chipped cream paint, the dirty smudge marks down
the thin bars. He was kicking hard. The blankets were tossed
up, flung about shapes; they didn't contain him. Then he looked
sideways through the bars. He looked towards her. He looked
very directly. The eyes seemed too large in his head. The nose
was small, flattened, the nostrils soft and spread apart; the lips
were pursed, they were making little jabbing, wet noises. The
lips seemed to address her while the eyes held back from doing

so. She stared at him. She had often stared at him like that before, but she had always managed to have empty eyes; eyes that didn't really see or engage in any kind of thought with the object within their sights. Now, maybe it was the bright light and the noisy sparrows, now she looked at him with all the drab, tired, dumped sound of herself. In some way, she wanted to hear her name. She wanted to be in a position to answer a call. She wanted to be a reaction; to be a moving creature like the sparrows in the gutters, not just a body in this tense, combined, blunder space, she had filled against him. His eyes grew still towards her, more intent than usual. She had learnt so well how not to see him when she stared; but this time she wanted to gather up this solid, drenched power they had made between them, she wanted to have it there in her eyes, she wanted to confront him with it. She crossed the room. She crouched down beside the cot, her hands outstretched, holding on to the thin, flimsy bars. She was his mother; the weapon, the power, was her. It had been dragged up out of her. It was entrails and force and blood. It was old. It was caked and pitted with other times. It was a gorgon's head. It was the gimlet moon grown bold and cheesed and lumped into every edge of her.

It is hard to break an internal silence that has escaped from its private buried moorings and then taken hold of an every day external space. The baby paused from its sucking. He stared at Dolly's short hair; pale spikes, up and out and round the full, circular form. He put his hand out vaguely towards her hair. But he had no control of it, it jerked backwards towards himself.

Dolly gripped the bars of the cot as if they were rungs of a ladder on which she must climb upwards. She held them hard, as if to gather from them some kind of strength or certainty with which to proceed. He gurgled, little bubbles of clear, bright, mouth water, flowing up over his chin. The bright light from the window was a great gash of warmth on her back, on the floor and the carpet, on the bundle of dirty clothes, and on the flung blankets, and the baby's round, pushing knees and little stabs of feet.

It might have been a moment of nothing that passed between them. The warmth of the sun certainly, with its full, wide awake, fresh morning disposition, it might have dowsed the fierce, sharp voice that in some way Dolly wanted to hear. She must have held the bars tighter than she knew. Her breathing was laboured and heavy, as if her whole body was in preparation for some onslaught, some peak action. Because of this, she must have shaken the side of the cot; suddenly it shook loose from the small metal clasp and shuddered down on to the floor. It was a loud, brutal, unexpected crash sound, surprising them both. The baby screamed. The scream was instantly there, with the sound of the crash, and the barrier of frail bars fallen from between them. His cry of panic broke into the thick, coagulated, blunder space, hurling the stiff, suffocating lumps of soundlessness into live, piercing fragments.

Then Dolly heard her voice. It drowned the sparrows. It pitted itself against the baby's scream.

'Don't! Don't!' she yelled. 'Shut up! Shut up shut up – shut up!'

She was standing over him, casting him entirely into darkness. Her body was directly between him and the light from the window. She was still yelling at him, but the sound of her voice only raced the tempo and strength of his own screams. She picked him up. She put her hands under his armpits, her thumbs pressing down on to his chest. She shook his head, close at her own; the two mouths were almost touching in a terrible adulterated unison.

Desperately he jerked his head backwards, as if he would throw his eyes out of himself to escape her mouth and frenzy so close to him. But her fingers pressed sharply back against his neck, so that he had no escape.

All the sounds in the room, all the violent, frenzied rage, driving

234

and being driven by the same bitter punch of dislocated need; it fed on its own disorder. With dervish intensity the two voices, and their rootless pathetic squall of leavened sorrow, rose and fell unchecked by any sense except small escapes from sound, for breath, to gather up and increase the momentum.

In the many days of numb silence and automatic movements, Dolly had hardly known who she was, or what, or why she moved; now she seemed to sense that she was breaking back into herself.

Still holding him like a lump of mandrake earth she had wrenched up out of the pit of their space together, she jumped on the spot. She ran about the room, pouncing into small spaces and then leaving them. She huddled in between the wardrobe and the wall, then she ran fast over the steaming patched sunlight on the dirty carpet. She ran to the window. She held him up over the sink. She shook him at his own reflection in the cracked mirror. Then she turned him back towards herself and shook him again.

Finally, she took the drenched, now almost dismembered weapon of their combined stillness, she took it up into her voice, into her arms, into herself. She climbed into the close, fractured skeleton of this perturbing baton, for which she was not ready or prepared. This baton flag of 'mother'. She had seized it on a false premise, more to furnish herself with being than to furnish another with the strength of becoming.

'Shut up! Spencer. Spencer. Please. There's no one here. We're alone. You have to hear me. You have to . . . You have to. You have to.'

They were both exhausted. The early brightness had gone from the sky. The room was back to its cluttered, shadowy self. She threw the child down on the divan bed, where he looked like some beached creature, breathless from a ruthless tide, and now banished among deposits of blankets, towels and the crumpled worn fringe of a grey sheet. Then for an instant he was still; very still. His mouth was open but motionless. His eyes seemed fallen back under the lids, the pupils rolled about in the little white clouds of moist tissue as if unattached. Dolly herself froze at the sight of him so motionless. She fell down on the bed beside him, and she cried. She cried from feelings of herself, feelings she understood. There was a strong pulse beating in the small neck. He was not dead. She ran to the sink. She turned on the cold tap, cupping her hands beneath the flow of clear water. The water seemed like a guardian angel. Dolly marvelled that from such a simple command as one slight, right angled turn, there was cold water flowing towards them both, to gather them back into the world of speech and time.

Dolly threw the cold water on his face. He flinched. She threw it again. He sniffed. His whole frame shuddered. Then the small bruised chest rose and fell. Dolly sat down on the bed beside him; she gathered up all his frail bewildered strangeness into her arms. She wound him gently in a shawl and holding him very close to her cheek, she rocked him to and fro.

'Spencer. Spencer. Little Spencer. Please, please forgive me. Please,' she whispered, and as she did so she let her lips brush gently against his cheeks and forehead and the sticky, dark mass of his hair. He made soft hidden little sounds, and then very soon he slept. When he slept deeply and the rhythm of his breathing was definite and assured, she got up and walked slowly in the narrow space between his cot and the bed. Then she walked up and down between the sink and the small Formica table. She even sang to him. The only tune that came into her head was the chorus from 'Who killed Cock Robin?' 'All the birds of the air fell a sighing and a sobbing when they heard of the death of poor Cock Robin . . . when they heard of the death . . . of poor Cock Robin.' Then she hummed the tune and watched the sparrows in the gutter.

The sun had moved on from their room. It was quite without sunlight now. It was altered. The drenched, solid power they had built between them had been dispersed. The spaces were empty. The objects were ordinary. When Tug came home she found Dolly asleep in the chair with Spencer in her arms. She thought how childlike Dolly seemed, but how crumpled and 'old manish' Spencer looked. His face was crushed in against Dolly's neck, the shawl had left a red pattern mark on his cheek. He was a thin baby. We must get him out into the sun, Tug thought, when he gets more chubby that old man look will leave him.

Soon after this, Dolly returned with Spencer to work in the pub. While she was in the bar, Spencer slept in the backroom. He was made a great fuss of. He was changed and fed and rocked by a great variety of people. He began to smell of the large, overfed Alsatian bitch, Lady, who lived on the premises, and he smelt of cigarettes and other pub smells, and the Johnson's talcum powder that Dolly sprinkled liberally over him to camouflage, and cast out a little, some of the other smells. It seemed, to all those casually concerned, that Dolly was coping. Only Tug remained uneasy, but she kept ahead of her, as the next goal, the great hope of Dolly being given a council flat. Dolly was certainly bothering with herself once again. Her nails were painted. Her hair was peroxided. Behind the bar she was the cheerful, chatty, outgoing person they had always known.

SIX

After that first pith spat slide into the glaring lights, the huge hands, the masked faces, the druid gowns, Spencer was like a summer insect, who, hatched out of season, cannot find natural sanctuary. With animal intent he searched for the responses he needed. In the rocking conditions of warmth and liquid and echoing even sounds, in that quiet white blindness of his mother's womb, he had no inkling of the cruel scarab roll, the headlong, brutal plunge he would have to make into the world. Birth; the slurry rush of a daunted, breathless creature into this wide, bewildered, jack-man tide of people; every kind of growth and emptiness, it was an unimagined, unasked for destiny.

The sense of mind and purpose, however skilful physicality manages to be in orchestrating the various organs into a fully flexed, united whole, still the meaning, the complete purpose, if any, of this full nature, remains a mystery. If the long lived are troubled, daunted, or inspired by this mystery, it is not surprising that a fresh fragment should be seen to be fragile, untaught, plagued simply by instincts, threads of command that seem to bewilder, even contradict. Within seconds of that first summary expulsion, even while still connected to the womb, this conglomerate of flesh and bones and panic must breathe. It must take in the dirty, tired gift of oxygen and all the rest, and then from that instant it must not cease that small metronome whisper of breath. With the breath, the life.

Spencer, born on a day of considerable cold in mid-winter in England, was one among millions. At first unnamed, he struggled for warmth, response and nourishment like all the rest. Just like all the rest, there were complex strands of other lives that were marching shadows in the making of his effect; in the making of himself. The name that was nothing to him for so long, just a sound in the minds and mouths of others, it gradually became a kind of standing and identity in the general emptiness. It could be scripted on to files. It could be registered on forms where it must be followed by the word male, because of the small, sideways little red organ that lolled about down there towards the wide limbs either side of it that were thighs. All of this was of course natural, obvious and commonplace. The birth was registered. Spencer Frampton was indisputably born. But there were other strands that had no obvious name, strands of trouble and fear and deeper being that came on thick and fast in an attempt to follow the instincts, and make safe the fragile sum of this small, working, unimagined life.

He sucked. He swallowed. He slept. He screamed. He defaecated. He urinated. He was normal in all these things. They were expected of him. But they were not anything like the full extent. They were not a description of the whole experience. Even those first breaths, the first suckle, the first scream and sleep; they were not the whole experience. Already the experience was complex. All people could do was handle and guide the housing of the experience. This housing of the experience known as 'baby' hid the experience itself. Just as later the 'boy' body hid the experience itself as it made the outer life manifest.

Spencer was six weeks old when his mother, overburdened by the reality of himself and its ancient reference to her as mother, his major perpetrator, his major cause; he was six weeks old when she shook him after spasms of choking and screams and flung him down on her unmade bed. He was six weeks old, a length of time in which already his yearning for touch and warmth and quiet shaded constancy had been repulsed. He was six weeks old when his small, bruised, exhausted body on his mother's low divan bed stiffened into a spasm, convulsed almost into a real length of pertinent breathlessness. He was six weeks old when a huge smooth skin shape, with two live sockets of eyes and a moving soft slit that spilt breath and sound towards him and other smells he knew; he was six weeks when this shape overwhelmed his fear and struggle as it came too close, and in that same second a giant noise stunned the frame of his senses with its crashing, sharp, alien, unknown sound, as the cot side fell to the ground. He was six weeks old when for the first time, with childish longing and tenderness, his mother folded the small extent of him close into her cheeks, into her deepest bounds. He was six weeks old. He was an illegitimate baby boy in a cold damp room in a high house, whose broken, rusted gutters were full of bright, deft, energetic sparrows.

He would not cease to grow in some measure; to learn, to need, to long, but the manner such things were manifest depended to a great extent on the hidden experience. The hidden experience was like a song, a dance, its nature was intense, its capacity limitless because its room was beyond the housing body. Its root was in the mystery and the mystery was by its nature unconfined.

The council offered Dolly a flat. It was above a run of small shops, which was very convenient. It was not high up and there was a good broad walkway balcony out at the back. There were regular buses, and not far away a small public park and in the other direction, the river. Dolly was delighted. But Tug had been offered promotion if she went away on this course. She helped Dolly to settle in. She made sure the neighbours were pleasant people, which they were, with kids and dogs and prams. The

Spencer Arms gave Dolly the loan of a van and driver for the move. They were most affectionate but they felt it was better for Dolly to be with Spencer now, full-time, because he really wasn't a baby anymore, he was a toddler, a real boy and into everything just as a boy should be. So Dolly was on her own. Everyone realised it wasn't ideal, but it wouldn't be that long before Spencer would start at playgroup and then school. 'You'll get to know the other mums,' they said. 'Then, once he's at school, come back in the bar, you'll always be welcome.'

But the dance without movement or call became pressed down, static, coal lumps of impending fire; and the song was mute, simply dumb, stacked sounds; it became brute thick without the warmth and flight of the tune.

The council flat was a fair size, but the lack of furniture, any ornaments or cushions and only the most meagre carpeting, made it seem larger than it was. Without Tug, her homecoming each evening, her general energy and bustling activity at weekends; without it Dolly and Spencer's life together had no particular shape. The days of the week or the times of the day were not important, there were no mealtimes or bedtimes; only the small black-and-white television set, the bleat of weathermen and newscasters through the grey snowstorm of poor reception, gave any sense of time to the day and its random interruptions of milk and rusks, tinned baby food, chocolate bars and cups of coffee. Dolly felt the shapelessness of things coming towards her like a giant mouth. She felt the approaching presence once more of the cage.

Spencer was fairly sturdy on his feet; he had a quaint, rather unbalanced way of walking, a kind of starfish sway, with his long arms outstretched, and the hands, frequently puffed and blue with cold even in quite mild weather, turned downwards, like flat fish pegged out in a space. He had a large head; it seemed out of proportion to the thin angular body. His hair was long and thick and tightly curled. If Dolly made any attempt to wash or brush it, Spencer screamed hysterically, so it remained a sticky, tight mass on the scalp, smelling of food and urine and sour milk. He seldom smiled. Only the fat Alsatian bitch, Lady, at the Spencer Arms was assured of a smile. Whenever she had waddled towards him and had lain her dry cracked nostrils on his tummy or shoulders, he had smiled. 'He really loves that dog,' they would say. And day after day it seemed he did. He pulled her ears, put his fingers through the mat of hair, poked and pressed at her; always she remained calm and steady as if she absolutely understood the language of his attentions. 'He'll miss Lady,' they all said. Dolly had no way of knowing whether he did or not.

Dolly was fearful to know him. Every close contact with him when they were alone together seemed to leach her; his very touch, the weight of him if he fell against her, the scrabble of him trying to get on to her knee or into her bed, seemed to threaten her, to accost her. She would push him back from her with increasing ferocity. When simply his presence became too much for her, she would keep him shut up in the small bedroom, while she sat alone biting her nails and smoking cigarettes in front of the flickering black-and-white television screen. The neighbours either side of her were noisy. Doors banged. Loud pop music played. There were shouts; children's fights and arguments, and then parents yelling out fierce orders and swearing commands. All their noise made Dolly even more aware of the long silences in her life. There was very little speech between her and Spencer. Silences would build up, until finally some small irritation would make her slap him; she would shout and he would scream. When he screamed, she would lock him in the bedroom. These repeated episodes took on a pattern from which they hardly ever deviated. The slap, the scream, and then the silence. At first, Dolly tried to make sure that they went out at least once a day. Spencer in the pushchair, herself behind him, out of his sight. In the shops;

at the post office and the small supermarket checkout, she was cheerful, full of talk and smiles. She had to hear the sound of her own voice speaking to someone at least once a day. She needed their looks towards her and their actual replies; such small phrases as 'Thanks love' or 'Will that be all?' 'You haven't got the penny have you?' became possessions she treasured and took back with her to the bleak emptiness of the flat. She never realised what a pale, withdrawn, listless child Spencer seemed to casual passers-by who happened to glance down at him in the pushchair. To Dolly, he was naughty, wild, rude, unruly, the dirty perpetrator of foul smells, spilt food and soap powder; he was like some festering splinter in the last fragile remnant of herself. She couldn't look towards him and see him simply for himself. She never saw a child. She saw the ugly mat of hair, the filthy face, she smelt his dirty nappy; it was always his needs, his threats, the ruthless intrusion of his demands, demands she could not satisfy because their satisfaction seemed to Dolly to mean the complete severance of herself from any kind of being in her own right.

There was a young fellow in the greengrocer's beside the supermarket who had a soft spot for Dolly. He was full of jokes and cheerful patter. He let her have things at special knockdown prices. He always put an extra potato or carrot or apple in, over and above the weight paid for. She started going down to the pub with him. It was called the Feathers. It was a more down-market pub than the Spencer Arms, but it was friendly. Dolly felt safe in there with the smoke and chat, the old men and the fat women, the salesmen and the site workers. She very soon became one of the regulars. They greeted her with a nod, a wink, a 'Hi Dolly'; it was the only real experience outside the caged and derelict emptiness of her life with Spencer. That life became increasingly like some cupboard stuffed with clothes and bulky items that have no purpose, but cannot for some reason be thrown out. But the cupboard door would not close, it kept creaking open, and the bulging ugly unwanted organs of these banished things would fall out again and again, demanding to be taken up and bothered with, or to be banished once again behind the door that would never really close.

Dolly left Spencer increasingly alone. In the mornings she fed and dressed him later and later. His pattern of demands began to alter. He cried less often. He cowered when Dolly came towards him. He learnt to turn his head defiantly from any mug or full spoon of food offered to him. He would not eat. The extent of his self expression was denial, refusal, silence. Then every so often he would suddenly, for what would seem to be no apparent reason, he would suddenly tear an object to shreds; a magazine or book or newspaper. Or he would throw a bowl of food he had refused to eat earlier, he would throw it in systematic slow drips on to the floor. In this way, he roused Dolly to the kind of bouts of physical fury that were really his only intimate contact with her now; the only occasions when he might be bodily held.

Dolly justified her nightly visits to the pub as a little life of her own to which she was entitled. The extent of her drinking was something she slipped into gradually. With each bout of drinking, the painful numb cage seemed to soften, to recede a little. She was less contained by it. There were gaps in the hard edges; there were jokes and laughter down in the pub, and there was real forgetfulness. There was even the odd night when a fellow might come back with her. Then she felt a woman in her own right, not a bloody mother. But in the cold, head-splitting light of late morning, the wingeing of Spencer, his bare bottom, his extremities blue with cold, his face pale as lard, would send her straight down the street for milk, cigarettes and a bottle of wine from her meagre funds; benefit money and occasional contributions from Tug or Lily. If the fellows came back, they usually left her gin or vodka. Spencer was like a wandering ghost figure who inhabited the hinterland of her senses. Many of the screams and knocks and confrontations she would not even remember.

Occasionally, she made visits to Sid and Lily. They found the child strange. He was unfriendly. He never responded to treats or presents. Lily had to admit he was an odd-looking nipper. In fact, the organisation of his face and limbs seemed uneven, a real job-lot mixture, with little co-ordination. His distant demeanour; he continually turned his back if he was being spoken to, all of it added up to an unsympathetic and extraordinarily ugly child. 'Those fish eyes,' Lily said, 'they'd haunt me. They're not the eyes of a child, no way.' But of course they were the eyes of a child. But a child who had to find some manner to contain within himself, within his small limbs and frail person, the stench, the refuse of all the attempts he had made to extend, to proceed, to find, which had always been instantly rebuffed and returned to him. Unable to receive, he would stagnate; he would stagnate with all the experiences, the sights and sounds and senses he could not give, buried into the little, dump housing of himself. Without exchanges, he was hidebound. Without movement for the dance, or tune for the song, he was a thin staring child that did not engage either sympathy or much notice from outsiders. More and more the things which engaged him had to be anything over which he had both access and control. The dirt and spit and biscuity gunge that gathered in the space between his cot mattress and the board beneath it. His own shit; free, soft stuff, ready to smear and make great curls and swings of shape on the walls, on books and papers, on any smooth surface available.

Dolly's drinking increased and with it her neglect of Spencer. His behaviour became so extreme, so anti-social that it seemed to justify in Dolly's mind anything she might do to attempt some kind of control and check on the child's peculiar, unnatural, savage ways.

Tug had taken a job in Manchester. She kept in touch. She

sent bright, cheerful clothes and colourful toys and picture books. On the telephone Dolly sounded cheerful. She seemed to Tug to have made some kind of life for herself. There were several women in the other flats with whom Dolly had a nodding acquaintance, but their own insurmountable problems; financial worries, unemployment, unruly teenagers, violent and abusive husbands, made them blind to this pert, peroxided young woman and her thin pale child.

Every so often something Spencer did would push Dolly towards greater violence. She rarely thought of Lumsden but sometimes she would pass in the street young men with the same kind of arrogant refinement. Then she would remember herself and the sunlight that had poured into the pretty rooms at the lodge. The brightness of it all, the slow clean pace of everything, the free fresh flowers, the early morning birds. Then she might look at the bruised body of Spencer, his pale taut skin, the spots, the red marks, and some understanding of her own part in the dilapidated nightmare of their world together might grip her. In her mind then, the battering sound of rain on corrugated tin would become the sound of vast and constant retribution to herself, like the thrashing smite of Sid's belt on her own body; the beating sound anyway of some kind of punishment for the mess that she carried with her night and day, but would never understand.

Sometimes, in the good weather, Dolly would walk for miles, street into street into street; the full, bustling, loud urban landscape made them both smaller, more insignificant; ordinary pedestrians. At a road crossing or on a park bench or staring into the bright interior of a shop window, they were a part of life without having to be named or responsible. But once they returned to the flat, only the drink could divide them from each other. It was the numb no-man's-land on which Dolly came to depend.

Spencer was two-and-a-half when Tug returned to London. She was stunned and horrified by the sight of the little boy. Dolly had done her best, dressing him purposely in the bright clothes Tug had sent him, but the cheerful clothes only served to make the staring pale face more pathetic than ever.

'He's too thin, Dolly,' Tug said.

'He won't eat.'

'Has the doctor seen him?'

'He's had his jabs and things.'

'But recently, has the doctor seen him recently?' Tug persisted.

'What could a doctor do?'

'Give advice maybe.'

'Advice. Advice. How fantastic. What a bloody helpful thing that would be.'

Tug realised she mustn't push Dolly too far, not at first anyway. But there was no getting away from the fact that the child was an under-nourished, neglected disaster.

'But you do need help, Dolly.'

'Do I? Do I really? What a revelation. This city is full of miserable shit-eating children who drive their battered bloody mothers insane. Do you know that? Well, the doctors do. They don't want their clean, well-organised surgeries to be fucked up with people like me. I'm just an unmarried mother. It's a kind of disease. A very expensive disease for everybody else apparently. They don't want to know if we're fucked up or not.'

'Dolly, why didn't you tell me things were so bad. I'd have come down, you know I would.'

'And what would you have done? Given off a little lecture, I suppose, and a good scrub of Domestos all round. And got a little slip from the doctor for Haliborange. It's a fuck up, Tug. I know that. Of course I do. He's not a baby. He's not a toddler or a boy. He's bad, Tug. He's bad. You don't know, you haven't been there. You haven't seen him tear things, throw things, destroy the place. You haven't heard his yells or cleaned up his bloody mess. He hasn't crawled into you, like some bloody maggot, night and day, nibbling at your body and your mind. He's not pathetic, Tug. He's powerful. He doesn't do anything he's told; he just fights or hides or stares. Normal children aren't like that. He's freaky. Come and stay. Come and see for yourself.'

Tug let Dolly rant on. Then she left her. She went into the kitchen, which was piled high with dirty clothes, congealed, burnt saucepans and unwashed dishes. Then Tug found the bottles under the sink, and more in the airing-cupboard, and she understood. But how to act on her understanding? She went back into the room. Spencer was lying on the floor, he was spitting on to the carpet and then licking the spit back again into his mouth. He seemed quite oblivious to his mother's voice, and her tears. The television was on, some panel game. Every so often Spencer went up to the set and put his lips against the screen. Each time he did it, Dolly pulled him back.

'Don't do that, Spencer. Spencer. Don't do that. It's dangerous. I've told you before. I've told you a thousand times. Spencer.'

Quite oblivious to her, the child moved forward and back to the television, a little run and then a staring pause, and then he would lick the screen. Dolly would get up and slap his bare legs, and then his face. He turned towards her, as she dragged him across the floor; his mouth contorted as if he might cry, but he remained silent. Then Dolly let him alone. He crawled away from her and went under the small Formica table. He lay there like a dog in a basket, curled up with his knees at his chin. Then he sucked his thumb and tugged on his willy, knocking his head forward and back against the leg of the table.

'Look at him. Look,' Dolly said. 'That's not normal, is it? Is it?'

'I don't know too much about children,' Tug said, remembering her own childhood of games and dares and laughter.

Tug realised she must do something. She couldn't have him herself, even if Dolly would agree to it. She moved in with them. She thought it best to begin with. She would get to know Spencer, maybe gain his confidence. Even if they took him into care, he wouldn't stand a chance as he was.

Dolly reacted to Tug's return to them by going out every evening and coming back later and later. She seemed careless to any kind of pride about herself. It was worse than anything Tug had imagined. The child remained resolutely distant, although he did begin to eat what Tug left out for him. She cleaned things up considerably. She even managed to wash his hair. He screamed throughout the operation, fighting Tug all the way, but he slept well afterwards and the next morning he even let Tug take a brush to it. The spots and sores, the bruises, the general overall condition of his body definitely improved. But Tug realised that these were only surface things. The child couldn't remain with Dolly; it was out of the question. If she got him into care it would take some time, and it would mean proving Dolly's negligence which she was loath to do.

Gradually, as Tug cared for Spencer, she noticed the strong likeness to Lumsden in his looks. Mostly it was the large eyes and the dark curly hair. He said few words: No, Don't, Shut up, and Fuck off, but something in the way he spoke reminded her of his father. It made Tug think of the way Lumsden had always managed to cop out of everything. But he'd gone on so much about his bloody family; maybe she should approach them?

With help from the local Catholic priest, who was Irish, she checked out Lumsden's address in Ireland. When she read the words . . . Farr, Rathmanagh, Ballynaule, Nr Claggan, Co Tipperary, she recognised it as the place Dolly said Lumsden had often spoken of, with its grand stables and grounds. She wrote to the parish priest in Ballynaule, and it wasn't long before she had a reply.

Father Bohane had, naturally, a nodding acquaintance with both Cecil and Violet Farr. Father Bohane was a quiet contemplative man, unlike his predecessor. By nature he was shy; public events, fund raising, school and hospital committees were not something he enjoyed. But he was well liked. In times of real stress he was a great support. People felt him to be someone of real sanctity and spiritual wisdom. They felt that his quiet ways and retiring character hid a man of great strength and deep kindness. Although he disliked argument and confrontation of any kind, he would never avoid an issue if there was any real Christian principle at stake. He had a great love of his fellow men. He was sure that there was no soul, however far gone in grace he might seem, there was no soul on this earth impervious to the great love of God, in which all created things were held. The love of God is yours, he would say, you have only, quite simply, to accept it.

Father Bohane had heard of the rather summary departure from Ballynaule of young Lumsden Farr. It was a story that lost nothing in the telling. But in spite of various lurid details that did come to his ears, he knew that the overall feeling in the parish had been in sympathy to some extent with this young man, who had been exposed to so much so young by being sent as a small boy to a school in England. Many people found Violet Farr a distant and rather arrogant woman, but no one doubted her intelligence and her considerable ability when it came to horse-riding, raising animals or running the estate. Both Donal and Maura, who worked full time at Rathmanagh, felt that the reserve, which was part of Violet's personality, was in a way a defence. As Maura said, 'There are times, Father, when a woman can be too strong for her own good.' She had known Lumsden as a small boy although she wasn't working up at Rathmanagh at the time. He had been a lively, cheeky child, full of spirit. She must, Maura always insisted, she must in some part grieve the loss of him. Because loss it was. Lumsden had not been seen in the village since his departure. And there were no photographs, nothing up at the house, to remind them of him. In a way he was more than dead to them, so it seemed. It was a mystery to both Donal and Maura, a mystery that two such lonely people would increase their loneliness by losing touch with their one and only child. It was a great sadness throughout Ireland for many families that the lack of employment forced so many young men and women to make their lives in other countries, but the Farrs did not have that problem. They were wealthy people. For them the loss of contact with their son must be a choice; it was certainly not a necessity. Naturally enough people wondered, as Cecil Farr became increasingly old and frail, if the boy would not come home to run the estate. Although no one could imagine his mother giving him an inch of authority until she was well and truly dead and buried.

It was against this background that Father Bohane received a desperate and unexpected letter from Teresa Gant concerning the life and whereabouts of a small boy called Spencer Frampton who was, so the letter said, the son of young Lumsden Farr, and so consequently the grandchild of Violet and Cecil Farr up at Rathmanagh. The letter enclosed two photographs of a small, thin child standing by some railings. The child had a mass of dark hair and very large eyes. He looked to Father Bohane more like a traveller's child than anything else. He showed the photographs to Donal and Maura. Maura instantly affirmed that about the eyes and hair there was a definite look of Lumsden. It was a great surprise to Maura, and also a considerable joy, that apparently the little lad's mother was a Catholic so the child had been baptised, so the letter said. 'Well, dear God, at least he has that one blessing, that one grace, poor little thing, it looks as if he badly needs much else besides,' Maura said. She had raised five of her own. Her heart went out to the poor creature who by rights, in Maura's view, belonged here in Ballynaule if there was no place else suitable. Donal shared the view that indeed the parish should feel some kind of responsibility towards the lad, who seemed unwanted by either of his parents, if the letter was true, and it sounded genuine enough. But Donal felt it would be a very hard thing, if not impossible in the circumstances, to raise the matter with Mrs Farr. Father Bohane was grateful to share the problem with both Maura and Donal who were so much closer to the family than he was. He thought the most important thing immediately was to give the poor girl Teresa some support; it was good of her to take the matter so to heart. Father Bohane said he would pray about it. He had a very particular devotion to Saint Francis. He was sure that the saint would guide them. In the meantime, Maura prepared a parcel of clothes and toys which Father Bohane sent off to Teresa Gant with his letter. He also enclosed twenty-five pounds from the parish funds. It was not so much, but it would help, and most of all it would demonstrate to this girl that she was not alone with the problem.

Tug received the letter and parcel with surprise. It was such a prompt reply. Tug was alone with Spencer when the post came. She wished that there was some way she could let the poor child know that there was this faraway place where people wanted to know about him. A place where people felt he belonged. Tug tried to imagine Ireland. She had only seen postcards. She had never been there. She knew it was a beautiful place, with lakes and mountains, donkey carts and small stone cottages. As the horrors of life with Dolly and the child increased, the vision of Ireland's peace and gentleness grew in Tug's imagination. In the jungle of inner city life, where and how could a child like Spencer survive? Once he was taken into care, he would simply be moved from place to place, foster home or institution; how would he ever find himself? He was just one among so many, that was the terrible thing. Tug felt pretty sure that Dolly, as well as everything else, was 'on the game', to all intents and purposes.

She went out every night. She had more or less abandoned the child, knowing that Tug would make sure the basic things were done for him. But it was always a worry for Tug trying to imagine what went on during the day when she was at the office. When Tug returned to the flat more often than not Spencer was lying on the floor under the table. If anyone tried to speak to him, he would close his eyes and shake his head and make for the nearest wall, and, like a criminal about to be frisked, he would press his face against the hard wall surface, his thin arms spread-eagled either side of him. He whined less often. He seemed to have given up any attempt to communicate. But every now and again, in the middle of the night, or suddenly while he lay on the floor, he would start to howl. He would throw back his head and make this wild, strange, hyena sound. If Dolly was there it drove her berserk. Tug was afraid then for them both; but if Dolly was drunk enough she would usually give up on him, once she had shut him into the bedroom on his own.

Several letters passed between Tug and Father Bohane in Ballynaule. It was the only slight comfort Tug had, this chance to share with someone else the horrors of life with Dolly and Spencer. When Tug sat down at the small Formica table with a Biro in hand and sheets of yellow paper from the Records Office, she felt as she wrote that she was literally throwing out a line; a rope from a dark pit or mine-shaft towards these real, kind, waiting people. She tried to imagine them in her mind's eye. As well as Father Bohane, there was Maura and Donal. They apparently both worked up at Rathmanagh and knew Mrs Farr. The letters made very little of Mrs Farr. Father Bohane had simply said that 'at this stage, we don't feel it would necessarily be in the little lad's interest to tell her.' Tug didn't know how to work that one out. Why not tell his grandmother? Was she senile or peculiar? One suggestion Father Bohane did make was that perhaps she could get a letter written from Lumsden to his mother. It could come via the parish priest. 'I would simply keep it by me,' Father Bohane wrote, 'and I would only show it to Mrs Farr if matters came to a real head. Maura is very fearful for the little lad and wants you to know that she would be there to welcome him if ever, simply for his safety, Ireland seemed to be the only place.'

When Tug received this letter, Spencer was beside her. He was more at ease than usual. Tug managed to gather him up on to her knee without too much resistance.

'Spencer. This letter's for you,' Tug said. 'It's from your Nan, Spencer. She lives in a big house in Ireland, where it's all quiet and green and beautiful. And Maura is there, and Big Donal.' The child's large eyes looked directly at her. He seemed interested but without any kind of understanding. Tug decided that whether he heard or not she would continually tell him of his Nana and Maura and Big Donal.

Following Father Bohane's request, Tug tracked Lumsden down again via Valentine Duckworth, who was now a fairly respectable and prosperous married man. She prevailed on Valentine to achieve some kind of letter from Lumsden to his mother that would acknowledge his indisputable paternity of this unfortunate child. Valentine did so, because his young wife insisted he should. Lumsden, now a veritable 'pot head', had less concentration and mental focus than before. When Valentine told him the saga of Dolly's alcoholism, and Tug's worry, he had some difficulty at first putting the story together. He had assumed the child had been adopted. But what the whole story did, as Valentine told it to him, what it did was bring back with some force the memory of Rathmanagh and Birkin, the red barn in which he had first started to smoke the men's cigarettes, pinching them out of their jacket pockets. He remembered the library, the smell of the Aga, the large sunny window in the nursery bathroom with its great view of Mount Murna, and the terrible hypnotic engraving of the stag that hung in its maple frame over the sideboard in the dining-room. And within the mixture of these vivid memories, was the sound, the texture, the very smell of Violet. He could see those piercing blue eyes, set so deeply into her skull, which must be edged with lines now. He could see the wisps of hair running loose and wild from the great rolled knot at the back of her head, that loose nest of gathered strands, kept fiercely in place by the dark spears of those very direct, uncompromising hair-pins. Probably the hair was grey. Maybe the voice, so imperious and precise, maybe it wavered, maybe somewhere within the ruthless, unwanting power of her there was by now a blemish or two somewhere or other; bruised, even fearful places, that might admit the very faintest yearning for some human touch, some blood-related memory. Lumsden was appalled to realise that the darkness and power of the nursery bag was still there, ready to devour him if she released her grip on the drawstring. With constant recourse to drugs and alcohol, Lumsden could summon to himself exotic and powerful charms, but their departure always left behind them ruthless, bleak stretches of despondent terrain. Long periods of despondency, if allowed, often mused on towards death. In some measure he felt, to his surprise, that he was drawn to the idea of somehow confronting his mother before either his or her death.

Valentine wisely let Lumsden take his time to absorb the news he had brought. Lumsden poured himself more wine. He swivelled the ridiculously large amethyst ring on his finger. He was obviously very preoccupied. He went over to the window. He looked out over the trim tops of the suburban trees. He was not thinking at all of a small son, with an inadequate, alcoholic mother. He was thinking of himself. He was thinking of his own mother. And, as he thought of her, it occurred to him that this child, apparently his, this strangely named 'Spencer', it occurred to Lumsden that he might be like a small, sharp stone in a leather sling. He, Lumsden, might, like David, from a million miles and cultures and waters away, he might swing a line in a great high hoop of direct flight, he might swing this sharp stone, this small child, towards that Goliath woman, his own mother. Always there, even if unremembered, always there with her power and constant taut pull on the drawstring of the nursery bag. The image of a sharp stone slung into one of those clear blue eyes lifted Lumsden from the anxious, despondent, downward curve that at first Valentine's surprising news had reduced him to. A small, unwholesome, unruly, Catholic child summarily dumped in that cruelly disregarding lap; it was a peculiarly deft piece of subtle justice. Blood will out had always been one of her favourite maxims. And my dear Mother, Lumsden thought, maybe blood runs as it will out, I'm sure you never thought of that.

Lumsden turned from the window and went straight to the small walnut desk at the back of the room. It was not his, it was owned by the generous lady with whom he lived. He sat down. He took pen to paper and wrote immediately to his mother, via Father Bohane, the parish priest in Ballynaule. He wrote how the child was proved by blood to be definitely his. He wrote that he had no contact with it. His circumstances didn't allow for it. He said how he had little knowledge of the mother, except that she was a mess, unhinged, as you would say, Mother, unstable anyway, and that apparently the child was in day-to-day peril, so he was informed on good authority. Then he added, with enormous delight, that the mother was a Roman Catholic, not of Irish origin, but from Aldershot. He said the odd name had nothing to do with him, but on the other hand there was an extremely civilised literary namesake if one chose to dwell on it. He went on for the final paragraph '. . . as I have often heard you say . . . blood will out! What a tiresome mystery it all is. Heirs of nothing and everything. My position at present is utter dereliction, but maybe at a later date . . .' And he left it at that.

Valentine was surprised by the letter. And even more surprised how little persuasion it had needed from him to get it written. Tug immediately sent the letter to Father Bohane. By now Spencer was three. Although still a strange and solitary child, he had the beginnings of a vocabulary. He listened attentively to Tug when she spoke. He followed her about. He watched her every move. Spencer never howled when Tug was in the flat.

As Dolly always left as soon as Tug returned from work, and as at the weekends she was always so hung-over, Tug and Spencer usually went out, not returning until late afternoon, by which time Dolly was beginning to prepare herself to go out again; there was very little opportunity for Tug to discuss anything at all with Dolly. Her moods were most extreme. She was either in a state of complete dejection; tearful, maudlin and incoherent, or she was suddenly buoyed up, her voice full of sharp little shrieks of fast crazy talk, full giggles and terms of endearment to Tug which sounded like sham, blousey little butts of fairground plastic. There never was a moment of calm, a pause of any kind, when Tug could really speak with her. She tried. Tug would make them both a cup of coffee and then say something like:

'Spencer's well past three now. We should think of his future ... I mean ...'

But Dolly would interrupt. She would turn furiously towards Tug, 'We. So it's "we" ... is it?'

'Well, it looks like it, doesn't it? I mean, day after day ... who cooks, shops, cleans, who minds Spencer every night ... come on Dolly?'

'You do, Tug. You do. Wonderful, bloody, interfering you. But no one asked you did they? You do it because you want to. What else could you do in the evening? There aren't exactly blokes lined up for you are there? I know you scorn me. You just think I'm a bloody little tart, don't you?'

Tug would try to keep silence. Any defence was useless.

'Well, maybe my life's a bloody sight more natural than yours.'

'Maybe,' Tug would say. 'Maybe, but I'm trying to talk about Spencer.'

'Sod Spencer. Sod him. You were right, I can't handle him. He and I, it's a fuck up. So what. It's not the first time and it won't be the last. You don't have to be here. We'd get by without you. Kids survive, Tug.'

'But they don't, Dolly . . . That's the point, they don't.'

'Well, the streets aren't exactly piled high with bodies, are they? They just get on with it. They grow up and then they just get spat out of their home like plum-stones . . . And they get on with it. One way or another, they get on with it. My mum was mad. She rocked herself to death in a stinking room; she didn't even have proper clothes on. So what? It happens. It happens all the time.'

Any attempt at talk Tug always found useless. But at least it was summer and she was able to take Spencer out into the park after work. They would feed the ducks and watch the other children on the swings and climbing-frames. Tug continued to tell Spencer that he had this nana in Ireland where it was beautiful; there were wild ducks, and instead of parks with paths and black railings there were hills and meadows and mountains. She never knew if he listened. She had no idea what he heard or noticed. His mind was like some hard shrivelled nut; a dead still emptiness in the huge staring dark of his eyes.

It was Thursday. It was a beautiful warm day. Tug got home earlier than usual. The great variety of music playing out of the open windows, the children in their flimsy summer clothes, with their chants and skipping games on the balcony at the back of the flats, it all gave the afternoon a light, celebratory feel.

Tug came to the door of the flat. She put down her bags of

shopping and searched for her keys in her jeans pocket, when she suddenly heard Dolly's voice.

'Bastard. You bastard.'

'You fucking little thieving bitch.'

Tug burst into the flat. The door into the bedroom was open. Dolly, completely naked, was screaming at this fat hairy bloke, who was at the end of the bed struggling into his clothes. As soon as he saw Tug he grabbed his T-shirt and shoes and left, with Dolly still screaming abuse after him.

Then Tug acted. She was certain now. She was certain what to do. It was over. This mess. It was over. It had to be. Ignoring Dolly, she started gathering up Spencer's things in various bags, his yellow crotcheted comforter, a knitted blanket. She took the brown envelope with his certificates. She took a few things for herself. Then she looked round for Spencer himself. She had caught sight of him in the front room as she came into the flat, but Dolly's noise and this great ugly man had taken her mind off him and on to this final, most urgent decision.

When she came back into the room with the bags packed, a clean shirt for him and a pair of shorts in her hands, she suddenly saw him. He was standing in the corner of the room. He was standing with his back to all the noise and mess and emptiness. He seemed to Tug like a little stick-insect, that can, by it stillness, completely hide itself in its environment. He might have been simply a shadow in the walls, a large dark stain across the paper. Gently Tug picked him up. Immediately he rammed his two clenched fists deep into the sockets of his eyes as if he would blind himself. He was stiff, so stiff. He made no sound.

Tug put the shorts on Spencer but she could not change the shirt, she could not move the tight little stopper fists that so effectively blinded him.

'I'm taking him, Dolly. I'm taking him to Ireland. Nothing can be worse than this. I'm taking him to Lumsden's mother.'

Dolly hardly seemed to hear. She had pulled on her shirt and

259

was sitting with her aching head in her hands. She felt that the weight of it was the bucket-swill of all the junk of her life. Her life, other lives, his life, any life; just the choking mess of life itself.

Tug borrowed a battered old van from the Spencer Arms. They gave her a mattress to put in the back and some cushions. She rolled Spencer up in a blanket, he seemed more inclined for sleep than anything else. Later, when they were well on their way, far out of London towards Swansea, then she would telephone Father Bohane. Maybe. Anyway, she would tell Spencer; she would try to make out some pattern of sense to him that she could somehow transfer into that grim, hidden little heart. Tug wondered if, in the end, feelings unused deserted people, or perhaps they simply stiffened into a frozen mass, like the atrophied lava victims of Pompeii. She wondered what in the end could possibly be the key to unlock so much incoherent suffering.

It was a long drive. Tug didn't know if Spencer slept or not but at least he was quiet. When they stopped at a service station, Tug found him lying there quite still, but with his eyes wide open just staring up at her. She lifted him out, she pulled him up into her arms and out into the rich evening light. They went into the cafeteria. Tug realised he had messed his pants. There was the smell, and the dark strident stain down his leg. She had a change of pants in her bag. She took him to the nursing mothers' space in the ladies' lavatories. The facilities were good and caring, plenty of space, and soap and hot water and paper towels. If only he was still an infant. If only he could be back at that beginning. Tug felt distressed at his obvious vulnerability; he was not an easy child. He gave out no warmth, no trust. It was as if he gave himself continuously these internal commands simply to not exist; not to be there; not to be a feeling body in a public space.

They were booked on a night sailing to Cork. It would be a difficult night, as the boat would undoubtedly be very crowded. There would be another long drive the next morning. Tug had thought of ringing Father Bohane from Swansea, but there wasn't time and Spencer was clinging to her with a new desperate frenzy. She could hardly get herself on to the lavatory he kept so close. Perhaps it was the bustle, the people, the piped music, the lights; but once on the boat, once the van had been parked, once they were up on deck he began to relax a little. Tug kept saying all these things about the sea. Spencer had never seen the sea before. He stared down into the dark bobbing water, little scoops of waves, cupping the reflection of the lights from the quay. There were three gulls swooping and diving off the end of the boat. Spencer watched their antics with fascination.

Fortunately the crossing was calm. The rows of high-backed leather chairs were full of people; snoring, drinking, chatting; little girls, sticky food marks still on their faces, lay across their fathers' fat stomachs, elderly women with neat bags and clean white cardigans talked intimately with one another. Everyone became careless of how they might seem to anyone else. The only need was some kind of sleep, a little snatch of respite before the next morning in Cork City.

Spencer eventually fell asleep on Tug's lap. She felt his hand slip into hers. She held it. She felt fearful because very soon she must betray his trust; a trust which she and he had so painstakingly evolved together. She had told him again and again of his nana, Mrs Farr, who lived in Ireland, in this house called Rathmanagh. She had tried to tell him of Maura and Big Donal. Although he listened intently, she knew he simply watched her face and heard the gentle sound of her voice. No sense in her words seemed to engage his understanding. Whatever transpired would be a surprise and a considerable shock. But it will be gentle and natural, Tug told herself. There will be physical safety and physical freedom. When all else is taken, then nature is the only reliable force left: wind, sheeting rain, moist earth smells, sunbursts on grass and animals and flowers. The fierce and tender lap of nature might be the last bastion that would be able to recharge and revitalise those numb and wounded areas of persistent violation.

But however much Tug went over everything in her mind, the pros and cons, the obvious good of her decision which she knew had been taken in haste albeit after months of careful consideration, she was still keenly anxious. Father Bohane had said so little of Mrs Farr. What was she like? Was she old and incapable? They hadn't said that or even inferred it. They had always been very insistent about how Maura would be there.

When they were well past Cork, making their way inland on the smaller roads, Tug decided that she must not burden anyone else with her decision. She would simply leave Spencer up at the house, then she would go and see Father Bohane. Perhaps she wanted to be sure that no one would put her off course; tell her the thing could not be done. She had taken the responsibility for so long. Surely family, blood ties, surely they stood for something, even in a society that pursued such a cult of the individual; individual rights, individual pleasures, individual freedoms.

Tug had never had a boyfriend. Fat and dumpy as a child, she had cultivated a manner in her own defence, a manner that gave the impression of independence and capability. She was certainly both independent and capable, but Spencer's birth and the subsequent three years of his life had made her aware that independence was more of a declaration than a truth. Alone was not a natural condition. Yet so much that was natural became distorted, like Dolly's life.

It was another fine day. They stopped in a small village. A single street of low shops, two bars and a garage. They bought bread and butter and sweet biscuits, lemonade and some slices of ham. Tug carried Spencer on her shoulders. They left the van and walked up a small hill from where they would get a fine view across the valley. Halfway up the road on the right was a large, stone-carved Celtic cross, set in a small square of neatly-cut grass. They went over to it and sat down to have their picnic. Beyond them, across the road on the opposite side of the valley, there were rolling hills, grazing cattle, small stone farmsteads. Various large white clouds in the sky cast particular dark moving shadows over the hills, like vast birds flying low over the meadows.

The cross was very beautiful. Spencer went up to it. He put his small fingers in between the rough gingerbread figures of apostles and saints, and into the mouths and over the ears of gryphons and monsters. He ate and drank well. He even laughed when, by mistake, Tug knocked over her can of lemonade. Tug stared in disbelief at the calm, powerful scenery, the blue sky, the empty road. This picnic was a small secret time; a hidden moment. Tug dreaded leaving him. Later in his life he would not even know that there had ever been a plump girl who cared for him. He would know nothing of this picnic and the stone cross in whose shade they were sitting. She would remember it. Fearful of her feelings, worried in case she lost her determined resolve, Tug quickly gathered everything up. Spencer was playing happily in the sun with various small sticks and stones. Tug had given up trying to explain or prepare him. It didn't work. Now all she thought of was to get this thing done as quickly as possible and just hope that it would work out. It couldn't be worse than Dolly and that flat; nothing could be worse than that.

Violet had been tying up plants, generally tending things, weeding, sorting and looking. It had been too hot during the afternoon to do anything very much, and she felt the heat more as she grew older, just as she felt the cold more in the winter. It was the long summer evenings she looked forward to. Everything seemed at its best in the evening light. She had just poured herself a glass of home-made lemonade. Cecil, as usual, was asleep in the library. Violet found the sight of him like that intensely depressing, those heavily creased, flickering eyelids, the little twitches of the nose, and the small red mouth lolled open like a button-hole in an old coat that has softened into a useless gap. If she paused at the library door to consider him, an edge of anger and irritation might invade the calm of the evening. With age, the difficulty and management of bitterness and anger became, to Violet's surprise, no less. It was simply that people assumed a certain calm and philosophy must prevail. And most of the time it did, to the outsider anyway; and there was no one in Violet's life who was not an outsider.

She picked up the newspaper. She was just about to go across the hall into the study when she heard the sound of a car engine. She looked out of the study window. It was not a car. It was a battered, blue van, one that she certainly did not recognise. She assumed it must be some tradesperson who had mistaken the house. She went out into the porch.

Tug had settled Spencer down in the back of the van with his blankets and things. She had hoped he would sleep. Anyway, without him beside her, without his small hand on her thigh, without his constant stares, she felt she could deal more effectively with the driving, and the manner of this meeting with his grandmother, which she dreaded. Her own nan was a cheerful person who lived alone in sheltered accommodation in Birmingham. She never forgot a birthday. Even now, she sent Tug parcels of chocolate bars, and handkerchiefs, and although Tug knew she was really hard up, she always enclosed some money. 'For a treat, dear,' she would write on the note-card in her thin wobbly script.

Ballynaule was very direct and easy to find after going through Claggan. Tug was tempted to go to the parish church but when she asked a man on the road the way to Rathmanagh, she realised she would get to the turning off the main road before she got to the village. That helped her to resist the temptation of seeking support. She turned up the hill. She passed the large oak tree and the start of the high stone wall of the demesne. She came to wide-open gates and a cattle grid. There was no house in sight. She went on up the hill, curving past meadows full of high grass and flowers. Then Tug saw this mountain on their left. It was far higher, and a more concentrated and distinctive shape, than the hills they had seen before. The van stalled. There is a definite strength and power in mountains, Tug thought. They rise up so purposely, as if declaring some sound, some certainty that is hidden in the deeper interior ground. Tug wondered if the mountain had a name. The van started up again. The drive curled to the right now leaving the hump of mountain behind them. Ahead of her, Tug saw tall trees, buildings covered with creepers, and a high stone house. The drive curved into a large, circular spit of gravel. The van bumped noisily up to the front of the house. Violet was standing in the porch. She was peering towards the window of the van, trying to make out the face and demeanour of the driver who had so carelessly and noisily disturbed both the evening and the gravel.

Tug saw this very tall, good-looking woman, her hair piled high into a loose bun at the back of her head. She was wearing a rather faded cotton shirt and a long brown skirt. Her skin was fair but weather beaten. There was no make-up, no powdered 'done' kind of look to the face, it was natural and strong like the bark of a tree. She seemed old and large and rather imperious.

Tug instantly felt like a criminal, a trespasser, an unwanted vagrant. She felt as scuffed and battered as the old blue van itself. She leapt out of the driving seat. She walked very directly towards Violet. Tug had not expected small, piercing blue eyes.

She had expected, maybe, frailty, age; not a woman like this, who seemed as strong and as remote as the tall trees beyond the drive and the very mountain itself.

'You Mrs Farr?' Tug said.

Violet nodded. She could not deny it even to such an ungainly, unattractive visitor.

'Then,' Tug paused for a second's breath. 'Then you've got to take the kid . . . you've got to take him now . . .'

'What "kid"?' Violet said, making the word 'kid' sound both alien and foreign to her, which of course it was. But the obvious Englishness of the girl, and her peculiar, distraught manner, made Violet reflect. Of course she had heard rumours. No one ever spoke to her directly. But inferences had been made to Lumsden having a child. She had ignored them completely. His life was not her business.

'Your . . . your bloody fucking grandson . . . that's what.'

It was the intransigent, unnatural disdain of the woman that made Tug's anxiety boil into a kind of frightened fury. Violet drew herself up. She stepped out of the porch on to the gravel. She came close enough to Tug to unnerve her completely.

'Please don't use that unpleasant language to me,' Violet said. But her carefully chosen words, spoken with unerring, pin-sharp fury were lost in the sudden pelt and drive of movement and whirlwind activity.

Violet, frozen with horrified disbelief, watched this bulky girl dump baskets and plastic bags and a filthy, multi-coloured knitted blanket on to the gravel.

'He won't do anything. He won't be difficult,' Tug said, shouting to force the quaver out of her voice. 'He's quiet. He's bloody stunned. She drinks. His mother drinks. These are his papers.' She waved the long brown envelope at Violet before putting it down on the top of the bags. 'Birth certificate and things. They've fucked him up enough, there's nothing left for him over there . . . so . . . I said I'd bring him here . . . Right?'

Tug paused for a second. She looked very directly at Violet. She wanted to pierce those cold, assessing blue eyes. She wanted to pierce them with the rough truth of Spencer. She wanted someone else to be spiked by the violation that so far had been Spencer's only human inheritance.

Violet felt as if she were witnessing some drama, some awful staged piece from aggressive political theatre that sought to alienate and disturb; the unwanted intrusion of mad, immoral minds bent on chaos.

Violet watched Tug go round to the back of the van. She wrestled apart the two dented doors. She clambered inside. Then she dragged towards her a huge bundle of blanket.

'It may seem tough to you . . .' Tug began, as she staggered towards the porch with Spencer in her arms.

'It seems quite absurd,' Violet interrupted, trying not even to acknowledge the long bundle . . . the small grey fallen sock, or the matted crown of dark hair.

'But, it's a fact,' Tug continued, as she struggled into the porch past Violet. 'You're family . . . kith and kin, all that crap about blood being thicker than water . . . that's why I've brought him. It has to be better than how it's been before. It has to be better than that.'

'It's ridiculous. We're quite unprepared.' Violet stood her ground. But she did not want to come too close to this mad bale of . . . of . . . she could not bring herself to think of what. Simply a dull, bale-weight in this fat girl's arms.

'Don't give me that shit,' Tug yelled. 'You've got a house and space: rooms, doors, fields, sky, water, cows, milk . . . priests!'

Then Spencer stirred. Another sock fell. Spencer himself was stiff, with tightly closed eyes. He was hidden, blind, in the dark heated tomb of the blanket over him. But he was heavy. Tug put him down. She just let him stand with the blanket still on his shoulders. She felt so nervous. So perplexed by it all; where and how was the root of caring and responsibility? But she had to go on. Tug bent down to him. She rested on her hunkers; her wide thighs apart; her knees just touching the strange shape of this small figure in the moulded cloth of blanket, with the hair just showing and the small spurs of those blue-white cheeks. One of the blankets fell to the ground. Tug took the other, a matted yellow crocheted object that had always been his comforter. Tug crumpled it into a ball on her knees. How could she leave him . . .?

'Spencer . . . we're here . . . Spencer . . . you know, your Nana's . . . We're here like I told you. Come on . . . come on.'

Tug's voice broke as she pleaded with him. But for what? What could he do? He was like a lay-by rag, a worn slump of litter, left for time to generally consume or gently dismember.

Spencer hung his head. With his eyes closed he could roll everything into it and leave it hanging there. Tug was seldom upset. Upset was usually loud. It was usually Dolly's noise. But there had been the sea, heavy white birds, hills, fields, and only single solitary cars. No longer railings, kerbs and crossing lines in between moving walls of lorries and buses and cars. Something was different. Too different to hear or feel.

Violet stood between them and the sun. Even through his crunched, closed eyes, Spencer could see her shadow. But naturally, it was nothing to him. Just a hung shape of dark, perpendicular air.

Violet struggled to find some word. She wanted to be inspired to make some definite, irrevocable gesture. But no part of her body seemed inclined to move. She found it hard even to master her breathing, which hastened as she wished she could hasten these people from her; immediately, directly. Then she heard, without having to turn her head, she heard the unmistakable, slow, painstaking footsteps of her husband across the hallway.

The only movement Violet could make was away. Away from the house. Away from this extraordinary tinker child and his foul, matted, animal hair, and those stubbornly closed eyes. Away from this fat girl, with her tight jeans and aggressive disposition. Violet could not see the hot, uncharacteristic tears streaming down Tug's cheeks.

'Come on, Spencer . . . Come on, fellow . . .' Tug said. She wondered what on earth she was asking him to do. Then she realised that it must be something for her. She wanted something of his to take away with her; a glance, a gesture. But it was wrong to want anything. All the needs were his. She could not imagine how he would make headway here. Maybe that mountain would close him into its wild hide; maybe it was the kind of ancient extent, that was, in the end, all anyone was left with, just a throw of circumference towards the sky.

Then Spencer moved. He turned his back on Tug. He turned his back on the wide sweep of gravel in the evening sunlight, and on the tall, perpendicular shadow of his grandmother. He walked slowly to the back of the porch. Here, against the white wall of the house, with its cobwebs and stains and flaking paint; against this new texture he leant in his accustomed position of blinding stillness.

Cecil came out on to the gravel. He had heard the commotion. The raised voices. He glanced towards the tinker child and the odd girl kneeling there beside plastic bags and blankets, and with the obvious understanding that all of this could not have anything to do with themselves, or Rathmanagh, he glanced towards Violet, who was standing out in the gravel some way from the porch. He went towards her, but she seemed distant. She seemed less assertive, less in control than usual. Even Cecil sensed the uncomfortable disarray of this glorious summer evening. Everything seemed brittle, stricken, uncertain; even the smell from the white tobacco plants below the library windows seemed to have withered into the general air of tense disorder.

'Can I do anything, my dear?' Cecil asked, as if there was nothing extraordinary, untoward or difficult going on. Violet looked directly towards him. The highly polished shoes, so anachronistic to the general tattered but careful confusion of everything else above them, the coarse blotched skin, the worn frayed cardigan, the missing button, the hard soup stains on the shirt front.

Violet would like to have pitched her voice higher than the mountain behind them. She would like to have screamed to him for all his ineffectual non-being. She would have liked her cry to have been: 'Drop dead, Cecil . . . just drop dead.' That screech of anger, which she did not make, reactivated her awareness of what was going on. The momentary stunned pause had passed. Now she must act. But it was too late. Tug, unable to bear the sight of Spencer so still against the peeling white wall of the house, had turned from him. To avoid Violet, who was standing quite near the blue van, she went round to the passenger's door. She opened it and clambered across to the driving seat. She cranked the van loudly into reverse, then she spun round, with the wheels throwing the small gravel stones in every direction. She went on as fast as she could down the hill, away from Rathmanagh and the mountain and that woman and Spencer himself. Spencer did not move. He heard the noise of the van, but it might have been a rush of wind, or simply a howl in his head. It was incumbent on him to be detached as far as possible from any signs or sounds. He must resist all experiences. The wall was cool, so were the tiles on the porch floor. It helped him not to register that Tug was gone from him. The cold tiles might make holes for his feet, the wall might billow inwards. He might soon become quite unseen.

Violet remained alone on the gravel. Cecil went indoors to lay the table for supper; his task every evening. He would soon be reassured by the feel of the green baize in the cutlery drawer, and the careful replenishing of the salt cellar. It simply didn't occur to Cecil that the child and the blankets and the plastic bags were of any relevance whatsoever.

Tug went straight to Father Bohane in the presbytery in Ballynaule. She understood to her relief that Maura would already have left for Rathmanagh, as she did every evening. Father Bohane assured her that she had been most brave, and before God she must have done the right thing. Whose concern was he, if he was not the concern of his own flesh and blood? Father Bohane said he would speak to Mrs Farr later in the evening, and that he would have by him Lumsden's letter. 'All shall be well,' he said. 'All manner of things shall be well.'

Maura, pushing her bicycle up the last stretch of the drive, was surprised to see Madam alone out there on the gravel. She would more often than not be weeding up on the border, or reading in the porch. But something about the way she stood set Maura thinking. She was angered. Maura knew Madam far better than Madam knew herself.

'Evening, Madam,' she said leaning against her black bicycle. Violet looked towards her but said nothing. She stared beyond Maura down the steep meadow, to the tops of the trees beside the river and beyond them to the quiet, impregnable steep curves of Mount Murna; the ridges and the deep grooves of sunken ground were very dark now against the evening sunlight behind the mountain. As Violet searched with her blue eyes for the furthest possible point of the horizon from herself, she could feel beside her, yards away in the shade of the porch, she could feel this child, that was nowhere near her sights, but that nevertheless encroached on her mind; he was to her like some bloated reptilian mass covered with hair and white-lice skin over the struggling, bubble runs of warm blood. She could feel this live mass coming towards her over the gravel; up into herself; up over the height of the house. The image was suffocating and powerful. She almost felt drawn to look towards the porch in order simply to dispel this monstrous, drowning vision.

Maura had already looked towards the porch. She saw the thin child, with a mass of dark hair, standing hard against the wall of the house. He had his back to the gravel, and the light; all of the evening. His small hands were pressed on to the dusty surface as if he would almost roll himself into it. Maura guessed at once. The rough tyre marks in the gravel. Madam's strange behaviour. And the photographs Father Bohane had been sent. It was the same child, most definitely.

Maura lent her bicycle up against the wall. She went across to the back of the porch and she gathered him up into her arms. She kissed him effortlessly, careless of his stiff, unresponsive body and tightly closed eyes. She stroked the pale skin. She whispered on and on, without regard either to Madam or to herself. It was not an occasion for talk or reason; it was simply an occasion for love. And love as Maura understood it was the most natural thing in the world. It flowed through words and gestures, glances and stillness. It was the very force of life itself.

'I'll take him to the kitchen, Madam,' she said. 'We'll have a good wash and a bite of something.' Maura didn't wait for an answer. Many of her servile polite suggestions were often quiet statements of complete command. Violet recognised this, although she would never have said as much. Maura was simply 'pure gold', 'a Trojan worker'. But this evening Violet knew that without Maura's prompt arrival she might have been unable to successfully hide the rage and contempt she felt for her son Lumsden; but most of all for this crude, evil manipulation of her life. In each hurried breath she made as she stood out there alone, she felt the violent, subtle burial of herself. There was something in this last mad event that was so mocking. It was a livid conclusion, out of all proportion to any part she might have had in the remote events that had preceded. The sharp David stone had certainly slung home. Violet was smarting from the sheer audacity of that gross girl; her language, her behaviour, was insufferable. She must be being paid by someone. Violet walked slowly into the house. It was a web of tricks and schemes, she was sure of that. Was nothing sacred? One's privacy. One's home. How could one tolerate the very depth of one's life strung out like a public clothes line, parading the gruesome laundry of feckless, completely irresponsible people? She was outraged. But she remained silent. She stored the pain and fury within herself, much as Spencer stored the dumb, unwanted scheme of his own life.

Maura very soon had Spencer sitting in the kitchen with a plate of fresh bread and butter and a little scrambled egg, and a piece of chocolate cake. He had opened his eyes. He stared at the food, at the cream Aga and the large brown steaming kettle. Gradually, he began to watch Maura, as she busied about in and out of the cupboards; heating things, mixing things, washing things, wiping things. Every so often she would wipe her soft hands on her apron and then she would take the edge of it and wipe her forehead, or her upper lip, then a spoon, or a mite of dust in the rim of a cup. All the time she spoke. It was tireless gentle talk, like a flow of fresh spring water. She purposely avoided looking directly at Spencer, especially when out of the corner of her eye she saw the small fingers squash their way carefully into the slice of cake and then quite eagerly eat up the broken pieces.

'Well, it's been a fine day, that's for sure. We've had a good spell for some time now. It'll be fine again tomorrow and I'll take you to meet Flora. She's an old donkey. Very gentle, very quiet. She's down in the meadow. We'll take her a bit of bread, she likes that, and we'll feed the hens and collect the eggs. They're not laying too well. They don't like the heat. But there'll be one or two for sure. Oh, we'll have a pile of things to do Spencer. And it'll be grand company to have you along

273

with me. What a journey you've had. The big boat brought you over the water, didn't it? I've been on that boat. It's a grand boat. Well now, we'll sail away ourselves, shall we? There's a fine little blue bed at the top of the house. It'll be grand for you, and there's a cupboard in there with some books and cars and things. They're your Daddy's. Well, they were. Now they'll be yours, won't they?'

All the time Maura spoke, she gauged exactly how near and then how far to be from him. It was a bit of closeness and real contact, and then a good bit of space to allow him to catch up as it were. It would never have occurred to Maura to think of her deft gentleness as a particular skill, it was simply the natural way anyone would be with a wounded creature.

Maura went ahead. She took the bags and the blankets up to the top of the house. Spencer watched her from the bottom of the wide central staircase. Then very slowly, when she called out, 'Oh, Spencer . . . Look at this. I've found a little car in this box and, good heavens, there's a cow too! Come on up and look.' Then, intrigued, he followed her until he was at the top of the house. Maura ran the bath and made the bed. All the time her chatter never ceased. Gradually, she said the word 'Spencer' more and more often and each time he looked more directly towards her. He wouldn't get into the bath, so she soaped his bottom and his back and his knees as he stood on the cork mat. He resisted her hand and the warm flannel anywhere near his face. Maura simply kissed the mat of unbrushed hair and said, 'Fine, that's fine, Spencer. We'll leave faces for tomorrow.'

He was soon into bed. Although there was still plenty of sunlight, Maura switched on the small bedside light, so that there'd be no chance of him finding himself alone in the dark.

Maura sighed and went back down the long flight of stairs very heavy hearted. It certainly wasn't a natural spot here for a little lad like that, but she would do her best. She could do no more than that. By the grace of God, it would be better than what he had been used to.

Tug was far from Ballynaule by the time Father Bohane telephoned Rathmanagh. Violet had already guessed that without doubt there was the imprint of popish interference in the whole business. She was furious; but she knew she must amass more facts and information before she could issue any kind of ultimatum. Certainly, it was not a situation that could continue.

Cecil was in the hall. He was restless. It was well past seven-thirty; well past suppertime. Schedules, the map of small irrelevant events, were the very structure of his existence. Like a card house, one slight move threatened the rest of his structure.

'Where is Maura?' Cecil said to Violet. 'She's definitely still here, her bicycle's outside.'

'She is here,' Violet said. She was contemplating the risk of ringing the presbytery. She looked with amazement at Cecil's stooped figure in the doorway of the study. Any idea that he should be involved in this bizarre event was unthinkable. How ruthless, how scheming, how full of deceits was the anxious dark of married beds. And now she had to acknowledge the well lit, cocksure extravagance of the unmarried bed. She loathed these two extremes. There seemed no mean, no civilised centre. The human condition seemed to hurtle pell-mell one way or the other, gross and vulgar, or sterile and unsung. Either way, Cecil was incongruous, and yet, if she was to be proved a grandmother, sadly, the subsequent truth was that he was a grandfather. She remembered Birkin. She remembered the power and strength of those summer evenings with him. Their late evening walks by the river and beyond, to Murna. She certainly had known perplexing strands of passion; she could sense what might have been. But with cruel indifference the structure, the definition of passion had been for her simply storm clouds circling her place with energy, pent-up drama, canticles of promise, but never, never did the storm break and spill their force, drenching and then resolving the site into a state of calm and quiet bliss. There was no more subtle light on ground than sunset after storm.

'Maura is upstairs,' Violet said. 'There is a boy with her, a boy who is three years old; a boy who is called, ridiculously, Spencer, like some bust-bodice or vest. A ludicrous name. However, that is his name and I suppose that just as it confuses dogs to change their names, it may also confuse children.'

'But why, my dear, is he here at Rathmanagh?'

'Because, Cecil, he has been dumped here. I have been given to understand that he is Lumsden's child. It is all most unsavoury and inconvenient. But for this evening, we shall have to eat late. We shall have to eat at eight, maybe later. Luckily, supper is cold, and Maura benefits from surprising duties, especially those that give her an emotional *carte blanche*. So we must be thankful that she at least is content. After all, we do increasingly depend on her.'

Violet knew that Cecil would pay little attention to any news, however flagrant and unimaginable, so long as the minute order of his regimes was in the foreground of all thought and plans.

'Well, if supper is to be late,' Cecil said, 'I shall have time to water the geraniums before I wash.'

Violet could not help envying him his absurdly unbalanced way of life. Even if his days were dull, at least they were never violent or threatened. There was no emotion, no blinding strands of lust or anger to create havoc . . . even mood. Cecil was the shuffling coil, unsprung.

Violet was sitting at her desk when the telephone rang. It was Father Bohane. At first the conversation was awkward because both of them were wise enough to wish to be the attentive listener, rather than the voice of authority.

'It's a sad affair, Mrs Farr. Very difficult for yourself, I know.'

Father Bohane had already read aloud Lumsden's letter and he had acknowledged the furious silence that followed it. Now he was intent on offering nothing but condolences and a degree of Christian congratulation that he hoped would make it awkward for Mrs Farr to follow with criticism and intolerance. 'Only a fine, good woman such as yourself would be able to cope at all with such a burden, and something not of their own making. I don't know you well, Mrs Farr, but people speak so highly of you in the parish, as do Donal and Maura. I realise you are a fine woman. The child is very fortunate to have such grandparents, with his own parents so sadly lacking in any kind of responsibility.' As the priest's voice went on, Violet's frustration became acute. She ended the conversation with the abrupt announcement that their meal was ready and waiting on the table. Father Bohane said he would drop in the letter, as it was important for them to have it. Neither of them referred in any way to where the situation might lead.

Spencer lay in the strange bed. He did not close his eyes. He stared out at the open doorway, at the landing floorboards, at the high wardrobe, at the books and chairs and desk and ornaments. The silence itself was like a fluttering bird, wings spread to the furthest emptiness. The great soft breast of the bird was an unseen weight, stifling, with its masterful close gentleness, the pores of his skin's circumference. It was firm on to the space of breath above the lips, and in the small whorls of coiled flesh in the ears, it was an ice-skim cool on the soft soles of the feet, it was firm, as flexed as deft muscle, on to his hands and arms and the sucked smooth fingertips, and the pink, mis-shapen, drool lump of the thumb. It was always there, a bulk of feathers, a throstle fullness ready to move, but never hearing the signal, never receiving the sound. It was both camouflage and captor. To be without it would be membrane raw; it would be an intolerable, dangerous nakedness. There would be no protection

277

then against the mouth gape, which sound cut loose into the bird. So the bird could not be done away with. Within its suffocating, closed embrace, silence was a kind of death. There were times when the silence lightened, when it shifted this way and that, like clear water in a wind. There were times when there were both heavy and light spaces, when the silence was a mosaic; then the feathers interlocked, slipped in and out of pattern rhythms that were almost comfortable.

In a strange bed, in the high room, unslept in for so long, the weight of the silence was a brutal force, a huge constraint, a quiet, choking scheme without pattern or movement.

Spencer kicked off the covers to make some space; to feel some sense on the rough skin of his legs and knees. He held his hand fast on the only sense agent still in his possession, he clung and wrung and rubbed his penis as if this movement could keep out the last final stiffness, that the weight of the bird and its stretched wings everywhere could reduce him to.

The spaces about him were so vast after the flat. Long arms of narrow corridors smelling of warm dust between bleached floorboards, and the height of the rooms, the curtains themselves were as tall as giants, and the stairwell, with its open doors and galleries leading out to other, lesser landing spaces. In the strange bed, in the high house, Spencer was like a kite that had been blown on to the top of a dead tree. No wind can blow it down, it is too tattered, too spiked with dead twigs and broken branches. It was unsafe in the high house with the bird of silence filling every smallest space.

Spencer knew he must howl. He knew he must gather up into his throat a real splinter of sound that would spear the bird; a sound that could cut into this weight over him. A sound that could reach out and out and out until some breath could thread back to him again; some space could moisten his lips, close his eyes, release the rough, ringing action of his hand on his penis.

Father Bohane had been with the letter. Violet had told him that conversation so late in the day would not be convenient. Maura had hung up her apron. She had assured Violet that she would be available for any extra duties while 'that little person is with us'. Violet ignored the warmth and caring in her voice. Indiscriminate charity was very common among simple, ill-educated people. It had to be countenanced, Violet supposed, in order that one could be availed of all the other skills. 'Thank you, Maura,' Violet said, with exactly the same evenness and finality of every evening.

Once the back door was finally slammed and Maura was free-wheeling down the drive on her black bicycle, Violet and Cecil sitting opposite one another in the dark dining-room, the cold beef and jacket potatoes on their plates, the cold water high in their glasses, the mustard, the salt, the butter and the bread in place, it was a picture of continuity, only the light in the sky was a reminder that it was later than usual. They discussed the bugs on the tomato plants, the broken pump in the yard, the exorbitant cost of servicing the car. No mention was made of Spencer, or his father, or the fat, angry English girl who so summarily had interrupted the late afternoon of such a glorious summer's day.

Violet was avoiding her anger and bitterness by careful slow speech concerning mundane subjects. Every time she said a word like 'mould' or 'blackspot', 'oil change' or 'carburettor', the stark, jousting press of bitter loathing which she felt for Lumsden himself and the subsequent lasso of his deceitful, profligate life over her was temporarily held back. Lumsden, and subsequent events beyond her control, had, so she felt, completely cut her off from the just inheritance that her fine father's blood, within her own veins, should have assured her of: a son of quality. Since Lumsden's departure, she had managed to construct a pall of dull, well-executed rural activities, community projects and committee procedures, to hide the gnawing gap of a dissatisfied life and an inappropriate destiny. She had moved from day to day demonstrating considerable skills. Then that child in the porch. He had seemed to her a fetid lump of wild existence. The scumbled resolution of all she had so successfully buried. She could see nothing in him, or about him, except the intolerable mockery he was to her.

Violet and Cecil had finished their supper. They had stacked the empty plates and glasses on to the trolley. They had wiped the faded mats; they had put the salt cellars and pepper pots back on to the sideboard. Cecil, as usual, said to Violet, 'Is that all, my dear?' And then, as usual, he replied himself. 'Yes, it is . . . I'm sure it is.' He began to wheel the trolley out of the dining-room towards the pantry door. It was a swing door. Cecil usually manoeuvred it with skill, by pushing his back against it until it was well open, and then he would pull the trolley in after him. There was a small rise between the hall floor and the stone flags of the pantry. One of the trolley wheels stuck. There was a jolt. Loose cutlery clattered down on to the stone flags. Ashamed at his clumsiness, Cecil bent down to pick up the spoons and forks, but as he did so he only made things worse. His elbow pushed the meat plate to the floor with a resounding crash of breaking crockery.

Violet purposely ignored the noise. She knew exactly how it would have happened. She was far too preoccupied with the very considerable problem of Spencer to allow herself to be diverted by Cecil's ineptitude. She walked away from the dining-room into the library avoiding any kind of glance towards the pantry door, the ship-wrecked trolley, and the splinters of food and crockery and the sharp shards of thick white china on the grey slates.

Upstairs in the strange bed Spencer heard the sounds. They were angry sudden sounds. They cut deep into the bird. They ravaged the weight of its breast on to him. They were intolerant pursuing sounds. His fear, his numb ship-wrecked stillness in the narrow bed in this strange high house; it felt discovered. He felt those sounds would come for him, like grinding teeth, like marching hands; they would gorge on him, greedy to expose him, to thrash his limbs out into all the object glares of these stairs and chairs, books and paintings, all the heavy mahogany, all the plumped cushions; the creaking shutters and the ticking clocks, the deep, under furniture shadows, the dark of the doors, the frail, faded weight of the curtains. They would dismantle him, just as they had so suddenly dismantled the weight of the suffocating bird. In an instant, Spencer knew he must make the sound, even greater now than it might have been. Louder. Further flung. He must hurl it out to press back from all the rest.

He sat up in the bed. He had kicked off the covers. He had nothing on but a T-shirt and pants. He shook his head, then he pulled it back down, between his thin shoulders. These little lumps of bone pressed in either side of his throat. And the sound came. It heaped itself up and up out from every scarred inch of him. It rallied all the forgotten emptiness of the small room and the great arm's length of the nursery corridor. It stripped out all the spores of anger and bitterness, the accumulation of over thirty years. The house rung now with nothing but the sound of the howl. The careful, avoiding silence of so many summers was punched into this great spire of sound.

Violet heard the howl. At first it was almost too loud, too strange, too utterly unknown for her to have any means of tracking it, or assessing it. There was nothing in her experience to regard it against. It was not the sound of a child. It was not a child's voice. It was blood curdling. Before that phrase had held no real meaning for Violet. It was simply a *Boy's Own* jungle description of some eerie sound. Maybe Conan Doyle had used it or Henty. Now Violet used it. She thought it as she ran out of the library to the foot of the wide central staircase. She gathered up her full skirt. Cecil was standing nervously in the pantry doorway. Violet ignored him. She ran up the stairs with unaccustomed speed. On the second landing she paused to catch her breath. The sound still rose, higher and higher. Then it seemed to peak. Like a sharp, narrow point it suddenly rested, as if homed at last into a most painful silence; the echo of the sound seemed to pin down into a flesh gasp every feeling that had ever been. It was no longer the silence of the house, their silence. A silence which had over the years collected the unwanted detritus of their thoughts and actions and had stored them quietly in dust and musty smells, in between ticking, rustling little jambs of sound. Now it was another silence. A peculiar live, poised silence. Pending. Strung.

As Violet paused for breath, paused to gather momentum again, she felt precipitated, not towards this thin child she must confront, but more towards some barren dereliction within herself.

Spencer had heard her feet. He had heard the material, soft, mush-sound of her skirt on the banisters. Now he heard her breath. He did not close his eyes. He stared out towards the landing and the fast fading patch of light that was reflected on to the floorboards through the open door of the nursery bathroom. He knew it was not Maura. And it was not the man. He knew it was the other person into whose sharp blue eyes he had purposely not looked. Like a dog who knows instantly who is pack leader, so Spencer instinctively knew that Violet was the command post, the cornerstone of this edifice in whose uppermost tract he was waiting. His face was flushed, although there were pale patches in towards the temples, the sticky roots of the dark curly hair. His left hand was up at his face, the thumb in his mouth, while with fierce regularity he pulled with his forefinger at the sore, puffy underlip. His right hand clutched the small swollen uncircumcised penis. It was as if this arc between thumb and thumb, one above and one below, it was as if it formed an unseen strand of power to cocoon the sum of his sense from attack. Like the gestures of hands, palm on palm in prayer, or the crossed ankles during Quaker silence to create a circle of protected calm, so the moving, clutching rhythms of Spencer's hands sought to protect him.

Violet was on the top landing. She presumed Maura must have put him in the night nursery, which had later become Lumsden's bedroom. It was at the end of the corridor. The small rectangle of sunlight on the dark floorboards outside the open door of the nursery bathroom reminded Violet of those evenings long since forgotten when Nurse Biddy had particularly asked that she should visit Lumsden in the bath, because he had been so good. Her visits to the night nursery had been deemed a treat, a privilege. Lumsden had always smelt so fresh. His skin had been so clear; his eyes so bright. Not the rancid, blotched skin of this child. Violet passed the bathroom door. The electric light was on in the night nursery, although it was not yet dark.

Spencer sensed her coming. The steps were slower. Then he saw her. He saw her brown leather shoes, the thick stockinged ankles, the deep hem of the brown skirt with flecks of dry mud on it. As Violet came forward towards the doorway, Spencer stared out harder and harder. He must push back the shape of her. But he must know her make and power. He had to know. Because there was the sound of her throughout the house. Every object and space and dust particle was in thrall to her. As she came closer the darkness of her body obscured the landing and the last ray of sunlight on the floorboards. Then the darkness of her rose up into the full height of the open doorway ahead of him.

Violet's breathing was still faster than usual. Spencer was sniffing. Clean warm liquid ran down over his upper lip and the sore there, and the red smooth tip of his forefinger, it ran down past his thumb and into his mouth. Each sniff shook his entire spare frame.

As Violet stood in the doorway, she looked towards the

blue-painted bedstead, the wardrobe, the chest of drawers, the nursing chair, the faded rug; a design of prancing lambs, their scuffed fleece now the colour of concrete where white wool had once been. In the dusty bareness of it all, she remembered now, not so much the small, smooth-skinned bathtime Lumsden of Nurse Biddy's era, but the later Lumsden. She remembered the cigarette stubs, the stains of coffee, and the huge carcass body full of strong, sweating smells that permeated the sheets and covers, even the curtains. She remembered his sloth, his lies, the way his bare feet stuck out at her over the bars at the end of the bed. She remembered these details and then suddenly a gust of violent, deeply troubling emotion took hold of her. Like a wave of stagnant water, it almost overwhelmed her. She thought at first it was on account of the sickening way the child pulled at his penis. As if utterly blind to her presence, he continued the ferocious, disgusting rhythm. She could see in the large swimming eyes some semblance of Lumsden. That recognition was like a curse. It seemed to mock that deep forgotten empty part of her, that had once been ready, but had heard no summons. It was too long ago now to name or consider. Violet felt somehow that her father's image, his hope, his claims for her; they were sullied, sour thoughts, inadequately buried. She felt physically in her dry throat, the contemptible dryness of those unlived, unknown moments of her own life; due to her, meant for her, but never realised.

'Never make that cry again. Never. Do you hear me? It is forbidden . . . utterly.'

Violet's breathing grew faster again, more specific, more laboured. Spencer sniffed and stared. She was so large and yet her eyes were small. Violet bent down and picked the covers up off the floor. She threw them back on to the bed. She threw them over the offending brazen part of him that both revolted and mocked her. How bleak and crumpled and pathetic he was . . . yet . . . he had this power. The power in

284

that howl. That dreadful animal sound which still rang in her ears, taunting her, drowning her out and back towards those extremes of herself that were unfelt, unsung; unrealised.

She had always thought Lumsden had mocked her, but this child seemed scooped up out of the very darkness civilisation must avoid. He was the taunting, scum surface that was engendered out of licence; the cursed turbulence that rank disorder brought to the surface from time to time when discipline and structure gave in to the wretched demands of rabid, free, indiscriminate feelings.

'Remember,' Violet bent down closer still to the pale, shivering face, 'never make that sound again . . . never. If you have something to say, say it. That sound was a threat. Nothing comes of threats, nothing.'

When she was very close to Spencer he closed his eyes. He turned his head aside towards the dark wall and the quiet there.

Violet left him. Her breathing gradually recovered its natural rhythm. On her way downstairs she went into her bedroom. She wanted in some way to repossess herself. She sat down on the tapestry stool in front of her dressing-table mirror. She took several long pins from the loose bun at the back of her head and laid them down on the smooth dressing-table surface. She ran a worn ivory comb through her greying hair. Then she pulled the various loose hairs out of the comb, and wound them round her thumb and forefinger into a tight ball. In spring or early summer she would have thrown these fine threads of her hair out of the window for the birds to find and wind into the neat precise comfort of their nests. Now in mid-summer she threw the small ball of hair into the wicker waste-paper basket.

It was Violet now who felt the silence. There was no sound whatsoever from the nursery landing. She felt less daunted. More in command. She felt she had achieved something. She had begun to staunch the flow that this peculiar, unasked for child, dumped in their midst, threatened to unleash from the order of their ordinary lives.

She did not allow herself to consider the future. Throughout all her life she had tried to follow her father's maxim of taking each day at a time. When she looked into the mirror she saw not a large, faded, country woman; she saw the remnants of a girl that she would never entirely abandon. She felt sure that her intense determination to protect herself was a flawless, civilised, constructive emotion. She did not feel the universality of the threat, the curse and that howl. She was not disposed to extend herself beyond the rigid rim her own life had drawn round her.

Even when a degree of calm seemed to have settled throughout the house, and her hair was reorganised, smoothed and knotted back as usual, even then she could hear the howl and see the pale, pale face of this weird insect child, apparently her grandson. Somehow to Violet a cruel stain of that cursed sound was forever marked on to his brow. Violet was never able to see Spencer simply for himself. Always some substance of that uncanny sound was marked for her in the pale tentative force of Spencer's face for as long as she looked on him.

Finally, when darkness filled the small nursery room, making the electric light a true warmth against the shadows, then Spencer slept. He never made that sound again. Never so loud or for so long. But he kept always in his strange silence some semblance of its pain and power.

SEVEN

Just as seasons meld effortlessly into one another, just as the chaos of storm damage becomes tomorrow's fence posts or wood-stacks, so the presence of Spencer at Rathmanagh became simply a fact of the place. There was no address to reach Lumsden, no telephone number, no concrete way to proceed; the whereabouts of the fat girl seemed to be unknown, the only course was the continual day-to-day organisation of life; an acceptance of what was still to Violet a mocking intrusion. The stain of that sound from the height of the house on the first evening never receded far from Violet's memory and imagination. Later, it was said by Maura to have been . . . 'Surely a nightmare, Mrs Farr. He probably didn't know where he was.' But that was never Violet's explanation. She knew he had been fully awake when he made that sound. She was sure of it. However there was no other course but to allow the child to take root, as it were, like some unwanted sapling that blown in on the wind suddenly strikes into life in ground not prepared for it. It was always Violet's certain determination that there would come a time when this sapling would be uprooted. It was a usurper, an alien person, not natural to Rathmanagh ground. He would never be her responsibility. Violet felt that her tasks were only derived from situations that she herself had chosen and created. She would not have foisted upon her situations that had been carelessly and irresponsibly engendered by others. It was a painful subject. But he did not belong. He was wild, random stock. Time, Violet felt sure, would demonstrate all of this in the end. Time would offer her the opportunity to express to others what was to her an absolute truth: the child was cursed. He was bad blood. Ill conceived. Bad blood will out. With all the care and love and kindness showered on him by Maura and Donal and many others in the parish, still there was, Violet knew, a definite streak in the nature of the child that could not absorb this uncomplicated affection. There was a repelling glaze in the child's eyes, and in his defiant silences. He never acknowledged the kindness offered to him. He hung back. He was not on course. There were deceits and darkness about him. There was definite pressure simply in his physical presence, a compelling, negative pressure. Violet knew these things and she knew a day would come when they would confound her and everyone else. She must simply bide her time for nature and its indomitable power to take its course.

Spencer for his part moved in and out of the great cave structure of the house like some night creature who is only safe in darkness. It was Maura who took responsibility for him. It was she who cooked, and planned and organised his days. She gave him chalks and bricks, odd cars and a small plastic watering-can. It was the kitchen and the pantry and the apple store that were Spencer's places; the laundry yard and the red barn. It was in the laundry yard that Big Donal constructed a sandpit. It was out on a piece of rough ground just above Flora's meadow that Donal built a small hut out of odd planks of wood left over from some building works. And it was at the top of the walled garden beyond the compost that Donal dug up a small patch of unused ground for Spencer to grow his own radishes and nasturtiums. The formal parts of the garden, like the front rooms of the house, were to Spencer uninhabitable places which were cut off for him by an unseen curtain that hung almost from the sky deep into the damp cellar ground. The unseen areas hid him, so he felt, from the uncompromising glare of these rooms and landings and corridors. It hid him also from the stooped man and the tall woman whom Maura referred to as his grandparents. Only occasionally as he grew older would he investigate the other rooms, when he knew there was no one else in the house. The heavy pieces of furniture, the ticking clocks, the faded fabrics, the baskets and books and cushions. They seemed to sigh out to him with her breath. They seemed to follow him with her eyes. In some way as he grew older, he wanted to break their spell. He felt drawn to understand the fullness and the waiting that seemed to be there in all the rooms of the house, and in the great diversity of objects. But he did not have the key. He was like a traveller walking on a strand, who keeps pausing to look out at the countryside inland, but who never quite finds the gap, or gate, or path to make entry, so he keeps on to the shore line which he knows and which will, he is sure, go on forever.

In the early days, it was Maura who minded him. It was she who laughed when he slammed the doors, or hid in cupboards, or took food, or broke plants and eggs and flowerpots purposely. 'My, we're so bold today,' she would say, clearing things up, always still smiling; still with open arms to him. Her constancy was so great that he began to forget to make these angry challenges. He began to take seriously and responsibly the little tasks she allotted to him; the collecting of eggs, the feeding of Flora, the filling of the wood-kindling basket, the stirring of pots and the drying of plates, and the cutting out into shapes of the dough each morning. He began to draw with the chalks Maura brought up to the house, colouring in the faces in magazines.

Every so often Maura would say 'Let's show Madam what we've done', and Maura and Spencer might process beyond the unseen curtain, towards the study or the dining-room, with a tray of biscuits or a posy of wild flowers. Madam would always pause. She would be attentive. Her voice and gestures might be gentle, but there was consistently an iron reserve towards the child. She scrupulously avoided coming physically close to him. She never addressed him directly. And so naturally the child hung back. He was stubbornly silent in Violet's presence. Later Maura would say to Donal 'But it is Madam's loss, Donal. It is a terrible thing, bitterness. It can get such a hold of you. It can blind you even to yourself, that's the devil of it.'

But the busy practical business of each day meant that Maura never dwelt for too long on the darker side of things. If Madam went away, Spencer spent the night with her in the village. Practical problems could almost always be solved one way or another. It didn't do to look too far ahead. Spencer was a fact in the life of Rathmanagh and in the parish of Ballynaule. People knew him and greeted him. They gave him sweets and coins, which Maura had to take for him, he never took them for himself. And despite his silence, which could seem surly and awkward, there was a quality about him which many people recognised. He had a way with animals. It was his quiet. His waiting. The children found him strange because he never joined in their games; he never spoke or smiled, but they all knew; they had all heard from their parents that he was without a real mother or father of his own, so they simply let him be. They let him come and go as he pleased. It was only much later that one or two of the older boys, particularly Liam Brennan, felt obliged to pick on him.

Whereas Maura had come forward to Spencer, Big Donal, sensing the child's natural anxiety towards him, let the boy gradually come to him.

Donal was a very big man. He had a huge frame, large wide shoulders and big rough hands that were dark with weathering and various scars. He had a deep voice. He spoke slowly and softly, usually looking ahead of him, never directly towards the person he was addressing. He wore a flat cap that, greased with age, came tightly down on to his high forehead. When he was in the kitchen for any length of time he might take off his cap and lay it there beside his mug of tea. Then the strange white rim at the top of his brow was very noticeable; a band of softer skin that was unweathered and in great contrast to the rough, reddened skin of the rest of the face. There was a calm and evenness, almost grandeur about the strong features; the large nose, the wide mouth, the long ears. It was a fine face full of folds and heavily creased worn skin. The chin was always rough with a strong beard mark, although the hair under the cap was not dark, but fair, soft strands going grey at the edges just above the ears.

Spencer loved to peer at Donal's face, to hear the small rasping sound when he ran his rough hand across his chin. He liked the slow way he dragged the chair from the table, the heavy sound his boots made on the floor. Spencer would watch the dry curls of mud fall out from the rubber soles. His shirts had no collar so Spencer could stare at the warm folded skin of his throat, he could watch the folds move as Donal spoke to Maura. Donal usually wore braces, they were fixed on to the trouser button with a leather thong. The trousers were great, bulky, bulging shapes over the wide knees, rippling down into the socks which rose out over the high, well-laced mouth of the black boots.

It was many months before Spencer took the large hand that almost daily Donal offered to him. When he did, when he went across the laundry yard one damp autumn morning, it was to go into the red barn, and find there in the deep dark muddle of straw and old crates and sacks, one of the farm cats, covered with these small blind mewing creatures, that gradually each day grew stronger and more striped with wide open eyes, and shoving, eager, greedy habits. It was there in the darkness of the barn that Spencer stood, letting himself lean purposely against the great leg of Donal, with all those warm farm smells of leather and feed and sweat in the thick heavy cloth of his trousers. Those smells and that dark mysterious place, and the pausing, slow discourse of Donal's speech about cats and tenderness and how she knew exactly how to mind them and give them what they needed; the sum of it to Spencer was a wondrous calm. It was the sound and smell at last of a great safety he would never forget. He even tugged at Donal's shirt sleeve and said:

'May I hold one?'

Spencer so rarely spoke. Donal knew the importance of that question. He knew what a watershed it was. He turned to Spencer. He bent down. He smiled as he gathered up one of the small furry creatures in his large rough hand and held it out to Spencer. Then, when he had laid the kitten back beside the cat, he said to her:

'Well done, Puss, well done, mother . . .'

Donal knew that at last there was some trust between him and the child. Now he could go on to show him the secrets and wonders of the natural world that are beyond belonging. He could lead the child towards the inheritance of God's earth, which was outside the nightmare of rights and tenancies; simply the unending cycle of nature itself which would never be silenced or arrested by the greed and torments of man.

Donal had never married. It was said he had loved a girl in Claggan who had gone to America with her cousin. It was said that Donal wrote and that she promised to return, but she did not. Whatever way it was, he had always seemed both gentle and content, which was more than could be said for many of the married men. He lived alone out on the Balligarry Road, in a small stone house with his dogs and pigs and ewe flock. The Balligarry Road was on the other side of Mount Murna. In the fine months Donal would walk across the mountain to Rathmanagh, by the goats' path as it was known, a narrow zig-zag route of bare track which led eventually on to the hard road.

Through Donal, Spencer began to see and feel and learn beyond himself. He learnt that there was no place in the world, however hidden or overgrown, however barren or dry, that was not habitat for some creature. He learnt that every sound, however small, had meaning. Every rustle, every twig crack, every blowing, sighing, chip or trill of sound. And the way things lay together, the way they were, tufts of hair, droppings, slime lines over a leaf, the wearing and marks in the ground, every gnawed stem or stripped piece of bark; everything had meaning. Spencer learnt that some of the most beautiful lives were the shortest: the dragon and the damsel fly. He learnt that survival was as Donal said 'a quiet work of art'. 'Nothing remains the same, all of it is change and motion, every creature has its time, every creature has its place somewhere.'

There were creatures that maddened Donal. The moorhens with their greed for the duck eggs. The slugs with their creeping, foul capture of good spring cabbage, the jays, the hooded crows. He could be maddened by a ewe who rejected a strong lamb after birth, or a flighty cow, wild eyed and restless. But his tempers, like storms or sudden gusts of biting wind, they had a place, they were there for a purpose.

Donal showed Spencer where he might catch sight of the kingfisher, that sudden dart of regal colour over the dark water. He knew the nesting places of the barn owl, of thrushes, wrens, redstarts, swifts and swallows, every bird that sang and nested in or around the woods and meadows of Rathmanagh. There was no small chip fraction of egg-shell that Spencer might find which Donal could not instantly name. He taught Spencer to fish for rudd and perch and minnows. He taught Spencer that there was even purpose in death; every carcass was someone's feast.

Later, when Spencer started down at the small village school in Ballynaule, he would come back up at midday to find Donal, because the classroom was so dull and confining. Donal always welcomed him. There was always a task to do; something to hold, or cut, or capture; something to shift or secure. Donal told them down at the school that sitting pegged to a desk wasn't what the boy needed, and they agreed, so Spencer's schooling became a very spasmodic, intermittent affair.

Spencer grew to love the sour milk smell of Donal's kitchen, the warm, muck earth feel that was in everything; the mugs and drawers, the towel on the back of the chair, and the sticky, rubber feel of the faded check oilcloth on the table. There was always milk and bread, butter and potatoes and cabbage, and a bit of boiled beef now and then.

Towards the end of every summer as Spencer grew older, Donal would drive him to Cork City in the small van, where they would collect Donal's sister Maeve. Then they would drive directly west to Kilbronan Bay, where they would stay for one whole week in Aunt Theodora's house. The house was very meagre and shabby now, but it was still in Violet's possession although she rarely went there herself. It was let, on and off through the season, and given as a holiday space to Donal or Maura when and if they felt so inclined.

The visit to Kilbronan was undoubtedly the highlight of Spencer's year. Here he had Donal to himself, to walk the bare mountains, to fish off the end of the pier. To scour the rock pools for crab and anemones and mollusc shells, to find huge fir cones under the pine trees, to watch the whooper swan fly inland to the lake each evening, and at low tide, to feel the warm worm casts and collect shells: cowries, dead men's fingers, razorshells, and the smooth, pearly, china man's hat. It was the freedom of the space, those wide, high skies, the sharp, salt smell on the wind, the shriek of the gulls and terns, the squelch, the giving, watery softness of the sand through bare toes. They always brought Donal's dogs with them. Two narrow sheepdog mixtures, Floss and Gyp, with their darting, low down, pointed noses and their eager wagging weaving walk at Donal's heels. Up on the mountain their coats became matted with burrs and ticks and cleavers, but nothing could daunt their sense of adventure, the breadth and excitement of the keen fresh smells in the rough grass. On the last day they would fill paper sacks of carrageen moss to take home and boil up for the pigs, Donal said that the cooked, glutinous mass was a fine tonic for them.

It was an unspoken, perfect passage of time between Donal and Spencer. It was so far from the heavily furnished rooms of Rathmanagh, with always somewhere in sight the stooping, slow figure of Cecil or the darker, busier shape of Violet, watering or weeding, sorting or simply staring. Spencer often saw her in the evenings. She would go to the front meadow where she would stand, staring out over the tops of the trees by the river towards Mount Murna. She would stare so intently, as if she saw something or someone most particular. Spencer would watch her unseen. She was so intent, he knew he was safe from a sudden turn or glance. Violet did perplex him. He wondered what it was he must have done to have her so disengaged from him. Wherever he was within the grounds of Rathmanagh, even if he were beyond the demesne wall, even if he was in the warmth and small safety of Donal's house, still the feel of her stare, and the searching need she seemed to have; it could always get to him. But out there, on the strand at Kilbronan, he was entirely free of her, so that the sounds of seabirds, and the constant slap of water became for Spencer like the breathing portals of heaven itself.

By the time he was ten, Spencer could read and write, but he had no particular taste for it. He enjoyed best to listen to the legends Miss O'Brien told them every Wednesday afternoon. Tales of Finn Mac Coul, the Hag of the Finger, a crone who had a gigantic son. She could only be slain with a silver arrow. She was slain by Finn. And there was Aine, a fairy Queen, whose dwelling place was in a hill, Knockainy, which made Spencer sure that there were fairies and other ancestors dwelling within Murna itself. There was Cuchulain and Donn, the Brown Bull of Cuailgne so desired by Maeve. There were Pookas, solitary demon spirits which could take any form. There was Tir na nOg, the land where everyone stayed young, it was an island somewhere, so Donal said, somewhere in the sea beyond Kilbronan Bay. Ossian, the son of Finn, had visited Tir na nOg. Because Spencer so loved these tales, he committed them easily to memory. It was the only thing he knew well and it considerably irritated Liam Brennan, who liked to think of Spencer as daft. He was jealous of the licence everyone seemed to give this lad who had nothing worthwhile to say for himself. Liam became bent on the downfall and humiliation of Spencer. Spencer sensed this and simply avoided him. But Liam, and one or two of the others, started trespassing in the woods and cycling up the back road into Rathmanagh, sometimes even as far as the stable yard itself.

Spencer's proudest task was the care of the several bantams and brown speckled hens that were kept in the run behind the red barn. It was he who minded them, shutting them up at night, last thing, and then letting them out again in the morning. It was he who knew if one was broody and might sit on a clutch of eggs. He had feared the rooster, but now his violent, colourful, domineering role in this small feathered community intrigued and fascinated him.

As the years had passed, certain understandings had established themselves between Violet and Spencer. Violet had made it quite clear to Spencer that Cecil was of no particular significance. Spencer helped Violet with the preparation of vegetables and plants for the Claggan market. He also had meals in the dining-room with his grandparents at the weekends. Although Spencer knew they were his grandparents, he never addressed them by name. He knew his position was different; unusual. To visitors he must always be absent. He would never assume himself to be a relative of the Farrs. He was more a creature within the demesne of Rathmanagh, like a dog or cat or servant's child.

Father Bohane had left the parish. He had been replaced by a much younger man, Father Gerard; he was possibly the only person who ever attempted any kind of direct approach that referred to Spencer's true circumstances. But Spencer was uneasy if his parents or future were ever mentioned. In his own mind he belonged more to the world of Finn and Ossian and Tir na nOg if he belonged anywhere.

But still for Violet he was an unnerving, continually appraising presence. She felt stalked by his pale face and its large empty eyes. He sometimes asked her about Birkin whose gravestone he had discovered. Violet found the name of Birkin on his lips deeply disturbing. It was as if he had dug open the very grave itself, exposing that great skull and the bright pointed teeth and the bare smooth bones.

There was no naughtiness now, no wild, contemptible behaviour. The hair was kempt, the body was clean, but the eyes were to Violet uncanny. They flushed her out. They mocked her. He simply stared in silence. He would never speak. It did not occur to her that Spencer might be seeking some kind of recognition of himself, some explanation for the strangeness of his circumstances. To Violet, the pale face, the expressionless eyes, derided her with increasing skill and cynicism. He was a ruthless, unbearable challenge to her. The more she sought to avoid confrontation, the more keenly he seemed to follow her.

As Spencer grew taller, as his limbs began to lose their round, chumped, child look, as his neck lengthened, and the veins stood out on the backs of his hands, Violet was aware of the sweating, sexual male that must emerge, something she could not bear to think of. She had even said to Cecil on more than one occasion that Spencer had about him the quality of a spy; some planted person, whose job was to discover unseen, the fullest possible and most private information about them. 'But, my dear, even if he were interested . . . there is nothing here. Nothing to find. Nothing to say.' Such a dismal response from Cecil only reminded Violet how trapped, how frog-marched her life had been by the dead stupidity of this man, who had spent a lifetime revelling in the utter emptiness of her destiny. In the depths of her many, many hours alone, Spencer became the image round which she coiled the vast unsprung rhythm of her life and being. It was his pale face framed in the thick dark hair that followed her like some sickened ghost seeking an appalling revenge; revenge for her barren life of tense intelligent control. Revenge for some lifelessness for which she felt he held her responsible. And the boy would grow. The face would increase. The mind might find words and then sounds. In his staring silence there was always for Violet the echo of that howl the first evening. She had lived through all these years certain that this curse, which his ill conception had brought into the world, this curse would finally show itself. Eventually the bad blood would run and then all Violet's store of bitter feelings would be released and she would be vindicated.

Violet had once said to Spencer 'I have never met your mother.' By inference, it was the only reference she ever made to Lumsden. Absence of either reference or information had made Spencer quite forgetful that parents should ever have been. The words 'Mother' and 'Father' were to him like two flat closed doors on an empty landing. The doors had neither handle nor keyhole. They were simply indents in an otherwise seamless high wall. It was within the secret chambers of Mount Murna's inner dark that Spencer's ancestors rested. For Spencer, Murna was a magic mountain. He often imagined a beautiful burial chamber there, lit only with candles. Here his guardian angel slept, with all his other ancestors; warriors and poets, a lion and a unicorn, and a beautiful woman who bent over a small cradle rocking a child who never slept. Because of this she always sang, but she did not turn her head from the child. Spencer had never seen her face, only her white hands and her long braided hair. But he knew the sound of her voice; it was a high clear sound, as easy, as effortless as a nightingale.

Violet's view of herself was of an intelligent woman, sorely tried, whose careful, iron control was sometimes breached, but those occasions, when her sarcasm and fury knew no bounds, were summarily forgotten by her. They simply piled up into the structure of injustices done to her. From these painful skirmishes she made the wounds and angry scars which became an extravagant cope of intense self-pity distancing her from other people, even the outer world itself; the whole vigorous trail of contemporary history. Increasingly the smallest irritations could bring about uncontrollable rage and indignation; mud on a carpet, dripping clothes on a polished surface, a message undelivered, gardening tools left out in the rain, the clatter of a loose window frame, Cecil's used handkerchief left at the back of a chair, unfinished food scruffily picked over on the plate, this was a frequent offence of Spencer's on the rare occasions he ate in the dining-room. Those who knew Violet Farr well felt anxious for her. The isolation. The bitter resentment of her grandson. Her obvious irritation of others less able than herself and her outbursts of anger at various committees and public occasions made her standing less. Her intelligence was never doubted, but her frequent sarcasm made her more of a liability than an asset in the affairs of the community.

It was a Saturday in early November. The day had been damp and heavy, the sky low and overcast. The laundry yard was backing up with leaves again from the fierce wind the evening before. The damp that had been fine and soft was beginning to have the cut of winter in it. Maura had left mashed potatoes and a rice pudding in the bottom oven of the Aga. A mutton stew simmered gently on the top. The table was laid in the dining-room, Cecil had done it a little earlier than usual. Violet at one end, with her back to the long windows, Cecil opposite her, just inside from the door into the hallway. Spencer's place was laid opposite the sideboard and the heavy engraving of the stag with the large oval eyes in the maple frame. No one had ever referred to Lumsden having sat so long before in exactly the same place in the dining-room; no one mentioned him either as son, or father of this child.

Spencer was chopping kindling in the red barn. He had just sat down for a pause on a pile of old sacks. He was stroking the thin black cat that lived in the stables when suddenly he heard a strange rush of sound. There were voices, general commotion. There was laughter. Then Spencer heard the unmistakable sound of bicycles being crushed down against the corrugated tin walls of the barn. He felt his stomach heave into a great lump. There was this knot of fear that almost leapt up into his throat and stifled his breath. He knew it was Liam Brennan. He knew it was Liam and the others. They had been up to Rathmanagh twice on the previous weekend, pinching apples and taunting and jeering. Sensing his anxiety the cat jumped down. He walked slowly across the barn to the open doorway. He was waiting for further sounds but there were none. Then suddenly there was a screeching clatter of squawks, and the hens and bantams scattered, coming down into the yard in front of Spencer. Flustered and hectic, they ran in every direction squawking and flapping their wings. They were everywhere. Spencer started to herd them round to the back of the barn into their run. The door of the run was wide open. Three bicycles were lying by the wall of the barn but there was no sign of Liam or the other boys.

Spencer, with his hands fanned wide apart, tried to coax the frightened birds back down from the muddy bank and into the run. Once he had the rooster the hens became a little calmer and followed. He was uneasy. There was no sign of the boys. Spencer felt pretty sure they would be up in the orchard. He decided he would leave them to it. He must simply secure the hens into the hen-house for the night and then secure the door into the run itself. He had just got them into the fusty dark and on to their perches when he made a quick count. There was one missing. It was the brown speckled hen. The darkness was closing in fast. He made the door of the run secure and then he went back down into the yard to look for her. The sight of the bicycles lying there like a loud clap of hands to taunt him made him nervous. Then suddenly he heard her. There was this racing mad cackle ploughed into the misty darkness. Then there were one or two spurts of sharp sound. Then there was silence. Then there was this small, faint, paltry sound unlike anything Spencer had heard before. Then there was silence again; a deep cold silence. The sounds had come from the orchard. Spencer raced up the muddy bank until he came in sight of the apple trees. The light was very gloomy, just a pale thin milk run behind the tar pitch, rough shapes of the trees. Then Spencer saw them. There were three of them. Liam was easy to see with his bright, thick, carrot hair. He was far taller than the others. He came forward towards Spencer. His arm was raised high into the air. He was swinging something up round his head. He swung it round and round like a bird scarer except it made no sound. He swung it harder as if it were a thing to hurl. Then Spencer saw the bright yellow claws that poked out beyond the rough grip of Liam's fist.

'Come on, fairy boy. Catch her. Catch her.'

And then Liam let go on the crest of a swing and this warm soft weight of feathers and claws hurtled through the air and landed with a thud at Spencer's feet. The bright eye was still open. There was blood coming from the beak. The boys ran off. They ran past Spencer laughing and spitting pips and apple cores out of their mouths in his direction. Then Spencer heard them take up the bikes. He heard their voices fade. He bent down and gathered the poor bird up into his arms. It was for him she had died. She had died for him. It was him, not the bird, that Liam despised. Spencer stroked the soft warm feathers. He could not believe it. He had seen death many times; rabbits, kittens, newborn lambs, a poisoned fox once up on Murna. He had always known, as Donal said, that death was just a part of things. But this death was different. He had never known a death like this, taken jeeringly, tauntingly, as a sport of derision. He felt shamed. They had gone now, and he had done nothing. He walked slowly back through the orchard grass and down the muddy bank, his shoes slipping and sliding on the greasy ground.

He went over to the large stone trough by the red barn. He sat on the edge of it. He let the bird's head dip down into the cold water. He wiped the blood from the sharp beak. He closed the bright eye. He had not known until this moment that he loved the hens. But as he held the bird, as he felt into the soft fine warmth under her wing, he knew he loved her. Love was not a word that belonged to him. Any love he had heard mentioned was remote, like the love of God or the love in ballad songs. But now, in the bitter damp shadowy dark of the laundry yard, he felt he understood it a little. He let his cool cheek rest against the feathers. He did not cry. He had never cried, not for as long as he could remember. But he had these feelings that pricked into his eyes, feelings that choked and swallowed in his throat, feelings like tight balls of clustered twine in his chest and stomach, feelings that wanted to spill out somehow. He should have known it was late because of the darkness. But he had forgotten time, and the stew he had smelt earlier, and the thick greasy mud on his shoes, when he should have worn boots. He had forgotten it all. The bird grew cold as the light faded; it seemed fitting for him to stay there, quiet and cold and damp, with the brown speckled hen across his knees, as he sat on the edge of the stone trough by the side of the red barn.

Violet had been upstairs in her bedroom for some while. She had been standing by the window watching the light gradually fade. She had seen Murna grow into a great dark lump of ground thrust up from beyond the river bed. Now in the darkness there was no definition of trees or scrub, or dips or gulleys. Simply the huge, strange bulk of the mountain itself. As Violet stared at Murna, she felt almost as if the lump of that mountain was there within herself, weighting her down, putting this dull pain into her legs and back and feet and fingers. She felt stiff and cold. The winter moved towards her, a cruel reminder of good seasons gone. The seasons of abundance and harvest, over and done with. Like her own life; gone; almost over and done, but without the harvest for which it was intended. In the dark of these bitter thoughts, she found herself increasingly attending to the presence of Spencer. His face loomed up towards her like some trickster or demon. She made his mockery of her, as she felt it to be, she made it the final wedge driving her towards this dull possessing interior dark.

And it was late now. Cecil was waiting in the hallway, his stiff white knuckle poised as usual at the glass face of the barometer. Violet came down the stairs.

'There's no sign of the boy,' Cecil said. He tapped the glass. The needle swung. 'Glass is going down,' he said. Violet went past him. She saw Spencer's wellington boots dry and unused by the back door. She saw the gathering late dark outside in the laundry yard. She went out into the dusky cold. She called. She shrieked the wretched name.

'Spencer. Spencer.'

She knew it was useless. Even if he heard he would pay no attention. She went across the yard towards the red barn. He spent most of his time out there with the cats and rats and sparrows.

'Spencer.' She called again. Then she saw him. She saw that pale, moon crust circle of staring face, over there in the dark.

'Spencer.'

He did not move. He was sitting on the large stone trough. She could see him quite clearly now. The staring pale face, the bare knees, the socks rolled down on to filthy muddy shoes. She raced across the yard. How dare he simply ignore her. How dare he.

As she came closer Spencer could hear her breath. He saw the drawn, thread flesh move in the long narrow neck. He saw her broad, shapeless chest heave forward towards him. Then she pointed her small head, like a javelin thrust, right up close to his own cool skin.

'How dare you . . .' she began again. Then she saw the yellow claws and the damp cold bird prostrate across the bare knees. She saw the loose flopped head dipped down into the water of the trough. She saw the bird's death. She saw in the death of the bird the bad blood of the boy; the bad blood running wild; running mad. Violet saw what she had always known. She saw the curse grown strong in this dangerous emerging young man . . . This miscalculation. This . . . illegitimate child. Illgotten. Ill. Sick. Mad. She had known it. She had always known it. Now they would know it. There might be reasons. There were reasons for everything, but madness seen and unregarded was irresponsible. Her responsibilities were clear. Her responsibilities were to this place, to Rathmanagh. They were to standards, decent, disciplined standards. The boy was mad. A killer child. She was not surprised. The pathology had been glaringly obvious to her all along.

Spencer tried to pull back from her face so close to him. He could smell her breath, a sharp dry smell. He pressed his fingers deep into the softest, most hidden feathers of the dead bird. He tried to gather some comfort up out of their innocence.

'I didn't do it. I didn't do it.'

He spoke so clearly, so precisely. She had rarely heard him speak like that before.

'That bird died of fright. That bird was killed,' Violet

said. 'Bring it with you. Follow me. Then wait outside with it.'

At last she turned from him. She walked in long strides across the laundry yard. Spencer slipped down from the cold ledge of the stone trough. He gently curled the head of the dead bird back up on to the breast. Then he followed Violet. It was all shadows now. It was all just lumps of darkness. He did not know how exactly, but he knew as he followed Violet towards the high stone house, he knew things would change; something would shift. Something would alter. Violet had gone inside. Spencer came round the house to the edge of the back meadow where he could look out towards Murna. It was too dark now to see the mountain, but he could feel it. He tried to feel for its magic, for the safety of the candle-lit chamber within it, that he always imagined there, with his buried ancestors, and his guardian angel, and the lion and the unicorn. He was fearful that somehow, the mountain might flatten and lose its shape. He was afraid that the whole horizon might be taken from him.

Then Violet came out again into the yard. She had switched on the light. Spencer saw the great slash of dark that was her shadow.

'Go and wait for me in the garage,' she said. Spencer cradled the dead bird up into his jersey. He used to carry the kittens like that. He felt strangely comforted by the weight of this innocent creature's presence, heavy and soft against him. He stood there with the bird, just inside the garage. He could smell oil and rags and warm petrol dust. As he looked out into the dark, listening for the sound of her voice again, or her footsteps on the yard, he suddenly understood what he must do. He must gather up this great dark silence of the night outside, he must gather it round him. It would be his turret. It would be his Murna. From within that silence he might survive. Donal had often told him that creatures sensed what to do, what to eat, where to go. He was a creature. He sensed as he waited, he sensed that he must gather up a deep, bidden silence. It would hide him, befriend him. In his circumstances any attempt at speech would be useless. Spencer knew that Violet must have made some kind of decision. He knew the patterns of her rage and certainties. There would be some kind of change. He had felt it in her heaving furious breath so close to him.

It was quite some time before Violet came with her coat on into the garage. She had telephoned Father Gerard. The continuous goodwill of the Catholic clergy over the years towards Spencer had always irritated her. Now she felt they could put their cardinal charity to some effect. They had meddled in the boy's life. They had been the means by and large of his arrival at Rathmanagh. Now they could put their Christian minds to his departure. Elderly people like herself and Cecil were no match for a child psychopath. This hen, this bleeding dead bird, it was, Violet felt sure, a precursor of other much more terrible deeds. But whatever deeds and violent misfortunes that were to come, they would not happen here at Ballynaule.

Violet drove the car towards the presbytery with menacing speed, bumping and braking as if the gears were the pounding, driving force of her fury.

She left Spencer for quite awhile in the car. Father Gerard could do nothing but listen. He heard and watched with dismay as this good-looking intelligent woman wailed with almost incoherent intensity about the evil, cursed, dangerous disposition of this child. She paced the room throwing her head this way and that, gesticulating with her hands. Two or three times Father Gerard, simply in order to calm her, suggested a chair to sit on. But when she did sit down she rose again almost instantly, as if she feared to be contained or stilled. At length, Father Gerard said the only thing he could in the circumstances: 'Of course I should be delighted for Spencer to stay here for a night or two, Mrs Farr. I shall be delighted to have a chat with him.'

'There is no longer time simply for talk and kindness, Father.

306

You have not seen and witnessed all that I have. You cannot have the grasp and understanding that I do.'

'Maybe not,' Father Gerard interrupted her. 'Maybe not,' he said, raising his voice against his better judgment. 'I have not the privilege of being his relative.'

'It is a very dubious privilege, Father, as you well know.'

'Circumstances of birth are irrelevant. We are not born into the world full of other people's shadows, Mrs Farr. We are simply children of God. One at a time, each on their own, each special and particular.'

'You would make a most unfortunate historian, Father. No wonder your Church relies on the suppression of reason. Unreasoning man is a glutton for the moods and rituals of your liturgy.'

'Please, Mrs Farr, please leave it. We achieve nothing by all of this. I am sorry you are distressed. I can understand that but . . .'

'There are no "buts", Father. There is only one way to resolve this. The boy must be returned to his parents. They must take responsibility now.'

'Well, certainly, since I now know how you feel, Mrs Farr. It is glaringly obvious to me that Rathmanagh is not ideal for Spencer.'

When Spencer came into the dark hallway of the presbytery carrying the bird still in the cradle of his jersey, he had so soaked himself in this great silence that he hardly heard Father Gerard's voice, when he said:

'Well, it'll make a fine stew for Donal.'

Father Gerard hoped by mentioning Donal he might lighten things. He wanted to relieve the boy of any guilt or fear he might have. He took the bird from Spencer. He wrapped it in newspaper. Spencer simply let him. He didn't hear the crackle of the newspaper or Father Gerard's voice. He heard in his head the sound of deer in a forest, the pounding of hooves, the scattering of loose ground. In his mind the dead bird lay like a swan sacrifice on a table of marble and the unicorn pawed the forest ground and then dipped its horn in coal fire and lit all the candles in the burial chamber. And there was no sound there but the echoing refrain of the woman with braided hair who rocked the cradle. The feathers of the bird would be down for her quilt, and the beak would be an emblem, with the bright eye and the golden claws, it would be kept forever in a jewelled casket.

Spencer sat very still within his silence, which was full of candle-light, and the deer, and the casket, and the feathers of the swan. Father Gerard was worried. The child would not speak. It was almost as if he heard nothing. Father Gerard took him up into the small spare bedroom. He gave him a towel and some cocoa and cake, but he did not respond.

'Your grandmother says that you told her you didn't do it.'

Father Gerard tried gently to coax some confidence from the boy. Spencer looked up. He would like to have spoken. But he could not. He had made the silence about him so well. He did not know any longer what he had ever done, or what he had never done. He did not know anything for sure. Even his cold knees, and muddy shoes, even the scratch on his arm from the wire in the run, they might all belong to someone else, and then again, although he touched them they might very well not even be there.

And the silence, so well made by Spencer, persisted. As the external actions and decisions about him increased, as he was questioned, left, taken here and there, so he became like a small stone in the depths of a whirlpool. The waters about him swirled and raced, were muddied, became thick, cold, never calm again. He remained safe within his strong silence. Safe like a smooth weight beneath all the turbulence and charge of the waters above him.

EIGHT

There were many people who tried their best. But Spencer's continual lack of response forced them to consider his condition as psychiatric, seriously disturbed. He was sent back to London. He was passed like a signal in a game. He was passed from priests to psychiatrists, to social workers, to hostels, and to foster-parents. His name was on a river-bed of forms. But with the strength of his silence he was able to remain apart. He waited in dull corridors, or on the edge of broken beds, he waited in overheated clinics. He was driven and checked, picked up and dropped off. But the weight of him slipped down always below the level of their care and control and understanding. They tried different schools, different homes, but without his co-operation they were made to feel foolishly inadequate.

Very occasionally he would speak. It was often nothing more or less than a murmur of politeness. 'Thanks' 'No thanks' 'Sure' 'No' 'No way' 'Dunno'.

In the beginning he kept his eyes downcast. He scrutinised their feet and his own, black scud marks on worn linoleum, thick dust, watery stains on wood or concrete or stone, swirling sick orange and brown on thin carpets. In the shapes and mood and smell of the surface into which he stared he began to see creatures; ants, lizards, moles, even now and then a damsel fly.

What he saw engaged his attention; in some way it fed him. And so he thought, if he saw a little earth or water, weeds or springy bank ground with furze and crippled roots and heather, if he saw a little like that, definite and keen, then surely if he looked up, if he raised his eyes, he might see the forest; the giant hide of Murna's open ground; the wide pounding drive of the ocean. He might see rocks and pools and the streaming emptiness of the sky. He thought carefully of this, but it was some time before he had the courage to dare to do it. He felt if he looked up too soon, before his silence had grown into even greater strength, he felt he might become impaled on their stares. He might become scared by their frenzied pens on the paper forms with his name; their folded, pale fingers, their waiting, waiting, waiting. They might close in round his breath, they might move in and destroy the safety of his silence.

Eventually he did look up. It was a bright morning in a very warm clean space. There was a man in the room with him. He had been waiting a long time. To begin with, he had simply said 'Well, you seem to be giving everyone a lot of trouble . . .' Then he waited. There was a small high window behind his head. There was the branch of a tree with birds on it. Spencer saw the warm square of sun on the brown carpet. And he heard the birds. The birds were sparrows. The word 'trouble' stayed in his mind. It grew like dark gnarled branches. It grew into a rough, contorted, creeper shape. It grew so that it took all the space. Only the smallest fragments of space were left between the rough winding limbs. But Spencer thought when it is spring and there are buds and leaves, then the dark difficult sinews will become hidden. Their patterns then will not be half so bold. There will be space then between the leaves and the leaves will be light and fresh, not heavy and dark like the trunk and the branches. He was seeing all of this when the soft large hands brought out these cards and put them down on the table. Spencer could just see that they were blot marks, rather like the mess of blood in the folded corners of newspaper, after plucking a bird. Donal plucked birds so fast. He never damaged the flesh. He knew how to pull the feathers without tearing.

The marks on the cards were not unlike branches, but they were softer. They were not unlike blood. They were liquid anyway. Spencer looked up, enough to see the stains on the cards and the clean square fingernails of the hands that held them. Then the man said 'What do you see?' Spencer thought of Donal plucking birds. He thought of the soft flight of the smallest, nail-paring, moon-curved feathers that flew out so fast into the dust at the edges of the room. And he thought of the shapes of blood under the carcass on to the paper. He said 'Blood.' The man said 'Anything else?' And Spencer said again 'No. Blood. Just blood.' The man shifted the cards. The blood on them was like butterflies and bellies and limbs; the blood was like Violet's hair strands, and the pierced, coiled knot at the back of her head. Spencer had not thought of Violet for a long while. Any thought of her might impair the silence. He was afraid to disturb the silence. These cards, these blood shapes might seep into it. They might take the silence from him. He tried to see the branches again instead of the blood. Something made him feel he must fight. He must fight for the strength of the silence to remain. To do this he might have to look up. He might need to stare face to face and then build the forest between them. So he looked up. He looked up at the man with the cards and the clean fingernails.

It was a very careful face. It was a man with cheese smooth skin and damp clean strands of hair. The eyes were ready like spikes to catch him; to impale him. To avoid the eyes so directly towards him Spencer stared at the forehead. He stared at the point between the eyes where nothing was, and as he stared, he remembered the unicorn that rested within Murna in the candlelit chamber. He remembered that the hooves of the unicorn are soundless; without sound the unicorn is suddenly there in a forest clearing. He remembered that spring and summer are the seasons when the unicorn has the power of the earth; the lion and its wrath and strength are less then. He thought that maybe it was the woman with braided hair who rocked the cradle, maybe it was she who drew from the unicorn his wisdom and calm. As Spencer thought the man stared.

After many sessions and much waiting, all he had from this boy was 'blood'. It was not much, but it was enough to be uneasy with. There might well be a predisposition to schizophrenia. Certainly, the boy was dangerously withdrawn. Dangerously out of touch with the real external world, and any practical sense of himself.

Then Spencer saw for the first time the lump on the clear forehead. Then from the lump he saw a brightness. The brightness grew outwards and upwards. It was a shaft of strong light. Then Spencer no longer saw the clean waiting man or the empty desk, or the blood-run cards. He saw the unicorn. A giant white beast with the body of a deer and gentle oval eyes and the bright horn of power; a driving power to keep all intruders from the weight and cloak of the silence. In the presence of the unicorn he was safe. He could look up. He could stare because they were nothing. They were no presence. There was only the white flanks, the strong quarters and the silent hooves, and a glow of moonlight and power; it threaded into the silence as small different leaves thread into the wide foliage roof of darkness that is the height of the forest.

Spencer stared. He was sitting upright. He was looking directly ahead at the tall clean man, but he felt quite comfortable because there was no one there, only the light and strength of the unicorn. His breathing was deep and regular. The clean man noticed it. He said 'Spencer.' He said it several times, but it sounded less than a name each time he repeated it. Eventually, he said 'Right. I think we'll leave things for today.' The clean man stood up. Spencer remained seated. He smiled. The clean man made a note of it. Spencer smiled because he was safe. He had mastered something. The unicorn was there. The forest was there. The emptiness, the tin sounds and bright shapes were theirs; they need not intrude on him.

As time passed, as he took pills and was moved from place to place, their urgent questions became less. He was not violent, so it seemed. He did not appear to be a danger either to the general community or to himself. The challenge was to persuade foster-parents to accommodate him, and for a suitable school to register him. All of these things were done. He remained withdrawn and strange. But he was not a pressing problem, like those who set fire to tables and mattresses or cut their wrists with razor-blades or ran riot in shopping centres, or absconded and were found drunk and partially clad on waste ground. Those were the pressing problems; they took the focus and filled the timetable of the authorities. Spencer receded into the background. He stared at large television screens, he stared at walls and yards and cupboards. Regularly his officer, sometimes a man, sometimes a woman, met him after school and gave him chocolate and money and talk. They tried to have ideas, they tried to sound alert, concerned, but Spencer's silence always finally exhausted them. He became increasingly less registered, less noticed, less monitored.

The school was a huge complex of rectangular rooms and wide corridors. Barren hard spaces smelling of sweat and ink and rubber. Occasionally groups of boys picked on him but his dumb lack of response was finally boring. He seemed fearless. And the fun was in the fear. There were girls intrigued by his silence who tried to get to him. But they got bored also. Spencer did not easily engage sympathy. His silence had, so people felt, an aggressive, claustrophobic quality. It was an unnerving, negative presence, and so people withdrew. The world withdrew, it fell back far enough from him and the turret silence within which he dwelt for him to regard it and assess it, in his own way, and at his own pace.

To Spencer, London reeked out street by street, concrete height after concrete height, like some vast fruit form, an interminable seamless interconnection of stems and leaf and flower structures, all grown up from a huge, hidden, smelted stem of iron from underground. The smelted stem must reach down into the red hot core of the earth itself. But this city fruit, this hydra, seaweed structure, globbed and bloomed and whelped these vast forms, foundation on to foundation. The building mass was divided by scurvy runs of tarmac where the insect panic of cars and buses and lorries loaded it. Only the park spaces were calm, and the wide ride of the river towards, so they said, the sea, but Spencer could hardly believe that. There was a great deal that was hard to believe. Somewhere or other, there was a Queen with small, stubby dogs, and giant barricaded houses; and there were politicians and game-show hosts whose large thrusting faces loomed up daily on the television screens. But they were incidental to the vast city fruit, whose structure hid and housed the real forging mass of people. The people fascinated Spencer, they were so various; it was as if this city fruit had been grown to capture, by its scent and the promise of its racing vitality, all the bugs and gnats and jungle-flies of the world.

The playground, the streets and pews of Ballynaule had one single face, one type of texture, like the cabbage-white butterfly in the walled garden, beautiful but not surprising. The face of Ballynaule made just one fully anticipated sound. But the faces found here on this city fruit were a continuous, constantly surprising, endlessly changing mass of difference and diversity. Because of the turret silence, Spencer could stare fearlessly in the hubbub of the school corridors and the open ground outside. He could purposely lean up against the wire-netting and watch these tall black boys with rose pink palms to their hands and a jet darkness to the rest. They moved with the ease of race-horses; liquid movements, feet, arms, trunk and thighs all one easy, ripple ribbon action. There were smaller, less dark Indian boys, with shining black olive eyes, sometimes they wore turbans to keep in the black stack of hair. The Indian girls had narrow wrists and fine ankles, turned like sapling branches, and long rich hair, unlike any girl's hair in Ballynaule. Some of the white guys were very fat, they talked with rough, cut grunt sounds and threatening exclamations. There were fat girls too, with loud scream laughs and huge bobbing breasts and thick bare legs. They all wore badges and crosses, heavy rings and dangling metal. There was as much variety of voice and walk, the feel of different flesh and different manner, as there were shells and creatures in the rock pools and shore line of Kilbronan Bay.

But Spencer skulked alone on the outer edge, so the way he saw and felt things was always several removes from the situation. The turret silence could baffle out external sounds, so he could ignore commands or questions made to him. But the turret silence could only contain a certain amount. As time passed, Spencer began to understand that even the turret silence had limits. And it was filled now. It was bulked up hard with so many actions and reactions felt, but never made. All the unsaid silent screams and fury and sadness were coiled up in there, mounting into a terrible dormant energy. As time passed, an urgency crept into the silence, it was so stuffed, so battened in by this bulk of feeling. It made Spencer move out and move on. He bunked off school to be alone. No one noticed. There were parts he would have liked to have come closer to. There were moments of life: loud music sounds and laughter, the nudging, joshing, spit and run tackle of harmless mucking about; all that he envied. The bulk weight of the turret silence became a heavy, almost suffocating load. His movements were sluggish, his skin solid, greasy and scarred. When he bunked off school, he simply slept in cold deserted spaces. But the sleep never grew into live energy like the others had. The sleep seemed to close up and muffle out every slit into light and air that the turret might have had. The sleep engendered nothing but a need for further sleep. He often muttered to himself the names, their names, the class lists from the notice-boards. Varied names like herbs or wild flowers, names of life's endless variety. Like a litany, Spencer murmured the names; names from a life to which he could never belong. Names of thrusting energy, names of tormentors, names of stunning, wanting girls, names of powerful guys who got no grief from the rest, names of scabs, names of wimps, just names: Basho, Wellington, Kimber, Jemma, Jess, Danielle, Seymour, Chima, Ifoma, Musole, Chuckwudi, Debbie, Marilyn, Ogbomnaya, Khalid, Andrew, Amber, Bethany, Kacy, Pod, Wang, Judd, Mark, Manuel, Mahmud and Hatch. Hatch was a tormentor.

Hatch was head of a gang. Hatch was heavy with power, and the fucking fear he could make happen. Spencer avoided Hatch. To stare into that pig face was to be bitten into and spat out. With Hatch and his thick gang the turret would be no protection.

*

Dolly's persistent struggle to avoid the bitter darkness and ugly dereliction which more than once she had come close to, had resulted finally in her marriage to Frank Pratt.

Frank Pratt had a substantial house and a sizeable, although rather dubiously earned, income. He was in cars. He was in antiques; clocks particularly. He was a large sticky middle-aged man, with heart trouble and high blood-pressure. He was a fixer, with a nose so he felt for a good deal. 'Fair's fair. My trouble, your gain. Good enough for me. We'll do a deal.' He had a mouth as wide and as flabby as his stomach which lay like a dead baby in the white shirt hanging out over the tight black trousers.

He had just been 'taken to the cleaners' by his last wife when he met Dolly. He was homeless. His wife had got the lot: house, dogs and children. He just had the car and a constantly changing address; various small flats and small hotels. He was almost a broken man. Dolly had chivvied him and cheered him. Because even without a house, he always had a good clean wad of readies in his back pocket. And he was generous. She grew to ignore the pungent, sickly smell of after-shave and anxious sweat, and the great hairy belly in the bed, with tight black nylon socks on the small feet. They were both hard drinkers and regular smokers, so in the foul, aching, early morning mist of nicotine stubs and empty glasses and bottles, they easily forgave each other for any railing, accusations, or physical uneasiness that might have passed between them the night before. Frank Pratt had good mates. Very soon they were more or less back on top. Some real estate now and then, thrown in with the clocks and cars. Diversity, flexibility, a bit of this, a bit of that. 'Never get stale,' Frank said. 'Get stale and you might as well be stiff. Get stale and you lose your grip.'

Dolly never told Frank about Spencer. She might one day, but past is past. She was fearful to go back to that time in any way. It was over and done with. Best forgotten. Now with the new house in Esher, her job, and Hollywood, she was closer to some kind of security than ever before. Hollywood was a large thin Afghan hound. She was a star. She had a pedigree as long and longer than her pointed nose, and fine pale coat of hanging hair. Of course she became known as Holly, and to return to her was the best part of Dolly's day. She gave the reproduction mahogany, the thick pile carpets, the gilt mirrors and soft velour suites, she gave them a final touch of real class. Dolly would change when she got home from work. She would get out of her cutting girdle and tight bra, she would have a bath and then put on her pink jump-suit and black velvet slippers and then, glass in hand, she would lie back with Holly in front of the vast, colourful television screen, believing that in the end, one way or another, she was a lucky girl. If there were niggling doubts, if Frank's wheezing ugliness got to her, she knew better than to let herself dwell on it. She would simply go shopping; cut-glass, a froth of pillow-cases and matching duvet covers, tins of prawns and pâté, any new lamp or rug or vast china ornament. It more or less worked. Thinking and remembering were no part of her life now.

It was with considerable difficulty that the Social Services tracked Dolly down. Spencer was now fifteen and it was felt that some kind of contact with the boy's parents might be helpful. It might break the dangerous silence and self-imposed isolation. The boy seemed to have little real contact with any adult, or any member of his peer group. And the signs of increasing puberty were becoming very evident.

Lumsden had already been appraised by his mother of the fact that this bastard child was now in London, apparently in the care of the authorities. Lumsden was married for the second time. His wife was an elegant Italian called Francesca. She owned a small boutique in Fulham called 'La Contessa'. She had two good-looking, sultry children from her first marriage. It was her social ambition that had made her decide on marriage to Lumsden. She had been brought up in Spain and had married a Spaniard first time round. Her own background was in fact rather dull and domestic, it had never inspired her, but the skilful presentation of herself was exotic and compelling. Lumsden's various friends in the west country found her 'an absolute stunner'. Lumsden, having lived for many years off others in the pursuit of his own pleasure, felt it a great stroke of good fortune that he should be gathered up, as it were, into the arms of a glamorous woman with decided views, and a thriving professional concern, who seemed to want very little from him. Overtly a hot number, Francesca's body raced with unconventional displays of physical need. She leapt on to the laps of unsuspecting middle-aged men, she stroked their legs and bit their ears, but always with impeccable control as if she were directed by an unseen guide who sought affect rather than any kind of conclusion. She amazed and beguiled, but remained aloof. Lumsden was the means from which she propelled her way into various rather amusing households. Without him, she might have remained simply a foreigner with a shop, with him she was nearly always the centre of attention.

Lumsden had told Francesca about Spencer. He had described it as a moment of bizarre untidiness. He was rather incompetent in bed these days and he wanted Francesca to know that in the full flower of his youth he had been deliberately wild. It never occurred to him, because he thought of it so seldom, that Spencer would turn up one day on the doorstep, a fully grown, silent, dour youth with a child care officer in tow.

The child care officer was an extremely conscientious man. He was very tall and thin, and he was almost bald. He had a most extraordinary Adam's apple that bobbed up and down the long neck like a lost marble with limited powers. He was called Jim Scott. It took him several months and various preliminary telephone calls before he could arrange the actual meetings.

After speaking to Lumsden on the telephone, Jim Scott's careful, prosaic, rather restricted tone of voice inspired Lumsden to call him Jim Snot. To the Farr family, Lumsden, Francesca and her lounging offspring, the whole idea of Spencer was simply a curiosity. It was obvious he would not impinge on their lives, Francesca had made her position there very clear indeed. They referred to the whole matter as 'The Snot Saga' and left it at that.

319

Dolly Pratt's reaction was quite different. It was a moment of horror for her when one sunny afternoon, with Hollywood sprawled across her lap, the telephone had rung and a very detached voice had said to her . . . Mrs Pratt, this concerns your son, Spencer . . . Dolly had gone cold from head to foot. She had wound her hand in and out of Hollywood's mane so nervously as she spoke and listened, that her rings became entangled in the long hair; she had to cut herself out of the tangle with a pair of nail scissors.

At first she was adamant. No way could she see him. No way. She had a new life now. A new marriage. Her husband didn't know. She couldn't be involved. She was sorry.

Gently, over the months, Jim Scott persisted. He visited her. He tried to explain that nothing was expected of her, simply an afternoon together, to help the boy in some way to anchor himself into the real world.

Eventually, a meeting was arranged. Spencer had not let the idea of parents as such enter the turret silence. He thought of Ossian reared possibly by a deer, he thought of Romulus and Remus. He thought of Tir na nOg and he thought of the unicorn. In his dreams, one day he would ride the unicorn; above the streets and forests, above the earth, together they would encircle the globe, their flight would be soundless, it would be so fast, so free that ultimately it would be beyond movement, it would reach the giant calm of stillness itself. They would reach that lap of gold beyond the stars where the woman who rocked the cradle in Murna's candlelit chamber would turn to face him, her hair loose and her child grown.

Spencer dreamt a great deal. His days were full of wide awake dreams. He ate through them, he stared through them, he walked and bussed through them. They were his life. So he made the journey to Waterloo Station with Jim Scott to meet his mother without any very real anticipation.

It was a short, difficult encounter. The boy seemed to Dolly, after all her anxiety and fluster, he seemed quite disinterested in her. There was little now to remind her of Lumsden; maybe the eyes, but they were so dead. Maybe the hair . . . maybe . . . but all that heavy denim, the bulky jacket, the poor shot blasted skin, the downcast expression. Dolly felt so alienated by him that it was less of an ordeal than she had anticipated. At the end she gave him a fiver. And she said 'Don't smoke. Filthy habit. I should know. I do it all the time.' No one smiled, so she laughed loudly, rubbing her lips together to get the soft, clinging, scented taste of the lipstick; it reminded her like the high leather collar of her coat, it reminded her that she was Frank's girl. She gathered up her bag and said 'Good luck then. I must dash. Promised I'd be back on the four-twenty.' Spencer just managed to nod a kind of farewell. But he stared past her as she ran for the train. He half closed his eyes. He listened to the loud, slap strut sound of people's feet on the hard surface, and he imagined herds of buffalo pounding towards a waterhole.

Depressed by the encounter with Dolly, Jim Scott hoped perhaps for a little more warmth and civility from the father. On the telephone, Lumsden Farr had an open, easy manner. He invited them to the house, which Jim Scott hoped was a good sign. But the invitation was based simply on curiosity. Francesca's children were riveted at the idea of Lumsden having a fully grown son. To them Lumsden was irritating and ineffectual; at least this proved he had done something apart from being a ligger and con man, with an embarrassingly dated and boring hippy cool.

But the second encounter was more disturbing for Spencer than the first. Lumsden was a name he had heard often. He had heard Maura and Donal speak of Lumsden and several others in Ballynaule. Lumsden had lived at Rathmanagh. Lumsden must have known Birkin. Spencer realised that he did want to look at Lumsden. He did want to hear him speak, but when it happened, the long precise drawl of words came too close to the turret silence. Their sound was some kind of threat. Throughout the ordeal, Lumsden poured drinks and talked effortlessly about nothing very much. Francesca, having been there in the beginning, soon made herself absent. The two young people managed to contrive some reason to enter the room. As soon as they left, Spencer heard their distinct giggles and whispers outside the door.

It was a green room full of smart things and very crowded bookcases. There were piles of papers and magazines and cushions and rugs. Spencer remembered the parlour at Rathmanagh which was green also, but paler, more faded, more dusky. Jim Scott spoke. Lumsden replied. Spencer longed to seek out the unicorn but he was afraid. He asked to use the toilet. Lumsden visibly shuddered and said 'Of course, old man, straight down and it's on your left.' When Spencer returned from the lavatory Lumsden felt it incumbent on him to ask him some kind of question.

'Have you any idea what you might want to do later on?'

There was a long pause. Spencer looked directly towards Lumsden. The skin was very loose on his face, the eyes were very large and blue. Spencer stared, then to Jim Scott's surprise he said 'Might hunt animals . . . I like animals.'

'Do you?' There was a definite tinge of sarcasm in Lumsden's voice. 'Well, any idea is a start, I suppose. But Fulham could never be described as a happy hunting ground. Too small. Too squashed. Too limited. No birds here you know, not even pigeons. They've been poisoned, I believe.' There was a long, careful silence. Instinctively, all three knew the encounter was over. 'Well, later on if I can be of use, let me know. You know where we are. Hunting's not quite my style, a bit too energetic . . . but good luck anyway.'

Lumsden was quite sure that this silent, denim-drowned youth would be unlikely to return to them. And anyway, what useful thing could he do? Life had to take its own course. Just as water ran by the easiest route to the lowest point, so did life. It was the natural order of things. Later Lumsden said to Francesca, 'Thank God for the welfare state.' After a few more jokes and one or two quite cruel observations, the 'Snot Saga' ended more or less there.

But when Spencer had left the room to go to the lavatory, on his way back, just as he was about to open the door again, he had heard Lumsden say in answer to some question or other 'Look, old chap, I couldn't care less. It's all yours. It's quite out of court for me. I couldn't care less. Couldn't care less.'

Spencer never knew what it was they were speaking of but the phrase 'Couldn't care less' stuck in his head, like a refrain, like a rhythm. It was the way the words ran, like the rumble of trains, like that. Couldn't care less. Couldn't care less. Couldn't care less. Then after the speed, the wheeze of the brakes and that little whine and the slower motion . . . Couldn't care. Couldn't care. Couldn't care.

Those words became for Spencer the rhythm and song of the trains, underground and overland; their constant refrain in the bolting, spinning, twisting, jolting dark.

Jim Scott had done his best, but the boy remained dangerously sullen and isolated. The foster-parents who had seven other, far more demanding, youngsters, left him to pretty well get by on his own. Spencer just came and went. He did any odd job when asked. He more or less kept the house rules, letting them know where he was, when he would be back; things like that. But where he was he hardly knew himself. He bunked off school so frequently, in the end he was hardly missed.

After the visit to his father he felt a certain urgency. He did not belong to this map of families: parents, brothers, sisters. He did not belong. But the edge of it all was a dangerous suffocating place. You had to get out. You had to hunt for another map. The turret silence was too crowded, too stifling thick with coiled up, unsaid things. Something had to happen. Something must shift or give way. On his mooching, wandering days, he felt some relief, some smell of freedom. He nicked now and then, mostly food and drink, sometimes records and earrings, which he could sell in school. The sour, stale, street flank became the animal hide against which he rested. Head down in winter, walking against the bitter wind, he picked his way over slough, junk places, the plastered-down rot edges of broken pavements and rough open ground. Like a beachcomber, he traced the flotsam of these human tides, the cans and rust and plastic, the bare trees blowing black plastic swipes on their branches instead of blooms.

Increasingly after a day on the streets and in the parks and shopping centres, he dreaded returning to the dull house where on paper he lived. He loathed the frying smells that greeted him, the fighting 'silly cow' noise of the other children, the droning voices from the television, the nagging questions of those in charge. More and more the cold, even the scabs on his skin, and the rot, damp, smoke smells in his hair, they were live details; they had some kind of breath and purpose in them. They were not dull emptiness, dry decay like the overheated school and house. He grew to welcome cold and wet. Shivering was body recognition, and his body was the dumb hut carcass that held the rest. If he coughed and spat, dragging up a gob of thick bile to pelt out on to some scrag of dirt and stones, he felt alive. A rusted can rolling the road sounded like a horse if you closed your eyes. There was a wilderness to be found; in its own way as rugged, as vivid and mysterious as Murna, and the forests, and rocks and strands beyond Kilbronan Bay.

There were heights and depths, great girder climbs, the soot wild railway embankments, the dump grounds by the river itself with swarms of gulls and cats and dogs, sniffing and mating in and out of the rubble. There were men and women who smelt of beer and fire smoke and sour sweat. Their smells reminded Spencer of parts of Donal's house. Beside them he could remember Donal. 'There's no place that's not some creature's habitat, no carcass that's not someone's feast.' When Spencer remembered these things he felt stronger, less fearful. There were creatures everywhere; woodlice, rats, flies, wasps, mud worms, and in the dumps and bins there was food and firewood.

He slept out rough a couple of times. He told them he'd gone to his dad's in Fulham. They didn't say anything. It was one less to feed and nag and he was practically of an age to make his own decisions anyway. He came back to the house less and less; just enough to get travel and lunch money and a bit extra if he asked.

When the weather was bad he travelled most of the day on the underground. These sulphur-smelling passages of power became a magic world. The cavern threads of an ancient kingdom. Like tides there was a shape to the flow of the creatures. There were full, high, jostling tides, then there was the medium flow of returning school-children and shoppers, and then, every so often in the middle of the day, there were long, still, dull spaces; empty platforms and empty carriages. Spencer felt sure that one day the unicorn would rescue these silent, worried people, who crowded and stared and never spoke as the trains rattled and wheezed their way in and out of the stations.

The refrain he had made in his head after he overheard his father speaking; the refrain had become more triumphant now. Couldn't care less. Couldn't care less. Couldn't care less. He wanted it to be his cry against them, instead of their cry at him. But it was only somewhere in his dreams that he felt any kind of strength. Underground, the rotting black bulging walls, the great weeping stains from the cracked curved roofs, the grey whale colours, the black wood escalator treads plugged with sticky dirt and cigarette stubs, this running cave environment seemed steamed and wrenched with the same kind of tattered

325

sadness as himself. It was bruised, exhausted, battered, only the words that flashed clean beyond the dirty windows had any celebratory ring to them. Monument. Angel. Barons Court. White City. Whitechapel. New Cross. They might all herald the light and power of the unicorn. They were all places marked with words of strength and hope ... when he read Bank, he could feel Murna's springy turf, its wild high ground, its smells and flowers.

There were so many faces. There were so many skins, some pitted and yellow, some red and thick, some smooth and clean, some black, almost burnished; they were like fruit peels, and their hair; stringy fine or jet wire, mattress stuff, like tufts of grasses.

There was no focus, no sense of time, no dimension of practical purpose, simply the route march of survival. The need was simply any means to carry the bulk weight coil of stacked up, unsaid, unfelt living that was the burden of the turret silence, and in its way the sum of Spencer himself.

There were awkward, dangerous moments, drunks and fights, runs to avoid the law, moments of confrontation; but he managed to keep them more or less under control. The power of the dreams drove away fear. The unicorn was master. Spencer could breathe into its soundless hooves and mighty flanks, he could summon the stub of brightness and wait then for the great horn to grow, until the beast was there, charged and waiting.

It was early spring when quite by chance he found the unicorn's stable. The spire, a fine, high point on the bell-tower was the landmark he followed. He ran towards it, past the blind, netted windows of the flats, towards the park itself. Not far from the Elephant, not far from Camberwell and the careful unexpected neatness of Addison Square, just back from there was this sudden real run of openness. That night it was not so cold. He was running because he heard a spot of trouble going on on the bridge. Then he saw the quiet cream spire and the burnt-out church itself. The high window spaces were girded with metal, but they were light because there was no roof on the building, birds flew in and out. Beyond the burnt-out church was this single red-brick building, with beside it the tall chimney which had been the steam stack when the building had been the public baths. Now it was a public library and sports centre. Both the buildings were out there, utterly alone, on this flat, free, open ground. Spencer would have run on, but he suddenly saw in brilliant colour on the side of the red-brick building this huge, magnificent butterfly. He climbed over into the cobbled yard to get a closer look. The butterfly was made out of shining tiles, it was very large; purple-brown with a yellow golden border to the outer edges of the wings. Underneath it, written into the brick, was Camberwell Beauty. Because it was so free and so strong and beautiful and different to all the other walls for miles and miles around, Spencer stayed. He wanted to wake in the morning beneath the wings of the butterfly. There was a single bench below the tall chimney stack, with a high hedge behind it. Between the newly-laid cobble-stones, fierce, healthy tufts of weeds and flowers thrust up as if the yard were really a meadow: ragwort, rosebay willow herb, buddleia, daisy, hawkbit, plantain.

Spencer slept on the bench beneath the magnificent butterfly. Then, in the early morning, before it was light, just at the beginning of the birds' sounds, he woke. He felt stiff and cold. He pushed the papers and card off his face. He was going to turn to look at the butterfly. Then he heard this strong, scraping, rustling sound coming from the burnt-out church, just across from him, over the meadow tufts in between the cobbled stones. He sat up. He stared at the high windows, the gentle warm stone of the church walls, and the triple-tiered bell-tower with daylight just showing through the empty window squares. He listened intently, the sound had been so strong, so particular. Then it came again, like a huge heave of body among dry leaves. Then he knew; within this church, just now, just beyond him in that clean, safe, burnt-out space, the unicorn slept. He could feel its great weight lying there, and the movement of the soft white flanks, and the shifting of the soundless hooves. As he looked up at the high open roof and the gridded squares across the windows he knew that the unicorn was like Pegasus; it would have wings. Because the forests had all been slaughtered there was nothing left but the sky from which to roam the earth. Now the unicorn rested, his huge powerful horn pointed up into the safe protection of the bell-tower. But he was here. He would ride out one day and take up the poisons out of the rivers and from the seas. Half in dream, and half in the cold stiffness of the early morning, Spencer felt small sharp tears prick into his eyes because he was here, with the unicorn so close. He would tell no one but he would return constantly.

But with the joy of that certain dream an anxious pain grew. It was harder to keep going. He was nicking more and more. He was noticed less and less. Scabs and sores and red, raw rashes competed with dirt to make the map of his face and hands. He began to realise he could not return either to school or the home, and although it was the freedom he had chosen, it pitched him further forward into a grinding, stupid fear.

In a sense he was waiting to be apprehended; found. Instinctively he was on the run. It was weeks later on a Saturday that he came round the corner of a street he knew well, to be confronted face to face by Hatch and his gang. He had seen him around from time to time. He had always avoided him. Now that was impossible.

'Shit. Shit if it isn't our old chum, Little Lonely . . .'

He grabbed Spencer by the collar. His breath stank of beer. His hard belly was tight against the loose folds of Spencer's coat. They circled him. They closed in on him, creaking, squeaky leather and chains and their mocking loud noise.

'Let's give him drinkies . . . Come on, get his fucking mouth open,' Hatch said, and he pulled Spencer by the chin forcing his mouth open with the pressure of his thumb on Spencer's lower lip. Their white faces, their foul breath, their punching, jostling bodies squeezed him into this narrow gulley space; he could barely see the sky. They tipped beer and all sorts down into his mouth, until he thought he would choke dead into their fat hands.

'Brace up, Lonely Boy. We're gonna give you some fun.'

Spencer wasn't sure how many there were. Four or five. They shoved him hard up against this wall on which was sprayed in white paint . . . You Can Fuck . . . You Can Win. They had their fists towards his face and stomach. Each time he flinched and cowered, ready for the blow they purposely didn't make.

'Fucking scared, aren't you? Bloody fucking scared.'

Hatch ran his open Stanley blade along the thick black leather arm of his jacket.

'Clean and sharp, isn't it? Couldn't say the same for you, could we, Little Lonely?'

The others laughed and opened cans of beer. Suddenly the cold air had gone. Spencer felt bruised, cooked dry by the crude warmth of their faces and bodies and fists so close.

'You need some fun, Lonely. Fucking little fun outing.'

Hatch ran the open blade along the edge of Spencer's chin. He could feel it cold and smooth. He closed his eyes, fearful even to swallow because the sharp point of the blade was so close.

'You'll shit fire soon, Lonely. Fucking scare pants, you'll have.'

The others laughed. They made gestures and noises as if there was a foul smell in the air.

'We're going to give you a treat. Bit of an outing. We'll take him on a fucking cow run . . . Scare the fucking cows, Lonely, and you'll scare less . . .'

Spencer hardly heard what they said. Above their heads the streetlights glared down, breathing a sick orange spit of light over everything.

Eventually Hatch was less close and the knife had gone. They were still drinking and swearing, and although their faces were not directly towards him, they made sure that he was firmly hemmed in. There were heavy boots treading on his feet and an elbow jutted into his stomach.

Spencer prayed for something to happen. Pigs maybe. Something, anything that would make them move on. But they kept drinking and they kept him pinioned. Then this police car drove by. Spencer didn't see it. He could see nothing but the black of their leather and the white of their skin; fat pimple faces, pudding-brown in the glow of the streetlights.

'Fucking pigs. The flats. The flats.'

They hurled and kicked away the empty beer cans and they ran on down this narrow pedestrian way into the maze of flats and small parcels of open ground. They carried Spencer between them as they ran, by taking his elbows, one on either side, so that his feet scarcely touched the ground. Belching and laughing they ran up this wide concrete stairwell which led to the flats. They ran on down the walkway. Many of the windows were boarded up. It was very quiet. Their noise seemed to scrape the blind concrete, it seemed to bleed it white.

'You're gonna see some fun, fucking Lonely.'

They paused. Spencer felt a hard pull on his lips again. Then this beer and sharp stinging liquid ran down into his throat and the dirt crevasses round his neck and hair. They were maybe three floors up. They seemed to know the place. One of them ran ahead. He had fire crackers. They started to jam them through the letter-boxes. There were loud bangs and then shrieks and angry shouts from the blind, still windows. By then, they were well past, down the next stairs and up towards the next block.

One man heard them coming. He threatened them loudly. They kicked at the door, then smashed in the window. The net curtains billowed out, but they were gone.

One pissed on the stairs. The rest ran on. There was no pause. No space. They raced on, riding high on every sound of panic or fury that came from behind the blind windows. Then they were down on to the grass again and across to a ground-floor run. They were quite near the railway; every so often a train thundered past, giving cover to any sound or screams or crash of breaking glass.

Spencer, realising that for the moment anyway he was not the butt and inspiration for their torments, simply ran with them. There was some excitement in the fear and screams of the chase. He had not run so far or so fast for a long time. Occasionally they butted him and said . . . 'Move. Fucking move.' Then there was a scream, a shrill, frantic sound. Hatch kicked at the door two or three times. 'Fucking, bloody cow,' he said and he kicked again. This time the door gave way. It was bright and small inside after the cold street dark. They seemed huge in the barely furnished room, where an old lady whimpered like a kitten as she sat in the deep tattered cup of an old brown chair. They kicked the chair. 'Fuckin' cow. Bloody fuckin' cow . . .' They were drunk. Spencer knew they were drunk. They hovered round her. It was the first pause. She whimpered again, a little moan of tight sound at the back of her throat. She was trying to lean forward, to grab a black purse that was lying on a small white napkin on a table beside a bird in a cage. The cage was covered with a cloth. Hatch hurled the cage to the floor. The woman's wails became loud, frantic. One of them held her down with his boot on her stomach. Hatch took the purse and tossed it to one of the others. She was choking now. She was hard down into the bottom of the chair, like a length of cloth, not like a woman at all. She was choking. Her teeth fell forward on their bright pink curve of plastic; they fell out of her mouth and on to the floor. One of the black boots crashed down on to them like a man on to a rat in a barn.

Spencer watched amazed. The black weight of them; her mewling, spluttering sounds. She seemed like she was already nearly dead. Then he realised what he saw, and what he felt, must be there very soon. Any second it might happen. Their punch down, skull crack on to her. Their drunk power and her slow, insect death. He almost waited for it. She was slumped, so down into the chair now. She was making less sound, barely breathing. One of them tore her thin cotton shirt and the worn vest, leaving the small flat puckered breasts bare. Hatch laughed, 'Fucking thin cow.' He made another noise. His throat seemed full of her death. Her lips just quivered. Spencer stared. The thin lips drooped a little like worn out elastic. The eyes were closed but the eyelids flickered fast like a moth trapped. Spencer remembered the speckled hen. He remembered that orchard scream and her bright staring eye in the cold scum of the stone trough water.

'Shut. Shut. Fucking old cow.'

One of them pissed in the corner of the room. Like a staling horse the foul stuff frothed down on to the mauve carpet. She made a new more desperate sound. Then the pissing guy swung round. The foul stuff sprayed across towards her, a filthy rainbow spurt at her small wet mouth. Spencer still stared. All the dying cries he had ever heard; rats, hens, pigs, they raced into this small woman's thin spilt mouth. There were sounds outside. Immediately they ran. They were gone. Spencer could hardly move. For several seconds he was there alone with her. Then he bent down and took this piece of cloth and threw it over her bareness. She took the cloth, she whimpered into the pale material, wiping her thin lips as if she would almost tear them from her frail face. She was not dead. Not stiff, still, insect dead anyway. Spencer ran then. He ran into the hungry empty dark. There were people coming towards the flats. Spencer ran. He made for the darkest shapes. He ran on, careless of direction. Eventually he came to lumpy rough ground, warehouses and stores.

He felt as he ran that he held the speckled hen's pain. He felt her death, wrung out again in the small woman's noise. He felt the small woman's noise and her cheeks, buried and torn in the dead bird's feathers. And he felt himself there, holding them down into the stinking, still waters of the stone trough. And he howled. He howled again. He howled aloud; an animal bellow. Shrieking sounds. Bolts of bleeding cries. They reeled out from his throat into the rough dark. He still ran on, stumbling, pausing now and then. His face was wet as if he were drowned. There was no sense, just bitter, unbearable shame in the long streaming wail of his cries. He picked his way over rusted pipes and sacks and oil drums. He came to a narrow gap between two buildings. Beyond he could see orange street lights. He could hear the cars and buses. Ahead was some major road. He was stumbling back towards people and places; all that restlessness. But he was unfit, unfit to return, unfit to be anywhere else.

Then, without hardly knowing why or what he did, he hammered at the cold glass of the store windows. He beat against the glass with his fists. He hammered at it. He howled once more with all the rage and pain he could muster; it was as if the glass was that hard barrier he had within himself. Then at last the glass gave way. There was a splintering crack like ice breaking. Then there were smaller sounds as the glass fell out on to the ground and on to the hard floor inside the building. Then at last there was the warmth of his blood running fast down his arm, on to his clothes and spattering out at the dirt and grass and stones. And with the blood running there was a stinging numb pain where the wounds were made. The pain was keen and real, it took back the cries and howls out of the sky. He was silent, shivering and empty. The coiled bulk was spat loose. The turret silence was torn. Dazed and quiet he was soon standing

333

on the pavement itself, back into the street and the sounds and the people.

He had no sense but the stinging pain and the dark rich flow of the blood on his arms and hands and clothes. Instinctively he held his hands upwards to control the flow of blood. He walked slowly now, completely careless of his surroundings. He was grateful for this new empty feeling; a drying wilt through the dark, moist, buried parts. With the coiled bulk unsprung, with the turret silence torn, he felt light, almost weightless. Vaguely he looked for some bench or low wall, somewhere he could stop, pause. He hardly remembered the rest. He must have fainted then. Later Jess told him he had been so white, as white as fish on the slab. But he liked the way she told it. He liked the way she remembered it all, as if it had been for her a special occasion; an amazing, unexpected thing. He didn't remember it like that. He remembered simply her voice, very clear to the other two girls, 'Get Mum. Get Mum. She'll know what to do.'

After that, Spencer remembered nothing. They said he fainted. Apparently the three girls and George carried him down the street, back into number 24 where Winnie was waiting. 'Bring him in,' she had said, when she heard from the girls how there was this lad out on the street, alone but covered with blood from cuts on his arms and hands.

Winnie had bandages and plaster, warm salt water and some antiseptic cream. It didn't look like a fight to her. It was usually fights at this time of night. The cuts were so random and jagged. She found some splinters of glass. He was lucky no vein was cut; he was very lucky. They were going to call an ambulance but the bleeding stopped. He obviously slept rough, that was clear from the smell on the clothes. There were more and more of them now, and they got younger all the time. 'They won't do much for him,' Winnie said. 'Here, where he is now would be the best place.' She knew they'd never keep him in the hospital, and where could he get to in this condition, and so late. They made him as comfortable as they could. They washed away the worst of the blood. A good pile of dirt came with it. 'He's so thin,' George said. 'He looks young to me, Mum, my age,' Jess said. She was proud of Winnie. Winnie was never afraid of things. She just got on with everything. She never gave a toss what other people said. How she took risks. How she trusted too much. She always had an answer for them. As she said, 'First, get on with the job. Leave all the talk and questions 'til later.'

George and Winifred Chappell had lived at number 24 for over twenty years, the length and more of Jess's life. Jess was sixteen. She was their youngest, the unexpected child of their old age. They had three boys. Two were married and working overseas. One they had lost with meningitis when he was only ten. Jess was more or less an only. She was a bright, cheerful girl with plenty of friends. She'd just left school. They'd taken her on in Smith's. It was a start anyway. Some of them had nothing. George was retired now but he worked part-time up at the school as caretaker. Winnie had been born in Nunhead. They moved to Peckham when they got married. She'd seen plenty of changes in that time. But to her, people were people the world over; troubles were troubles, and jobs were jobs. She got on with life as it happened, each day at a time. She'd seen every kind of sickness and violence. It would take a lot to surprise her now. Things were different. People kept so to themselves; they used to be more of a community. But there's still plenty that's good; plenty that'll last. As she always said, 'No government can take your spirit. Spirit's your own. They can make it harder for you of course. They can wear you down; but there's nearly always one worse off than you if you look around.'

Winnie worked up at the hospital three days a week and on the other three days she ran the Red Cross secondhand. There were several old people who couldn't get about. Winnie did shopping for them, stopping in for a chat afterwards, which was what they needed most. She was never idle. As George said, 'If she stopped now it would probably kill her.' The three of them were quiet and comfortable together. They were fond enough of the roof over their heads, a council house which they had no intention of buying. People in their circumstances couldn't think of doing a thing like that. 'Maybe one day,' Jess often said, 'maybe one day I'll buy it for you.' But Winnie only laughed. 'Future's a fickle thing my girl, you never want to try and tie it down.'

They'd seen a lot of violence in the street. Fights, domestic troubles, break-ins; all sorts. But that night had been quiet. 'Those cuts look self inflicted to me,' Winnie said later, when Spencer slept and she and Jess were washing out his shirt in the sink. 'He's certainly been sleeping rough.' Winnie was fearful to call the police in case it only made things worse for him, as was often the way. 'Well, he looks weak as a kitten to me,' George said, 'so I agree with Mother, let him be. Let him be.'

So they settled him down that first night on the settee. They gave him sweet tea and some tablets for the pain. He slept fitfully. Winnie kept an eye on him. He looked so pale, so washed out. He looked through with life already, poor lad, and yet he hardly looked old enough to have begun it. What kind of people could they belong to, to choose a life like this. Peculiar migrant creatures they seemed; just youngsters, and more and more of them all the time. She pulled the blanket up over him. She left the hall light on and the door open in case he woke and needed anything. When she was a girl, two or three times they'd rescued a pigeon with a broken wing, now it was lads like this one. Still, same as the bird, that was probably all he needed, a pause, a warm safe place, no questions, just a chance to recover, just a bit of breathing space.

To Winnie, it was a natural, practical thing. Some of them down the street would be shocked. They'd think it stupid. You don't know anything they'd say. You don't know who he is or where he's been. But to Winifred knowing wasn't the issue. The boy's need was the thing. Just like any creature, if it didn't suit him he'd soon get up and go. So it was decided and Spencer stayed. 'One day at a time,' Winnie said, 'and no questions. He'll say what he wants when he's ready, when it suits him.' There were neighbours who were sure he'd rob them. 'Nothing's worth taking,' Winifred told them. She was more or less right. The television was black and white, everything was small and useful, nothing was valuable. The valuables were love and care; uncomplicated, ordinary, practical tenderness, the kind that cost more or less nothing; only the inclination, only the time.

Spencer was very quiet in the beginning. He felt immensely shy to be there, clean and warm in George's loose, spare clothes. Winifred was quiet also. She made him feel usual; not odd or awkward. Each evening Jess chattered on. She brought him various clothes and things from her friends that were more suitable. Spencer didn't know how it was, but Winifred had this smile, when she cleared the cups, or stirred the teapot, she had this way of just looking, just acknowledging; never calculating or appraising. Just when Spencer thought he should ask for something, Winnie would seem to know what was in his mind and say it first. 'Just take your time, Spencer. Heal up a bit. Get your strength.' She never asked anything, not even his second name. Spencer was enough for Winnie. Jess asked. She was eager to know, but she didn't pester. They let him be. They came and went, always easy, always friendly. In the beginning, he felt a bit awkward and strange, but gradually he gained confidence. He dried the dishes. He swept the yard. He made the tea. But he never cut the bread and butter, Winifred did it so fine, so thin. Maura would have marvelled at her way with the bread knife. Spencer thought of Maura and Donal. He remembered Rathmanagh a little. It was the first time for a long while that he had let it occupy his mind. He knew they

337

would like to know. Jess often asked. But although the turret silence was broken, it was still too soon to share its spoils; all those years of muddled memories and uncertain identity. All the London years piled up like a stack of refuse, blocking the way either forward or back. But always, without Spencer speaking, Winifred seemed to know what it was he might like to say or ask.

'Why don't you sign on, Spencer? Use this address. You can if you like.'

It was such a big thing, but the way she put it she made it seem small, ordinary, everyday.

'If I could . . . I'd like to. I'd like to very much.'

'Fine. That's settled then. You go down there on Monday. You may have a job by the end of the week. Who knows.'

Winifred smiled as she set the cloth. She seemed pleased. She was always bending and busy. She was so small. Like a sparrow. She moved in quick, sharp, keen ways. She had very small feet. She wore black lace-up shoes with bulges where the bunions were. She always wore stockings, brown stockings, and a brown coat and a small blue hat, almost always the hat. In the evenings, after the meal was cleared away she was never idle. She crocheted blankets and baby clothes from old wool she unwound herself, from things that came into the Red Cross shop. When she scrubbed down the steps at the back she sang. They were old songs. Jess laughed. Warbling Winnie, she called her, but Spencer could tell that she cared a lot for her mum. He never thought of his mother. But he sometimes thought of the unicorn and the woman with braided hair; and he thought of those maidens into whose lap they said the unicorn leapt. He would like to have told Jess of the burnt-out church and the unicorn stabled there; but it was too soon. It would sound stupid. Sometimes Spencer walked back, to the cobbled yard and the magnificent butterfly. It wasn't so far.

He was still silent but it was no longer the oppressive, threatening silence that had been before. It was more a stillness. It was as if he were waiting in order to be ready.

He got a job in Safeways. It wasn't far from Smith's, so in the mornings Spencer and Jess went down there together. At first he was just sweeping up and stacking shelves. Then he was with fruit and vegetables, sorting, pricing, and stamping out the small sticky labels. He paid Winifred rent. He bought himself clothes now and again, usually with Jess's advice and encouragement. 'Do you fancy Spencer?' the girls would ask Jess. 'He's different,' she would say, 'I like that. He's quiet, he's gentle; a bit mysterious in a way. He's nice.'

George had this old motorbike out in the shed. It had belonged to one of the boys. Together George and Spencer, with the help of a neighbour, did the bike up. They had it ready and licensed for Spencer's seventeenth birthday in July. After that Spencer rode out most evenings; round the Rye, up the Forest Hill Road, through to Penge and Crystal Palace. Sometimes he went as far as Bromley or Croydon; always on the way home he would make sure to pass by the library, the burnt-out church and the brilliant butterfly. On the bike, out there in the centre of the streets, the rough, reeking days of dumps and waste-ground gradually became forgotten. He was almost there in the fast-forward part of the map, but there were still niggling shadows, there were still empty, uneasy stretches. But as the weeks and months passed, they became less powerful, less greedy for his attention. Spencer noticed Jess more. Her jokes, her schemes. He listened to records with her but he was still shy to join in with her friends and go to clubs and discos and concerts. 'Give him time,' Winifred said. 'In the end, he'll have a lot to say. I'm sure of that.' Winifred had noticed how observant he was with the plants in the house, any insect or moth he found and stray cats and dogs. He had a way with them all, and a fair knowledge too. Winifred felt sure that there had been a time in his life when he'd lived well and truly out of town.

It was during the long summer evenings that Spencer spent most time alone with Jess. He knew she'd had a few boyfriends, but she seemed keen to be with him. They joined the library. They went to the parks and to the Horniman Museum. Gradually, Spencer told Jess more and more of himself. In the museum, staring into the cases of masks and strange dancing figures and the great white ivory cow, Spencer felt less awkward. He told Jess of Rathmanagh, of Maura and Donal and their summer visits to Kilbronan Bay. He told of Mount Murna, the river and the woods. She loved to listen. He told it so well.

'Well, with all that, why ever did you come back over here?'

Whenever Jess asked that, Spencer clammed up. He didn't know why himself. It was somewhere there in the orchard scream of the brown speckled hen, and her bright eye and yellow claws. He didn't want to remember. Jess guessed there was really much more to it all; she longed to know. She wondered so much what his people were like. She felt increasingly drawn to this strange, quiet boy that lived with them now as their lodger. This boy that had been found by her, fish white and bleeding, well over a year ago. In the beginning, she had thought he was like a brother, but now she felt sure she could really care for him. She began to want him to want her. She saw less of the others. He had so much more to him; and he had so much to say, just as Winifred had always said he would, when he was ready.

Spencer told Jess of Finn and the Fianna. He told her of Ossian and Maeve and Cuchulain. He told her of Tir na nOg. One day he would tell her of the unicorn. But not now, not yet. When they passed the burnt-out church hand in hand, he wondered about telling her, but something told him it was still too soon.

NINE

Winnie sensed it first. She sensed that there was this special ease between Jess and Spencer. From the start Jess had been warm and outgoing, it was her nature. A friendly, smiling child full of life and vitality, that had always been her way. She had made those first months easier for him than they might have been. She always filled any awkward gap or shy silence with her jokes and laughter. But in these recent months Winnie noticed a change. His silence now seemed softer, full of gentleness. Spencer seemed pleased now when Jess badgered him with questions. He teased her with those wild Irish tales. He was well able to stand up for himself. They knew that for some reason, as a very small child, he had been taken over to Ireland to be reared by his grandmother, Mrs Violet Farr. He never spoke much of her except to say she was very tall, with small blue eyes. He spoke more often of her place, Rathmanagh, of Donal and Maura. The mountain Murna, the river, the forests and woods. He told them that he had been in care. He told them that he had once met his father, who was called Lumsden. He never mentioned his mother. Jess grew excited about this father in Fulham with the weird name. 'Why don't we visit him?' she said. 'He'll be proud. He'll see you're so well, and you've got a job and a bike. He'll be really proud of you.' But Spencer would never talk of it or discuss it further. 'No. No Jess. He's world's apart from me.' Then the refrain . . . couldn't care less . . . couldn't care less . . . couldn't care less came into his head. The trundle and slow wheeze of the brakes . . . and couldn't care. Couldn't care. Couldn't care. Spencer would tap his spoon on the table thinking of the rhythm of the trains and the sulphur smells. Jess would try to get his attention. She would try to persist: 'But come on, he's your father!' 'Well, blood isn't the whole story,' Winnie would interrupt. 'Your people in the end are those you love, and those that love you.' She said these things fiercely and practically. Love to Winnie was a natural thing, like a well-swept floor, or a good risen sponge; having the whole place sorted and clean and bright; it was putting a kind of natural order into things, making rough edges and darkness impossible.

Jess had altered. She had really grown up in the past year, she'd lost her puppy fat. She'd never be beautiful, she didn't have the bones for it, but she was a striking girl. That smooth skin going a golden brown as it always did in the summer months, even here in the city.

It was thinking like this and seeing the two of them together that gave Winnie the idea of writing to George's cousin in Suffolk. She had married a farmer. He was a small farmer, fruit and some corn, no stock, but they were not far from the sea and they had considerable space as it was an old house. Maybe they could see their way to letting these two have a holiday. Winnie felt it would do them both some good. The space and freedom. A bit of fresh air away from all the dirt and fumes. They could be quiet together and they would have the bike to get around on. Winnie wrote the letter. She had long, even slanting copperplate writing. She kept a small pad of lined paper under the work-basket.

It was not long afterwards that Winifred had a reply. Very soon it was all arranged. They would take the bike on the train as far as Ipswich. 'Mind you,' Winnie said to Spencer, 'there's no mountains up there, I can tell you straight off.' Jess had been there as a small child. They had a snap of her on the beach being blown to bits by the wind but happy as anything.

Winnie and George saw them off early on the Friday. They were a great pair together. Spencer looked so eager; full of smiles. Winnie had never seen him like that. He belongs out there, where it's free and a bit wild, she thought. He won't mind the bitter wind. And she kissed them both before they had strapped on the heavy helmets. Winnie had to be on her toes to reach for Spencer's cheek, and he had to bend to her, she was so small. 'Like a sparrow, your Mum,' Spencer said to Jess, 'with the might of an eagle.'

It was only to be for a week. The first days were cold but bright. They explored the pubs and the churches. They walked the various shingle beaches and back up into the high sandy cliffs that were falling fast into the sea. Then along the estuaries, on the narrow muddy tracks between the tall rushes, with duck boards every so often over the wide ditches. While they were walking among the high marsh grasses, as high as their waists, Spencer told Jess of Cuchulain and his love for Emer the Fair and how her father told Cuchulain he must first go across the sea to be trained by the fierce warrior woman Scathach. He told Jess how the route there was so treacherous, across wide bogs of boiling pitch and through fields of high rushes, with edges sharp enough to cut off a man's thighs.

They stopped in at the pub below the church, where the devil, as a black dog, had left huge paw marks on the church door. The marks were still there to be seen. In the pub Spencer continued with his tale of Maeve and Finn, King Conchobor and the champions of the Red Branch. 'All these women warriors and mad heroes,' Jess would laugh and tease him, but she loved him to go on telling, because he held her hands then, easily in his own. All these fierce lives; these cruel, dark adventures. Spencer looked so alert when he told her. His eyes were brighter now. For so long they had seemed quite dead. In the evenings they walked back down from the farm into the small orchards. Spencer was shy at first to kiss her properly. She had to lead all the way. She felt when she kissed him that she was really warming him, calling him up somehow out of terrible bleak plains and swamps like those in the stories. She knew he was shy and a little fearful, so she just took his hands and put them on to her bare breasts, and held them there until he was easier with it all. 'Come on, hero,' Jess would say. 'Slaying's over.' She remembered the story of Cuchulain after his warrior training with Scathach, how he took the fierce woman warrior Aine in single combat by a trick, diverting her attention, and how he then laid her, leaving her carrying his son, who long afterwards in combat Cuchulain killed, not realising the boy was his child until he saw the ring on his finger. They were terrible dark tales really. Jess understood that maybe Spencer had known a kind of darkness as a child and perhaps these tales of overcoming and valour gave him a kind of strength. Gradually, after each orchard evening together he became more soft, more supple, less stiff and fearful. 'You great hero, Spencer . . . I love you. I really love you,' she said as they came through the dark trees towards the lights of the farmhouse. He said nothing. But he stopped walking and kissed her properly then, without her leading him to it. He buried his face in her fair hair that smelt of salt and wind and sea. He felt this new compelling rhythm unlike anything before.

He had been afraid of the power of these physical things. He hated the raw driving panic of those dreams that had so often taken him, and overwhelmed him. In the billowing cocks and balls and cunts on the walls round number 24, and by the park, and on the warehouses, he felt these signs jeered at him. They made him even more fearful of this special thing he longed one day to do. He knew he was behind the rest. He guessed Jess was way ahead of him. And in a way he was glad.

After the first cold bright days, it was suddenly windless; brilliant sun with real midsummer heat. They had three days to go. They packed a picnic, then they took the bike straight down towards the sea. Back from the beach, behind the upturned boats and small fish stall there was a café. They bought beer and crisps. Spencer couldn't swim. Jess could, more or less. They just messed about jumping the curled tongues of foam as they slapped up on to the sand. Skidding and sliding as the water tugged back in smooth swirls, full of small sharp stones and shells. The beach was fairly crowded. Dogs kept coming up and licking their legs. Small children eating ice-creams wandered by, pausing to stare. Boys bounded past towards the water, scattering sharp grains of sand all over them and into Jess's careful, smooth coating of sun-tan cream. 'Let's go back up the estuary,' she said. So they took the bike and a few more beers and went up on to the road and through the forest. 'Not like an Irish wood,' Spencer said. On the bike, with Jess's hand on his hip and the wind, a rush of warm power into his face, Spencer felt strong and confident; almost in command. They left the bike on the headland, up against a tree, but hidden from the road. Then they picked their way through the bramble edge of the field, down towards the great wide band of estuary below them. The sun was high in the sky. There were several very white clouds below the brilliant shimmering blue of the rest. Beyond the black barn just ahead of them was this small clearing off the track. They had been there before. It might be private land because there were no beer cans or litter. There was just this small pile of soft ash where someone had made a fire. The grass was almost clear of thistles. Under the leaves of some wild cherry trees there was dappled shade. They made this their space. Spencer picked off the dry twigs and several stones. It was too hot to eat. They drank beer. The thick hedges of thorn saplings and briar hid them from the fields and the hard, dry paths. There was only the heat and the sky. 'It's a magic clearing, Spencer,' Jess said. 'It would suit your unicorn.' 'It might well. It might well,' he replied. Spencer could imagine those soundless hooves, and the powerful moon-white creature, gentle and still, in this small space of grass and flowers.

Jess was sitting with bare feet and her shirt unbuttoned. She wore no bra. Spencer could see the firm breasts he had held in the dark of the orchard. They felt these sharp signs race between them as they sat together on the grass; just a little apart. Jess wanted him to know that she'd done it before. She was sure he would be too shy, but she wanted him to know so she said 'All those poor maidens left out for your unicorn to leap into their laps!' Spencer looked up from the grass and the dry twig he'd been scuffing it with. They looked directly at one another. There seemed in that second to be nowhere else in the world but this small clearing, and the full sun beating down into it. 'Well, you can keep me from your unicorn,' Jess laughed. 'I'm no maiden! Maybe the unicorn wouldn't notice. Maybe he'd grow calm and still just the same.' Spencer moved close to her. She lay back down on the grass. Her breasts seemed to him like two blooms with this small, keen centre. He bent down over her, shading her from the bright light. Then he kissed her, and he kissed those two keen blooms. She smelt of sea salt, like a mermaid he thought; a mermaid might smell like this. Then all the awkwardness, all the anxiety, all the tattered, small remains of the turret silence, all the last trip coils of the unsaid things, all of it floated past as if it had hardly been. All of that was over now, less than the soft ash beside them where a small fire had been. Jess leant forward. She pulled down the zip of his jeans. It was a loud noise in the stillness. She knew that if it had been one of the others, they might have used something. It might have been better. But sometimes things just don't belong. They just must happen as they are. She wanted such closeness for them; such a binding of love between them in this hidden summer space, where nothing must intrude, not even heroes. 'It's easy,' she whispered, 'it's easy.' In the midst of his reaching and feeling he saw the Murna chamber and the maiden with braided hair, he saw her here on the grass, he saw her fade, it was as if all the candle flames flooded into this deep reach between them. 'I love you,' Jess said. In that second he knew beyond anything he had ever known.

They lay there afterwards. They lay there until the shade moved and there were different shadows. As they lay there together, he told her about the burnt-out church. He told her about the night he had spent below the butterfly. He told her about the cold first light and the bird sounds. He told her about the scuffing rustle of moving flanks among dry leaves. And he told her as he looked up into the blinding sun, he told her how he knew it was the unicorn hidden there, waiting to fly out like Pegasus, ready to dip its magic horn into the poisoned seas and rivers, ready to heal the waters of the earth. As he told her, as the sun warmed them into one single piece of summer ground, like one leaf, one impression on the worn grass, as he told her, she could hear the rustle of those dry leaves, she could see the white, moon flanks resting; a billow weight on the dry church stones. She could see the bright horn up into the bell-tower. 'It's true,' she said. 'Your unicorn is true.' And he stopped all his telling and they just held hands with their eyes closed against the brightness of the sun.

It was getting towards evening when they made their way back to the bike, and then after that out on to the open road. The sun was low in the sky. The shadows were rich and long, but there was still considerable warmth in the air. The road ran inland above and parallel to the estuary. It was a wide, open road with clear views either side across the standing wheat, and plough and burnt stubble. Church towers rose above the corn like silent echoes of a lost certainty. Few of the churches were open, many were sad, stale places, although from any distance they still were the master shape over every village cluster, reaching well above the modern roofs and chimneys. The road dipped and turned

347

now and again, it was like a wide, ribbon length thrown out from the centre towards the sea. By odd gateways there were wooden painted signs: Herbs for sale, Farm fresh eggs, Rhubarb, Lettuce, and sometimes Rabbits. The rich evening light on the leaves and flowers, on the roofs and signs and towers, seemed spilt out from the charge and happiness between them. Just as the turret silence had so contained him, now Spencer felt that he was every light space, every bird sound; he was the freedom of the wind into their faces, he was the fine rose threads of light in the sky. He was the standing corn, the draughts of blue smoke from allotment bonfires. He felt Jess so close, he felt the weight and shape of her behind him on the broad seat of the bike, that was the bounding wide berth of their unicorn. With soundless hooves on the open road the bike surged effortlessly on. It seemed almost a natural thing for the bike to have wings, so that it could mount like Pegasus into the clear space of the sky. Because, without that space and all its nameless freedom, how could there be room for so much sudden hope, and feeling?

Jess had not expected Spencer to be so close, so soon. But it had been right. It had been given to them in that small briar circle of worn, unicorn ground. She had no misgivings. But as the bike swerved and sped, as the banks and trees and corn shot past; flashes of skimming shapes, flying off the ground, she called to Spencer, 'Hey Spencer . . . Hey hero . . . Not so fast. Not so fast.' But on the wind her voice was as soundless as unicorn hooves. Spencer opened the throttle as if it were the cover of some deep well that was now no longer a cavern reaching into silent, stagnant dark, but a clear bubbling froth of surface water, running ready, like evening tides towards the calm edge of the shore. Edges were the property of fear. Feelings free, must be boundless. In a purring salmon leap of speed, the bike rose suddenly into the air. From some skid it spun round, leapt, and then fell hard into the dark, trapped edge of the verge, leaving deep, crude scars in the warm road surface.

Very soon, slow ordinary cars on either side of the road stopped. Anxious, horrified people stumbled out and went over to the dark verge, where the two young people lay; scattered, tossed up and fallen like great birds out of the evening sky. The bodies were quite far from the bike. They lay at right angles to one another. Her hand reaching out for his, even though neither could have thought of such a thing in that split second of speed. A man pulled the bike further into the verge so that it would be no danger to the passing traffic. People gasped and stared. They knew the boy was dead. He must have hit the stump as he fell. But the girl seemed to be breathing. They covered her brown, summer limbs with rugs and cardigans. A woman knelt beside her in among the docks and nettles, ready to comfort her, to hold her hand, to be with her during the waiting that must happen now. The man who had brought the bike off the road stood for several seconds staring at the boy. The helmet had gone; it was fallen ahead in the long grass. The hair was thick long dark curls. He had a pale face, with large blue eyes. There were no cuts, no bleeding, no outwards signs. The man closed the boy's eyelids over. It must have been a blow to the head. It was death on impact anyway. He put his jersey, stuck with straw and wisps of hay, he put it gently over the boy's pale face. He wondered where the parents would be tonight to hear this terrible news. He had three sons of his own, grown and married now. He prayed in his heart for the grieving people of this son, and he thought of that saying 'Those whom the gods love die young.'

TEN

It was late evening after what had been a hot, stuffy day. George and Winnie were together in the kitchen. Winnie had been all day in the Red Cross shop. They hadn't been busy. She was knitting as usual. The needles clicked out this polka-dot pattern of sharp time. The wool was blue, quite fine. George slept. His mouth was open, his hands loose weights in his lap. Then there was this loud knocking on the door. It was not the knock of a neighbour, it was too powerful for that. It was not kids either, it was too definite. Winifred went to the window. As she got up the knitting fell from her lap to the floor. Several stitches ran off the end of the grey needle. Winnie didn't consider rescuing them. Something told her then they were no longer of the least importance. She pulled back the lace curtain. A policeman and a policewoman were standing on the step outside. Winnie glanced round the small neat kitchen, as if it were for the last time. Also, she sought to summon from its peace and calm some strength. She was so fearful. And so certain that her fears were justified.

They said these things. They spoke calmly and carefully. They seemed so young themselves. The boy is dead. He died instantly. Your daughter is concussed. Nothing else. She is suffering from shock. She is sedated in hospital in Ipswich.

She's comfortable. They found nothing damaged. She will be fine.

As they spoke, Winifred saw him as he had been the first night. The blood all over him. Matted into his hair. Spattered down on to his shoes. She saw the terrible distress and emptiness in those large eyes. She could see that drained face so clearly as it was then. Sheet white. As pale as death. Those were the very words that had come to mind when she first saw him that late night. She had known at once, because they came like that into the hospital, she had known that those cuts were most probably self inflicted. Now, so the policeman said, there were no cuts; nothing. Winnie saw his face again, as he left the house only days ago; so cheerful, so strong in himself at last. The waste. The terrible waste. The mystery of it all.

They went at once. The police fixed the transport. Even though it was summer, Winifred took her brown coat. Jess was in a side ward alone. Poor mite, poor child. They could do nothing but be there, and tell her again and again that even if his life had been short, he had known in the end good times. 'You gave him that,' Winnie said. But Jess could hardly hear; in her aching, stiff body, there was nothing but a gorge of dry emptiness. Tears continually burnt out all over her face. She could see him there above her, in that small unicorn space, with the high bramble hedges and the brilliant sun. As the hours passed, her distress became a frantic anger. It could not be so. It could not be so.

Winifred and George identified the body. They stayed for several minutes in the grim, cold calm. He seemed so complete, so peaceful, and yet so utterly empty of himself.

Whatever had been, whatever had passed, Winifred and George felt that his people must be told. They contacted Social Services. Then they in their turn were contacted by Jim Scott. It was he who called on the parents personally. In his job you

351

judged no one. In his job everyday must be a second chance. No door must be closed.

Dolly was sunbathing when Jim Scott called. She was wearing large sunglasses with bright pink frames. Her body glistened with oils and creams. She had just plucked some offending hairs from her legs. The news of Spencer's death came as everything about him had always come, awkwardly; intrusively. They were to go out that evening. And there was a dinner-dance at the club on Saturday. She sniffed loudly into her towel. She felt suddenly so exposed; somehow degraded. Surging, rotten memories of her early life battered down on her. Sid and Lily, those terrible doughnuts, the gimlet moon and Sid's thrashing, her mother's rag-end, wretched life. And her own attempts to fly from it all; to leave it all behind. She took Jim Scott into the kitchen. When she ran water from the cold tap into the kettle, she remembered the rain and how it had thundered down on that barn. She remembered the sound of that storm in the running water. And she remembered those few moments of trust. Rotten, stupid, childish trust. Trust me, Mrs Noah. Trust me.

Fat and soft with the gluttony of empty treats day after day, she wept loudly. Jim Scott was not surprised. In her bitter, wretched, angry tears she tried to find some sorrow for the boy's death. But what she wept for was herself, and somehow or other, the loss of her own life in the way she had wanted it to be.

Dolly and Frank agreed to come to the funeral. It would be an end of it all. After Dolly had met Spencer in the station, she had told Frank and he had not minded as she supposed he might.

It was Lumsden and Francesca who made the funeral arrangements. Spencer's baptism had always entertained Lumsden. Francesca and her sullen, good-looking children were Catholics. They had a cottage in Wiltshire where they were in the parish of a small baroque Catholic chapel which was attached to a

352

substantial private house, although it was now no longer a family home. The house had known many lives. It had been a girls' school and after that an international sixth form college. Now it was divided into apartments. Homes for the exclusive and elderly. More than considerable financial assets had to be offered to have one of the apartments in the house. International high-powered Catholic lineage was a good thing. On account of this, every Sunday boasted a most unusual congregation of exiled Europeans as well as local Catholics. Francesca felt extremely appropriate in these surroundings. She was definitely considered one of the most exotic of the faithful. The priest who ran the parish was formerly a Benedictine monk so he was suitably at ease with these founded people. He was from a civilised background himself. Theologically he remained very much a man of the nineteenth century. The horrors of central altars, dreadful fellowship, and the new liturgy, with its vulgar, intrusive sign of peace, were always scrupulously avoided by his congregation.

He was a little surprised to hear that Lumsden had a son, but if he had been baptised a Catholic, which was apparently the case, then there seemed to be no very good reason why he should not be buried in the small private cemetery just below the house.

Lumsden telephoned the news of Spencer's death to his mother. He spoke to her annually. She never initiated any contact or conversation herself, but she would always add at the end of the call, 'Your father is older, but unaltered in any other respect.' That was all. She made no comment when Lumsden told her of Spencer's death; but he could almost feel her stare from the study window out across the meadow, over towards Mount Murna. That strange, powerful receptacle for all the unsaid things. The heaving, solid shape of that mountain might almost be the compound form of the rejected and buried thoughts of generations.

The burial took place on the Thursday after a simple Requiem Mass at the chapel. The congregation was small. Francesca, flamboyant in designer black, knelt close to the communion rail with Lumsden. Lumsden felt that black was really rather excessive. He wore a loose grey suit and a long claret silk scarf. In the beginning, when he had agreed with Jim Scott to make the arrangements, it had seemed to him the only decent thing to do. Somehow or other, it was like that last act, that struggled to put things together at the end of rather an indifferent play, that had got out of hand in the beginning. Lumsden had never seriously considered that Dolly might be there. Just possibly, the good people from the Elephant and Castle, with whom, so Scott said, Spencer had been lodging.

Before the event, it had seemed to Lumsden that what he had arranged was pretty straightforward. But from the moment they parked the car in the grounds outside the chapel under the cedar trees, Lumsden felt peculiarly disadvantaged. It was as if for some reason the occasion, like a wild card, would not remain easily within the pack of social convention. Dom Martin had been most uncomplicated and accommodating, as well he might, he had devoured many excellent dinners at the cottage over the years, and he was a man who only tolerated a really good brandy.

The day itself was blustery and extremely unseasonal. Perhaps it was the vulgar white BMW with unreal, fluffy white covers over the upholstery that Lumsden had noticed parked there already, when he and Francesca arrived; perhaps it was that jarring note of incongruity that had somehow got to him. It certainly never occurred to him at that stage that the car might have some connection with Dolly. However, when Lumsden and Francesca made their way up the aisle past the coffin and the candles, a waft of impossibly cloying scent, running riot with a most defeating smell of aftershave, made it almost impossible for him not to glance at the pair who were perpetrating these dreadful odours. Francesca did not look. It was customary for her to be looked at. But Lumsden saw out of the corner of his eye a small stout pair, dressed from head to toe in black. The woman was nearest to the aisle. She had a patent-leather bag. She wore a tight, fitted coat and a small pill-box hat with a veil. She was wearing dark-glasses and she was sniffing into a small scented handkerchief. Unmistakably Mrs Noah. Lumsden was amazed. He would like to have looked for longer but he was glad that the circumstances made it impossible, at that juncture anyway. But he felt a jolt of worrying discomfort. A kind of anxious, grey dismay, unlike anything he had felt for a long time. Almost a small spill from the nursery bag. It was certainly not regret. Nothing as specific as that. Certainly not sorrow or sadness. Nothing maudlin or particularly reflective. Just a sudden huge distaste for what he had arranged, the general palaver of everything. It was rather similar to regretting having ordered a dozen oysters because you couldn't really believe that your true inclination was for steamed white fish. It was perhaps the recognition that 'the morning after' really never left you, if the conditions immediately preceding it were continually prescribed, you could hardly go back to a soft-boiled egg and bread-and-butter soldiers.

Lumsden stared ahead at the gilt and white, the carousing angels, the over-painted narrative scenes from the Old Testament. He didn't attempt to engage mentally with the dull intoning of Dom Martin. The priest made no mention of the boy by name. He only referred to the 'deceased'. A rather bland way to go on about any human being, Lumsden thought.

There were two or three locals in the congregation, regular daily communicants. And Lumsden had noticed a tall, heavily-built man standing just inside the doors at the back of the chapel. He had his cloth cap rolled like a paper in his large weather-beaten hands. There was a pale white line high on his forehead, where the skin presumably was hidden under the cap, and never saw the sun. He was obviously an agricultural worker, someone who was out in all weathers anyway.

A neighbour drove Winnie and George and Jess down from London. They arrived just after the service had begun. Jess was in no fit state really to be there, but she had insisted. She had sobbed so much these last days. Winnie longed for the funeral to be over for her sake. But she felt, to see him laid to rest in good country ground, she felt it might help Jess later on. She would take a good while to get over it, they both knew that. They stayed together at the back of the church supporting Jess between them as best they could. Jess could see nothing and she heard even less. But she did know that there were these four candles lit beside the coffin. In her mind, it meant that Spencer was already within Murna now, in his great, imagined burial chamber, with his poets and ancestors, the unicorn and the woman with braided hair. Jess clung to that thought. Spencer had told her so often of Mount Murna. Soon, through her tears and the flickers of the candle flames, nothing was distinct; nothing had form or sound. She felt in her pain so close to him, closer perhaps than they might ever have been if his life had gone on as it should.

After the service, the priest came forward to the altar rail and said to the small fragmented congregation that the burial service would be in the graveyard, just beyond the grounds of the house, and would the four men present like please to carry the coffin down to the cemetery.

So it was Lumsden Farr, Frank Pratt, George Chappell and Big Donal who moved forward to the coffin and together lifted the remains of Spencer Frampton, the deceased, on to their various shoulders and bore him slowly out of the chapel and down the drive to the small gate into the private cemetery.

There were few to witness these unlikely pall-bearers, who had each played such differing parts in the life of the deceased. The four women followed the coffin, their heads hard down against the rough wind; Francesca and Dolly had to hold on to their hats. As the coffin made its way, tilting now and then on account of the differing heights of the four men, the wind gusted and spluttered as if it would drive the proceedings out of its extreme control, which was in such contrast to the life of the boy who was about to be interred.

The grave had been dug up at the north end of the cemetery, back under the high hedge. Francesca and Dolly stood beside Dom Martin as the four men lowered the coffin into the ground. The priest wore a heavily decorated cope; he carried incense and holy water. Once the coffin was still in the ground, the priest continued with various litanies and prayers to which Francesca piously responded, assisted now and then by Donal's deep voice, for only they were accustomed and at ease with the manner of the ceremony. Dom Martin, aware of the uncontrollable distress of the young girl, assumed that there might be some intimacy between herself and the boy, so, as was customary, he came forward to her and guided her to the edge of the grave beside him, so that after Lumsden had waved the aspergillum, the blessed horse-hair tail of holy water, over the coffin in the sign of the cross, she might also make her final gesture in the same way.

Jess, having sobbed in the church uncontrollably, was almost calm. The fierce wind, these roaring, tearing, unseen teeth that seemed to grab at her hair and clothes and all the surrounding leaves and branches, momentarily stunned her into a kind of stillness. But then, finding herself alone beside the priest and these strange people, and staring down into the dark ground where this length of pale wood stared back towards her, where Spencer's face should have been, she broke down completely, competing with the wind in her angry, bitter confused state. Where were his heroes now? Could they not break apart his lifelessness? Couldn't she once more see his face?

Dom Martin was embarrassed and made uneasy by the girl's noise and complete lack of control. He regretted having thought to involve her. He had simply wanted to give this unfortunate boy some final dignity to what had been, apparently, a most restless life, full of turmoil and endless demands on the state. Dolly was silent. She had done her weeping. She was looking at the sticky clay on the heels of her shoes. Francesca simply stared ahead, her gloved hand on the wide brim of her hat. She looked, as always, calm and elegant. She looked as if there could not possibly be a girl in a flimsy cotton dress and worn cardigan who was crying in this loud, loose, ill-bred manner, so noisily interrupting this dismal, cold service.

It was an awkward pause. The mourners, most of them having so little to mourn, simply longed to be back in their comfortable cars, with their heads out of the abysmal winds.

Then Winnie, who had been standing well back below the grave, not wanting to intrude on those she thought were his closest relatives, now she ran forward, completely careless of these well-dressed, stiff people, and this adorned priest. She ran forward to her child. Her small, black shoes, bulging where the bunions were, slipped on the long grass. Her brown coat, the nap quite worn away at the edges, flapped like goose wings as she ran up the hill to Jess. She had to jump on her toes to reach the cold, red cheeks of her daughter. 'Love, my love,' she said quite simply and she pulled the knotted, windblown head towards her. She held the cheeks in her hands until Jess grew calmer. Then, with Winnie's hand to guide her, they waved this dripping thing of holy water over the coffin and then quietly they left.

Donal walked back down towards the road after them. His flat cap on his head and the good news in his heart to tell Maura and some of them back in Ballynaule; Spencer had, so it seemed in the end, found some fine people over in England.

Lumsden and Francesca waited for the odd unknowns to leave before they suggested to Dom Martin that he might like to come back to the cottage for lunch and a strong drink. Dolly had hesitated, wondering if simply good manners meant

358

she should have addressed Lumsden. But Frank had received what he thought were very clear signals from Francesca that their presence was not wanted. So he guided Dolly firmly back towards the white BMW under the cedar tree.

*

Gradually, as autumn gave way to winter, Jess spent less time alone in her room playing the same records again and again. She began to see her friends as before. She got a new job in the bank. She had always been good at mathematics. She also signed on for evening classes in computer studies. It was Winnie's idea. She'd thought it would take Jess out of herself a bit. Give her something new and fresh to get on with. And it worked. Jess enjoyed the course and did well at it. But almost every Saturday, without fail, she went down to the library. She walked round the side into the small cobbled yard between the burnt-out church and the high red-brick wall with the magnificent Camberwell butterfly shining out from the coloured tiles. She would sit there for some while on the wooden bench below the old chimney and the wall with the butterfly on it. She would sit there just as she had done so often before with Spencer. She felt so glad that she had this place to come to. It was much better than visiting a grave. She would sit and listen hard until she felt sure she could hear the regular, even breathing of the unicorn in the burnt-out church. It was probably her own breath, but in the strength of that beat and that listening she felt Spencer's life and strength again. She could remember all his heroes. All those dark, wild, slaying tales. Many of those heroes in their incredible daring had died young. Perhaps to die young was a natural thing for some. Perhaps they were fulfilled and ready even if to the rest of the world it might not seem so.

As the evenings began to close in, getting dark earlier and earlier, Jess thought more and more of the brilliant hot afternoon and their small space of worn grass, the high bramble hedges, that briar circle of their unicorn ground, the soft ash beside them where a wood fire had been. Jess thought of them lying there together. How close and easy it had been. In the beginning after the accident and those first months after Spencer's death, she had not been able to let herself think at all of that afternoon. But now, in the dark of winter, she could begin to let herself remember. She remembered Aine with whom Cuchulain had lain. And she remembered how Aine had been left with Cuchulain's child. She had once thought, just once, if maybe missing a period or two meant anything. But Winnie said that the shock and the accident would be quite enough to cause things to go amiss and not to worry. Then past Christmas, Jess knew she was putting on so much weight, but she had been pigging sweets and chocolates and coke. Then Winifred wondered. She was surprised at herself for not having thought of it earlier, but the sadness and the shock had been everything.

One late evening after George had gone to bed and she and Jess were quite settled together with a cup of tea, she said to Jess 'Could there be a chance, love, just a chance you might be carrying his child?' Jess didn't reply for a while. She looked down at the steam spiral from her cup. She stirred the tea. She had just begun to wonder that herself. But she'd thought she was simply imagining it; imagining that she, like Aine, was carrying his son. Because she had wanted that to be so, she had felt quite sure in her own mind that of course it would not be. And when her mother said the thought aloud, it made her own, private, vague dream real. Then Jess knew. She knew absolutely that it was true. Suddenly it was a fact. There was no doubt in her mind at all. So she looked up at Winnie and said 'Yes. Yes. More than a chance, Mum.' Winnie looked across the table at her daughter; the last; the baby. 'Oh Jess, Jess, we'll manage fine,' she said. 'And I know, I absolutely know, that this one will be a truly blessed little person.'

For Winifred it was yet another practical thing. Another

purpose. Another event. Another natural proposition to be grown accustomed to, prepared for and celebrated. It was simply the way things were. The unquestionable shape of life and its various mysteries. Things might have been otherwise. Many people might have wanted it differently. But once a thing was, once the die is cast, you go with it; you see it through. It was obvious to Winnie that Jess badly wanted the child. When it was all confirmed, she was delighted. And there were many friends who had known Spencer, who shared the Chappells' joy that in a sense a part of that young lad's life was still with them.

It was a spring baby. It was a little boy. He was a good weight, over eight pounds at birth and a very easy child from the start. Jess wanted to call him Spencer. He was registered Spencer Patrick Chappell. With Patrick as his second name, Jess said he would never forget that a part of him belonged in Ireland. As soon as she could after they were home from the hospital, Jess pushed him in the buggy over to the burnt-out church and the butterfly. She told him, as he slept in the sun out in the small cobbled yard with the weeds and flowers pressing up in between the stones, she told him that in there, in that burnt-out church, in there the unicorn was waiting, with its soundless hooves, to fly out one day over the earth, to heal with its horn all the poisoned seas and rivers of the world. Jess was going to make sure that as he grew he would learn from her all those fierce and favourite tales of his father's.

Spencer Patrick, in contrast to his father, was very fair, but he had the same wide eyes. His face was never pale. He caught the sun easily just as Jess did and so even in London he had a good strong colour most of the time. He was a thriving child, into everything and something to say to everyone. Winnie noticed quite early on how he took an absolute delight in any living creature; spiders, worms, moths, butterflies, any grub or stray.

She used to say to Jess, 'One day we should take him over to Ireland for a visit.'

Increasingly, the child gave them nothing but joy. However many grand-children there were, and Winnie had four already overseas, there was something particular about this one. 'It's so often the way,' Winnie would say to George, 'the ones least expected have the most to give.'

It was her great joy in the life of the child that prompted Winnie one summer to think that perhaps she should let his people know. She felt they had no right to keep the joy of this child's life simply to themselves. After all, he was a new beginning. Anyone would want to rejoice in that, after the struggles his young father had known, and then his terrible, sudden death that summer.

It was a few weeks after the third anniversary of Spencer's death. Winnie decided she would write to his parents and also to his grandmother in Ireland. His grandmother might well be dead. But anyway she would write. She would simply let them know of Spencer Patrick. She had all the addresses with Spencer's papers. They had been given to her by Jim Scott after the funeral.

She wrote the same letter to all three. She wrote the letters late one evening while George slept and Jess was out with friends and Spencer Patrick was safe upstairs in his cot. Winnie always found the small clean kitchen at the end of the day the most calm place. She took the pad of lined writing paper out from under her work-basket and she wrote in even, slanting, copperplate handwriting these short letters:

'It is three years now since the sad occasion of Spencer's sudden death. All our family miss him very much, but we have the great joy of having his son, my daughter Jess's child, with us. Spencer Patrick is a wonderful, healthy boy. We just wanted you to know of his life here with us.'

She signed the letters . . .

'Yours sincerely . . . Winifred Chappell.'

Then she addressed the three small envelopes: Mrs Pratt; Mr Farr; and Mrs Farr, Rathmanagh, Ballynaule, Claggan, Co. Tipperary, Ireland. She felt it was rather like putting a note in a glass bottle, and then throwing the bottle out to sea. Mrs Farr might well have died. The others might have moved on. Winifred had no way of knowing. She posted the letters next day. It was late September.

Dolly and Frank had moved to Leatherhead but the letter was forwarded on to them. They were both surprised by the small cheap envelope. The handwriting was very old fashioned, all those loops.

Dolly opened it, her bright red fingernails tearing at the thin paper. She had to read the letter two or three times to make any sense of it. Then Frank read it and they remembered the girl in the flimsy cotton dress who had sobbed so uncontrollably at the grave. 'That's them,' Dolly said. 'That's them, the girl, and there was this tiny little woman, remember Frank?' Dolly became petulant and then furious. Her head ached as usual. She was on a mass of pills for various odd discomforting ailments. She had enough on her plate. How dare they track her down like she was some sort of criminal. 'It's not like that,' Frank tried to interrupt. 'What then? They want money, Frank. They want money. I can smell it. This is just the beginning. Very nice. Very neat and small. But afterwards. They want money, Frank.' And she stormed off into her bedroom. She stared at her puffy face in the glass; the red lips, the plucked eyebrows, the open pores, the dullness of it. It was being found. That was the worst. The very thought 'baby' made her stamp and howl. The greed of them, the whole wet mess of their endless, frantic, dribbling lives.

Frank knew the signs. He knew how easily something might trigger one of those storms. But he could afford to be generous. He was rarely at home these days. He gave Dolly purchasing

363

power, which was more or less all she wanted. Because of that, Frank figured he'd bought his freedom as far as other women were concerned. He came into the bedroom.

'Look, Doll.' He held up the small, narrow sheet of lined writing paper. 'Nothing. It's nothing.' He tore it into small pieces. 'It never got here. You never read it. Right? All over and done with. Now take the car, get that pair of spotted dogs you were so keen on. Those china hounds or dalmatians; the ones with the pink tongues sitting on the green cushions.' 'Oh, Frank!' Dolly cheered instantly. 'For the hall. I thought for the hall.' 'Yes. For the hall if you like. Just get them.' And Frank felt with his small red hand for the large wad of crisp notes in his back pocket.

The Farrs were just unpacking the car after a weekend in Wiltshire. Francesca and the children were arguing as usual. Lumsden with his exquisite skill for never carrying in anything, even his own jacket, unlocked the front door empty-handed. There were several letters on the mat. He bent to pick them up. 'Any post?' Francesca called. 'A few sumptuous envelopes; all for you, darling,' Lumsden said. He put three letters for Francesca on to the hall table. There was a fourth letter. Very odd. A most insignificant envelope addressed to him, in this even sloping hand. Lumsden was intrigued. He went into his small study, where he spent most of his time sleeping and smoking and listening to compact discs, although officially he was thought to be researching for a book on 'Obscure Pleasures'. It was to be an anthology. It was not yet commissioned, but he remained hopeful. He went over to the window and opened the envelope.

Spencer Patrick. A healthy child. Lumsden's first thought was how unbelievably fecund young women were at the lower end of the social scale. He knew this news, if it was true, would madden Francesca. In a way it entertained him, this feckless little thread, still persisting against all odds. Still pursuing a random, groping kind of history. Lumsden decided that he might as well keep the letter. He was not altogether sure why, maybe it had some significance for him. It was all part of the sure escape from Violet and the nursery bag. How irritated she would be to know that Fitzpatrick genes were thriving in the hinterland of the Elephant and Castle. Lumsden took down one of the small pocket editions of Lamb's *Essays of Elia* from the bookcase. The one he had taken as a young man from his grandfather's library at Rathmanagh, on the day of his banishment out of Ireland. It was the one published by the Knickerbocker Press. He opened it at random. He opened it at the essay on Poor Relations. He glanced down at the text and read with some amusement:

> A poor relation is the most irrelevant thing in nature – a piece of impertinent correspondency – a preposterous shadow – a drain on your purse – a rebuke to your rising – a stain in your blood – a frog in your chamber – the one thing not needful – the hail in the harvest – the ounce of sour in a pound of sweet.

Francesca called. Lumsden left Winifred's letter in this excellently apposite page.

Violet received little correspondence now that she had more or less retired from most of the committees in the area. There were circulars and there were bills, all easily recognised. But a small cheap envelope with a London postmark was something unusual, something not anticipated. There were so few surprises these days, so few fragments of demand that ever deviated far from the dull course of life at Rathmanagh. Only nature provided any kind of resonance or monumental drama, with its storm sand squalls; its oozing piles of rotting produce; the horror of unwanted apples, blemished fruit shining like brash baubles in the dark, long grass.

Violet had been on her way up to the orchard when the post came. She had been weeding just in front of the house. She wiped the mud from her hands on to her faded skirt. She hardly glanced at the envelopes as she took them from the postman. She was certain that there would be nothing in them to seriously concern her. She put the three letters into the pocket of her skirt. She went on up to the orchard to start on the daily chore of trying to clear the thudding mass of unwanted fruit from the damp ground.

Just before opening the gate into the orchard, she paused to turn and look down, below the house and yard, past the red barn, its doors now fallen on their hinges and stuck permanently open into the ground, past the broken pump, the peeling dry paint on the kitchen door and window-frames, the overgrown, almost grassed look of the weeds and moss over the stones of the laundry yard. She heard the garage doors creak in the wind. She saw Sally pushing her bike up the hill. She was such a plain, lifeless girl, totally devoid of any initiative. It was interesting that although she was so much younger than Maura, she managed so much less. Violet missed Maura, even though it was years now since she had retired. It irritated Violet to realise that it was her humanity she missed. Violet tried to persuade herself it was her cooking and her singing, but she knew it was more than that. Donal came up to the house now and then, not to work exactly. He simply called. He would do odd, difficult things, mend this or that, cart or carry things that were too much for Violet.

The cat, Shiva, ran up through the dilapidated hen run. There were no fowl these days, but Shiva seemed to like to lie on the felt roof of the hen house. So like everything else it stayed where it was quite resigned to growth and decay combining to give it a new, impractical, but nostalgic identity.

It was when Violet bent down in the orchard to pick up the apples that this small cheap envelope fell on to the long grass. She picked it up, surprised by the London postmark. She didn't open it because without her glasses,

366

which were in the study, she would not be able to make any sense of it.

Something about it made her go down into the house sooner than she might have done. She left her boots inside the back door. She walked slowly through the dusty house. The autumn sunlight over everything was a cruel reminder of fading decay everywhere; the unpolished dining-room table, the clouded, steamed and sticky windows, grit and wood fragments over every floor surface.

Cecil, as usual, slept in the library, the paper open and unread on his knees. Violet opened the letter. She was quite alone. Shiva had not followed her. Sally was upstairs in the bedroom. Violet could hear the heavy, clumsy movements over her head. So much noise, so many bumps and clatters with such little effect, waste-paper baskets unemptied, nothing dusted above waist level, sheets and towels never changed unless specifically asked.

As always with unexpected correspondence, Violet first read the signature at the end of the letter. Winifred Chappell. It meant nothing to her. It made her think of rosewood pianos, nothing else. She glanced back to the top of the page and she read on. But her mind remained in those three words, so incongruously calm in this neat looped handwriting. Those three words: Spencer's sudden death. Spencer's sudden death. She felt Shiva suddenly there against her leg, arched and purring. The noise poured into the warm, still, dusty silence. Sudden death. Sudden death. It had happened long before. Not three years ago. It had happened here. In this house. It had been marked already in that mad banshee howl that first evening. She could still remember the sound. A curdled sound making the empty silence sour.

As she held the small piece of lined writing-paper, she sought to think, to wonder, to remember, to react. But she could do none of these things. She felt simply the great weight of flesh and age. Stagnant days stretching ahead into the grey struggle of winter months. Without knowing why, without any considered reason, she kicked the cat away from her. Gently but firmly. The purring was so live, so intruding. She wanted to be in an empty place. Rathmanagh, for all its silence, for all its dull routine, it was not empty. Her father's books in the library, his face from the faded sepia photographs, he was still vivid to her. But his fine quality was dismissed from life. It had not been brought by her to any kind of fruition. Cecil, her gargoyle husband, so happily grown old into his dithering, dribbling, stumbling body, loped like some discarded nursery toy from chair to chair. Birkin was dead. Birkin, the one life.

She put the letter into her pocket. If she had read the rest, if she had read the words 'Spencer Patrick is a wonderful, healthy boy', they had not become gathered into any concrete impression. They had not become in any way, as the letter intended, a fact of life, to be told and known and understood.

Winifred Chappell was fiction to Violet Farr.

It was simply the words 'Spencer's sudden death' that had propelled her back into the mysterious, angry pain she had sought so many times to reject, to abandon. In old age Violet had discovered to her surprise that random, buried feelings were more persistent than cold logic. All her life, in her own estimation, she had acted coherently, from a position of intelligence.

She took Cecil his lunch on a tray. She had none herself. She felt restless. During the afternoon she wandered from room to room, staring out of the dusty windows. The dead blue-bottles and spiders lying on the various sills seemed to buzz decay out of their dry desiccated bodies. In every room, in every space, she found the ferocious noise of uneasy memories. She found empty medicine bottles in the nursery bathroom, a single sock; in the attic under the eaves, with the heavy leather trunks of Capt. Farr, there was a small wooden tuck-box, with L FARR painted in heavy black capital letters. She found wrinkled apples, broken toys, and a cigar box. She picked it up. She opened it, expecting more spiders, more emptiness, more stifling tired smells. She found a small parcel made from the clean smooth page of a child's exercise book. Violet undid the folded piece of paper. In it was the skull and the sharp white bones of a small bird, probably a sparrow. On the edge of the paper in a very poor uneven hand were written the words: 'this little bird is dead'. Beside the cigar box there were several tattered books and a chipped magnifying-glass. They were not Lumsden's things.

Violet did not know why, but she folded back the white bird bones into the smooth sheet of now crumpled paper. She put it into her pocket, where the letter was. She tried to concentrate on other things. The day seemed absurdly long to her.

In the evening she went out and stood at the edge of the porch. She stood in the last rays of the sun. It was late September but there was still considerable warmth. She had read the letter two or three times during the afternoon. Now she took the crumpled piece of paper torn from a child's exercise book, she took it out from her pocket.

'It's too late,' she said aloud to the long grass and distant evening shadows. 'It's too late. It's all too far gone.' She was staring as she so often did towards Mount Murna, that ageless continuum of definition, that put the miserable change of human time firmly in its place.

Shiva came out on to the porch. Violet, regretting her treatment of the cat earlier in the day, said to her 'What is past is really quite beyond one. Out of the way. Different. And what is now . . .' she sighed. The cat came closer to her. 'What is now is almost without any presence whatsoever. But then, nothing is as it seems, so they say . . . and who knows . . . who knows anything.'

Then suddenly she crumpled in her hand that piece of paper torn from a child's exercise book, she crumpled its contents until she heard the small, mocking sound of those frail bones shattered.

Later that evening after supper with Cecil in the dining-room, she decided that, having never told him of Spencer's death, she could in no way contemplate referring to this other life and this unknown woman, Winifred Chappell.

She did not destroy the letter. She simply put it with her other papers in the blue blotter in the bottom drawer of her desk. She did not know why she kept it. She had no longer sufficient energy left to pursue the subject and its terrible distracting trail of memories. She had had enough for one day. Maybe some part of her felt that there might be a time when to consider it again would be appropriate, but not now, not this September.

ELEVEN

I t was over two years later that Cecil died. Suddenly, and most mercifully, he had a heart attack on his way to the bathroom. It was all easily dealt with. An uncomplicated burial at Claggan followed. Violet wrote briefly to Lumsden to avoid any possible decision on his part to attend the ceremony.

Cecil's death was in the spring. Violet was grateful for that. It was her favourite season. She had anticipated some sense of release from Cecil's death. He had been no kind of companion to her for so long. She had imagined that possibly without the drear demands of his routine she might find new energy, new interests. But a strange futility seemed to become the sum of everything. There seemed little point in weeding, watering, tying back, constructing and controlling. She found she almost longed for nature, like some violent, powerful wave, she longed for it to sweep the demesne from her. To take the house and land, the earth and trees all back into itself. What had all her struggles meant in the end? She could never flourish again with the same tenacity and force as a single blade of spring grass.

Donal came by most evenings. It was kind of him. Violet wondered why he cared, or if indeed he did. It was pleasant to speak once in a while as if someone or something mattered. It was reassuring to hear the sound of one's own voice.

It was while Violet was sorting through various papers of Cecil's that she came upon the blue blotter in the bottom drawer of her desk. She wondered about Winifred Chappell. In the end they were both simply women; like blades of grass. At the end of life identity seemed to fade. Time was careless of particularity in the grave. It was only while the idea of identity was stoked, stated, remembered, propositioned, that it really existed. Without all that noise, one was more or less dead already.

Without further thought, Violet Farr wrote to Winifred Chappell. She said how her husband had recently died. She said that she lived alone, but if Winifred and her family should ever visit Ireland, then if they wished they might certainly call on her.

Winifred was surprised and delighted to get Violet Farr's letter out of the blue. Spencer Patrick was now five, full of chatter and doing well at school. Jess had a good job in computer demonstration. Altogether things were well. George had a heart condition, but it was under control. Jess and her mother planned to hire a car and go to Ireland; Jess had an old car but not one that could stand such a journey. They would go to Kerry, but they would drive first through Tipperary and maybe stay a night on the way. They were surprised that Mrs Farr was still alive. They had never expected to hear from her. Jess longed to see Rathmanagh; but most of all Mount Murna.

When the arrangements were made they sent a card to Mrs Farr suggesting that perhaps they might call on her in the afternoon of the Thursday.

Violet was surprised when she received this card. She was surprised, not that they were coming, but that she had invited them. She found herself most anxious of the event. She began to regret it. But she firmly told herself that if she could not cope with this one woman and her daughter and their child then she must be past it altogether.

Violet asked Sally to prepare tea in the dining-room, with something suitable for a child. Sally was surprised. It was unlike Mrs Farr. Sally baked a chocolate cake and made some fresh scones. On the Wednesday evening Donal came by. Violet was out in the porch. He found her more talkative than usual. It was as if she had something more to say, but could not find the way to it. He had heard from Sally that Mrs Farr was expecting company. So Donal asked her outright. 'Sally says you're to have company tomorrow, Mrs Farr. That's good. I'm glad.' 'Yes, Donal. Yes indeed. In fact I wondered if you might care to join us?' Donal could make no sense of it. There was something more to it than she said and it seemed to matter to her. 'Certainly, Mrs Farr,' he said, trying not to express his surprise, but to carry on as if it was altogether normal.

Donal came, as Mrs Farr suggested, at four o'clock in the afternoon. He came up to the front of the house. A small white car was parked out on the gravel. Donal could see no one. Then he heard voices from the wood above. He saw this small party come out into the sun. It was Mrs Farr and a very short woman, and a young girl with fair hair. Then Donal heard a rush of noise and a small boy came bowling down the bank towards him. In that second he instantly understood. He recognised the woman now and the girl. He hardly needed the introduction that Violet nervously made.

'This is Mrs Chappell,' she said. 'And Jess.' Then she paused, 'And this is Spencer Patrick, Donal.'

Donal shook both Winifred and Jess by the hand. Then he grasped the little lad. His fair curly hair; the wide, laughing eyes. Donal picked him up and swung him round. 'Welcome. Welcome to Rathmanagh, Spencer Patrick. You've certainly a fine string of names for any lad.'

373

Spencer, delighted with all the space and freedom, ran wild. Donal took him and Jess up into the orchard and round behind the red barn where he knew a thrush was nesting.

Winifred remained with Violet. She had recognised Donal from that windy graveside, just as he had recognised her. She sensed an awkward restraint from this tall, still good-looking woman who, although she obviously suffered from the stiffness and pain of old age, had a very commanding manner.

They boiled the kettle. They discussed the quality of Sally's scones. Violet described to Winifred the tiresome rigmarole of the Aga, its various moods depending on the direction of the wind and the quality of the coke. Winifred said she cooked on gas and found it very good, very even and reliable for baking. No mention was made of Spencer; either his life or death. But it was not necessary. There was more feeling between them without the questions.

Winifred and Violet were already sitting down at the dining-room table when Donal and Jess came through from the kitchen. Violet was in her usual place with her back to the window. She was pouring the tea into the cups when Spencer Patrick ran in. He came straight to her. He leant against her, much as Shiva might have done.

'Look, Mrs Farr. Look. We found a nest with teeny squeaky birds and I found this.' He held out a large piece of speckled shell. 'May I keep it? May I keep it?'

Violet was unused to free, fearless children, let alone a child in any way related to her. His openness took her by surprise. His weight against her was impossible to draw back from.

'Of course keep it,' Violet said. 'Donal knows all the secrets round here. Every animal haunt and need. He knows all creatures very well indeed.' Violet continued to pour the tea. The child ran delighted to sit beside Donal, the precious piece of eggshell in his hand.

After tea they walked down the top meadow towards Mount Murna. Violet told them of Birkin. What a loyal friend a dog could be. She took a stick now to walk the mountain. 'For many, many years', she said, 'Birkin and I came out here every evening. We always walked towards the end of the day, when the chores were done. The evening is a wonderful time on the mountain.'

As they walked Spencer ran ahead, darting this way and that, finding things, collecting things, jumping from stones, throwing twigs, and smelling flowers. Jess and Donal tried to keep up with him. Winifred and Violet followed more slowly. There was quite a wind coming from the east and that, combined with the great difference in the height of the two women, made conversation difficult. Winifred only said again and again what a beautiful, magic spot it was. They paused when they were more or less at the top of the mountain. The two women sat for several minutes on this wide, flat stone. It was then that Violet said as she poked the ground with her stick, 'Of course, Mrs Chappell, of course one day all this will be his.' Violet was about to point to the child, but Winifred had run to him where he had fallen. He got up laughing. But Violet knew that the wind had taken her words. Winifred Chappell had not heard what she said. Nevertheless it would be so. One day, Rathmanagh, all this ground and old house and yards and trees and memories, it would all be his. She would see to it. There was little else left for her to do. She would do that one thing well. It was a way into the future and a way out of the past.